Competitive Swimming Manual
for Coaches and Swimmers

Competitive Swimming Manual for Coaches and Swimmers

Dr JAMES E. COUNSILMAN

*Swimming Coach and Professor of Physical Education,
Indiana University*

PELHAM BOOKS

London

First published in the United States of America by
Counsilman Co., Inc.
2606 East Second Street
Bloomington
Indiana 47401
1977

First published in Great Britain by
PELHAM BOOKS LTD
52 Bedford Square
London WC1B 3EF
1978

ISBN 0 7207 1092 8

Printed in Great Britain by
Hollen Street Press Ltd at Slough, Berkshire
and bound by Hunter and Foulis, Edinburgh

Contents

List of Tables

Preface

When I wrote *The Science of Swimming*, I unrealistically included over four hundred pictures of the basic swimming strokes taken at various angles, out of water and under water. Prentice-Hall, the publisher, requested that I delete a majority of the pictures in the interest of keeping the purchase price of the book under twenty to thirty dollars. As pictures illustrate far better than words, I was disappointed, but I had to agree that at a price of twenty dollars or more we would not sell many books.

Since then I have become more of a camera freak than ever, and I take movie, sequence, and still pictures of champion swimmers here and abroad, when and where I have the opportunity. Some are good and some are not so good, depending on the conditions under which they were taken and, of course, on the limited ability of the photographer. This manual was therefore designed to be the vehicle by which I could share the opportunity to learn from some of these pictures. I am sure that many of you will see and interpret things in these pictures that I have not been able to.

In addition I have tried to make the material on training, the organization of practice, and diet and exercise as up-to-date as possible.

I am indebted to many people for their contributions to the manual. Because so many coaches lack information about what constitutes good pool design, I have asked Joe Hunsaker, a pool consultant, to write two articles on this topic. Dr. David Costill and Dr. Robert Bartels have permitted me to use two very good articles which I thought contained important information for the coach and swimmer. From the late Lloyd Percival's *Sport and Fitness* publication, articles by Roberta Angelino and Joe Taylor have been selected for reprinting. Two articles by Dick Schleihauf, which are in my opinion the best written on the "lift effect" in swimming, are presented, and I must express my appreciation to the author.

The patience and cooperation of my wife, Marge, who read and reread, corrected my spelling, and typed the manuscript without ever totally losing her composure, deserve mention. The final job of assembling the entire mass of pictures and typewritten pages into logical and readable form was given to John and Catherine Vint. They are responsible for the copy-editing, compilation, and design of the finished product, for which I thank them.

Bloomington, Indiana   James E. Counsilman, Ph.D.
May, 1977

Competitive Swimming Manual
for Coaches and Swimmers

Part One

TRAINING

ONE

Practical Considerations of Training

SECTION 1.1
METHODS AND PRINCIPLES OF TRAINING

Nearly everyone understands some of the basic concepts of training. For instance, when you train (or work out), you get into "condition." The exercise that you do in your training program places a stress on your body, which adapts to this stress by changing itself in order to be better able to handle this *particular* stress.

These changes are physiological changes that permit the body to function more efficiently. If you swim long distances, your heart will improve its efficiency and be able to pump more blood to the muscles. This blood will bring oxygen and glycogen to the muscles, remove the fatigue products, and, in the process, improve endurance.

In this instance the stress factor is the training program of *long-distance or overdistance swimming*; the change or adaptation that is made as a result of this stress is increased cardiac (heart) efficiency, and the final effect on your performance is that endurance is improved. Many other changes occur in the body as a result of overdistance swimming, but to illustrate this point, only the improvement in heart or cardiac efficiency will be mentioned at this time. Overdistance swimming will bring about changes that will enable a person to swim long distances better, but it won't result in the necessary changes that will permit him to sprint short distances at top speed. To bring about these changes some *sprint training* must be introduced into the program. Sprint training imposes a stress factor that is of shorter duration but that is more intense than slower and prolonged distance swimming and that causes the muscles to adapt by improving their ability to contract quickly against a greater force—in other words, the muscles become more powerful (see Table 1.1).

Once again let me mention that many other changes occur as a result of the different methods of training. They will not be mentioned here but will be discussed in detail in Chapter 2, "Theory and Research of Training." If a swimmer wants to be conditioned for both speed and endurance races, he must introduce both overdistance and sprint training into his training program.

Table 1.1
Specificity of Training

Stress Factor (Method of Training)	Adaptation	Effect on Performance
1. Overdistance swimming *Example*: continuous swimming of 2 to 4 miles	Improved cardiac efficiency	Improved endurance (to swim long races)
2. Sprinting *Example*: swim 8 × 25 all out	Muscles get stronger	Improved speed (to sprint a 50)
3. Swimming middle distances fast *Example*: swim 5 × 200 very hard with long rest	Ability to tolerate high levels of oxygen debt	Ability to swim middle distances at a fast speed

4. Combined program
    1. Overdistance swimming— swim 2 × 800
    2. Sprint 4 × 25
    3. Swim 2 × 200 very hard with long rest
	1. Improved cardiac efficiency
	2. Muscles get stronger
	3. Ability to tolerate high levels of oxygen debt
		1. Improved endurance
		2. Improved speed
		3. Ability to swim middle distances at a fast speed

Theoretically, it is possible for a swimmer to be conditioned to perform well in a long-distance race such as a 4-mile swim, to also be conditioned to perform well in a sprint race (50 yards) and at the same time not to be conditioned to swim a good middle-distance race (200 meters).

Swimming a middle-distance race well depends on the ability to work at a fast pace for a moderate length of time. During an all-out middle-distance race the swimmer is not able to take in as much oxygen as he is burning. To be in condition for the middle distances his body must change to be able to take in more oxygen and to be able to operate more efficiently when in oxygen debt. This type of change is brought about only by swimming middle distances at fast speed.

Specificity of Training

The fact that the body makes specific adaptations or changes to specific types of training is called *specificity of training* and is one of the most important principles to be aware of in designing a training program.

If you want to swim a good sprint (50-meter race), a good middle-distance race (200- to 400-meter race), and a good distance race (400 meters and over), all three types of training methods that have been discussed must be used. While there is some transfer of training effect from one type of training to another, the amount of this transfer is dependent upon the similarity in the types of training. For example, a swimmer who is using only overdistance training will probably sprint faster than he would if he were doing no training at all, but he will not sprint as fast as he would if he were doing sprint training, nor will he sprint as fast as he would if he were doing some middle-distance training.

It becomes obvious that you must train a distance swimmer with a program that has a different emphasis than that of a sprinter. In reality, however, swimmers (particularly young ones in age-group swimming) swim several events which are between the distances of 50 and 200 yards. The programs for different swimmers on a given age-group team need not be extremely different. In college and senior AAU or international competition one swimmer may be concentrating on the 50- and 100-yard events and another swimmer on the 500- and 1650-yard races. In this case it is important that they be given different programs. While both of these programs may use the three methods of training already mentioned in a *mixed program* of training, the emphasis will be different for the distance swimmer doing more overdistance swimming than the sprinter, and for the sprinter doing more sprinting than the distance swimmer. Both of them should use some middle-distance training, because this training will give the sprinter more endurance to swim his 100 race faster and it will give the distance man more speed to swim the 500 faster.

While all of the above statements seem so obvious that it may seem ridiculous to discuss them in detail, we tend to forget or to overlook them in planning a training program.

The real questions that must be answered in designing a training program are the following:

1. How far should you swim—i.e., 5000 yards a day, 10,000, 12,000, or 20,000?
2. How often should you work out? Once a day? Twice a day? Three times a day?
3. How hard should you swim? How much effort? Should you swim all-out efforts all the time or should you do some moderate and some easy swimming?
4. How many months out of the year should you train? Three months? Ten months? All the time?
5. What methods of training should you emphasize—sprint training, overdistance training, middle-distance training, etc?

There is no definitive answer to any of these questions. Many of the answers must be based on such factors as how much time in the swimming pool is available, how good you want to become, and how much time and energy you have to devote to training.

I would like to devote the rest of this section to a discussion of some of the principles that can be used as guidelines in setting up a training schedule.

Intelligent Planning That Includes Progression in Intensity and Duration

Any training program should include provisions for a steady, progressive increase in the stress factor as the swimmer's training progresses. The swimmer who ultimately will be training a total of 12,000 yards in two workouts a day at the height of his training program (December, January, February, and March) should start with considerably less yardage at the first part of the season, such as in October—5000 yards a day, in November—7500 yards a day. Early in the season he should use the less intense methods of training to a greater extent, i.e., *overdistance training* and *interval training* (we'll discuss this latter method of training soon). As the season progresses, the swimmer's physiological processes adapt to the training stimulus and the body is more capable of handling the more intense methods of training, that is, *sprint training, repetition training,* and *maximum-effort time trials.*

The Use of Intermittent Work and Its Application

Most of the physical activity in which humans engage is of an intermittent nature—very little can be characterized as continuous. We engage in short bouts of activity interrupted by periods of light work or rest. This is true of most of our sports activities—football, baseball, tennis, etc. It is also true of vigorous work, such as digging ditches, working on an air hammer, and so on. Children and animals play their games in this manner. This type of intermittent physical activity is so common that it could be characterized as an inherent pattern of behavior.

Man and animals can work at very intense levels of maximal effort for only short periods of time. They must, therefore, if they are to work continuously, pace themselves and work at lower levels of intensity, or if they do work at high levels of intensity, must alternate these work periods with rest or diminished work. Fatigue during intense activity results from the build-up of fatigue products in the muscle—primarily lactic acid—plus depletion of muscle glycogen and the inability of the body to supply enough oxygen to the muscle. When periods of rest are permitted between the bouts of exercise, the body is able to recover from some of the effects of fatigue by decreasing the level of lactic acid and raising the level of glycogen and oxygen in the muscle. This type of intermittent exercise permits the athlete to work at a more intense level of stress without suffering as much from the cumulative effects of fatigue.

As we will see when we examine the training schedule of champions, most of their training is done with some form of intermittent work.

For many years swimmers trained almost exclusively on continuous types of training, and thirty years ago the workout schedule of a champion might have consisted of the following:

> Swim 1 mile
> Kick ½ mile
> Pull ½ mile

This workout would be an application of the one training method we mentioned earlier—overdistance training. As he got near the bigger swimming meets at the end of the season, a swimmer would probably add some sprints, such as 4 × 50-yard all-out efforts, to his training program.

Interval Training and Related Methods

After World War II—in the late 1940s—champion swimmers started using an intermittent form of training that runners had been using since 1939—a method known as interval training.

Interval Training. Interval training is a method of training in which the body is subjected to regularly repeated submaximal bouts of exercise interspersed with controlled periods of rest. The rest periods are relatively short, and while they do permit partial recovery, they do not permit complete or even nearly complete recovery of the body from the fatigue of the previous bouts of exercise. An example of an interval-training routine would be to swim 15 × 100 yards with a rest interval of 10 seconds between each 100-yard swim.

A great deal of confusion, misinformation, and controversy exists concerning interval training. A more comprehensive review of this method of training and related methods will be found in Chapter 2, "Theory and Research of Training."

The term *interval training* is often erroneously used to describe any training method in which a series of bouts of exercise is interspersed with a series of rest intervals. The term *interval training* obviously has its origin from the use of rest intervals, but to qualify as interval training the method must meet the following criteria:

1. There must be a series of bouts of exercise at submaximal effort.

2. The interval of rest must be short—short enough to permit only partial recovery from the previous bouts of exercise.

If the swimmer were to swim 5 × 100 with 3 to 5 minutes rest between each effort and if each effort was at maximal effort, this would not qualify as interval training but would be categorized as *repetition training*.

Repetition Training. Repetition training is a method of training in which the body is subjected to a series of bouts of exercise at maximum or near-maximum speed interspersed with controlled long periods of rest in which there is relatively complete recovery of the body from the fatigue of the previous bouts of exercise.

The average speed at which the swimmer swims the 15 × 100 with 10 seconds rest interval would be slower than when he swims 5 × 100 with 5 minutes rest. For example, Mark Spitz swam 15 × 100 with 10 seconds rest with an average time of 55.2 seconds, whereas when he swam 5 × 100 with 5 minutes rest his average time was 47.8 seconds.

Repetition training is the ultimate method in terms of intense training stress and should be used sparingly. A small amount of it can be used each day, but if large doses of it are used in each training session, the body will fail to adapt to this level of stress and the swimmer will become overstressed and will be pushed into the stage of failing adaptation.

The proper use of repetition training conditions the body to swim for a moderate length of time at an intense speed, whereas the use of interval training adapts the body to swim at a moderate rate of speed for longer periods of time.

It is desirable to use both methods of training, but the total amount of interval training used in a mixed program of training will be 5 to 10 times greater in total distance than the amount of repetition training. Table 1.2 lists the differences between the two types of training, using sets of repeat swims as done by Olympic champion Jim Montgomery as examples.

When using either method of training, the swimmer or coach has to make decisions concerning four factors before setting up the workout routine. These factors can be easily remembered by remembering the cue word DIRT:

> D—distance to be swum
> I—interval of rest between each repeat swim
> R—repetitions or how many bouts of exercise or repeat swims
> T—average time the distance is to be swum in

The difference between the two methods may be summarized under each of these headings as follows:

1. *Distance.* Both methods can use the same distances (50, 100, 150, 200, 300, etc.).

2. *Interval of Rest.* Interval training uses short rest intervals (5, 10, 15, 30 sec.) while repetition training uses long rest intervals (1, 2, 3 min.).

3. *Repetitions.* Interval training involves the use of many repeats, such as 30 × 50, 20 × 100, 10 × 200, etc., while repetition training uses considerably fewer repeats, i. e., 10 × 50, 5 × 100, 4 × 200, etc.

4. *Time.* In interval training the times used are much slower than those used in repetition training. Repetition training times should be 5 to 15 percent faster than interval training times for the same distance.

Table 1.2
Comparison of Interval Training and Repetition Training

Method	Pulse-rate Average	Quality Developed	Physiological Change
Interval Training			
Example: swim 16 × 200 yd. with 15 sec. rest (average time for Jim Montgomery, 1:56.3)	Before swim 146 After swim 178	1. Primarily endurance 2. A small amount of speed 3. A small amount of tolerance to working at an intense effort when the body is in oxygen debt	1. Improves the efficiency of the cardio-circulatory system by (a) increasing cardiac efficiency—the heart can pump more blood, (b) increasing the number of functional capillaries in the muscles 2. Improves the ability of the muscles to work aerobically 3. Increases amount of glycogen stored in the muscles 4. Improves enzyme action in the muscles that help endurance
Repetition Training			
Example: swim 4 × 200 yd. with 5-min. rest interval (average time 1:45.3)	Before swim 92 After swim 188	1. Some endurance but not as much endurance as is developed above 2. More speed than is developed above 3. Tolerance to working at an intense effort for a moderate length of time (ability to swim middle distances fast)	1. Increases strength of muscles 2. Improves enzyme action in muscles that permits the body to work more efficiently in the absence of adequate oxygen (anaerobically) 3. Improves the ability of the body to tolerate the pain and discomfort associated with fatigue

In a training program a swimmer might also want to swim some of his repeat swims with a moderate amount of rest. For instance, he might swim 10 × 100 with a 45-second rest interval. Would this be interval training or repetition training? It actually is not important what we call it. In distinguishing between the two methods of training I was trying primarily to develop a concept, and it is really not important what the methods are called as long as the reader remembers the following concepts:

1. The shorter the period of the rest interval between repeat swims, the greater the effect on building endurance and the less the effect on speed.

2. The longer the period of the rest interval, the higher the quality of the repeat swim.

3. A swimmer can tolerate large volumes of low or moderate-quality work such as overdistance or interval training, but large quantities of high-quality work such as repetition training or all-out time trials can cause overstress.

Figure 1.1 shows how a swimmer can determine his pulse rate. The use of pulse rate helps the swimmer and coach to evaluate

1. How much effort the swimmer used in swimming a given effort. The higher the pulse rate, the harder the effort has been, with most swimmers reaching maximum pulse rates of 180 to 200 beats per minute.

2. The condition of the swimmer. When the swimmer is in poor condition, a given effort (for example, 60 seconds for 100 yards freestyle) will cause a higher pulse rate than when he is in good condition.

3. His state of fatigue. It may even show when he is ill or becoming ill. Under any of these conditions (fatigue, illness, or incipient illness), the swimmer will have a higher pulse rate than his average. This is particularly true after a moderate swimming effort.

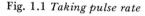

Fig. 1.1 *Taking pulse rate*

Figure A shows the swimmer taking his pulse by placing his right hand on the left side of his chest over the heart, where he can feel the beat of the heart against the rib cage.

Figure B shows that the swimmer can also place his hand on his neck under the jawbone, where he can feel the pulsation of the carotid artery. The swimmer should take his pulse for 6 seconds and multiply by 10 (or take it for 10 seconds and multiply by 6). The pulse should be taken as soon as possible after an effort since the pulse rate decreases very quickly.

Speed-Play Training. Speed-play training is a method of training that is closely related to interval training. In this type of training the swimmer swims continuously but varies his speed from slow to moderate to fast, etc. Frequently referred to as pyramids, a typical workout routine might go as follows:

Swim 1 length slow, 1 length fast, 2 lengths slow, 2 lengths fast, 3 lengths slow, 3 lengths fast, 4 lengths slow, 4 lengths fast, 3 lengths slow, 3 lengths fast, 2 lengths slow, 2 lengths fast, 1 length slow, 1 length fast.

Another variation of a speed-play routine could be used:

Swim 1000 yards by swimming 2 lengths slow, 1 length fast; repeat this routine until you have swum 1000 yards.

The advantage of the use of the intermittent work training methods discussed here is obvious:

1. It permits the athlete to use a more intense training stimulus than continuous training methods.

2. It permits the athlete to be exposed to the stress he will encounter in race conditions not just once but many times in a single workout.

3. It permits unlimited opportunities for changing routines and consequently avoids the boredom associated with continuous training methods.

4. Intermittent type of physical activity is probably more basic to man's nature than is prolonged continuous work.

Figure 1.2 summarizes the differences in the five methods of training that have been discussed.

Fig. 1.2. *Five types of training*

Relative percentage contributions of the various methods of training to speed and endurance.

Source: Counsilman, *The Science of Swimming* (Englewood Cliffs, N.J.: Prentice-Hall, Inc., 1968).

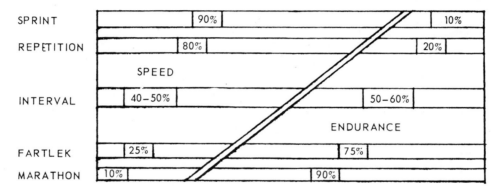

1. *Fartlek Training* (speed play). Fartlek training consists of swimming relatively long distances of one-half mile and over continuously, using a variety of speeds.

2. *Overdistance Training.* Overdistance training consists of training at distances greater than the distance of the event for which the swimmer is training and, naturally, at a speed slower than that he will use in the actual race.

3. *Interval Training.* Interval training consists of swimming a series of repeat efforts at a given distance with a controlled amount of rest between efforts. The rest interval is long enough to permit partial, but not complete, recovery of the heart rate to normal.

4. *Repetition Training.* Repetition training consists of swimming a series of repeats of a shorter distance than and at a greater speed than that swum in a race. The rest interval is long enough to permit almost complete recovery of the heart and respiratory rate.

5. *Sprint Training.* Sprint training consists of swimming all-out efforts at top speed, either in a series (6 X 50 all-out efforts with a long rest) or as isolated efforts (1 X 75, 1 X 50, 1 X 25).

A Mixed Program of Training

Nearly all world-class competitive swimmers use a combination of at least three or four methods of training. When a combination of methods is integrated into a single program of training, it is called a *mixed program*.

Tables 1.3, 1.4, and 1.5 provide three workouts that combine three, four, and five methods into a single workout.

Table 1.3
Early-Season Mixed Workout
(Using Three Methods)

Procedure	Type of Training	Pulse-rate Range (Low-High)	Quality Developed in Percentage Endurance Speed
1. Warm up 800	Overdistance	130	Endurance 90%, speed 5%
2. Swim 16 × 100, 10 sec. rest	Interval training	130-170	Endurance 80%, speed 20%
3. Kick 1000	Overdistance	130	Endurance 90%, speed 10%
4. Pull 5 × 200, 15 sec. rest	Interval training (hypoxic breathing)	130-170	Endurance 80%, speed 20%
5. Swim—1 slow, 1 fast, 2s, 2f, 3s, 3f, 4s, 4f, 3s, 3f, 2s, 2f, 1s, 1f	Speed play	120-170	Endurance 85%, speed 15%

Total Distance: 5000 yd. The primary emphasis is on endurance.

Table 1.4
Midseason Workout
(Using Four Methods)

Procedure	Type of Training	Pulse-rate Range (Low-High)	Quality Developed (Approx. Percentage)
1. Warm up 800	Overdistance	120	Endurance 95%, speed 5%
2. Swim 8 × 200 with 20 sec. rest, 8 × 200 with 10 sec. rest, 4 × 200 with 5 sec. rest	Interval training	140-180	Endurance 80%, speed 20%
3. Kick 500	Overdistance	140	Endurance 90%, speed 10%
4. Kick 5 × 100, 15 sec. rest	Interval training	135-175	Endurance 80%, speed 20%
5. Pull 500	Overdistance	140	Endurance 90% speed 10%
6. Pull 10 × 50, 10 sec. rest	Interval training (hypoxic breathing)	135-175	Endurance 80%, speed 20%
7. Swim 5 × 150, 3 min. rest	Repetition training	95-180	Endurance 50%, speed 50%
8. Swim 8 × 25, all-out effort, 1 min. rest	Sprint training	85-160	Endurance 10%, speed 90%

Total Distance: 7500 yd. In this workout the main emphasis is on endurance, but a greater percentage of speed is introduced than in the early-season routines.

Table 1.5
Late-Season Workout
(Right Before the Taper Begins, Using Five Methods of Training)

Procedure	Type of Training	Pulse-rate Range (Low-High)	Quality Developed (Approx. Percentage)
1. Warm up 800	Overdistance	120	Endurance 95%, speed 5%
2. Swim 8 × 200, 15 sec. rest; 8 × 100, 10 sec. rest; 8 × 50, 5 sec. rest	Interval training	130-180	Endurance 80%, speed 20%
3. Swim 20 × 25 variable sprints, 20 sec. rest	Sprint training	95-170	Endurance 20%, speed 80%
4. Kick 10 × 100, 20 sec. rest	Interval training	130-180	Endurance 75%, speed 25%
5. Pull 1000 yards, 2 lengths slow then 1 length fast, etc.	Speed play (hypoxic breathing)	120-170	Endurance 85%, speed 15%
6. Swim at a very fast speed, 2 to 3 rest intervals: 200, 150, 100, 75, 50	Repetition training	95-180	Endurance 50%, speed 50%
7. Loosen down 500	Overdistance		

Total Distance: 7125 yd. Here a greater emphasis is placed on speed than in the previous two workouts.

Hypoxic Training. Hypoxic training is a method in which a swimmer practices controlled breathing and breathes fewer times than he ordinarily would.

For instance, if he breathes once every arm cycle when swimming a 200-meter repeat swim, he might breathe only half as often by breathing every second arm cycle, or he might even try breathing only one third as often by breathing every third arm cycle. It is really not so much a method of training as it is a type of breathing that can be used with the different methods. This type of breathing can be used when doing any of the five methods of training mentioned earlier in this chapter. When the swimmer takes in less air, the level of oxygen debt in the body is increased and becomes a stress factor that brings about certain desirable physiological changes. Several research studies show that this type of training has desirable effects and improves the athlete's ability to extract more oxygen from the inhaled air. In our practice at Indiana University, approximately one third of our total workout is done with hypoxic breathing, and all of the pulling drills are done with hypoxic breathing, (breathing either every second or every third arm cycle). For a more complete discussion of hypoxic training read "Hypoxic Training and Other Methods of Training Evaluated" (Section 2.1).

Types of Sets of Repeat Swims

While much of the discussion of repeat swims has mentioned the use of rest intervals of 10, 15, 30 seconds, etc., swimmers very seldom use exact rest intervals in their training. Rather than use exact intervals of rest it is much easier to use departure times. That is, a swimmer is swimming 10 × 100 yards with 20-second intervals of rest and he swims each 100 yards in 60 seconds, he can leave every 1 minute 10 seconds, but if he swims each 100 in 58.5 seconds he must start the second one 68.5 seconds after he started the first one. The third one he must then start 2:17.0 after the first one, etc. The bookkeeping becomes staggering. It is much simpler for him to start a 100-repeat swim every 1 minute 10 seconds. For this reason the rest intervals as they are given in this book are only approximations, and each swimmer must work out his departure time so that it gives him approximately the desired rest interval. All of the sets mentioned can be done in an interval or repetition training method.

Straight Sets. A straight set of repeat swims is a set in which the swimmer holds the distance, the rest interval, and the time of each repeat swim constant. *Example*: 30 × 50 meters, departure time 45 seconds, average time to swim distance 28 seconds, average rest interval 17 seconds.

Typical Straight Sets

10 × 50 or	10 × 100 or	8 × 200 or	5 × 400 or	3 × 800 or
20 × 50 or	15 × 100 or	10 × 200 or	8 × 400 or	5 × 800 or
30 × 50	20 × 100	14 × 200	10 × 400	8 × 800

75s, 150s, 300s—in fact any distance can be used

Descending-Time Set. In a descending-time set of repeat swims the swimmer tries to swim each successive repeat faster than the previous one.

Example: 6 × 400 meters, departure time 6 minutes

	1	2	3	4	5	6
Time	4:40	4:38	4:34	4:30	4:28	4:22

This type of set is particularly popular with most world-class swimmers at this time and is used by such world record holders as Mark Spitz, Tim Shaw, Jim Montgomery, Shirley Babashoff, and others. It enables the swimmer to impose various intensities of stress on his body and is physiologically sound. Typical descending-time sets are the same as above in straight sets.

Out-Slow—Back-Hard Set. In this type of set the swimmer swims the first half of each repeat swim slower than the second half; i. e., swim 8 × 200, departure time 3 minutes on each 200. Swim first 100 in 1:08 and second 100 in 1:06 or better for a total time of 2:14 or better. This type of swimming gives the swimmer confidence that he can come back hard in the second half of his race, and it teaches him to pace himself.

Typical Out-Slow—Back-Hard Sets

4 × 200	3 × 400	3 × 800	3 × 1500
8 × 200	5 × 400	6 × 800	
	8 × 400		

Decreasing-Rest-Interval Set. The most popular variation of the standard set of repeats that has been developed recently is the set of repeats in which the interval of rest is decreased as the set progresses, i.e., swim 20 × 100 meters.

> 1. The first 10 × 100 meters is swum with a departure time of 1:20 (this must be adapted to each swimmer—1:20 would be used for a world-class man freestyler) average time 1:10 or better, average rest interval 10 seconds.
> 2. The next 5 × 100 would be swum with a departure time of 1:15 (average time 1:08 or better).
> 3. The last 5 × 100 would be swum with a departure time of 1:10 (average time 1:05 or better).

The world-class male freestyler could do the same type of set using 200 meters as the distance swum with the following departure times:

5 × 200	departure time 2:35
5 × 200	departure time 2:30
5 × 200	departure time 2:25

This type of set varies the stress on the individual and is very challenging. As the season progresses and the swimmer gets into shape, the departure time is gradually decreased. This type of set is particularly good early in the workout because it gives the swimmer a chance to warm up before he really has to exert himself. The swimmer can also measure the improvement in his conditioning by being able to use a shorter departure time.

Typical Decreasing-Rest-Interval Sets

20 × 50 meters on 45	4 × 150 on 2:00	4 × 400 on 5:00	3 × 800 on 10:00
10 × 50 on 40	4 × 150 on 1:50	4 × 400 on 4:50	3 × 800 on 9:30
10 × 50 on 35	4 × 150 on 1:40	4 × 400 on 4:40	

Increasing-Rest-Interval Set. If the rest interval between sets is changed enough, it is possible to combine training methods into one set of repeats. For example, if a swimmer is assigned to do a set of 20 × 100- yard repeat swims, the first 5 × 100 can be done with a 10-second rest interval between each 100, the second 5 × 100 with a 20-second rest interval, the third 5 × 100 with a 30-second rest interval, and the last 5 × 100 with a 1-minute rest interval. As the rest interval is increased, the swimmer is expected to swim at a faster speed, and the method changes from the first set, which is strictly interval training, to the last set of 100s, which has a 1-minute rest and which qualifies as repetition training (in reality the swimmers will not use exact rest-interval times but will use departure times as described in the previous set of repeats).

Typical Increasing-Rest-Interval Sets
(Using departure times for good male freestyler)

10 × 50 m. on 40	4 × 200 on 2:30	3 × 400 on 5:00
10 × 50 on 50	4 × 200 on 2:45	3 × 400 on 5:30
10 × 50 on 60	4 × 200 on 3:00	3 × 400 on 6:00

It is important to restate here that the different stroke swimmers on your team will all have different take-off intervals. Even swimmers using the same stroke will have to use different take-off intervals, depending on their ability.

Varying-Distance Sets. A set of repeat swims that many swimmers find challenging is one in which the distance of each repeat swim is changed.

> *Example A.*
>   1. Swim 400, look at 300.
>   2. Swim 300 faster than you were at the 300 on the way
>   to the 400—look at your 200.
>   3. Swim 200 faster than the 200 above in 2, look at 100.
>   4. Swim 100 faster than above in 3.
>
> *Example B.   Typical Varying-Distance Sets*
>   1. Swim 4 × 400, 30-sec. rest interval.
>   2. Swim 4 × 200, 20-sec. rest interval.
>   3. Swim 4 × 100, 10-sec. rest interval.
>   4. Swim 4 × 50, 10-sec. rest interval.
>
> *Example C.*
>   1. Swim 100   Allow 30 sec. to 1 min. between each swim.
>   2. Swim 200
>   3. Swim 300
>   4. Swim 400
>   5. Swim 300
>   6. Swim 200
>   7. Swim 100
>
> *Example D.*
>   1. Swim 10 × 50, 10-sec. RI.
>   2. Swim 4 × 100, 15-sec. RI.
>   3. Swim 4 × 200, 30-sec. RI.

This type of set of repeats offers limitless opportunities for variety. The swimmer and coach must be careful not to use these sets exclusively, because they do offer a smorgasbord of bits and pieces and cannot be substituted for the use of straight sets or broken sets. We use them in our program two or three times a week (when doing one workout a day). They can be done either in interval-training or in repetition-training methods.

Broken Swims. A method of training that we use at least twice a week during the hard-training phase of our program is referred to as *broken swims.* If the swimmer is training for a 200-meter race he might want to work on his 200 pace of perhaps 2 minutes for 200 meters. He can do this by swimming 4 × 50 repeat swims, and swimming each 50 meters in 30 seconds and allowing 10 seconds rest interval between each 50 swim. This permits him to swim his broken 200 at the same tempo he will want to use in the 200-meter race. The 10 seconds rest between each 50 permits enough recovery to maintain a fast tempo for the entire 200 meters.

Broken 300s. Broken 300s usually consist of 3 × 100 repeats, with 10 seconds rest interval between each 100. This gives the swimmer a total of two rest periods of 10 seconds each, or a total elapsed rest-interval time of 20 seconds. If the swimmer is using a pace clock he can start when the second hand hits 20, and then his actual swimming time will show up on the pace clock.

Broken 400s. Broken 400s can be swum as 4 X 100 with a 10-second rest interval between each 100 for a total elapsed time of 20 seconds, and once again a swimmer can cancel out this rest-time interval by starting his broken swim when the second hand hits 30.

They can also be done as 8 X 50. If the swimmer is doing 400 with a 10-second rest interval between each 50, he will have a total of 7 rest intervals or a total rest time of 70 seconds. He must therefore start his broken swim on 50.

Broken 800s. Broken 800s are usually done as 8 X 100 with a rest interval of 10 seconds between each 100. The swimmer should start when the second hand hits 50.

Broken swims can be of any distance the swimmer or coach wants to make them, i.e., broken 100—4 X 25, broken 1500—15 X 100. The rest interval can be 5, 10, 15, 20 seconds, etc. If the set of repeats is short, such as 4 X 50 (broken 200), and the rest interval is short (such as 10 seconds), the type of training would qualify as a cross between interval training (because of the short rest interval) and repetition training (because it will probably be swum at a very fast speed).

Typical Sets of Broken Swims

Swim 8 X broken 200s (4 X 50)	These can be swum with the swim-
Swim 5 X broken 400s (4 X 100)	mer trying to keep them at the
Swim 3 X broken 800s (8 X 100)	same time or trying to go each
Swim 2 X broken 1500s (15 X 100)	succeeding one faster as in de-
	creasing time sets.

The swimmer can also do his kicking or pulling in the same manner such as 2 X broken 400 kicks (4 X 100—10 second RI).

Mixing Broken Swims and Straight Swims

A combination of two methods is the use of alternating broken sets and straight swims as follows:

Example A.
1. Swim a broken 200 (4 X 50—10 sec. RI).
2. Swim a straight 200.
   Repeat the above 3, 4, or 5 times so a total of 6, 8, or 10 X 200 has been swum. Allow approximately 1 min. between each 200.

Example B.
1. Swim a broken 400—4 X 100 (or 8 X 50).
2. Swim a straight 400.
   Repeat the above 2, 3, or 4 times until a total of 4, 6 or 8 X 400 has been swum.

Example C.
1. Swim a broken 400—4 X 100—10-sec. RI.
2. Swim a straight 400.
3. Swim a broken 300—3 X 100—10 sec. RI.
4. Swim a straight 300.
5. Swim a broken 200—4 X 50—10-sec. RI.
6. Swim a straight 200.
   Allow 1 to 2 min. between each swim.

Example D. A Mixed Set for a Distance Swimmer
1. Swim a broken 1500—15 X 100—5-sec. RI.
2. Swim a straight 1500.
3. Swim a broken 800—8 X 100—5-sec. RI.
4. Swim a straight 800.
5. Swim a broken 400—4 X 100—5-sec. RI.
6. Swim a straight 400.
   Allow 1 to 2 min. between each swim.

I find mixing broken swims with straight swims is a good method to use when the swimmers get tired of doing straight sets. The general pattern we follow is for the swimmers to do them by decreasing their time as the set progresses. In a set of 200s, the third broken 200, for instance, is faster than the second, and the second is faster than the first. The third straight is faster than the second straight, and the second is faster than the first. In other words, the times on the broken swims are compared only to the times on the other broken swims, and the times on the straight swims only to those on the other straight swims. The time on the broken swims would generally be faster (cancelling out the rest intervals) than those on the straight swims.

The swimmer and coach can devise their own combination of swims and can use any distance, any rest interval, or any number of repeats they wish. The most common ones are those I have mentioned previously.

SECTION 1.2
PLANNING A YEAR'S TRAINING PROGRAM

Careful planning of a season's program consists of establishing a general outline of a program for the entire season that is based on a sound physiological concept. This outline does not have to be followed rigidly, and the fact that the swimmer or coach has set the plan down in writing does not commit him to staying with the plan if he decides it is not "doing the job." A preseason planning session with the coach and the team is a necessity in my opinion, and should consider all of the training concepts and principles discussed in this section. In Table 1.6 I have outlined the program that we use with our swimmers at Indiana University.

Each program varies one from another. The program I have outlined for the swimmers I coach can serve as a guide, but each coach must make adaptations that will suit his team and its particular circumstances. In Table 1.7 I have provided a blank chart for the reader to use in setting up his own program. I would recommend you have photocopies of this chart made as you may want to make corrections or use them for several years.

Table 1.6
Plan for a Year's Training Program, 1975-1976

	September	October	November
Number of Workouts per Week	Workouts are optional.	5	6
Total Time and Distance per Week A.M. P.M.		1 hr.—3000 yd.	2 hr.—6000 to 7000 yd.
Dry-Land Exercises How Often and How Long	Administer strength, flexibility, and power tests.	1 hr.—4 days a week—mostly isokinetic exercise	45 min.—5 days a week—isokinetic exercise
Type of Training **Type of Sets**	Either stay out of water *or* play water polo *or* Swim easy—no formal training.	Overdistance and short-rest-interval training Do sets of 150s, 200s, 300s, 400s, 800s—stay away from short-distance and sprint training	Overdistance, short-rest-interval training, repetition training, and some sprinting Add 50, 75, 100 repeats plus some 25 yd. sprints
GENERAL PLAN	This is the best month to take it easy, to get away from the pool—play some tennis or paddle ball. The body needs to rest—use this time for a change of pace.	Practice begins this month. Concentrate on building strength and doing some swimming. This is a good time to work on stroke mechanics, for team members to look at movies and work on weaker strokes.	The tempo of practice picks up and more high-quality work is introduced into practice. Still keep up the isokinetic exercise, but reduce time by 15 min. Continue stroke work and talks on training.
	March	April	May
Number of Workouts per Week	8 to 10	6 to 10	5 to 10
Total Time and Distance per Week A.M. P.M.	45 min. to 1 hr.—2000 to 3500 yd. 1 hr. to 2¼ hr.—3000 to 7000 yd.	Short loosen-up workout 1 hr. to 1½ hr.—3000 to 4000 yd.	1 hr.—3000 to 4000 yd. 2 hr.—6000 to 8000 yd.
Dry-Land Exercises How Often and How Long	20 min.—3 days a week	15 min.—3 days a week	30 min.—4 days a week
Type of Training **Type of Sets**	Mixed training—avoid too much high-quality work. Do lots of easy swimming, some slow interval training, some sprinting and pace work.	Mixed training—just enough to stay in shape to swim in National AAUs in mid-April.	Mixed training—as in Jan. and Feb., but concentrate on endurance work.
GENERAL PLAN	This is the time for tapering. Start taper 2 to 2½ weeks before big meet. Gradually reduce yardage until 3 days before meet when it should be 2000 to 3000 yd. Prepare mentally for big meet.	Swim for first 2 weeks until National AAUs, then lay off for 2 weeks before beginning training for summer season.	Swimmers work once or twice a day, depending on academic schedule. (At Indiana University classes end the first week of May and swimmers begin twice a day in 50-meter pool as soon as exams are over.)

December	January	February
11	11	11
1¼ hr.—3000 to 4500 yd.	1¼ hr.—3000 to 4500 yd.	1¼ hr.—3000 to 4500 yd.
2¼ hr.—6000 to 8000 yd.	2¼ hr.—6000 to 9000 yd.	2¼ hr.—6000 to 9000 yd.
30 min.—4 days a week—isokinetic exercise	30 min.—4 days a week—isokinetic exercise	30 min.—4 days a week—isokinetic exercise
Mixed training—a combination of all methods. Break team into 3 groups: sprinters, others, and distance. Do all types of sets.	Mixed training—introduce broken swimming into workouts; start doing more sprints. The swimmers should start feeling tired.	Mixed training—have swimmers try to do best repeat times. Watch for good performances in repetition sets of repeats.
For next 3 months the swimmers work out twice a day. Exercises continue. Swimmers should improve times in repeats and begin reducing take-off times on short-rest-interval training repeats.	Continue hard work, keep interest high by varying workouts. Don't break training for dual meets. Get a few swimmers ready to make cut-off times in their events. Continue stroke work.	This is the month in which swimmers are most likely to get sick. Watch for colds and other respiratory infections. Tell swimmers to dress warmly, get plenty of sleep, and eat properly.

June	July	August
12	12	8 to 11
2½ hr.—7000 to 9000 yd.	2½ hr.—5000 to 9000 yd.	1-1½ hr.—3000 to 5000 yd.
2 hr.—5000 to 6000 yd.	2 hr.—3000 to 6000 yd.	1-1½ hr.—2000 to 3000 yd.
30 min.—4 days a week	30 min.—3 days a week	Eliminate all dry-land exercise
Mixed training—emphasize improving times and decreasing departure times for the various sets of repeats.	Mixed training—more time spent on pace work and sprinting. Avoid too much high-quality work.	Mixed training—decrease number of repeat swims. Increase pace work and sprinting.
This will be the hardest month of the year. Swimmers must get plenty of sleep and rest and must watch diet. Coach must plan workouts carefully and watch for signs of failing adaptation.	This is the last full month of training because Nationals occur in mid-August. This should be a month of moderately hard work in which swimmers are not pushed so hard they can't recover by the National Meet.	Tapering begins around first of August (assuming Nationals, discontinue training for two weeks).

Table 1.7
Plan for a Year's Training Program, 19 -19

	September	October	November
Number of Workouts per Week			
Total Time and Distance per Week A.M. P.M.			
Dry-Land Exercises How Often and How Long			
Type of Training			
Type of Sets			
GENERAL PLAN			

	March	April	May
Number of Workouts per Week			
Total Time and Distance per Week A.M. P.M.			
Dry-Land Exercises How Often and How Long			
Type of Training			
Type of Sets			
GENERAL PLAN			

December	January	February

June	July	August

SECTION 1.3
PLANNING EACH WEEK'S TRAINING PROGRAM

Each Sunday I try to find time to sit down for an hour or two and plan the following week's workouts, day by day. I do not necessarily commit myself to these workouts, come what may; in fact, I usually change them by the end of the week.

This kind of planning is beneficial for several reasons:

1. It forces the coach to reflect on what he is going to do for the week and to adopt a plan that conforms to the scientific principles of training.

2. It permits the coach to balance the entire week's program in terms of the amount of sprint work, overdistance, interval training, and repetition training he will use.

3. It assures the coach that he will not duplicate the same set of repeats inadvertently, and it provides the variety that is needed in a training program to prevent boredom.

4. At some time during the week the coach may find himself without the time to plan that particular day's workouts. If he has already done some planning earlier in the week, he will not be forced to make up the workout as he goes along.

I never post the entire week's schedule. I list only one workout at a time. I have found that most swimmers don't want to know exactly what they will be doing tomorrow or the day after. They do like to know the general plan of the workouts, but they prefer to allow the specifics to wait their turn in the general scheme.

General Plan—Winter Season

In the program at Indiana University during the academic year the morning workout is the shortest (1¼ to 1½ hours) and the afternoon workout is the longest (2¼ hours). The reverse is true in the summer, with the morning workout being the longest (2½ hours) and the afternoon workouts the shortest (1¾ hours). The swimmers are classified in three groups: sprinters, others (all flyers, backstrokers, and breaststrokers, and most crawl swimmers), and distance swimmers.

Overall Plan for a Week's Workout

Morning Session (total distance between 3500 and 5000 yards, workout time between 1¼ and 1½ hours). Although the general overall plan will be as outlined below, I believe the coach should occasionally break away completely from the plan and do an entirely different workout just for variety. Following I have listed the items done in the workout and their sequence:

1. Warm up 500 to 800 yd. (any combination of easy swimming, kicking, and pulling).
2. Swim a set of short (5 to 20 sec.) rest-interval-training repeats that total 1000 to 1500 yd., such as 20 to 30 × 50, 14 to 20 × 75, 10 to 15 × 100, 7 to 10 × 150, 5 to 7 × 200, 4 to 6 × 250. Plan to use a different set each day of the week. Some days mix up the sets, i.e., 8 × 100, then 8 × 50.

3. Kick 500—one day kick continuously, the next do the kicking in an interval-training method, such as 20 × 25, 10 × 50, or 5 × 100.
4. Pull 500—on the days you kick 500 continuously, do the 500 pulling in an interval-training method, and vice versa.
5. This segment of the workout may be one of the following:
   a. An overdistance swim (500, 800, 1000, or 1650 for time—out-slow—back-hard).
   b. A series of short-rest-interval-training repeats totaling about 800 to 1600 yd. Do a different set than was done in the second segment of the workout.
   c. A series of high-quality repeats (anaerobic work) with a long rest—3 × 150 with 3-min. rest interval.
   d. Sprints—swim 10 × 50 leaving every 1½ min.

The type of repeat swims done in this part of the workout depends to a great extent on what is planned for the workout in the afternoon. If a high-quality workout is planned, this section of the morning workout should not be high quality, but should be overdistance or short-rest-interval training.

Distance swimmers. Distance swimmers should do around 5000 yards in the morning. They do almost the same workout as the other swimmers, but double the length of the repeats in Sections 2 and 5 of the workout. For example, if the *others* are going 10 × 100, the distance swimmers should go 10 × 200. In Section 5, if the *others* are going 800, the distance swimmers should swim 1650.

Stroke swimmers. The flyers, backstrokers, and breaststrokers must make adjustments of the total number of repeat swims they accomplish in Sections 2 and 5 of the workout by reducing the total number slightly. That is, if the freestylers are going 10 × 100, the flyers and backstrokers will go only 9 × 100, and the breaststrokers only 8 × 100. This is done in order that all swimmers may finish that section of the workout at approximately the same time and may start the next section of the workout together. The distance men have to operate pretty much on their own and can do only part of the workout at the same time as the rest of the team.

Fig. 1.3. *Kicking and pulling*

Kicking and pulling are important parts of a swimmer's training routine. They permit the swimmer the opportunity to isolate and overload the muscles of the legs and arms. They also add variety to the swimmer's workout routine.

Figure A. Three pieces of swimming equipment: the pulling tube (a tractor tube with a 7-inch inside diameter), the plastic foamex kickboard, and the pull buoy.

Figure B. Many swimmers prefer to use the tube because it creates more drag than does the pull buoy. I allow the swimmer at Indiana University the choice of either the tube or the pull buoy.

Table 1.8
Weekly Plan for January 19, 1976 to January 25, 1976

	Monday	Tuesday	Wednesday

MORNING	1. W.U.800
	2. Swim 16 × 75 Hyp.
	  on :55 (Fly on :60,
	    Back on :60,
	    Br. on 1:10)
	3. Kick 500 continuously
	4. Pull 5 × 100 on 1:15
	  Free to 1:45 Br.Hyp
	5. Swim 1000 for time
	  split negative
	  Dis. Men—W.U.800, then
	  Swim 4 × 1000
	
	Total Distance
	Others—4000
	Dis.— 4800
		1. W.U. 500
		2. S.10 × 125 Hyp.
		3. K.5 × 100
		4. P.500 continously
		  Hyp.
		5. S.5 × 300
		  Dis.—4 × 500
		
		Total Distance
		Others—4250
		Dis.— 4750
			1. W.U.800
			2. S.3 × 200
			  3 × 150
			  3 × 100
			3. K.500 continuously
			4. P.10 × 50 Hyp.
			5. S.12 × 25
			  Dis.—S.1650
			
			Total Distance
			Others—3450
			Dis.— 4700

AFTERNOON	1. W.U.1200
	  S.Hyp.
	  10 × 100 on 1:10 Free
	    1:15 Back
	    Fly
	    1:25 Br.
	  5 × 100 on 1:05 Free
	    1:10 Back
	    Fly
	    1:20 Br.
	  5 × 100 on 1:00 Free
	    1:05 Back
	    Fly
	    1:15 Br.
	3. S.12 × 25 Every other one
	  fast from a push-off
	4. K.400-then 3 × 200
	5. P.400-then 4 × 150 Hyp.
	6. S.4 × 500 on 7 min.
	  Dis. 2 × 1000
	
	Total Distance
	Others—7500
	Dis.— 8500
	Spr.— 6000
		1. W.U. 800
		2. S.5 × 200 on 2:20
		  3 × 200 on 2:15
		  2 × 200 on 2:10
		  Dis.—8 × 400
		  Spr.—Go 100s
		3. S.800—negative split
		4. K.800—then 8 × 25
		5. P.1000 Hyp.
		6. A. S. broken 400, 4 ×
		  100—10 sec. R.I. be-
		  tween 100s
		  B. S. straight 400
		  C. Repeat A and B for a
		  total of 6 × 400
		  Spr. 300s
		
		Total Distance
		Others—8000
		Dis.— 8600
		Spr.— 6400
			1. W.U.1200
			2. S.
			  6 × 150 on 1:45 Free
			    1:55 Back
			    Fly
			    2:15 Br.
			  4 ×150 on 1:40 Free
			    1:50 Back
			    Fly
			    2:10 Br.
			  4 × 150 on 1:35 Free
			    1:45 Back
			    Fly
			    2:05 Br.
			3. S.16 × 50 variable sprints
			4. K.600 continuously, then
			  8 × 50
			5. P.600 continuously, then
			  2 × 200
			6. S.1000 continuously, con-
			  centrating on working
			  turns hard and swimming
			  easy
			7. S.5 × 200 Repetition
			  Training (with long R.I. of
			  3 min.)
			  Spr.-150s
			  Dis.-4 × 500
			
			Total Distance
			Others—7700
			Dis.— 8900
			Spr.— 6450

Note: Most workouts outlined for "Others" are for middle-distance freestylers, breast, back, and butterfly swimmers. In repeat swims the sprinters do either half or three-fourths of the distance assigned the "Others," and unless noted otherwise, the distance men double the distance, (i.e., if the "Others" are doing 10 × 100, the sprinters would do either 10 × 50 or 10 × 75, and the distance men 10 × 200)

Thursday	Friday	Saturday	Sunday

1. W.U. 500
2. S. 10 × 100
3. K. 500 continuously
4. P. 500 continuously
5. Complete the workout with anything you want to do to a total of 1500
 	
Total Distance
Others—4000
Dis.— 5000
Sp.— 3000
	1. W.U. as you would before prelims. of NCAAs
	For example:
	  A. S.K. or P. a total of 800 yd.
	  B. S. 4 to 6 × 50
	  C. K. 300
	  D. K. 2 × 50
	  E. Sprint 2 × 25
	  F. Loosen down 200
	2. S. any of the following:
	  A. 1 × 400 B. a pace
	    1 × 300 1650
	    1 × 200 C. 20 × 50
	    1 × 100 on :60
	
	Total Distance
	2450 to 3000
		Dual Meet at 2:00 P.M.
		
		All swimmers must work out before the meet.
			Morning off unless you want to be videotaped for underwater stroke analysis, in which case be at the pool between 10:30 and 1:30.

1. W.U. 1200 :40
2. S. 20 × 50 on :45
             :50
             :35
  10 × 50 on :40
             :45
             :30
  10 × 50 on :35
             :40
  Dis. 30 × 100
3. S. 1000 split negative
4. K. 1000 continuously
5. P. 1000 continuously Hyp.
6. S. 1 Broken 400-10 R.I.
    1 Straight 400
    1 Broken 300-10 R.I.
    1 Straight 300
    1 Broken 200-10 R.I.
    1 Straight 200
  Dis. 1 Broken 1500
      1 Straight 1500
  Spr. 200-20-0-200-150-
  150-100-100
 	
Total Distance
Others—7000
Dis.— 9200
Spr.— 6100
	1. W.U. 800
	2. S. 8 × 100
	    8 × 75
	    8 × 50
	  Dis.—Double
	  Spr.—Half
	3. K. 10 × 100
	4. P. 10 × 100 Hyp.
	5. S. Others 3 × 500
	    Dis. 3 × 100
	    Spr. 3 × 300
	6. Work on Starts and Relay Take-offs
	
	Total Distance
	Others—6100
	Dis.— 7600
	Spr.— 5500
		Dual Meet at 2:00 P.M.
		
		Swimmers come in at 12:30 P.M. and do the following warm-up:
		
		1. W.U. 800
		2. S. 20 × 50 (Dis. 12 × 100)
		3. K. 400
		4. P. 400 Hyp.
		5. S. Sprints, such as 2 × 25
		After the meet, team members who go 20 × 100 will receive credit for one workout
		
		Total Distance
		Others—4650
		Dis.— 4850
		(Not including distance swum in races)
			4:30—6:30 P.M.
			
			There will be a make-up workout for those who have not done 11 workouts this week
			
			1. W.U. 500
			2. S. 8 × 50
			3. K. 400
			4. P. 400 Hyp.
			5. S. 3 × 800
			
			Total Distance-4100
			All swimmers do same workout

Code: W.U.—Warm up, S.—Swim, K.—Kick, P.—Pull, Hyp.—Hypoxic, Dis.—Distance Swimmers, Others—Middle Distance Swimmers, Spr.—Sprinters, Fly—Butterfly, Br.—Breaststrokers, Back—Backstrokers, on 60 sec. refers to departure time, R.I.—Rest Interval. Distance is measured in yards.

Table 1.9

Weekly Plan For _____ to _____

	Monday	Tuesday	Wednesday
MORNING			
AFTERNOON			

Thursday	Friday	Saturday	Sunday

Sprinters. The sprinters will also change Sections 2 and 5 of the workout, but in the opposite direction by reducing the distance of the repeats. That is, while the *others* are going 10 × 100, the sprinters will go either 10 × 75 or 10 × 50.

Afternoon Session (total distance between 7200 and 9000 yards, workout time 2¼ hours). A typical plan is as follows:

1. Warm up 800 to 1200 yd. (¼ swim, ¼kick, ¼ pull, ¼swim)
2. Swim a set of short-rest-interval-training repeats with a total yardage of between 1800 and 3000 yd.
   Use a decreasing-rest-interval set, that is:
      Crawl—10 × 100 on 1:10 + 5 × 100 on 1:05 + 5 × 100 on 1:00
      Breast—8 × 100 on 1:25 + 4 × 100 on 1:20 + 4 × 100 on 1:15.
      Fly and Back—9 × 100 on 1:15 + 4 × 100 on 1:10 + 4 × 100 on 1:05
      Distance—8 × 200 on 2:20 + 4 × 200 on 2:15 + 4 × 200 on 2:05.
         On other days of the week, other sets of repeats may be done at these distances: 50, 75, 100, 125, 150, 200, 250, 300, 400.
3. On alternate days use the following type of efforts:
   a. Swim a set of sprints—12 × 25 with 30-sec. rest)
      or
   b. Swim an overdistance effort—out slow/back hard (400, 500, 800, or 1000)
4. Kick a total of 800 to 1200 yd., half easy and the rest in repeats (kick 500 easy, then kick 10 × 50 on 50 sec., or 5 × 100 on 1:40).
5. Pull the same distance and in a similar manner to the kicking, except do a different set of repeats (if you kicked 5 × 100, then pull 3 × 200 or 10 × 50).
6. Swim a set of repeats. This is probably the most important part of both the morning and the afternoon workout.
   a. Two days a week (Monday and Wednesday) do a high-quality set of repeats (repetition training) with a moderate rest interval and composed of any of the following: 20 × 50 on 60 sec., 10 × 100 on 2 min., 7 × 150 on 3 min., 5 × 200 on 4 min. Keep a close check on the times and record them in a daily log.
   b. Two days a week (Tuesday and Thursday) do a set of broken swims (4 × broken 200—a broken 200 consists of 4 × 50 with a 10-sec. rest interval between each 50).
   c. If the swimmers are tired and appear to have had too much high-quality work, give them a low-pressure, low-quality workout, such as (a) a continuous 1000 easy swim for no time, (b) a 3 × 400 progressive swim (each one faster than the previous), or (c) work on starts and turns.
7. On three days a week (approximately) finish the workout with some sprinting. These sprints should be done on the days when you have done overdistance in Section 2 of the workout. For example,
   a. Swim 10 × 50 EOOF (every other one fast), moderate to long rest interval, starting a fast 50 every 2 min.
   b. Swim 12 × 25 with 30-sec. rest interval.
   c. Time three all-out 50s from a dive.

Table 1.8 is a weekly plan for an Indiana University team for midseason. Table 1.9 is a blank copy of the same table suitable for reproduction by a coach or swimmer (see pp. 24-27).

SECTION 1.4
TRAINING THE DISTANCE SWIMMER

Earlier in this chapter the difference between the type of workouts used for distance swimmers and those for the rest of the team was discussed. The difference is probably obvious to the reader, but he will gain more insight into the necessity for different types of workouts if he reads "Hypoxic Training and Other Methods of Training Evaluated" (Chapter 2, Section 2.1) and "Power: What Is It, How Do You Measure It, and What Does It Mean to the Coach and the Swimmer?" (Chapter 2, Section 2.2).

The main differences for the distance swimmer are as follows:

1. More aerobic work
   a. Overdistance swimming
   b. Short-rest interval training
2. More work: The swimmer should go 20 to 40% more total distance in each workout (providing the time is available).
3. Longer repeat swims than the rest of the team is doing. If the rest of the team is doing a set of repeats such as 8 X 150, the distance swimmer should double this distance and go 6 or even 8 X 300.

Some of the typical sets of repeats for senior-level distance swims, as used in separate workouts, are listed here:

```
     20 to 40 X 100
     10 to 20 X 200
      8 to 14 X 300
      8 to 12 X 400
      4 to  8 X 800
     1, 2, or 3 X 1500
```

In "How Champions Train" (Section 1.10) the reader may examine some workouts of distance swimmers. It will be noted that even the better distance swimmers do not eliminate all speed work, such as sprinting, or high-quality work, such as repetition training, from their training programs. *All swimmers need a mixed program of training—* the distance man, however, must put more emphasis on those types of training that develop endurance.

SECTION 1.5
TRAINING THE SPRINTER

The sprinter needs more explosive power and less endurance than the middle-distance and distance swimmers. Since he swims the 50-, the 100-, and sometimes the 200-yard distances he needs good endurance and he should thus not eliminate all endurance work from his training program. He also needs to do some overdistance swimming and some short-rest-interval training. He, however, should put more emphasis on the types of training that develop speed. In general his training program can be adjusted from that of the rest of the team in the following manner:

1. Do more anaerobic work
   a. Sprinting
   b. High-quality repetition training
2. Do less work—the sprinter should do 20 to 30% less than the middle-distance swimmer, but he should increase the speed of the work he does.
3. Use shorter repeats than the rest of the team, and in general use longer rest intervals. If the rest of the team is going 8 × 150, the coach may want the sprinters to go 8 × 100 or even 8 × 75 on the same take-off interval as the swimmers who are swimming the 150s.

The sprinter needs to train his system to release energy fast and to be able to operate in oxygen debt. To do this he has to expose his body to these conditions almost daily. Some high-quality work each day is indicated. The sprinter should also read Chapter 2, "Theory and Research of Training," to gain a better insight into why he has to train in a certain manner.

SECTION 1.6
TRAINING FOR THE INDIVIDUAL MEDLEY

Individual Medley swimmers are faced with a problem of whether to train all four strokes each day or to train one stroke in one workout, another stroke in the next workout. I believe they should adopt a plan that will give them a fairly even distribution of time among all strokes, but I also believe they should not work the same amount of time on each stroke every day. In Table 1.10 I have listed the workout pattern I devised for Gary Hall and Fred Tyler, both National champions and holders of the American records in the individual medley (see p. 32).

SECTION 1.7
ADJUSTING WORKOUTS TO FIT THE VARIOUS AGE-GROUP LEVELS

Frequently, after talking about training methods at a clinic, I have had coaches come to me and say, "You told us how to train world champions—now tell us how to train age-groupers or high-school swimmers." While it is true that too many of us get intrigued with the manner in which champions are trained, I believe that all of the material I have covered in this book is as applicable to the age-group swimmer as to the National or Olympic champion.

I too have coached age-groupers and have done so for my entire coaching career. I give them almost the same workouts I use with our champions except that I adjust the workouts for the younger, less experienced swimmers in the following manner:

1. Decrease the total time and the total distance they swim.
Example: If the team is divided into three levels, the following schedule might be established:

Green Team (beginning competitive swimmers): 1 hour a day, 5 workouts a week, cover about 2000 yards in a workout.
Red Team (intermediate level): 1½ hours a day, 6 workouts a week, cover about 4000 yards in a workout.
Blue Team (advanced level): 2 hours a day, 6 workouts a week, cover about 6000 yards a workout. During the summer season and part of the indoor season these swimmers will work out twice a day for a total of 11 workouts.

2. Decrease the number of and the distance of the repeats.
Example: If the championship swimmers were doing 20 X 150 repeat swims on a departure time of 1:40, this could be adjusted for the various levels in the following manner:

Blue Team: 20 X 100 on 1:30
Red Team: 12 X 100 on 2:00
Green Team: 12 X 50 on 2:00

I would recommend that a coach should use a mixed program of training which will combine all five methods of training no matter what level of age-group swimmer he may be training.

An age-group coach cannot usually break up the team into three groups—distance, others, and sprinter—but must break the group into skill levels. Even then he will not have a very homogeneous group. He must then assign the better swimmers to a certain lane, the next best to the next lane, etc. In this manner he can assign a different number of repeat swims to each lane and use different departure times. For example, Lane 1 (the better swimmers) will swim 10 X 100 with a departure time of 1:30. Lane 2 (swimmers with a level of skill that is slightly lower) will do 8 X 100 with departure time of 1:45. Lane 3 will do 7 X 100 with a departure time of 2 minutes, etc.

When I work with an age-group team I have one assistant who does nothing more at this stage than set up the lanes in which each swimmer will swim. As the swimmer becomes more skillful and better conditioned, he can be moved into a faster lane if the move is warranted. Of course, this must be at the expense of someone who will have to be moved down, so such a move can only be justified if the latter swimmer is holding up the faster swimmers in his lane and if they are bumping into him as they swim circles.

The main limiting factors in how far and how hard a coach can work any team—whether it is age-group, high school, or college—are

1. The length of available pool time
2. The degree of organization of the program
3. The level of motivation of the swimmer
4. The type of program the coach believes in and presents to the swimmer
5. The level of skill of the swimmer

I watched a high-school team spend two hours in the pool area at a practice session in which the team went less than 2000 yards. The average age-group swimmer should go at least 2500 to 3000 yards per hour, whereas high-school and college swimmers can go 3000 to 4000 yards per hour. Any coach who succeeds in accomplishing only 1000 to 2000 yards per hour is not doing his job. I know a 59-year-old master swimmer who averages 3000 yards per hour in his workouts. I use this fact to illustrate the absurdity of achieving as little distance as some teams do and to show the reader that it is easy for the average young swimmer to do 3000 yards an hour. The purpose of a workout is not just to grind out yardage, and I don't want to leave the reader with that impression. However, swimmers come to the pool to swim, not to sit on their derrieres on a poolside bench or to spend time throwing kickboards or discussing the latest record releases. They deserve a well-organized practice that will enhance everyone's feeling of accomplishment and will contribute to team spirit.

Table 1.10
Training for the Individual Medley

Workout Pattern for All Swimmers—Minimum of 11 workouts per week: 6 afternoon practices
(2¼ hrs—6000 to 9000 yds.) and 5 morning or evening practices (1 hr. 10 min.—3000 to
5000 yds.)

Monday	*Tuesday*	*Wednesday*
Warm up 400 Swim 12 × 100 on 1:15 Kick 400 Pull 400 Swim 2 × 500 Entire workout done free-style	Warm up 400 Swim 6 × 150 Kick 4 × 150 Pull 4 × 150 Swim 18 × 50 Entire workout swum back-stroke	Warm up 400 Swim 6 × 100 Kick 200, then 3 × 100 Pull 200, then 3 × 100 Swim 400, 300, 200, 100 Entire workout swum breast-roke
Warm up 800 (200-s, 200-k, 200-p, 200-s) Kick 100, pull 100, swim 100—repeat 10 times alternating strokes Swim 800 free Swim 8 × 200 on 3 min.-1st 200 fly, 2nd IM, 3rd back, 4th IM, 5th breast, 6th IM, 7th free, 8th IM	Warm up 1200 Swim 20 × 50 fly 10 × 50 free Kick 500, then 5 × 100, free and fly alternating Swim 30 × 25 sprints, free and fly alternating Swim 16 × 100 on 2 min. in 4 sets of 4 × 100—1st set fly, 2nd free, 3rd fly, 4th free	*Switching workout** Warm up IM Swim 3 broken 400 IMs-4 × 100, 10 sec. rest Sprint 30 × 25—1 kick, 1 pull, 1 swim, alternating Kick 600 IM, then 12 × 50, alternating strokes Pull same as kick Swim 4 × 200 from dive—1st 2 IM, 2nd 2 fly
TOTAL: 7000 yd.	TOTAL: 7000 yd.	TOTAL: 6000 yd.

*Switching Workouts: In this type of workout, emphasis is placed on working on switching
from one stroke to another. For example, if the swimmer swims a 400 IM, he might switch
strokes every 25 instead of every 100. Broken swims are also done so that the swimmer will not

Policies for Individual Medley Swimmers
1. Each I.M. swimmer must work on his weakest stroke or strokes at least one whole workout per week.
2. He must *not* practice the I.M. every day.
3. He must do at least two stroke-switching workouts per week. Over half of the Indiana University team swim the I.M. in some meets.

Thursday	*Friday*	*Saturday*
Morning off	Swim 3500 any style, concentrating on weakest stroke and breaststroke	Warm up 500 Swim 4 X 400 free progressive Kick 400 fly Pull 400 free Swim 20 X 50 fly
Warm up 800 Swim 6 X 150 concentrating on back and free Kick 400, then 8 X 100, free and back alternating Pull same as kick Swim 6 X 300 on 4½ min. Swim all-out 50	*Switching workout** Warm up 1200 IM Swim 10 X 100—1st fly, 2nd IM, 3rd back, 4th IM, 5th breast, 6th IM, 7th free, 8th IM, 9th fly/back, 10th breast/free Kick 400 IM easy kick 10 X 25 all strokes, kick 400 IM for time Pull same as kick Swim broken 200, 10 sec. rest 1 straight 200/repeat 6 times	Warm up for meet: 1. Warm up 800 2. Swim 8 X 50—2 of each stroke 3. Swim 1:55.7 for 200 IM in meet 4. After meet swim 20 X 100 freestyle
TOTAL: 6550 yd.	TOTAL: 6400 yd.	

become accustomed to switching only after a rest inverval (i.e., if he swims a broken 400 or 4 X 100 with 10 sec. rest between each 100, he will swim as follows: 1st 100—50 fly/50 back, 2nd 100—50 back/50 breast, 3rd 100—50 breast/50 free, 4th 100—50 free/50 fly.

SECTION 1.8
WARMING UP FOR PRACTICE AND FOR COMPETITION

Warming up for practice can be done partially on land by using such exercises as arm-swinging and stretching. Some swimmers also find it advisable to stretch their legs—this is particularly true for breaststrokers.

Warming up in the water can be accomplished by swimming, kicking, or pulling a total of 800 to 1000 yards. It is a good policy to have the first sets of repeats of the day done in a short-rest-interval-training manner such as 10 X 200 with 5 to 20 seconds rest interval. This permits the swimmer to do relatively low-quality work at the beginning of practice before he is warmed up. Such low-quality swimming loosens up the muscles (stretching the connective tissue) and lessens the chance of injury. After the first set of repeats most swimmers will be sufficiently loosened up to go all-out in sprints if they wish. Swimmers who don't warm up sufficiently frequently develop such disorders as tendinitis or bursitis. Breaststrokers in particular should loosen up their legs by kicking easy breaststroke at first, gradually increasing the pressure on the feet until they are sure they have warmed up the muscles sufficiently.

If the swimmer has worked out once in the morning and then swims again in the afternoon, he will not need as much time warming up since the warm-up effect carries over for several hours.

Warming Up before the Preliminaries
of a Big Meet or before a Small Dual Meet

Before a swim meet a swimmer should establish a standardized warmup that he has evolved for his needs and has used many times and in which he has confidence. It is good procedure for the coach to have the swimmers practice warm-ups during the year. Before some practices I put up a workout sheet in which the first part will read as follows:

Workout Thursday P.M.

1. Warm up as you would before the prelims of the NCAA. For example:
   a. Swim, pull or kick a total of 800 to 1000 yd.
   b. Swim 4 to 8 X 50 on 60 sec. Go each 50 faster than the previous. Distance men go 4 to 6 X 100 on 1:30.
   c. Kick 200 to 300 yards then kick 2 X 50 to loosen up legs.
   d. Swim 2 to 4 X 25 yd. from a dive. Distance men swim a couple of 50s (hard, but not all-out).
   e. Loosen down 200 yd.

The swimmers may adjust their warm-ups, doing a little more or a little less than the guide I have provided. Let me repeat: It is important that the swimmers have confidence in their warm-up which they have used with success before some practices and before small meets during the season.

Warming Up before the Finals

The swimmer can reduce the warm-up he uses before the finals to as little as one half as long as the one he used before the preliminaries. The effects of the preliminary swim plus the previous warm-up will have some carry-over value.

Here is the warm-up Mark Spitz used before each final event in the 1972 Olympics:

1. Warm up 400 easy swimming—a little of each stroke.
2. Swim 2 X 50—not all-out, but at about 85% speed.
3. Kick 100 to 200 meters.
4. Swim 1 or 2 X 25 meters.

Distance men should swim farther and work more on pace than should the sprinters or middle-distance swimmers. Individual-medley swimmers should warm up by doing some swimming and kicking of each stroke.

SECTION 1.9
TAPERING: GETTING READY FOR THE BIG MEET

The term *tapering* is used to express the decrease in work level that the swimmer does in practice in order to rest and get ready for a good performance. I think there is no phase of a coach's program of which he is less sure than the taper.

The length of taper the swimmer should use depends on many variables: how long he has been training, what event he is training for, how hard he has been training, and most important of all, how he, as an individual, responds to a decreasing work load.

Nearly every year I will receive at least one letter from a young coach which goes like this:

> Dear Doc:
> We had a great dual meet season this year—we won all of our meets and worked out hard through all of them. I never tapered them for a single meet. Two weeks before the state meet we stopped working hard and I sprinted the hell out of them. In the state meet they stunk.
> From now on I won't use a taper but will work them out right through the state meet. What do you think?
>
> Sincerely,
> Frustrated Coach

This coach, like nearly all of us at some time, has had the miserable experience of leaving the best performance of his swimmers in the pool the last week or two before the big meet by oversprinting them.

If the swimmers had been doing some sprinting at least several times a week before the taper started, then "sprinting the hell" out of them during the last two weeks would have resulted in less shock to their systems.

Here are a few guidelines to use in devising a taper:

1. The biggest temptation is to do too much work—don't leave your race in the pool.
2. Use a plan for tapering such as the following:
   a. Do a fair amount of loosening-up type of swimming.
   b. Do some sprinting, but not too much more than you have done during the past month.

c. Do some controlled pace work.

d. Do some repeat swims with longer rest intervals, but don't eliminate completely all short-rest-interval type of work.

e. Avoid too many all-out efforts in anything longer than 50 yards. Too much high-quality work at middle distances can exhaust a person for a couple of days.

f. Require that the distance men do a lot of easy swimming plus some pace work and not much sprinting unless they are also going to enter the shorter races or swim a relay leg.

g. Build confidence during the taper period by going hard occasionally and trying to achieve a good time. For example, Jim Montgomery, 1½ weeks before he set the world record in the 100-meter free, went 5 × 100 on 2½ minutes. I told him to go them progressive (each one faster than the previous). His first one was very easy at 63 sec.; his second one he dropped to 61 sec.; the third, 58 sec.; the fourth, 56 sec.; and the last, 53.7 sec. This particular set did not tire him excessively, and swimming the last 100 in 53.7 made him believe he could break the world record in a race.

h. Use some broken swimming during the taper. This type of repeat helps the swimmer work on pace and also builds his confidence, because as he becomes rested he will swim them faster than he did during the entire season.

That Terrible Feeling. When swimmers have been training very hard and they start their taper, they sometimes feel terrible. This feeling may last for a week or so before the swimmer begins to feel good. The reason for this is not clear. I don't know how valid my reasoning, but I explain it to our boys in this manner: "If you have been training hard, your body must adapt to a new stress—that of rest. This is a strange and maybe cockeyed concept. I compare it to the situation in which a doctor who normally works twelve to fourteen hours a day takes a vacation. He can't relax, he has a guilt feeling and gets nervous not working. He must adapt to relaxation. Perhaps the swimmer's body has to adapt to a decreased level of work, and until it does the swimmer gets 'that terrible feeling' that eventually goes away and leaves him ready for a big race."

Different Tapers for Sprinters, Others, and Distance Men

The principles mentioned earlier in this chapter between the three types of swimmers apply also to the taper:

1. *Treat each person as an individual.* Everyone responds a little differently to a taper. If most of the swimmers are responding as the coach expects them to do, but a few seem more tired than he would expect, he should have the tired ones take a shorter workout or get out of the pool after a short loosen-up swim.

2. *Watch what the swimmers do out of the pool.* It doesn't do much good to reduce a swimmer's work load if when you let him out of the practice he plays three games of handball and stays up late that night. The whole season can be made or ruined during the taper period. A team meeting at least once a week or even a short meeting every day to reinforce this point to the swimmers may be necessary. They should also watch their diet and try to get enough sleep.

3. *Cut down on the total distance during the taper.* Most world-class swimmers never taper for the small meets and their final taper lasts from 1½ to 2½ weeks. During the taper period the total distance is decreased to as little as one quarter or less of the total yardage they did during the peak of their season. An example is Fred Tyler's

taper during the last two weeks in the summer of 1975. Fred averaged 12,000 meters a day during his hardest training period. The last 14 days before the United States World Games Trials he reduced the total daily distance (in two workouts) as shown in Table 1.11. As a rule, the last two or three days before the meet the total yardage should be markedly decreased. Avoid the temptation to oversprint at this time.

Table 1.11
Fred Tyler's Taper before the 1975 United States World Games Trials

Days before Meet	14	13	12	11	10	9	8	7	6	5	4	3	2	1
Distance (in meters)	10,000	9500	8000	7000	6200	day off	6000	5600	5400	5000	4000	3600	3400	3200

The last two or three days before the meet the total yardage should be markedly decreased. Avoid the temptation to oversprint at this time.

SECTION 1.10
HOW CHAMPIONS TRAIN

This section of the manual is devoted to helping the coach and the swimmer plan their workouts by providing sample workouts of various champions. It is not meant to be a comprehensive compilation of the workouts of all champions, since these alone would fill a volume. It is designed rather to show the reader how some of the champions train and to give some idea of the variety of workouts that are used by various swimmers and coaches. While there are distinct differences in the way swimmers work out, it will be noted that all of these champions observe the principles of training mentioned in an earlier section. This section is divided into nine parts: (1) Sprinters, (2) Middle Distance swimmers, (3) Distance swimmers, (4) Butterfly swimmers, (5) Backstroke swimmers, (6) Breaststroke swimmers, (7) Individual Medley swimmers, (8) Age-group swimmers, and (9) Team workouts. I don't believe a breaststroker should look at only the breaststroke workouts and the backstroker at only the backstroke workouts, etc., but that each swimmer should look at the various stroke workouts to get ideas for his own routines.

Sprinters

James Montgomery. Olympic record 49.99 for 100 meters freestyle.

Indoor Season Workout, January

A.M.
1. Warm up 500
2. Swim 6 X 125 on 1:30, hypoxic breathing
   4 X 125 on 1:20, hypoxic breathing
3. Kick 400 then 2 X 50
4. Pull 4 X 125 on 1:30

     5. Swim 500 under 5 min.
          400 under 4 min.
          300 under 2:55
          200 under 1:55

Total Distance: 4150

P.M.

1. Warm up 800
2. Swim 5 × 200 on 2:15, hypoxic breathing
      5 × 150 on 1:40, hypoxic breathing
      5 × 100 on 1:00, hypoxic breathing
3. Swim 12 × 1 sprint every other one
4. Kick 400—then 8 × 75 on 1:15
5. Pull 400—then 6 × 100 on 1:10
6. a. Swim a broken 300—3 × 100, 10-sec. rest interval
   b. Swim a straight 300
   c. Swim a broken 200—8 × 50, 10-sec. rest interval
   d. Swim a straight 200
   e. Swim a broken 100—4 × 25, 10-sec. rest interval
   f. Swim a straight 100—under 48 sec.

Total Distance: 6550

For a more complete understanding of how Jim trains refer to the sample chart on planning a week's workout in Section 1.3.

Kim Peyton. Kim has won the women's National AAU title long course in the 200 free. She swims a two-beat crawl stroke.

TYPICAL TRAINING
January, 25-meter pool

6:00 to 6:15 A.M.

Pulley machine—200 to 400 pulls

6:15 to 7:45 A.M.

200 swim	200
100 kick	100
3 × 1000 swims, 1-min. break, pull the last one. Average time 12:10	3000
1 × broken 1500, 10-sec. break at the 100. Time for this is normally about 17:30	1500
8 to 12 × 50 on 45-sec. pace	400 to 600
	Total 5200 to 5400

3:15 to 5:15 P.M.

400 swim	400
200 kick	200
8 × 100 free first four offside breathing;	

second four alternate breathing	800
6 × 450 swims on 6:30 pace; quality set—average per swim, 5:14 (We relate this to a 500-yd. swim in a yard pool)	2700
8 × 100 kick on 2:30	800
4 × 200 pull on 4:00, backstroke	800
10 × 100 free on 1:30	1000

Total 6700

February

6:00 to 6:15 A.M.

Pulley weights

6:15 to 7:35 A.M.

200 swim	200
100 kick	100
2 × 1500 swim	3000
15 × 100, 10-sec. break	1500
Average time 1:09	

Total 4800

3:15 to 5:15 P.M.

400 swim	400
200 kick	200
8 × 100, 10-sec. break	800
4 × 1000 swim with 1-min. break, pull last two	4000
4 × 100 kick on 2:30	400
30 × 50 swim 10-sec. break	1500

Total 7300

Jerry Heidenreich. Jerry was second in 100-meter freestyle in the 1972 Olympics and has won the national championship in the 200-yard freestyle.

An example of two days of early season workouts are as follows:

Tuesday

A.M. (1 hr. 50 min.)

Warm up	12 × 50		12 min.
Pull	12 × 100	@	1:30
Kick	6 × 200	@	4:30
Swim	1 × 800		12 min.
Swim	2 × 400		7 min.
Swim	4 × 200	@	3:30
Swim	8 × 100	@	2:00

P.M. (1 hr. 45 min.)

Warm up	10 × 100		20 min.
Kick	1 × 500		10 min.
Swim	12 × 200	@	3:00
Kick	5 × 100	@	2:00

Stroke	4 × 50		5 min.
Sprint	8 × 50	@	1:30
Warm down	1 × 500		8 min.

Wednesday

A.M. (1 hr. 50 min.)

Warm up	3 × 300	@	5:15
Pull	300		Repeat this
Kick	300		4 times—one
Swim	300		each 16 min.
Stroke	4 × 50		5 min.
Swim	3 × 800	@	14:00
Stroke	8 × 50		10 min.

P.M. (1 hr. 48 min.)

Warm-up	16 × 50	@	1:00
Swim	100		2 min.
	200		4 min.
	300		6 min.
	400		8 min.
	500		10 min.
	400		8 min.
	300		6 min.
	200		4 min.
	100		2 min.
Kick	6 × 250	@	6:00
Stroke	3 × 100	@	2:00

Sonya Grey. Sonya is the Australian champion at the 100- and 200-meter freestyle.

Training Program

A.M.

    1 × 800 m. freestyle
    12 × 200 m. freestyle every 3:15, average 2:20
    16 × 50   m. kick every 65 sec.
    32 × 50   m. freestyle every 45., average 34.0
    32 × 25   m. freestyle every 30., average 15.0

P.M.

    1 × 800 m. freestyle
    24 × 100 m. freestyle every 1:30, average 1:09.0
    32 × 25   m. freestyle kick every 35
    32 × 50   m. freestyle every minute, average 32.0
    1 × 800 m. freestyle

One month before the Championships, Sonya started her taper, gradually reducing her mileage and increasing her efforts and having more rest. Following is one of the day's programs that she would do in this period:

Taper Program
(One Month before the Championships)

A.M.

    1 × 800 m. freestyle
    16 × 100 m. freestyle every 2 min., average 1:05.0

8 X 50   m. kick efforts every 90 sec.
16 X 50   m. drive freestyle every 2 min., average 30
1 X 800 m. freestyle

P.M.

1 X 800 m. freestyle
8 X 200 m. freestyle broken 5-sec. spell, average
          2:25 less 15 sec.
16 X 50   m. freestyle kick on minute
8 X 100 m. freestyle every 2 min., average 1:07.0
1 X 800 m. freestyle

One week before the State Championships, Sonya went to one session a day. This is one of the workouts used in this period:

1 X 800 m. freestyle
16 X 50   m. freestyle on minute, average 32
8 X 100 m. freestyle effort every 5 min., 1:03.0
8 X 50   m. freestyle kick
8 X 50   m. freestyle dives every 3 min., average 28+
1 X 400 m. freestyle

Warm-up before a Meet

1 X 800 m. freestyle
4 X 50   m. freestyle, average 31
8 X 25   m. freestyle, average 13

Middle-Distance Swimmers

Shirley Babashoff. Shirley is probably the best girl swimmer America has ever had. She has won numerous national championships in the freestyle events and is also outstanding in the individual medley.

SAMPLE WORKOUTS
Midseason

8-10 A.M., Long Course
Warm up 400 m.
Swim Locomotive to 4 and back down
          1 length fast   1 length easy
          2 lengths fast   2 lengths easy
          3 lengths fast   3 lengths easy
          4 lengths fast   4 lengths easy
Pull 6 X 200 on 3:00, descending 1 to 3
Kick 10 X 50 on 1 min. freestyle
Swim 20 X 100 10 on 1:15, 1 to 5
               5 on 1:12, 1 to 5
               5 on 1:10, 1 to 5
4 X 50 sprints of each stroke 1 to 4 on 1 min.
400 easy

P.M.

5:00 to 5:30 weight training
5:30 to 7:30 swimming

Swim 20 × 50 on 50 warm-up
Pull 4 × 400 on 6:00, 1 to 4
Kick 3 × 100 of each stroke 1 to 3 on 2:10
Swim 8 × 250 IM (100 fly, 50 back, 50 breast, 50 free)
      10 × 50 on 50 sec. breathing every 7 strokes, descending 1 to 5
      10 × 50 on 45 sec. breathing every 5 strokes, descending 1 to 5
      10 × 50 on 40 sec. breathing every 3 strokes, descending 1 to 5
400 warm down

Taper Workouts

A.M.

1,000 swim
Pull 8 × 100 on 1:40
Kick 8 × 100 on 1:15
Swim 6 × 200, descending on 3:20
3 × 50 of each stroke on watch
300 easy

P.M.

500 swim
500 kick
500 pull
Swim 20 × 50 on 40 sec., descending 1 to 4
Swim 3 × 400 1 easy
        1 broken 10 sec. at 100
        1 broken 10 sec. at 50
          descending
4 × 50 sprint on watch
400 easy

Kathy Heddy. Kathy won the 1975 World championship in the 200 individual medley, but actually trains more for the middle-distance freestyle events and also swims a good 100 free. She is probably best at the 400-meter distance.

Typical Long Course Workout

A.M.

15 × 400 swim
10 × 100 kick
30 × 100 pull
  Total   10,000

P.M.

25 × 200 swim (may go as many as 30 × 200)
1,000 kick
2,000 pull (may pull 3,000 in various ways)
Sprints
  Total: 8,000 to 9,000

Typical Short Course Workout (One per Day)

Preseason

3,000 timed swim
20 × 100 swim
1,000 kick
2,000 pull
  Total: 8,000 yd.

During Season (January, February, March)
> 12 to 15 X 500
> 5 X 200 kick
> 15 X 200 pull
> Total: 10,000-11,500 yd.

Distance Swimmers

Rick Demont. Rick was World champion in the 400-meter freestyle and the first swimmer to break 4 minutes on the 400-meter. Rick uses what his coach Don Swartz calls cyclical training—going hard one day and easier the next. Following are samples of an easy day and a hard day during the indoor season:

Monday

A.M.

Warm up, 400 each: pull, kick, swim	1200
Kick 4 X 250, rest interval 30 sec.	1000
8 X 300 swim, negative split, rest interval 60 sec.	2400

P.M.

Weights—30 min.	
Warm up	1000
Pull 8 X 125, rest interval 2 min.	1000
Kick 10 X 50, rest interval 60 sec.	500
10 X 150 IM, no freestyle	1500
	Total 8600

Tuesday

A.M.

Warm up	800
Pull 3 X 1000, negative split, rest interval 2 min.	3000
10 X 50 on your time	500

P.M.

Warm up	500
20 X 200 on 2:30 pace, progressive 1-5, 6-10, etc.	4000
1 X 2000, each 500 faster	2000
25 X 100 on 1:15 pace	2500
Easy	200
	Total 13,500

Jo Harshbarger. Jo has been national 1500-meter champion and was formerly the world record holder at the 1500 and the 800 meters.

Typical Workout Day (Summer)

A.M. (1½ Hours) Short Course   Yardage

1 X 400 back, warm-up	400
1 X 1000 free	1000
5 X 100 fly on 1:45	500
1 X 1000 free broken 200s, 20-sec. RI	1000
3 X 200 breast on 4 min.	600
10 X 100 free on 1:30	1000

8 × 50 kick choice on 1 min.	400
Warm down	100
	Subtotal 5000

A.M. (2 Hours) Long Course

5 × 880 free on 15 min. (9:17-9:26)	4400
8 × 110 free on 1:45 w/paddles	880
1 × 440 IM kick	440
	Subtotal 5720

P.M. (1½ Hours) Long Course

1 × 880 IM warm up	880
5 × 440 free on 5:30 (avg. 4:43)	2200
8 × 110 kick on 2 min.	880
10 × 55 free sprints on 1 min. (33+)	550
1 × 220 warm down	220
	Subtotal 4730
	Total 15,450

Taper Workout
A.M. (2 Hours) Long Course

1 × 1100 free warm up	1100
10 × 110 free on 2 min. easy/hard	1100
10 × 110 free on 2½ min. (1:06.8-1:07.8)	1100
20 × 55 free accelerating	1100
Easy kicking and warm down	600
	Approx. Total 5000

Butterfly Swimmers

Peggy Tosdal. Peggy is a National AAU 100-yard butterfly champion. During her early season workouts she swims mostly freestyle. During the midseason phase she does much of her workout butterfly. Her taper phase begins three weeks before the Nationals when she reduces the distance gradually. Eight days before the Nationals she begins coming in only once a day and doing only 3000 yards a day of easy swimming with very little sprinting during the last six days.

Typical Early-Season Workout
June 8

7-9:30 A.M., Long Course
Warm up 800 m. swim
Swim 20 × 100 m. free (10 with 5 sec. rest, descending 1 to 5)
                    (10 with 10 sec. rest, descending 1 to 5)
Kick 600 m. (300 free on side, 300 fly on side)
Pull 4 × 400 m. with 30-sec. rest freestyle (last 400 m. fly 1 length, free 1
    length)
Swim 1000 m. free, rest 15 sec. Swim 800 m., rest 20 sec.
    Swim 600 m. free, rest 25 sec. Swim 400 m. free, rest 30 sec. Swim 200
    fly (check heart rate after each swim).
Swim 10 × 50 m. on 50 sec., descending 1 to 5

200 easy free to warm down
   Total: 8700 m.

5-7 P.M., Long Course
   Warm up 400 m. swim, 400 kick (fly), 400 pull (free)
   20 × 50 (5-sec. rest) free with last 5 fly, descending 1 to 5
   Kick 6 × 100 fly with board on 2:20
   Swim 3000 m. for time (not Peggy's favorite!)
   Swim 8 × 200 m. on 2:50 free, descending 1 to 4
   400 easy to warm down
      Total: 7800 m.

Typical Midseason Workout
July 16

7-9:30 A.M., Long Course
   Warm up 10 × 100 m. on 1:40
   Pull locomotive to 3 and back down, freestyle (1 easy, 1 fast, 2 easy, 2
      fast, 3 easy, 3 fast, 3 easy, 3 fast, 2 easy, 2 fast, 1 easy, 1 fast)
   Kick 10 × 50 m; 50 fast fly, 50 easy free on 1:20
   Swim 10 × 250 m. on 4:40, descending 1 to 5, free with each last 100 fly
   Swim 8 × 50 m. on 1 min., descending 1 to 4 every 4th fly
   Swim 8 × 50 m. on 50 sec., descending 1 to 4 every 4th fly
   Swim 8 × 50 on 40 sec., descending 1 to 4, free
   Swim 10 × 100 on 2 min. (100 fast fly, 100 easy free)
   200 easy warm down
      Total: 5100 m.

5-7 P.M., Short Course
   Warm up 500 yd.
   Pull 100 free, kick 100 fly for 800 yd.
   Swim 5 × 125 yd. on 1:30 free descending
   Swim 5 × 125 yd. on 1:45 free descending
   Swim 5 × 125 yd. on 2:00 free descending
   Kick 12 × 50 yd. on 1:20 (6 free and 6 fly) with board
   Swim 800 yd. for time
   12 × 75 yd. on 3 min. every 3rd 75 fly
   300 yd. easy to warm down
      Total: 5775 yd.

Taper Workout

5-6:30 P.M., Long Course
   Workout 500 m.
   Kick 300 m.
   Pull 300 m.
   Swim 12 × 50 m. on 1 min., descending 1 to 4
   Swim 4 × 50 m. fly on 200-m. race pace (2 min.)
   Swim 1 × 100 fly broken 5 sec. at 50
   Starts—Turns
   400 m. easy to warm down
      Total: 2400 m.

Mark Spitz. Mark Spitz, while he was outstanding in both butterfly and crawl strokes, trained mostly for the crawl stroke events and did less than one fourth of his workouts using the butterfly stroke. This is true of many of the butterfly swimmers I have coached, i.e., Gary Hall, Fred Schmidt, and Larry Schulhof, all former national champions. Other butterfly swimmers that have swum for me, such as Olympic Champions Mike Troy, 1960, and Kevin Berry, 1964, have done as much as 75 percent of their practices using the butterfly stroke. Each swimmer must determine in close relationship with his coach how much butterfly he should swim in his training program. Early in the season Mark did very little butterfly swimming but concentrated on his crawl stroke. About once a week he would do one set of repeats butterfly. Throughout the entire season, however, he would do approximately half of his kicking drills using the fishtail kick. His fastest time for a 100-yard fishtail kick on a kickboard was 58.8 seconds.

Once Mark got into fair shape and we started training twice a day with a total of eleven workouts per week (six afternoon and five morning workouts), we adopted the following plan:

1. He had to do at least two afternoon and one morning workout per week where at least 75 percent of the total distance swum was done with the butterfly stroke.
2. He had to do some butterfly in every practice—at least a minimum of 200 yards. If he felt good he would do more.
3. At least half of his kicking drills in every practice session was to be done with the fishtail kick.
4. He never had to do long repeats fly, i.e., 800s or even 400s, although occasionally I would have him do an isolated 400 fly.

Below I am listing Mark's workouts for three days: (1) Early season, November 4, (2) Midseason, February 12, morning and afternoon, and (3) Taper workout, March 16. These workouts were used the year he went 47.9 for the 100-yard and 1:46.9 for the 200-yard fly.

Early Season Workout
November 4

We were doing five workouts a week of 2 hours duration in the afternoon plus ½ hour of isokinetic exercises.

1. Warm up 800
2. Swim 8 X 200 on 2:15, average time 2:01
   4 X 200 on 2:05, average time 1:59
3. Swim 800—out slow/back hard—final time 8:01, out in 4:10
4. Pull 800 continuously—he used a 7-in. inside diameter rubber tube. He didn't like pull buoys and used no paddles.
5. Pull 800 continuously
6. Swim 400—swim first 200 fly, last 200 free
   300—swim first 150 fly, last 150 free
   200—swim first 100 fly, last 100 free
   100—swim first 50 fly, last 50 free
   Total: 6,600

Midseason Workout
February 12

A.M.

1. WU 800 (200 S, 200 K, 200 P, 200 S)
2. Swim 20 X 50 (first 16 X 50 free on 45 sec., average time 27 sec.; last

4 × 50 fly on 45, average time 28)
3. Kick 5 × 100 dolphin on 45 (average time 1:15)
4. Pull 500 crawl for time; time 5:37
5. Swim a moderate effort:
> 400 IM, time 5 min.
> 200 IM, time 2:21 min.

Total: 3,400   Time: 1 hr. 10 min.

P.M. Fly Workout (Must Be at Least 75 percent Fly)

1. WU 1000 (250 S, 250 P, 250 K, 250 S) one half of warm-up done fly
2. Swim 20 × 100 on 1:15 (every other one fly, the others crawl; average time for fly 61 sec., for crawl 65 sec.)
3. Swim 12 × 25, every other one fast (all of the fast ones fly, the easy ones crawl; average time for fly from push-off, 11.5 sec.)
4. Kick 400 fly, then 3 × 200 fly on 3 min., average time per 200 kick, 2:47
5. Pull 400 crawl, then 6 × 100 on 1:30, every other one fly, no time recorded
6. Swim 4 × 200 on 6 min. If Mark broke 2 min. on each of the first three 200s then he didn't have to do the 4th one. His times: 1st, 1:58+; 2nd, 1:57+; 3rd, 1:54+. Total distance: 5900.

Total Distance Fly: 3250 or about 55%

As you can see from this workout, considerably less than 75 percent was butterfly. I was always pleased to get this much fly out of Mark in a practice, so I always felt I was psyching him out. He in turn also knew it was less than 75 percent fly and he thought he was pulling one over on me.

Taper Workout

Mark liked to taper at least two weeks before the NCAA meet. During the taper he would come in eight times a week—six afternoon practices and two morning practices. The morning practices were nothing more than a 2000-yard workout with no formal organization and with each swimmer doing what he wanted to do. The afternoon practices were organized and lasted 1½ hours.

Afternoon Taper Workout
March 16

1. WU 800
2. Swim 6 × 100 easy crawl on 1:30, average time 1:03
3. Swim 4 × 100 moderate crawl on 1:20, average time :59
4. Swim 8 × 25, every other one fast—the fast ones fly, the slow ones crawl
5. Kick 400, then 2 × 50, average time 31 sec.
6. Pull 300 easy
7. Swim 4 × 50 fly on 60 sec., average time 27 sec. (from push-off)
8. Swim 4 × 50 fly on 1:30, average time 23.6 (from a dive)
9. Loosen down 400 easy crawl

Total Distance: 3500   Time: 1½ hr.

Warm-up

Mark's warm-up has been discussed in detail earlier in this section under *Warm-up*.

Bruce Robertson. Bruce is a Canadian swimmer who took second place in the Olympics in the 100-meter fly in 1972. Compared to the average American swimmer he works out fairly lightly. He swims the 100 fly and the 100 free, but goes a poor 200 fly.

TYPICAL TRAINING

Monday, July 10, 1972
Short Course

400 warm-up swim
16 X 50 swim and 50 sec. warm-up
1 X 1500 free swim with paddles, 18:10.0
1 X 800 free pull, 10:40.0
1 X 400 free kick
  Total: 3900

Wednesday, July 12, 1972
Long Course

1 X 400 swim warm-up
8 X 50 free, 50-sec. turnover, descending from 35.0 to 31.0
8 X 50 free, 45-sec. turnover, descending from 35.0 to 32.0
1 X 200 kick
8 X 50 kick at 1-min. pace, descending fly 42.0 to 38.0
8 X 400 free swim at 5:30 pace, average time 4:45
4 X 100 kick at 2:30 pace, average time 1:30
8 X 50 free at 45-sec. pace, descending from 38.0 to 34.0
4 X 50 free kick at 1-min. pace, descending from 43.0 to 40.0
4 X 50 free at 35-sec. pace, 33, 33, 33, 33.
  Total: 6200

July 30, 1972
Long-Course Taper

1 X 200 kick
8 X 50 free at 50 sec. warm-up, descending from 35.0 to 31.0
4 X 100 kick fly warm-up at 2:30 pace, 1:30, 1:27, 1:24, 1:21
1 X 400 easy individual medley, with single-arm butterfly leg
4 X 50 free at 1-min. pace 33, 33, 33, 33
1 X 200 easy swim
1 X 50 free hard, push-off 26.8
1 X 250 easy swim
1 X 50 fly hard, push-off 28.1
1 X 250 easy swim
  Total: 2400

Backstroke Swimmers

John Naber. John is World record holder for all distances in the backstroke and is also American record holder on the 500-yard and the 1650-yard freestyle. He can outwork almost any swimmer in practice. John goes on an average between 12,000 and 14,000 meters a day, doing most of the workout freestyle but always doing part of it backstroke.

Typical Outdoor Season Workouts
A.M. Long Course for 2 Hours from 8 to 10 A.M.
  Warm up—800 swim

400 kick
400 pull
4 × 800 (2 back, 2 IM)
15 × 100 pull with paddles
8-10 × 100 kick
10 × 50 sprint
1 × 200 easy swim
    Total: 7800 to 8000 m.

P.M. Short Course for 1½ to 2 Hours from 4:40 to 6:30 P.M.

Warm up—1 × 400 swim
          1 × 200 kick
          10 × 50 working on stroke
4-5 × 100 descending each time, 10-20 sec. rest after each one,
    working on individual strokes
5 × 250 kick descending series
10 × 25 leaving every 20 sec.
8 × 25 leaving every 18 sec.
8 × 25 leaving every 16 sec.
4 × 25 leaving every 15 sec.
1 × 1000 working on turns
    Total: 4500 to 4600 yd.

Other Examples of John's Main Series

20 × 200 in sets of 5, each one faster than the one previous
8 × 400 on individual strokes
30 × 100 at various intervals
60 × 50 with 15 of each stroke
6 × 600 IM

Steve Pickell. Steve is a Canadian and was ranked number one in the world in the 100-meter backstroke in 1974 with a time of 57.6. During the heavy training season Steve trains 14,000 to 16,000 meters a day. Starting a month or so before the Nationals he starts doing more speed work.

Pickell's Favorite Workout
Long Course, Middle of the Season

A.M.

20 × 50 on the 1:00, descending
10 × 100 kick, working on the last 25
10 × 100 pull, with the last 25 hard
8 × 200 back, descending 1 — 4 with 2:00 rest
400 swim down
    Total: 5000

P.M.

400 swim, 400 pull, 400 kick, 400 swim
10 × 100 kick, descending 1-10
30 × 50 back every 45 sec. or freestyle every 40 sec.
10 × 400 free
400 swim down
10 × 50 backstroke kick
10 × 100 backstroke with the last 25 hard
300 swim down
2 × 50 all-out backstroke
    Total: 10,400

Breaststroke Swimmers

Stu Isaac. Stu is primarily a breaststroker but also swims and trains for the individual medley so that he has variety in practice. Below is a workout that he used over Christmas vacation. Ordinarily he does not work this hard during the time school is in session.

Monday

A.M.

500 easy—warm-up	500
4 × 200 kick/ 3:30 (av. 2:40)	
4 × 200 swim/ 3:30 (av. 2:20)	1600
8 × 400 or 300/ 5:30 pulling alternate 400 back and 300 breast pull	2800
(As one series) all freestyle	
5 × 50/ 60 sec.	
4 × 100/ 1:30	
3 × 150/ 2:00*	
2 × 200/ 2:30*	
1 × 250 swim down	1750

Subtotal   6650

4:00 — 6:00 P.M.

500 swim—loosen up	500
10 × 50/ 60 sec., breast (build-ups)	500
10 × 100/ 2 min. breast quality set (1:10, 1:10, 1:08, 1:08, 1:06, 1:06, 1:04, 1:03, 1:04.5, 1:03.5)	1000
500 swim easy	500
20 × 50 kick, av. 37-39 sec./ 50	1000
20 × 1000 freestyle-av. 0:59-1:01	2000

Subtotal   5500

Total   12,150

*Stroke setting in early sets working into pace. (This series can also be done breaststroke—increasing interval by 5-10 seconds at 150s and 200s.)

Sets of 100s on the 2 minutes are one of Stu's favorites. He feels this gives him the time and rest to feel his way into the stroke and to work easily toward speed while still maintaining a hard series.

Sample Workouts
(For Dual-Meet Stage of Training)

15 × 100/ 1:20 freestyle (av. 1:01)	1500
3 × 400/ 5:20, 1 each back, free, back	1200
1 × 400/ breast split 10 sec. at 100 (av. 1:08)	400
7 × 200/ 3:30 kick (av. 2:40)	1400
30 × 25/ 30 sec. (15 fly and 15 back)	750
5 × 75/ 1:20 breast-pull	375

Total   5625

500 easy	500
10 × 200/ 2:30/ free	2000

10 × 100 kick/ 2 min.	1000
10 × 150/ 5 min. split 10 sec. at 75 and 125 1st 5 av. 1:35, 2nd 5 av. at 1:32-1:34	1500
500 swim down	500
Total	5500

Non-quality Work: Quantity

20 × 75 free/ 60 sec.	1500
10 × 400/ 8-min. breast stroke (av. 4:48-5:00)	4000
Total	5500

Allison Grant.   Allison swims both breaststroke and freestyle in national competition. She works up to as much as 16,000 meters a day in the summer time.

WINTER WORKOUTS

25-yard Pool

1. Warm-up: Swim 200 free, 200 reverse IM, 200 breast, 200 IM, no rest
   Workout: Pull 4 × 100 breast on 2:00
   Kick 3 × 30 breast on 5:00
   Swim 3 × 800 breast on 14:00
2. Warm-up: Swim 400 free—400 breast
   Workout: Kick 20 × 50 breast on 1:00 (no board)
   Swim 8 × 200 free on 2:30
   Swim 24 × 50 breast on 1:00
3. Warm-up: 1000 freestyle
   Workout: 6 × 100 breast on 2:00
   Pull 300 breast
   Swim 200 free—200 breast, 5 sets on 5:30
   Swim 100 free—100 breast, 6 sets on 3:00
4. Warm-up: Swim 600 free
   Workout: Kick 10 min. of mixed strokes
   Swim 100 fly—100 back, 6 sets on 2:45
   Swim 100 back—100 breast, 6 sets on 3:00
   Swim 100 breast—100 free, 6 sets on 2:45

Short Course, P.M.

Warm-up: Swim 500, kick 10 × 100 on 1:45
Workout: Swim or pull 10 × 400 free on 5 min.
Swim 10 × 100 free on 1:20
Swim 20 × 50 free, 5 on 50 sec., 5 on 45 sec., 5 on 40 sec. and 5 on 35 sec.
Total: 7,500 yd.

MIDDLE SEASON WORKOUT

Long Course, A.M.

Warm-up: Swim 500, kick 500
Workout: Swim 1500—1000—500—400—300—200—100 free with increasing effort on each swim (30-sec. rest interval, all freestyle
Swim 10 × 100 free on 1:30
Swim 20 × 50 fly on 1 min.
Total: 7,000

Short Course, P.M.

Warm-up: Swim 500, kick 500, pull 500
Swim 4 × 10 × 100 free on 1:30, 1:20, 1:15, 1:10. Each set is descending
Pull 1000 free for form
Swim 10 × 50 fly
    Total: 7,000 yd.

PRE-TAPER WORKOUT

Long Course, A.M.

Warm-up: Swim 500, pull 1000 for form
Workout: Swim 10 × 200 on 5 min. with 2 easy 50s at 3 and 4 min.; or
    10 × 100 on 4 min. with 2 easy 50s at 2 or 3 min.
Kick 1000 broken in any way desired
Swim 10 × 50 fly
    Total: 5100 m. or 4100 m.

SUMMER WORKOUTS

1. Warm-up: Swim 200 free, 200 back, 200 breast, 200 free with no rest
   Workout: Kick 10 minutes
    Swim 8 × 200 free under 2:45 with 30 sec. rest
    Swim 20 × 40 breast with 15 sec. rest
    Swim 10 × 40 fly with 20 sec. rest on 5 breaths per 40
    Swim 800 free with paddles
2. Warm-up: 600 free—600 breast
   Workout: Kick 6 × 120 breast with 20 sec. rest
    Pull 6 × 120 breast with 20 sec. rest
    Swim 12 × 80 breast with the first 40 easy, the second 40 hard with 30 sec. rest
    Swim 12 × 40 build-up breaststrokes with 30 sec. rest
    Swim 12 × 40 free on 3 breaths, 30 sec. rest
3. Warm-up: Swim 1500 free
   Workout: Kick 2 × 400 breast with no board with 1:00 rest in-between kicks
    Pull 10 × 40 breast with 20 sec. rest
    Swim 10 × 300 free under 3:45 with 30 sec. rest

Individual Medley Swimmers

Mike Currington. Mike is a great all-around swimmer, having placed in the Nationals in the fly, the freestyle, and the individual medley events. He trains mostly for the fly and freestyle races but does mix in some of the other two strokes.

EARLY SEASON WORKOUTS

Long Course, A.M.

Warm-up: Swim 500, pull 1000, kick 500
Workout: Swim 3000 freestyle
Pull 5 × 200 free, 30-sec. interval
Swim 5 × 200 free on 3 min.
Swim 10 × 50 fly on 1 min.
    Total: 7,500 m.

High-Pressure Workout (Longer Rest Intervals)
Short Course, P.M.

Warm-up: Swim 500, kick 10 × 100 on 1:45
Workout: Swim 5 × 400 free on 6 min. The first three are are descending,
     and the last two are broken with 10-sec. rest intervals
     Swim 10 × 200 on 3:30; the last four are broken with 10-sec. rest
     intervals
     Swim 20 × 50 fly on 1 min.
       Total: 6,500 yd.

Jill Symons. Jill trains for the individual medley and has placed in the national
championship in this event in both 200- and 400-yard distances. She swims her workouts
using the various strokes in a balanced manner.

SAMPLE WORKOUTS

Short Course (Both Workouts in 25-Yard Pool)
Early Season

Morning
    Swim 800, kick 400
    10 × 100 on 1:30 (odd-free/even-choice)
    Kick 10 × 50 on 1:15
    25s on 45 sec.

Evening
    Pull 500, kick 500
    3 × 1000 (1 broken 200s; 1 broken 100s; 1 straight)
    Kick 400 IM
    20 × 50 on 1:00 (5 each stroke)
    Easy 200

Midseason

Morning
    Pull 800, kick 400
    3 × 500 (broken 100s)
    15 × 30 on 15 sec.

Evening
    Pull 800, kick 400
    3 × 1650
    Kick 2 × 300
    10 × 50 on 1:15
    Easy 300

Long Course
Early Season

Morning—33 1/3-yard Pool
    Pull 1000 free
    Kick 600 breast
    Swim 1000 free
    Swim 400 breast
    Swim 400 back
    Swim 1600 in special stroke drills

Afternoon—25-yard Pool
    Pull 800 back
    Swim 400 breast
    Kick 5 × 100 fly on 2:00
    Swim 3 sets of 4 × 200 on 3:00 (fly-back, back-breast, breast-free)
    Kick 300 back
    Swim 2 sets of 10 × 50 on 1:00 (swimmer's choice)

Midseason

Mornings—33 1/3-yard Pool
    Pull 6 × 133 free on 1:45
    Kick 266 back
    Kick 266 breast
    Kick 266 breast
    Pull 10 × 66 on 1:15 (one arm back)
    Swim 3 × 200 on 3:00
    Pull 4 × 133 on 2:15, breast
    Swim 400 breast
    Swim 400 IM
    Swim 6 × 133 on 1:45, free
    Swim 8 × 66 on 1:15, fly

Afternoon—25-yard Pool
    Pull 500 free
    Swim 5 × 300 free on 4:30
    Kick 200 back
    Swim 10 × 50 on 1:00 (one arm back)
    Swim 5 × 100 back on 1:30
    Pull 2 × 200 breast on 3:30
    Kick 300 breast
    Swim 5 × 150 breast on 2:30
    Swim 20 × 50 on 1:00 (5 of each stroke at 200 IM pace)

Age-Group Swimmers

Teri McKeever. Teri is a national record holder in the eleven- and twelve-year-old 50- and 100-meter butterfly. I include a sample of her workouts here in order that you may see how hard a twelve-year-old can work.

Typical Summer Workout Day
A.M.
    500 free (warm up)
    200 free (swim, kick, pull, swim)
    10 × 50 free on 50 sec. (progress to fastest)
    200 back (swim, kick, pull, swim)
    6 × 50 back on 1 min.
    5 × 100 back on 2 min.
    200 back (swim)
    2 × 400 IM (swim, kick, pull, swim)
    3 × 75 each stroke on 1:15
    3 × 200 IM on 3:30
    10 × 100 free on 1:30
      Total: 5,800 yd.

P.M.
  300 free (warm up)
  1 × 400 IM kick
  5 × 200 fly on 3:30
  6 × 100 back on 1:45
  5 × 100 breast on 1:45
  Kick sprints: 4 × 25 on each stroke, 5 sec. rest
  5 × 200 free on 3 min.
  5 × 100 IM on 1:45
  4 × 50 each stroke on 1 min.
  4 × 25 each stroke (rest 10 sec.)
  200 free (wind down)
   Total: 6,100 yd.
    Total day's work: 11,900 yd.

Team Workouts

I personally believe that with any group of senior swimmers (age 13 years and up) the team should be divided into three groups and each group be given a separate workout which all can do at the same time. The division of the group is based on:

1. How much work each person is capable of handling
2. What events the individual is training for.

I break our team up into the following groups:

 a. Distance swimmers
 b. Middle-distance swimmers
 c. Sprinters

This is also the distinction made at Mission Viejo, California.

I am listing here some sample workouts as given to the Mission Viejo team by their coach Mark Schubert.

SAMPLE SENIOR WORKOUTS

Mid-January

Morning (Short Course), All Groups
  Warm up 20 × 50 on 50 sec.
  Kick 4 × 200 on 3:50, descending
  Pull 800 negative split
  16 × 150 (8 on 2:20 stroke, 8 on 2:00 free, descending 1 to 4)
  8 × 50 stroke on 1 min., descending 1 to 4
  Warm down 300 yd.
   Total: 5,700 yd.

Afternoon (Short Course)
 Distance Group
  Warm up 1000 yd.
  Kick 10 × 50 on 1 min. (1 to 5)

Swim locomotive up to 4 and back (1000 yds)
Pull 4 X 400 on 6:00, descending
8 X 200 on 2:30 (1 to 4)
6 X 300 on 3:40 (1 to 3)
4 X 400 on 4:50 (1 to 4)
2 X 500 on 6:00, descending
4 X 50 sprints on watch
Warm down 400 yd.
    Total: 10,700 yd.

Individual Medley and Middle Distance
Warm up 1000 yd.
Kick 10 X 100 on 1 min. (1 to 5)
Pull 5 X 200 on 3 min., descending
8 X 100 weak stroke on 1:50 (1 to 4)
8 X 100 best stroke on 1:30 (1 to 4)
16 X 50 on 50 sec. (1 fast stroke, 1 easy free)
Warm down 400 yd.
    Total: 5,800 yd.

Sprinters
Warm up 1000 yd.
Kick 10 X 50 on 1 min.; breaststrokers 8 X 100 on 1:50
10 X 125 stroke on 1:45 (1 to 5)
Pull 5 X 200 on 3:00, descending; breaststrokers 8 X 100 on 2:00
8 X 75 on 1 min. free (1 to 4)
8 X 75 on 1:15 stroke (1 to 4)
8 X 75 on 2:00 with 50 free between (stroke), (1 to 4)
5 X 50 on one breath, at own pace
Warm down 300 yd.
    Total: 6,100 yd.; 6,200 yd. for breastrokers

Early July

Morning (Long Course)

Distance Group
Warm up 800 m.
4 X 800 on 10:30, descending
Pull 600, 400, 200; 10 sec. rest
Kick 6 X 100 on 2:00 (1 to 3)
30 X 100 (10 on 1:30, 10 on 1:20, 10 on 1:10), (1 to 5)
4 X 50 on sprint
Warm down 400 m.
    Total: 9,400 m.

Individual Medley and Middle Distance
Warm up 800 m.
Pull 600, 400, 200, with 10 sec. rest
Kick 6 X 100 on 2:00 (1 to 3)
4 X 300 on 5:00, descending, stroke
24 X 100 (8 on 1:30, 8 on 1:20, 8 on 2:00 stroke), (1 to 4)
4 X 50 sprint on 2:00
Warm down 400 m.
    Total: 6,800 m.

Sprinters
  Warm up 800 m.
  Kick 8 × 50 on 1:15 (1 to 4); breaststrokers 16 × 50 on 1:00
  Pull 400 m.
  4 × 200 on 3:00, descending
    Total: 2,400 m.

SECTION 1.11
STRESS, SLEEP, REST, AND DIET

In order to swim fast a swimmer must not only train hard and intelligently in workouts but must also observe good training principles out of the pool. He must eat properly, get enough sleep and rest, and avoid overstress.

When one of the swimmers on our team complains of being constantly tired and run down and has recurring bouts of illness, I sit down with him and we try to determine the cause or causes. How is he eating: nourishing, well-balanced meals, or does he indulge a taste for junk foods and ignore his nutritional needs? Has he lost weight lately, is he sleeping enough, are there too many stresses operating in addition to the stress of training?

When we have isolated the factor or factors that are causing the fatigue and/or illnesses, we can do something about them.

I have learned from experience that the major causes of fatigue and increased incidence of illness are not the intensity of the workouts alone, but one or more of the other factors added to the stress of workout. The combination often constitutes overstress, and the result is the fatigue and illness syndrome.

This phenomenon usually takes the following course: the swimmer is trying to do too much and has imposed too many stresses upon himself. He is trying to do well in school and is studying hard; he is trying to swim well and is training hard and he has certain demands that stem from other areas. He may be trying to do part-time work to earn money, he may have social demands being made on his time by his girl friend, his parents, or his friends. He may be involved with outside activities that dissipate his energy, such as fraternity meetings, and so on. A swimmer who is in the hard phase of training (two workouts a day) must realize that he is not superhuman; he must eliminate some sources of stress that he could normally handle easily in order to tolerate the physical stress of training, if he wants to swim successfully. His parents, girl friend or wife, and friends must also recognize these facts and cooperate with him and his coach by making fewer demands on his time and energy.

I have found that most swimmers who are well organized and who use their time effectively can handle school work and training with little problem. They cannot handle both if they spend a lot of time watching television, participating in bull sessions, dating every night or, in general, wasting time. I try to help any swimmer who is having the problem of organizing his day by asking him to establish a regular schedule of going to bed at a certain time, working out at a given time, studying at a given time, and so on.

Major Types of Stress

There are two major types of stress: physical and psychological. Physical stress is typified by training hard, not sleeping enough, and eating poorly. Psychological stress results from worrying about grades or fretting about being admitted to medical or law school. The psychological pressure of worrying about a girl friend or wife or pleasing his coach or parents is also typical of the stresses to which a swimmer is exposed.

Both physical and psychological stresses are accumulative. As they pile up, a swimmer who is under the hard physical stress of a vigorous training program should try to reduce the psychological stress he must undergo.

Why? Because too much stress results in failing adaptation. The body exhausts its resources to fight off illness, especially upper respiratory infections such as colds. Another typical disease of failing adaptation is mononucleosis. That is why, as I said at the outset, it is important to recognize the symptoms of failing adaptation, to try to identify the stress factors that are operating and to do something to reduce the stress and reverse the course of failing adaptation.

Sometimes workouts must be shortened or stopped until the body can return to normal. Coaches, parents, a girl friend or wife, who constantly keep a swimmer under psychological stress probably contribute more to the swimmer's inability to adapt than all the hard physical work he does in the pool. As I mentioned in the coaching chapter, the psychological environment in the pool area should never be one of tension, anxiety, and fear of reprisal should the athlete fail to meet the coach's expectation. It should be a supportive environment in which everyone is relaxed yet highly motivated, an atmosphere that emphasizes cooperation and common goals.

Sleep, Rest, and Biorhythmic Patterns

When a swimmer trains hard, he needs more sleep than when he is not training. Not everyone needs the same amount of sleep. I usually get by on six hours a night and feel no harmful effects. Olympic swimmer John Murphy normally sleeps ten hours a night and sleeps twelve hours when he trains hard. These examples are extremes; the average person needs seven to eight and a half hours of sleep under normal conditions. When a person trains hard (two workouts a day), he will need to add one to two hours to his normal sleep habit. This is true of me when I train hard for masters competition. Thus, there is no magic number of hours that can be recommended for swimmers to sleep. Each person must find what best suits him.

The pressure of study or perhaps just poor self-discipline causes many swimmers to sleep insufficiently. Many of their problems of adaptation can be traced to this factor. Certainly it can be listed as one of the major problems during hard training.

A swimmer in hard training should not burn the candle at both ends. He should cut down on activities that demand a lot of time and physical effort. For example, he should not get heavily involved in intramural sports during the period of hard training. He should organize his day to do the essential things—studying, attending class, training hard in the pool, and so on—but during his free time he should not run madly about expending his remaining energy reserve. Many swimmers take a short nap of a half hour to an hour daily between practices. This is fine if it does not interfere with sleep at night. As I have said before, this is an individual proposition; each person must find the rest and sleep patterns that are best for him. If he cannot take a nap, the swimmer should at least spend some time resting. There may also be some merit in the suggestions of Dr. Herbert Benson's book *The Relaxation Response*.

Biorhythmical patterns have been mentioned a great deal recently as a factor in the performance of our lives, and certainly it is true that the body adapts to circadian (daily) and seasonal biorhythmic patterns. Swimmers need not worry that they will be at the bottom of one of these patterns when the state or national championship meet occurs. These patterns are easily overridden by the emotional response (the adrenal mechanism) of the occasion. That is the reason most swimmers perform their best times at the biggest competition.

The reason for discussing biorhythmic patterns here is that they influence performance and that the swimmer can adapt his cirdadian rhythm to help his performance. For example, a swimmer is working out only once a day in the fall from 4 to 6 P.M. He forms the habit of getting up at 8 A.M. Then double workouts begin and he must now workout from 6 to 8 A.M.. This necessitates rising at 5 A.M. instead of at 8 A.M. and forces a change in his circadian rhythm. For some people this presents a real problem. Our swimmer will have to go to bed three to four hours earlier and get up three hours earlier. Some people adjust to this change in a few days, while others take a week or two. Some give up after a few nights of staring at the ceiling with wide-open eyes; they rationalize by saying, "I function better late at night, I guess I'm just a night person." If this happens, the person should keep going to bed at the new time even if he doesn't sleep well, and should keep getting up at the new time. Eventually he will break the old pattern and will adjust to the new circadian rhythm.

Diet

The swimmer should be concerned with two phases of his diet: his daily diet and his precompetition diet. The daily diet should be adequate in both nutritive and caloric values, i.e., established requirements of vitamins, minerals, protein, and so on, and sufficient calories to maintain normal weight. The precompetition diet should be concerned with food ingestion for two days prior to competition right up to the final meal before the competition.

There are many misconceptions associated with diet. Most conscientious swimmers train as hard and as intelligently as they can to improve their performances. They even concern themselves with such small details as the fraction of an ounce difference between the weight of one swim suit as compared to another. It is only natural that they should worry about the food that they eat and try to get every advantage they can from eating properly or taking dietary supplements. It is just this concern that makes them so susceptible to any dietary claim that comes along. In a few exceptional cases some have been know to resort to drugs to improve performance. Unfortunately, or perhaps fortunately, there appears to be no way an athlete can eat himself into condition. An athlete conditions himself by training hard and intelligently, observing good training rules, and eating a well-balanced diet. While it is true that an athlete can eat improperly and hurt his performance because he lacks even minimal nutrition, it—repeat—appears there is no way an athlete can eat himself into condition.

The following is a discussion of the misconceptions concerning diet that I mentioned previously:

1. Protein is a good source of energy, particularly before a meet. True or false? *False*. The meal, in fact all the meals for two days before a meet, should be relatively low in protein and high in carbohydrate. The reason is explained thoroughly in the next two sections and I would recommend that coaches and swimmers read them carefully.

2. A diet that is high in protein, especially if a swimmer wants to put on muscle, is desirable since muscle is made of protain. True or False? *False*. A diet with a protein content of 10 to 15 percent of the total calories consumed is sufficient. Extra high protein diets do not build muscle tissue any better than does a normal mixed diet. In all my years of coaching I have never seen a swimmer in the United States suffering from protein deficiency. I did see a case in Mexico of a financially deprived swimmer whose daily diet consisted of tortillas and beans and who exhibited symptoms of protein insufficiency.

3. Honey is a good source of energy before a race and will aid performance. True or False? *False*. This is a custom that athletes have followed for years in the belief that it would raise the level of blood sugar and thus benefit performance. It has been proven to be false, and while honey or any other form of sugar might help in a marathon swim, such as swimming the English Channel, it is of no value in the normal competitive distances of 50 yards to 1500 meters. Ingestion of high levels of sugar, honey, and so on, may result in a drop rather than a rise in blood-sugar level due to insulin shock. More about this later.

4. Special vitamin supplements can help improve performance. True or False? *Once again false*. There is no evidence to show that any special supplements, i.e., vitamins, minerals, protein, and so on can, improve a swimmer's performance. In fact, excessive amounts of certain vitamins can have a toxic effect.

There are many other fads and fallacies, some of which will be mentioned later. I have singled out the four above to reinforce my belief that a normal mixed diet is the best for all humans, and for the athlete, even more so.

I would now like to list some guidelines in planning a diet for the two areas I have mentioned: the daily diet of a training athlete and the precompetition diet.

All persons—athletes or nonathletes—should receive their nutrients from the food they eat and not from taking food supplements, such as vitamins, minerals, protein tablets, wheat-germ oil, etc. The daily diet should consist of approximately 15 percent of the calories to be derived from protein, 35 percent from fat, and 50 percent from carbohydrate. If the following daily food guide is followed carefully the above proportion will be satisfied.

Daily Food Guide

The following guide to good eating is recommended by the National Dairy Council and presents the foods in four groups. Anyone following this plan can be assured of a well-balanced diet and that all of their dietary needs will be met.

1. *Milk Group*

   Three or more glasses of milk. Cheese, ice cream, and other milk-based foods can supply part of the milk.

2. Meat Group

   Two or more servings of meat, fish, poultry, eggs, or cheese with dry beans, peas, nuts as alternates.

3. *Vegetables and Fruits*

Four or more servings, including dark green or yellow vegetables, citrus fruit or tomatoes.

4. *Breads and Cereals*

Four or more servings made from enriched or whole grain.

Everyone needs the nutrients from all of the four groups. A person should eat enough of these foods to maintain proper weight. If he must eat more to maintain his normal weight, he should include a similar proportion from each of the four groups in order to assure that the nutrient recommendations will be filled.

When training hard, an athlete will burn many more calories than normal and should do so by observing the proportionality suggested above rather than by adding calories that are empty of nutritive value.

A Supplementary List of the Common Foods from the Four Groups
1. *Milk group*—milk shakes, sherbet, cottage cheese, processed cheese, yoghurt
2. *Meat group*—hamburgers, sausage, steak, chicken, turkey, shell fish (lobster, shrimp, oysters, clams), eggs, baked beans, peanuts, fish
3. *Vegetable and fruit group*—apples, bananas, pineapple, peaches, grapefruit, pears, strawberries, oranges, carrots, cauliflower, string and lima beans, celery, lettuce, spinach, squash, peppers, onion, potatoes
4. *Breads and cereals*—dry cereals, oatmeal, corn grits, crackers, cake, cookies, rolls, toast, macaroni, rice—either whole grain or enriched

Mixed Foods. Many of the foods we enjoy the most are a combination of foods from two or more of the recommended groups. A combination pizza, for example, combines cheese from Group 1, sausage from Group 2, peppers, tomatoes, onions, and mushrooms from Group 3, and the crust from Group 4. A Mexican taco has a similar composition, depending on its content. To maintain a proper diet when eating these foods, try as far as possible to order the type of pizza, taco, hamburger, and so on, that contains the most nutrients.

Junk Food and Empty Calories. Americans are eating more and more often at quick-serve places. While it is possible to maintain fair nutrition at such restaurants, it is also possible to end up with nothing but a junk-food diet, one in which few of the dietary needs are met except in terms of the total number of calories. A typical junk food meal would be (1) A hot dog with mustard, (2) French fries, (3) a coke, and (4) a candy bar. Try to substitute the following quick meal in place of the typical junk food menu: (1) a cheeseburger with lettuce, tomatoes, and onions, (2) a baked potato with butter or sour cream, (3) a glass of milk, and (4) a piece of fruit, some raisins, or peanuts.

The following is a list of junk foods that should be avoided because they contain little nutritive value. An occasional piece of cake or candy bar will not do much harm unless it substitutes for the foods which supply important nutrients, such as vitamins, minerals, proteins, and so on.

1. All forms of carbonated soft drinks
2. Candy
3. Ice-cream cones or freezes

4. Anything containing a high percentage of refined sugar
5. Popcorn, potato chips, crackerjacks
6. Beer and other alcoholic beverages

The Meal before Competition

I have already mentioned some prevalent misconceptions about the precompetition meal (i.e., that it should be high in protein). The precompetition meal should actually be normal or lower than normal in protein and fat and high in carbohydrate. Carbohydrates come primarily from Group 4 (breads and cereals), but also include foods from Group 3 (vegetables and fruits), particularly potatoes.

Certain foods require a long time to digest and thus slow the emptying of the stomach. They should be avoided. Other foods may dehydrate the stomach and cause discomfort.

Foods to Avoid in the Precompetition Meal

These foods fall into five groups:

1. *Greasy foods*—any fried foods, such as French fries, pies, and doughnuts; meat fried in grease, such as chicken, fish, breaded tenderloin, sausage; large amounts of cheese, whole milk, peanut butter, nuts of any kind.

2. *Highly seasoned foods*—pizza, spaghetti, highly seasoned meats, chili, and so on.

3. *Salads*—cucumbers, radishes, raw carrots, corn on the cob. These foods are relatively hard to digest and may cause stomach distress when the athlete is nervous.

4. *Any food that causes flatulence*—beans, junk food such as candy, pop, popcorn, peanuts.

5. *Foods that are too sweet*—foods containing large amounts of sugar, candy, dextrose or fructose, honey, and so on. These foods draw fluid into the intestinal tract and may cause dehydration of the tissues. High levels of sugar in the blood may also cause the pancreas to secrete excessive levels of insulin, which will in turn cause the liver to take sugar out of the blood, leaving the person with a lower than normal level of blood sugar. This phenomenon is referred to as insulin shock and is another reason for the athlete to reject foods of high sugar content before competition.

The Timing of the Pre-event Meal

The final pre-event meal should be eaten at least three hours before the athlete is to compete. If the swimmer is to swim one event in three hours and another two hours later, he may experience some hunger pains before the second event. He may also need more fluids. A limited amount of noncarbonated soft drink or fruit juice with a teaspoon of sugar per hour given in small amounts will provide the fluid, relieve the hunger pangs, and cause no discomfort. Some athletes can also tolerate such commercial liquid preparations as Sustagen or Nutrament. These also should not be consumed at one time, but should be taken over a period of time. Once again, let me repeat: *Avoid junk food.*

Fluids. A glass of water or even two glasses of water plus the drinks mentioned in the plans that follow may be taken with each of the meals. Skim milk is preferred to whole milk because of the high butterfat content of the latter, which somewhat slows the emptying of the stomach.

Salt. Food should be unsalted or only lightly salted, although more salt may be added during hot weather. Salt causes water retention, and a person can gain an unwanted pound or two very quickly.

The following menus can serve as a guide for the swimmer planning his own precompetition meal. He should study them carefully and substitute only when the substitute conforms with the principles stated earlier in the text.

Precompetition Meal Plan

Breakfast

Plan 1
1. Glass of orange juice or half a grapefruit
2. Dry cereal, sugar, skim milk
3. Scrambled eggs
4. Toast with margarine and jelly or jam
5. Glass of skim milk

Plan 2
1. Glass of tomato or apple juice
2. Lean ham slice
3. Three or four pancakes, margarine and syrup, or a sweet roll (don't take the pancakes if they are greasy)
4. Canned peaches
5. Skim milk

Plan 3
1. Serving of prunes or Kadota figs
2. Bowl of oatmeal with sugar and skim milk
3. Waffle, margarine, honey or jelly
4. Hot tea with sugar and lemon

Lunch

Plan 1
1. Hamburger patty (with grease absorbed on a napkin as much as possible)
2. Bread roll or bun
3. Tomato soup made with skim milk
4. Fruit juice (orange, pear, or apple)
5. Plain cooky or cake
6. Skim milk

Plan 2
1. Roast beef
2. Baked or mashed potato with margarine
3. Bread and jelly
4. Green beans
5. Fruited gelatin
6. Skim milk

Plan 3
1. Toasted cheese or chicken sandwich, made with two slices of bread or a bun
2. Mashed potato with margarine
3. Vegetable or vegetable soup (with fat skimmed)
4. Pudding, gelatin, or fruit
5. Skim milk

Dinner

Plan 1
1. Small steak (absorb grease with napkin, and trim fat)

2. Spaghetti or rice (small serving)
3. Roll or bread
4. Vegetable
5. Plain cake
6. Chocolate milk

Plan 2

1. Fruit juice or bowl of soup (broth or tomato soup made with skim milk)
2. Lean meat (no gravy), fish or chicken (baked)
3. Vegetable
4. Baked potato, margarine
5. Corn bread, margarine
6. Sherbet with plain cooky
7. Skim milk

Plan 3

1. Fruit salad
2. Baked fish
3. Vegetable
4. Boiled potato, margarine
5. Whole-wheat bread, margarine
6. Banana
7. Skim milk

Snacking between Meals

This practice has become an American tradition and is not a good one, because it tends to consist of junk foods. If you do snack, try to avoid the empty calories, and choose something from the list below:

1. Fruits—oranges, apples, bananas, pears, peaches, grapes, etc.
2. Vegetables—raw carrots, lettuce, celery, raw cauliflower, etc.
3. Dried fruits—raisins, apricots, prunes, apple, etc.
4. Small sandwich—chicken, ham, cheese, etc.
5. Canned fruit or gelatin with fruit
6. Whole-grain crackers with cheese or sour-cream dip
7. Milk shake, ice cream, or sherbet
8. Bread with peanut butter and jelly
9. Only if nothing else is available, resort to cake, cookies or pie. They are not as good as the seven items mentioned, but are preferable to candy, pop, chips, or popcorn

SECTION 1.12
"THE FACTS ABOUT ERGOGENIC AIDS AND SPORTS PERFORMANCE,"
BY WILLIAM L. FOWLER, JR.

The use of ergogenic aids in an attempt to improve performance in sports has plagued coaches, trainers, and physicians for many years. Whether nutritional, physical, or pharmacological, there is little evidence that these aids have a significant beneficial

This article is based on Dr. Fowler's paper delivered at the Ninth National American Medical Association Conference on the Medical Aspects of Sports, November 1967, in Houston. It is reprinted from the *Journal of Health, Physical Education and Recreation* Vol. 45, No. 10, (November-December 1969), AAHPER, Washington, D.C.

effect on physical performance. Furthermore, the use of many of these substances, such as drugs, results in undesirable and often dangerous side effects, and the legal and ethical implications of healthy individuals using a drug in the quest for advantage in sports cannot be disregarded.

Ergogenic is defined as increasing the capacity of bodily and mental effort, especially by eliminating fatigue symptoms. Ergogenic aids, therefore, would include nutritional, physical, and pharmacological agents. In addition to the ethical and legal implications of using aids to increase physical performance in normal individuals, several principles should be considered in evaluating the effectiveness of an ergogenic agent.

First, is there any physiological need for a particular substance? An example of this is the use of vitamins to supplement a normal well-balanced diet. Since exercise does not increase vitamin requirements and it is impossible to supercharge the cells by providing an excess of vitamins, there is no logical reason to use them. On the other hand, salt and water replacement has a sound physiological basis, since profuse sweating can result in a depletion of sodium chloride.

Second, is the methodology used in evaluating an ergogenic aid objective, valid, and reliable? There are many variables involved in sports, such as skill, training, and motivation, and it is impossible to subjectively evaluate the effect of a substance upon team or individual performance. Any study should be viewed with caution if it does not utilize controls and quantitative measurements.

Third, are the changes reported pertinent to the topic under investigation? For example, the reasons for evaluating anabolic drugs would be to determine their effect on strength and physical performance. The fact that weight might increase is interesting but immaterial. Indeed, to equate increases in weight with a possible increase in strength could be erroneous, since there is considerable evidence that much of the increase in weight is due to water retention.

Fourth, are the known side effects of an ergogenic aid severe and frequent enough to outweigh any potential benefits? There should be little doubt that the marked physiological effects of anabolic drugs in women and prepubertal males precludes their use in young boys as well as in females of any age. In the postpubertal athlete, the possibility of testicular atrophy, change in libido, liver damage, and edema would also appear to outweight any possible increases in strength.

Nutritional Ergogenic Aids

Nutritional ergogenic aids are specific foods, vitamins, and inorganic substances added as supplements to a normal well-balanced diet in healthy individuals. Although there is a sound nutritional basis for optimal performance, there is no evidence that any special food or vitamin can improve athletic ability.

Protein and Carbohydrate

Protein or amino acid supplements to the training diet have been traditional for many years, although several studies have shown that protein is not metabolized in significant amounts during exercise in well-nourished individuals. Gelatin, an incomplete

William L. Fowler, Jr., is associate professor and chairman, Department of Physical Medicine and Rehabilitation, School of Medicine, University of California, Davis. He received the B.S. and M.Ed. degrees from Springfield College and the M.D. degree from the University of Southern California.

protein rich in the amino acid glycine, or glycine itself, is still frequently advertised as a source of instant energy. The increased work output and decreased fatigue reported in preliminary studies has subsequently been shown to be due to training. Use of protein supplements to increase strength is also doubtful. Both Nelson and Rasch and Pierson have shown that additional protein added to the diet of either football players or normal males receiving resistive exercises failed to improve performance on motor tests or to increase weight, girth, and strength.

It is more logical to understand why increased performance has been attributed to the use of sugar as an ergogenic aid, since there is an increased utilization of carbohydrates during strenuous activity. The capacity to endure prolonged muscular work is enhanced if carbohydrate stores are replete prior to the exercise. There is no evidence, however, that sugar as a pre-event supplement increases athletic performance. Both Pampe and Karpovich were unable to find any effect from the ingestion of sugar on tests of short duration, and Haldi and Wynn showed that performance in swimming 100 yards was the same regardless of whether a high or low carbohydrate meal was taken three hours before the event. During brief periods of very strenuous exercise, muscular efficiency is dependent upon energy reserves and training and not on the composition and size of any pre-exercise supplement.

Vitamins

Vitamins are essential for the maintenance of normal metabolic functions and must be furnished from exogenous sources since they are not synthesized by the body. A healthy individual ingesting a well-balanced diet receives adequate amounts of all vitamins. Therefore, the use of vitamins in normal individuals without a specific deficiency represents nothing more than expensive placebos. A vitamin deficiency may result from inadequate intake, disturbance in absorption, faulty utilization, or increased tissue requirements in terms of growth. When vitamins are used in such exigencies, they are considered as drugs. The rationale for vitamin supplements apparently involves the assumption that vitamin requirements are increased during exercise, or that it is possible to supercharge the cells of the body by providing an excess of vitamins. It is, of course, impossible to "oversupply" the tissues since most vitamins cannot be stored, and any excess amount is rapidly excreted. In addition, vitamin requirements are not increased before or during strenuous exercise.

The effects of vitamins C, nicotinic acid B, and E on physical performance have been extensively studied. Supplements of C and B, separately or in combination, have failed to produce increased endurance, muscular efficiency, or motor performance in well-controlled studies. Vitamin E, wheat germ oil, and octacosanol are probably the most popular ergogenic aids in this country and are advertised as "cure-alls" for improving mental and physical fatigue.

Seven related compounds exert vitamin E activity. Of these, alpha tocopherol is the most potent. Quantities are present in a wide variety of foods, although the richest sources are some types of vegetable oils. Tocopherols are natural antioxidants of foods and are believed to be effective in preventing oxidation of fats. Vitamin E deficiency states have been induced in many species, although no pathological counterpart to the muscular dystrophy of vitamin E deficient animals has been found in humans. Deficiencies have been induced in humans through the feeding of polyunsaturated fatty acids from which most of the tocopherols have been removed. A disturbance in absorption or utilization of tocopherol is also found in children with steatorrhea due to cystic fibrosis, portal cirrhosis, and biliary atresia. Serum tocopherol concentration in these children ranged from 50 to 75% of normal. Although the administration of vitamin E increased tocopherol levels, there was no change in muscle strength. It is difficult, therefore, to imagine how the administration of vitamin E to healthy athletes with a normal diet could possibly improve their strength, endurance, and performance when the administration of vitamin E failed to improve strength in patients with a severe deficiency.

Many experiments have been carried out in both humans and animals concerning the value of wheat germ oil as an ergogenic acid. Cureton and Pohndorf presented data showing that subjects taking a wheat germ oil supplement made greater gains in physical fitness measurements than did subjects taking vitamin E, a placebo, or exercise alone. Studies on athletic teams, however, failed to produce any conclusive evidence in favor of wheat germ oil. Percival reported a decrease in the recovery pulses of men after a step test or following a 440-yard run. Ershoff and Levin found that diets containing wheat germ oil prolonged the time it took guinea pigs to swim to exhaustion. Rats fed wheat germ oil did not, however, increase their swimming time when compared to a group fed corn oil. Consolazio and associates also found that the performance of rats receiving vitamin E or wheat germ oil or octacosanol did not differ from that of control groups. The failure of wheat germ oil to produce significant results with athletic teams in competition or with rats in swimming tests casts considerable doubt on its usefulness.

Other Nutritional Supplements

Potassium, calcium, magnesium, phosphorus, and sodium chloride supplements have been used as ergogenic aids. Even with minimal dietary conditions, humans are rarely subject to any deficiency in these elements, and excess amounts are rapidly excreted from the body when renal function is adequate. However, excessive sweating in hot weather may bring about a sodium deficiency resulting in heat cramps and hyperpyrexia, and work capacity in a hot environment is markedly reduced when salt is restricted from the diet. The addition of salt as a supplement in hot weather is only a precautionary measure, of course, to prevent heat cramps and hyperpyrexia. Under normal conditions it is not a source for extra energy and endurance.

Lecithin, a phosphatide, was originally thought to be associated with increases in strength, but controlled studies have showed no beneficial effects. Phosphates have been used as ergogenic aids with conflicting results. As is the case with most ergogenic supplements, beneficial results reported in early subjective studies were not confirmed by subsequent objective experiments. Alkalinizing procedures with sodium citrate and bicarbonate as well as fruit juices have also been used in an attempt to prevent the lactacidemia and ketonemia of exercise. Although reports in the early literature indicated increased performance and endurance, subsequent studies concluded that any changes produced in the alkaline reserve by dietary manipulation would have little influence on the ability of normal individuals to perform muscular work.

Other substances have been tried in various combinations, the latest being the potassium and magnesium salts of aspartic acid. Its use is apparently based on the observation that exercise causes an elevation of blood ammonia, that this increase contributes to fatigue, and that the mixed salts of aspartic acid, aspartic acid alone, or ammonium carbonate would prevent the rise of blood ammonia. Conflicting results have been found in both animals and humans. In animals, Barnes and Laborit found that the mixed potassium and magnesium salts of aspartic acid prolonged the time required for rats to reach physical exhaustion due to forced swimming. Similar experiments reported by Rosen were equivocal, and Matoush found that aspartic acid salts had no effect upon the swimming performance of rats and dogs. In humans, beneficial reports have been mostly based on subjective relief from fatigue. In well-controlled objective studies, the potassium and magnesium salts of aspartic acid produced no significant changes in fatigue, strength, or physical performance.

Physical and Mechanical Ergogenic Aids

Physical ergogenic aids include breathing oxygen, or the use of massage, mechanical devices, and ultraviolet light. Most of these aids fall into the category of fads in that they represent exaggerated claims for some technique that might be beneficial if used in moderation. An example of this is isometric exercise, which is a convenient and effective way of increasing muscular strength. Its limitations, however, must be recognized since isometric exercises do not assist range of motion or cardio-vascular-pulmonary endurance.

All objective experiments regarding the effect of vibrating cushions, belts, and other mechanical aids have shown that these machines have no influence on performance, weight, or metabolic fitness. Several studies have indicated a beneficial effect from ultraviolet irradiation on physical performance in runners, swimmers, oarsmen, and stationary bicycle riders. The explanation for this is not clear and is probably due to a psychological effect in most cases. Hettinger, however, feels that ultraviolet light affects muscle by mediation through the adrenal gland and subsequent mobilization of the sex hormones.

Oxygen

Since one of the main limiting factors in physical performance is the amount of oxygen which the organism can take up, it would appear logical to assume that breathing pure oxygen might increase the capacity for exertion and recovery. Unfortunately, it is impossible to store oxygen.

During the early 1900's, several investigators reported that the administration of oxygen before and after athletic events increased speed and endurance in running, reduced lactic acid accumulation, and quickened recovery from fatigue. The remarkable success of the Japanese swimmers in the 1932 Olympics with the use of oxygen established its reputation as an ergogenic aid even until today.

Karpovich explained the reason for the apparent beneficial effect of preliminary oxygen inhalation when he demonstrated that swimmers increased their speed because they were unable to hold their breath longer and, therefore, immobilize the chest. He also reported that it was impossible for prolonged breathing of oxygen to be more effective than the traditional three preliminary deep inhalations, since only 20 percent of the oxygen remained in the expired air two minutes later. Other studies have also shown that oxygen inhalation prior to exercise does not have any effect on work performance, speed of running, or rate of recovery. Work loads can be maintained for longer periods of time, however, if oxygen is administered during the exercise period.

Massage

Müller has shown that massage allows quicker recovery from fatigue in the rest pauses following a period of work. Under conditions in which exhaustion was reached after one hour without massage, the maximal working time was tripled by the use of massage during the rest pauses. This was only temporary, however, for several work-rest cycles, and the subject had to pay for it later with a subsequent slow recovery. Asmussen and Boje and Hale were also unable to show that massage had any beneficial effect as an ergogenic aid.

Pharmacological Ergogenic Aids

Pharmacological ergogenic aids are drugs, and a drug is broadly defined as any chemical agent which affects living protoplasm. To both layman and physician, the use of drugs implies the prevention or cure of a specific disease. While a physical or nutritional supplement may be dismissed as a useless but harmful fad, it is difficult to find any legal or ethical basis for the utilization of drugs in the quest for advantage in sports. Unfortunately, the use of an ergogenic aid seems to depend on whether or not the substance is a stimulant or is habit-forming. If the drug is not a stimulant, its use apparently does not contravene the rules on doping of the Amateur Athletic Union or the International Amateur Athletic Federation, at least as interpreted by many athletes.

This interpretation is, of course, open to question. Stimulant is defined as producing stimulation by causing tension on muscle fiber through the nervous tissue. In addition, drugs only stimulate or depress cellular activity since they cannot impart new functions to cells or tissue. It would also appear that habit-forming is being confused with addiction. Habituation usually refers to the psychic and emotional dependence on a drug, while addiction signifies a more basic physiological dependence and tolerance. Few, if any, drugs are nonhabit-forming, and most drugs produce undesirable and often dangerous side effects depending on dose, tolerance, cumulative action, and individual idiosyncrasy or hypersensitivity.

Central Nervous System Depressants and Stimulants

The major central nervous system depressant is alcohol. Although seldom used by athletes as an ergogenic aid, it is important to determine its effect on performance since it is customary in some countries to drink wine or beer with meals. The apparent initial stimulation from alcohol results from the unrestrained activity of the lower centers of the brain which are freed by the depression of higher inhibitory control mechanisms. It increases neither mental nor physical ability, although familiar and habitual mechanical tasks are less affected than work requiring skill and attention. There is only a minor direct effect on respiration, circulation, and skeletal muscle activity, but the total amount of work accomplished may be increased due to lessened appreciation of fatigue. Karpovich, in a review of the literature, notes that alcohol has a deleterious effect upon speed in swimming or running short distances, but that work output may be increased or oxygen debt reduced depending on the amount consumed.

Central nervous system stimulants that have been used as ergogenic aids include caffeine, camphor, cocaine, coramine, strychnine, and metrazol. Amphetamine also directly stimulates the brain but is primarily classed as a sympathomimetic drug.

Caffeine is a powerful central nervous system stimulant which produces a keener appreciation of sensory stimuli, increases motor activity, decreases reaction time, and allays fatigue. It is the least active of the xanthines in its effect on respiratory and cardiovascular function. With large doses, however, pulse rate, blood pressure, cardiac volume, respiratory rate, peripheral vascular resistance, and A-V oxygen difference decreased while cardiac output, stroke volume, left ventricular work, metabolic rate, and respiratory volume increase. Its central and peripheral actions are antagonistic on the blood vessels, but a peripheral vasodilatory action predominates with therapeutic doses resulting in increased blood flow. Central stimulation is responsible for increased capacity for work by preventing the perception of fatigue, although there is also a direct action on skeletal muscles. Several studies, reviewed by Karpovich, showed that caffeine increases work output but does not affect speed in running short distances.

The increased capacity for muscular work with cocaine is also primarily due to a lessened sense of fatigue. Action on the medulla results in an early increase in respiratory rate, but this soon diminishes. Heart rate is increased after moderate doses due to an increased central and peripheral sympathetic stimulation. Vasoconstriction occurs due to central vasomotor stimulation and results in an initial rise in blood pressure. There is no direct action of skeletal muscle, so the ability to relieve fatigue results from central stimulation. Several studies have shown that cocaine increases endurance and the speed of recovery after bicycle riding.

Coramine is primarily a respiratory center stimulant through its reflex action on the carotid chemoreceptors. It also causes peripheral vasoconstriction by central vasomotor stimulation, but increases coronary blood flow and cardiac output in large doses. Metrazol acts at all levels of the cerebrospinal axis. Early, there is an increase in respiratory minute volume through stimulation of the medulla. The vasomotor and vagal centers are also stimulated, and reflex activity of the spinal cord is increased. Its activity also extends to the neuromuscular junction producing an increase in tension and duration of the twitch response. Peripheral action on the circulation and heart is negligible although splanchnic and cerebral vasodilatation occur due to its action on the medulla. There have been no controlled, objective work studies using coramine or metrazol.

Drugs Acting on Autonomic Effector Cells

Certain drugs mimic the effect of nerve stimulation on muscle or glands. Their action can be efferent and central as well as efferent and peripheral. They may stimulate or block structures innervated by adrenergic nerves, stimulate or block structures innervated by cholinergic nerves, or inhibit skeletal muscle and autonomic ganglia. Amphetamine, benzedrine, and epinephrine are examples of drugs used as ergogenic aids which stimulate structures innervated by adrenergic nerves. Amphetamine differs from epinephrine in that it is also a potent central nervous system stimulant.

Amphetamine stimulates the respiratory center in the medulla, causes excitation of the brain stem reticular activating and arousal mechanisms, and facilitates mono- and polysynaptic transmission in the spinal cord. More work can be accomplished but the number of errors is not decreased, and it does not enable subjects doing exhausting work to perform longer or recover more quickly. It increases the rate and depth of respiration through its action on the respiratory center plus a dilating action on the bronchioles. Cardiac output is increased by direct myocardial action and peripheral constriction of arterioles. There is also an increase in systolic and diastolic blood pressure, although these changes are inconsistent as is the heart rate. Reports on its effect on physical performance are conflicting and apparently depend on factors such as fatigue, motivation, and sustained attention. Smith and Beecher reported that amphetamine improved performance in a variety of athletic events, tests of strength, and psychomotor and mental performance. Others found no effect on performance in essentially the same tests and athletic events. In some of these studies, it was noted that heart rate and blood pressure were increased in the resting state and that the recovery of both were retarded after exercise.

Epinephrine also acts directly on effector cells. Some autonomic structures are stimulated while others are inhibited, and it has very little effect on the central nervous system in therapeutic doses. It has a marked vasopressor action on blood pressure, accelerates the heart rate, and increases cardiac output. The arterioles of the skin, hands, and feet are constricted, resulting in a decreased blood flow in these areas, although overall peripheral blood flow is increased. Oxygen consumption is increased, blood sugar and lactic acid levels are elevated, and the glycogen content of liver and muscle decreased. In both animals and humans, the use of epinephrine has failed to produce an increase in work capacity, although it may make the subjects feel more energetic.

Nicotine inhibits skeletal muscle and autonomic ganglia but exhibits complex and often unpredictable changes. It is a central nervous system stimulant for the respiratory, vasomotor, and emetic centers, but a primary transient stimulant and secondary persistent depressant of all sympathetic and parasympathetic ganglia. It also manifests a curariform action on skeletal muscle in the secondary stage. Nicotine apparently has no effect on a variety of neuromuscular and cardiovascular performance tests, although Karpovich felt that performance was better in nonsmokers after a two-year study.

Cardiovascular Drugs

Cardiovascular drugs as well as other pharmacological substances causing peripheral vascular vasodilatation have been widely used as ergogenic aids, especially in cyclists. There have been few controlled studies regarding their effect on work performance in normal subjects. In patients with muscular dystrophy, however, the cardiac glycoside, digitoxin, failed to increase strength, reaction time, or working capacity.

Many drugs cause vasodilatation, including choline esters and adrenergic or ganglionic blocking agents. There is also a miscellaneous group including nitrites, thiocyanate, veratrum alkaloids, rauwolfia, hydralazine, and khellen. Most of these drugs are extremely potent, and the deaths of several athletes have been attributed to their use.

Androgenic-Anabolic Steroids

The most popular drugs used at present by athletes are the androgenic-anabolic steroids. Thus far, no nonsteroid androgen has been discovered, although many derivatives of testosterone have been prepared and tested in the search for compounds that might promote general body growth without masculinizing effects. Such compounds are often called "anabolic steroids," a term which is somewhat premature since a complete dissociation between androgenic and anabolic effects has not yet been achieved.

The normal function of testosterone at puberty affects the skeleton, skin, muscles, sebaceous glands, subcutaneous fat, and speech as well as the sex organs. The role of androgens in developing muscle size and strength is based primarily on laboratory studies in animals and clinical observations in humans. In animals, skeletal muscle mass decreases following the removal of the testes or hypophysis, is restored by replacement therapy, and can be increased by excesses of androgen. Dogs trained on a treadmill compared with those receiving testosterone showed no differences between the effect of muscle training and the androgen in histological and chemical analysis. When compared to control animals, both groups had an increase in total muscle weight, cross-section of muscle fiber, number of nuclei, and protein content. In humans, it is presumably the presence of androgens in increased quantities in the male that is responsible for the greater muscle mass. During adolescence, muscle groups such as the hip flexors, rotators, and extensors and the gluteus medius attain maximal strength in the male, while performance in the female remains at a lower level.

Several well-controlled studies investigating the effect of androgens on strength and performance have produced conflicting results. Simonson, Kearns, and Enzer used methyl testosterone in males over 48 years of age with complaints of excessive fatigue and found that endurance, flicker frequency, and back muscle strength were increased. Hettinger administered testosterone to older male subjects between 65 and 70 years of age and also reported increases in strength and physical working capacity. A combination of isometric exercises and testosterone produced even greater increases in strength. Samuels, Henschel, and Keys, in a study of young men between 21 and 30 years of age, reported that methyl testosterone failed to increase strength. Fowler, Gardner, and Egstom also were unable to show any increases in strength, motor performance, vital capacity, anthropometric measurements, and physical working capacity after the use of an anabolic steroid, androstenolone, in young men. A combination of a training program and the drug also failed to change these measurements. Fowler and associates also studied the effect of twelve months of androstenolone treatment, with or without therapeutic exercise, on children and adults with muscular dystrophy. There was no improvement, subjective or objective, in muscle strength and other measurements.

The difference between subjective observations and objective studies and even between well-controlled experiments may be due to several factors. The type and degree of response to androgen is age-dependent. Increased muscle strength occurs to a greater extent when androgen is given before puberty than when given at or after puberty. After 50, increases in strength in response to androgenic drugs again appears to occur. Before puberty, testosterone production has not yet reached a maximal peak. Although not as well documented, androgenic steroids may be more effective in increasing strength in men after 50 because testosterone levels might again be reduced. The response to androgen is also dose and time dependent. This may explain the difference between subjective statements of increases in strength and the lack of confirmation by objective studies. In the reports in the literature, only therapeutically recommended doses were used. The amount used by athletes is usually much greater. For example, the maximum recommended dosage of dianabol is 20 mg per day for three months. Yet it is not uncommon to find athletes on two to three times this amount for as long as one year.

There is little doubt that many athletes are currently taking these anabolic drugs. In 1966, 38 weight lifters or field event men in the Southern California area were surveyed: 50 percent had taken or were receiving one or more of the anabolic steroids; 47 percent had received the drug from physicians and 47 percent were on a dose that was two to four times greater than the recommended therapeutic amount. All of the men expressed the belief that their performance had improved. Only five denied any side effects. Most of those on the drugs had been taking them for at least one year.

It must be remembered that the anabolic-androgenic steroids can also produce serious side effects. Large doses of testosterone suppress the secretion of gonadotropin and may cause atrophy of the tubules and interstitial tissue of the testes. In some species, androgens also exert a direct effect on the testes. The growth promoting effects of androgens may also be seen in the prostate, and prostatic hypertrophy is an occasional side effect.

Methyltestosterone, methandrostenolone, nortestosterone, oxymetholone, stanozolol, and norethandrolone have been reported to cause cholestatic hepatitis. Frank jaundice does not always occur, but there is usually some increase in bilirubin and transaminase with reduced elimination of bromsulphalein. The response is dose-dependent and becomes a frequent complication when large amounts of androgen are taken. Even small doses of many androgens, such as methyltestosterone, are metabolized with difficulty by the liver. Large doses probably have a cumulative effect and may result in the accumulation of large amounts of the substance or its metabolite in the body. Large doses of androgens can also cause excessive erythropoiesis leading to moderate polycythemia and reticulocytosis.

Hypertrophy of the musculature in response to testosterone requires retention of nitrogen. There is also retention of potassium, sodium, phosphorus, sulfur, and chloride associated with a gain in weight, which can partially be accounted for by the water held in association with the retained salts and protein. Indeed, edema is often a troublesome side effect when large doses of androgen are used.

Androgens accelerate growth in pre-adolescent children but may decrease the height which they would ultimately attain. The bone age increases more rapidly than the height age, since androgens accelerate the ossification and eventual fusion of epiphyseal cartilages. All of the anabolic drugs share this property. The result of such a developmental pattern will be that the ultimate height attained will not be increased and may even be decreased.

Summary

Of the nutritional and physical ergogenic aids, only carbohydrates have any physiological effect on performance. Sodium chloride, of course, is a necessary supplement during vigorous physical activity in hot weather. Contrary to popular belief, there is no evidence that the requirement for vitamins may be increased during work or that it is possible to supercharge the cells of the body by providing an excess. There is also no evidence that breathing oxygen hastens recovery from fatigue or improves performance.

There are no pharmacological ergogenic aids which can be safely used. The undesirable and often dangerous side effects of using drugs far outweighs any questionable benefit. If these considerations are not convincing, the legal and ethical implications of healthy persons using a prescription drug in the quest for advantage in sport cannot be disregarded. Whether done unknowingly, tacitly, secretly, or openly, the use of ergogenic aids in sports should be unequivocally condemned.

SECTION 1.13
"A SYMPOSIUM ON NUTRITION," BY GEORGE V. MANN, SC.D., M.D.

Nutrition-Performance Link?

The meetings, with English-Russian translations, were opened by Prof. Victor Rogozkin, director of the Leningrad Research Institute of Physical Culture. Rogozkin and his colleagues are especially interested in what they call the molecular biology of physical exercise. But Rogozkin soon focused attention on the central question of this meeting: Is there some nutrient formula or feeding regimen that will augment physical performance? All competitive athletes are well aware of the asymptotic character of the performance of international-class competitors. As Kazharov observed in the *Moscow News*, the first four places in the 90-meter ski jump at Sapporo were only 0.7 of a point apart on a scale of 12. In the 500-meter men's skating there were ten competitors who finished within a second of the winner. When many competitors are very good and almost equal, attention turns to training factors that will give some small advantage, and one of these may be nutrition. Now the question of the best diet for competitors is the same one the Greek wrestler Milo asked his trainer 2,400 years ago. Milo got no good answer either; he did it with meat and wine.

The meeting began with a paper by Alexei Pokrovsky, professor of biochemistry at the Third Medical School in Moscow and director of the Institute of Nutrition, Academy of Medical Sciences of the USSR. An attractive, dynamic man, Pokrovsky expressed the opinion that athletes often eat too much protein, an opinion emphasized later by Dr. Anna Ferro-Luzzia with Italian data showing that their athletes average about 3 gm/kg body weight daily of protein.

The speakers in the symposium were often given to tedious classification of sports according to daily energy requirement, although no one was prepared to demonstrate that appetite alone is an insufficient guide for an athlete's energy requirement. The Italians showed the astonishing fact that their athletes average 5.5 percent of their daily energy requirements supplied as ethanol. This may explain some fiascoes in Italian performance.

Manipulating Muscle Glycogen

The organizers invited Hultman and Saltin to review their work with manipulation of the glycogen content of muscle. Saltin did not appear although his abstract was fascinating. He made the following points: Only water replacement has been shown beneficial for long-term exertion. The failure to demonstrate any advantage of solutions of sugars and various electrolytes during competition may be a result of gastric retention. Both hyperosmolality of the stomach contents and heavy muscular exertion will inhibit gastric emptying. Saltin said that solutions as dilute as 2.5 percent glucose will reduce the rate of gastric emptying by 10 percent, and solutions of 5 percent to 7 percent glucose will reduce it by half. Since neither water nor glucose is absorbed from the stomach, the widespread use of salt and sugar solutions may be neither helpful nor harmless.

Dr. Mann is career investigator, Vanderbilt University School of Medicine, Nashville, Tenn., and a member of the editorial board of *The Physician and Sports Medicine*.

This article is reprinted from *The Physician and Sports Medicine*, Vol. IV, No. 1 (1976).

Erik Hultman, well known for his work in Stockholm on muscle glycogen, began by reviewing the energy stocks of muscle. Muscle has a maximal rate of high energy phosphate production of about 2 mm/sec/kg. This rate is probably limited by the V_{max} of phosphorylases in the tissue. It is in fact somewhat higher than the maximal demand, but at maximal rates of exertion the phosphogen supplies of muscle are exhausted in a matter of seconds. A wider choice of fuel substrates is possible at submaximal rates of work, and this choice of fuel is influenced both by training and the nature of the mixture of muscle fibers, a characteristic which is probably determined by heredity. Thus as rate of work decreases from maximal levels the fuel is progressively phosphogens, glucose, and glycerides. There is no known way to alter phosphogen stores. But as Hermanssen, Bergstrom, Saltin, Hultman, and others have shown, stores of muscle glycogen can be manipulated. Either starvation or a carbohydrate-free diet will halve the glycogen content of skeletal muscle, and exercise will virtually abolish it. If, then, carbohydrate is fed, supernormal levels of muscle glycogen can be reached. While work performance has been shown in the ergometry laboratory to be increased by this maneuver, it has not been established that these super levels of muscle glycogen will augment the performance of competitors. Hultman remarked that these means of maximizing the content of muscle and liver glycogen may not necessarily be useful for the competitor. A gram of glycogen is associated with three grams of water in tissues and these deposits may both stiffen and weigh down muscles for best physical performance. Nevertheless it is becoming apparent that training involves the modification and indication of enzyme systems which change the efficiency of utilization of fuel substrates.

Does Fat Help?

Shinjiro from Japan discussed the role of various diet mixtures on the performance of rats. He observed that few sports require a great surplus of body fat. Japanese sumo wrestling and perhaps American football are the exceptions. The traditional obesity of the largest weight lifters seems to have no basis in augmented performance but is instead a convention.

N. N. Yakovlev of Leningrad described studies with rats that were tested by swimming. He could not change the glyceride content of muscle with diet, but he did show some large changes of muscle phospholipids with work. Parizkova from Prague also showed higher rates of lipid metabolism in trained rats and she found these effects persisted for several days after the training had ceased. But the changes could not be produced by simply adding fat to the diet. The sense of these papers dealing with the effect of training on fat metabolism was that fat is the broad-based fuel for all but short, intense exercise. The present problem is that except for conventional training, which increases the rate of fat catabolism, no one knows how to manipulate the fat content of muscle or, by such manipulation, to augment performance.

A number of the studies reported were done with rats. The translation of these studies to human affairs poses difficult problems. The Swedes, always sangfroid in human research, seem to think it impossible.

Professor Macaraeg, the Filipino, examined the use of a liquid pregame meal for competitors. For this he used the US commercial mixture called Sustagen, giving each man 240 ml several hours before competition. X-ray studies showed that the stomach was empty in two hours and that digestion was essentially complete in four hours. He reported less nausea and vomiting and indigestion during competition.

Electrolyte Supplements

A frequent debate in the discussion periods revolved around the advisability of attempting to correct changes of water and ion composition produced by exercise until there has been either a demonstration of functional impairment produced by those changes or proof of augmentation of performance by the supplementations. While it was not much discussed, many observers seemed to feel that the effect of electrolyte and food supplements for athletes is mainly a placebo effect. That is, it is real and measurable but explained by emotional and psychic forces rather than by physiological, chemical processes.

Gawronska of Poland described studies of the manipulation of muscle glycogen in Polish Olympic athletes who were training at 3,000 meters elevation. She could not demonstrate an augmentation of performance by preloading the muscles with glycogen.

Dr. Barry Brown of the University of Arkansas could not show an effect of vitamin E supplements in 22 middle-aged subjects who were trained and measured for various physical parameters. He used a novel design tactic. While the subjects were told that one-half would receive placebos, in fact all did receive the treatment. Thus there were no controls although the sample size was doubled.

Professor Böhmer of West Germany examined the changes of body potassium after exercise using whole body counting of ^{39}K for his calculations. He showed that body potassium is lowered and renal clearance is increased by exercise even as the intracellular potassium went down and the extracellular potassium went up. The changes he described emphasize the need for recuperation between exertions. A marathoner may lose 9 to 12 liters of sweat in his race, and this will contain 5 to 7 mg of potassium per liter. This loss is in addition to the urinary loss, so the quantities of potassium involved are large. But no one knows if potassium replacement during competition is useful for performance. The empirical observation that athletes, whether equine or human, need several days' rest between competition suggests that this period may be necessary to restore ion equilibriums.

"Sports Anemia"

Kvanta of Sweden considered the iron deficiency associated with training that is sometimes called "sports anemia." He argued, although he did not demonstrate, that anemia is common among male athletes. He believes this comes about through two mechanisms. Sweat contains 0.3 to 0.4 mg per liter of iron, so a vigorous athlete losing 9 to 12 liters of sweat daily would lose 2.7 to 4.8 mg of iron above his usual losses. His iron loss would be equal to or greater than that of a reproductive woman. The other mechanism of sports anemia which Kvanta postulated is an interference with the absorption of non-heme, dietary iron. This is caused by such dietary components as phytates, oxalates, carbonates, phosphates, and certain siderophilic protein materials in animal foods, especially eggs, which bind iron and prevent its absorption. His solution is to administer a daily capsule of beef hemoglobin supplying a highly absorbable form of iron. He reported that runners given this supplement increased their hemoglobin levels by 20 percent to 40 percent and their serum iron levels by 25 percent to 30 percent. The report emphasized the importance of keeping some surveillance of body supplies of iron in athletes. Kvanta used serum iron and blood hemoglobin for that purpose, but this can now be better done with measurements of the serum levels of ferritin, which is an index of the body pool of iron.

Prof A. I. Pshendin of Leningrad described his experience with a sugared electrolyte mixture resembling Gatorade that was given to athletes during competition. The philosophy again was to make the supplements match the losses, but his athletes did not perform better.

The Brazilian Settineri described the use of capsules of potassium chloride (500 mg) to prevent muscle cramps in swimmers. The cramps were lessened by this therapy after a few days, although the Americans commented that these capsules of KCl had been banned in the United States because of local damage to the intestinal mucosa.

Lactate Clearance and Fitness

I described a lactate tolerance test that Dr. H. L. Garrett and I had used to study the nature of physical fitness in dogs and men. Lactate clearance was correlated with fitness in adult men. We found that either physical training or a low carbohydrate diet would cause the rate of lactate clearance to increase. Most astonishing was the demonstration that men given 20 gm of sodium L(+) lactate orally each day in four divided doses would show a significant improvement of physical fitness even without training. We interpreted this to mean that disposal of lactate is one limit of fitness and that this can be augmented by feeding lactate. In the discussion, Dr. Hultman preferred to believe that the effect demonstrated is more likely to be an augmentation of an oxidative step of lactate dispersal. I believe it more likely that the augmentation of clearance induced is due to the induction of some limiting enzyme in gluconeogenesis. Whatever the mechanism, the phenomenon needs more study, because it may offer a dietary means of augmenting physical capacity.

Dr. A. Venerando could not demonstrate that supplements of vitamin C would improve work performance, although it did contribute to the lactic acidosis associated with work.

The conference was summarized by Professor Rogozkin. The evidence that athletic performance can be improved with nutritional supplements seems insecure at this time, if one requires proof of physiological mechanisms. The placebo effect of nutrition is large, however, and it is often confused with physiological effects. A sufficient amount of body fat, the main fuel for work, seems always to be available. Overfattening may impair performance by increasing the inertia of the body and the energy cost of performance. A better noninvasive and more sensitive index of body fat reserves is needed. The role of the various lipids in supporting work efficiency is just being approached at the molecular level, a task now well underway by Yakovlev and his colleagues at Leningrad. The manipulation of tissue glycogen by programs of work and diet is well developed, but it should not be assumed that super levels of glycogen in muscle will automatically result in super performance. The proposal from America that oral lactate will augment both lactate clearance and physical fitness needs to be carefully examined. Coaches are likely to think this is a threat to their suzerainty.

The Athlete Wants Performance

The efficacy of electrolyte replacement is now only vaguely understood. A distinction should be made between changes produced by exercise which are harmful to further performance and those which are in fact facilitative or conducive to better performance. The phenomenon of second wind is probably an example of the latter. At the present stage it is foolhardy to correct or overcorrect all the changes because we can measure them.

The athlete, like Milo the wrestler, is concerned with performance, not with esoteric, physiological chemistry. He seeks regimens that will help him win and he deserves advice that will guard his health. The symposium emphasized the primitive state of our knowledge about the optimal feeding of athletes, but it may mark the beginning of a new wave of research.

Professor Pokrovsky asked me to name the leading US expert on nutrition for athletes. I could not think of one, and at the end of the Leningrad Symposium I still could not name one—anywhere. But Leningraders like to think of themselves as innovators and changers and to prove it they will show you a statue of Lenin at almost every turn. Perhaps they have made a beginning with this symposium. Milo would say, "It's about time."

SECTION 1.14
"WHAT SHOULD ATHLETES EAT? UNMIXING FOLLY AND FACTS," BY RALPH A. NELSON, M.D., PH.D.

Proper nutrition often loses out to food fads, quackery, and superstition, and this is as true for athletes as for the general population. While the principles of physical training are properly understood by coaches, trainers, and athletes, they have neglected the equally well-developed principles of nutrition. Thus, many trained athletes engaging in highly competitive sports ascribe special properties to foods and food supplements which to them seem to improve their athletic performance but which, in fact, have little nutritional merit. If they succeed in sports, this unfortunately reinforces their convictions. They then spread their ideas to others, and within their school or athletic group a particular diet may become popular. If the athlete is performing well, coaches, trainers, and team physicians, recognizing psychologic benefits, at least, are reluctant to interfere. So the habit is not discouraged, even if it is suspected that it is nutritionally useless. But those who overlook such habits are not merely indulging an athlete's harmless whim. Nutrients have potent effects on the physiologic and biochemical adaptions of the body. Therefore, changes in dietary habits or inclusion of great quantities of highly purified nutrients in the diet may have significant consequences, some of them deleterious.

How Much Protein?

More than any other food, protein is regarded by athletes as having particularly healthful properties. They reason: Meat is muscle; a person is what he eats; therefore, he will increase muscle mass and strength if he eats meat. However, studies in animals and humans have not demonstrated any benefits from eating excessive amounts of protein. In

Dr. Nelson is consultant in nutrition, Department of Internal Medicine, Mayo Clinic and Mayo Foundation, and assistant professor of physiology and associate professor of nutrition, Mayo Medical School, Rochester, Minn.

This article is reprinted from *The Physician and Sports Medicine*, Vol. III, No. 11 (1975).

fact, one of the most impressive developments in clinical nutrition in the past decade has been the treatment of chronic renal disease by *lowering* protein intake. The program has kept people out of hospitals, working, and feeling well even though they may have severly impaired kidney function. If such good results are possible by restricting the intake of protein, is excessive protein intake healthy for normal human beings? Is there perhaps even danger in overconsumption of protein?

Various animal studies indicate such peril. High-protein diets have produced acute, subacute, and chronic nephritis in rabbits. In rats fed high-protein diets all of their lives, mild to severe chronic nephritis has developed, with azotemia, urinary cast formation, and increased daily urinary excretion of albumin. In dogs with an Eck fistula (diversion of portal blood flow away from the liver into the inferior vena cava), the feeding of usual rations has produced "meat intoxication," encephalopathy, and death. These animals will live normally, however, if dietary protein is restricted.

In several species of animals, life span can be increased by decreasing protein intake; for example, rotifers nearly double their life spans when protein intake is halved.

In man, an increase in dietary protein has been shown to increase blood urea concentration: At a protein intake of 0.5 gm/kg the blood urea concentration averaged 19 mg/d1; at 1.5 gm/kg it averaged 39 mg/d1; and at 2.5 gm/kg it averaged 45 mg/d1. In children and adults, albumin synthesis and catabolism increase when dietary protein is increased, but the concentration of circulating albumin is unaffected. In adults, increasing dietary protein with no change in caloric intake greatly increases total protein synthesized and turnover rates of protein metabolism.

Life Span Question Open

There are no reliable data on the effect of protein intake on life span. Some societies that appear to have large numbers of active centenarians have a protein consumption only about half that currently recommended for our own society. But the precise ages of the centenarians are in doubt.

An intriguing hypothesis is the possibility that increased protein consumption in men may be one factor responsible for the shorter life span of men as compared with women. Protein consumption has been shown to be 40 percent greater in men than in women based on the total daily intake, and about 20 percent greater when related to body weight. The amount of dietary protein ultimately converted to urea by the liver was 31 gm in women and 42 gm in men per kilogram of liver tissue. Thus, women presented, through their diets, 36 percent less daily protein load to their liver metabolism than men. Since the metabolic cost of obtaining calories from protein exceeds the cost from carbohydrate and fat, excessive protein consumption "idles" the body engine faster, while producing no demonstrably favorable metabolic effect. Therefore, considering the animal studies and reports that men and women eat similar quantities of protein as children but not as adults, protein consumption may in some way affect life span in human beings. There is no place, therefore, in the training program of athletes for high-protein diets or protein or amino acid supplements.

Some athletes, usually football linemen and defensemen, improperly relate size to strength, not understanding the difference between weight gained as muscle and that gained as fat. This misunderstanding is often shared by coaches. Unfortunately, just eating more only adds fat to the body mass; muscle protein cannot be increased by eating high protein foods. The only way muscle mass can be increased is by special exercises.

If the athlete wishes to increase his muscle mass, he needs no more than 0.8 gm/kg of protein during a 24-hour period, as recommended by the Food and Nutrition Board of the National Academy of Sciences. The ordinary diet, therefore, provides enough protein to meet the requirements for muscle hypertrophy. Again, it is important to stress that exercise, and not eating more protein, builds muscle mass.

Those who equate weight increase with strength must fashion a very strenuous eating program for themselves in order to gain weight, because 1 lb of human fat contains approximately 3,500 kcal, about the same as 1 lb of butter. To gain 1 lb of weight, therefore, an athlete must eat 3,500 kcal of food above his normal weekly requirements. Thus, an athlete who expends 3,500 kcal daily must take in 4,000 kcal each day:

$$4,000 - 3,500 \text{ kcal/day} \times 7 \text{ days/week} =$$
$$3,500 \text{ kcal}$$
$$\text{excess per week} = 1 \text{ lb fat}$$

Not only does the athlete achieve no more than a gain in body fat, he also establishes excessive eating habits that tend to endure into later life. In the young growing athlete, the abnormally increased caloric intake may also stimulate an increase in the number and size of adipose cells. Available data indicate that these cells do not disappear, so the athlete has increased his fat-storage capacity. Increased food intake tends to keep these cells filled with fat and cause obesity as he grows older. The athlete also will tend to become obese early in his athletic career, and this tendency, if not checked, will hamper his performance.

The athlete who is eating more will find it all the more difficult to decrease food intake as he grows older. Many professional athletes have difficulty in preventing weight gain and obesity. Coaches who are successful in professional sports tend to favor athletes who do not have body weight problems; one football coach will not sign contracts with players who have difficulty in maintaining normal playing weight.

Thus, the athlete who eats more with the intent of becoming stronger and playing better only becomes fatter, develops excessive eating habits, and may stimulate fat cells to multiply and enlarge.

Carbohydrate Loading

Carbohydrate loading is a technique in which athletes exercise strenuously while eating a low-carbohydrate diet and then exercise lightly while eating a diet very high in carbohydrates. This technique has been shown to more than double the glycogen content of muscle and to increase the endurance of track athletes. The use of such a dietary program is not without risk, however. Increased glycogen deposition is associated with deposition of three times as much water as glycogen. Glycogen and water can be deposited in muscle to such a degree that a sensation of heaviness and stiffness is produced. Recently, the carbohydrate loading technique was used by a marathon runner who then suffered angina-like pain and electrocardiographic abnormalities. Glycogen is deposited in cardiac muscle and with it, water.

Athletes using this dietary practice should be informed that glycogen can destroy muscle fibers. Although this tends to occur only in disease states (for example, acid maltase deficiency), we do not know what happens to the muscles and heart of the athlete who does not use all of the muscle glycogen he has stored as a result of loading.

The effects of using the technique over a competitive lifetime are also unknown. Some athletes, after using the carbohydrate-loading technique, experienced what may have been myoglobinuria, presumably as a result of muscle destruction. Recently, the technique was shown to alter the supply and utilization of fat-derived fuels during exercise. It decreased glycerol and plasma free fatty acid concentrations and increased ketone body concentration and insulin and growth hormone levels. The procedure, therefore, does more than add carbohydrate to muscle; it exerts metabolic effects on other substrates used for energy during exercise.

Hazards of Starvation

Another problem in nutrition and physical fitness is the starvation and semistarvation practices of young wrestlers. Starvation not only dehydrates the body but also produces weight loss in the form of losses in protein, glycogen, potassium, sodium, phosphorus, sulfur, ribonucleic acid, enzymes, minerals and trace elements, and other important cell constituents. Fifty percent or more of the weight loss induced by total starvation involves fat-free protoplasm. The tissues that lose this protoplasm are those active in protein synthesis, such as liver, pancreas, small intestine, and muscle. The depletion is due to several mechanisms. With sudden starvation there is no dietary protein to meet daily requirements. Although the body responds to this change fairly promptly by decreasing the amount of protein synthesized, breakdown of protein continues at a rate almost equal to that when the athlete was eating. The starving athlete in training uses muscle tissue as a source of calories even more than a starving person not in training. The body fat stores are so reduced in the highly trained athlete that he draws on his stores of protein (see Table 1.12).

Table 1.12
Body Composition and Predicted Tissue Losses in Acute Starvation (Based on Overnight Fast)

	Highly Trained Semi-starved	Highly Trained Normal*	Normal†	Obese
Weight (kg)	54	63	63	128
Lean Body Mass (kg)	53	59	54	78
Body Fat (kg)	1	4	9	50
Basal Metabolic Requirements (kcal/day)	1,300	1,700	2,000	2,350
Body Tissue Utilization in 24-hour Starvation (gm/day)				
Protein	108	125	84	115
Fat	74	77	132	115
Carbohydrate	31	120	110	206
Percent Protein from Body-Tissue Stores††	51	39	26	26

*7% of body weight estimated as fat
†15% of body weight estimated as fat
††Percent of tissue lost as protein (gm)

Further, semistarvation coupled with a diet low in carbohydrate could, by producing ketosis and its associated dehydration, result in a weight loss of 3 to 4 lb of water within 24 hours. Such procedures are used by athletes (or recommended by coaches) to achieve a lower weight classification. Often associated with this practice is voluntary dehydration, salt deprivation, and use of diuretics and cathartics. Dehydration from four sources—ketogenic diet, water deprivation, salt deprivation, and drugs—leads to impairment of circulatory function and poor athletic performance.

The result is diminished body reserve for athletic demands—which more than offsets any advantage gained in competing in a lower body-weight classification. Predictably, continuation of the starvation and semistarvation process over an entire season in the youthful competitor could affect normal growth.

Vitamin supplements are used routinely by many athletes, both amateur and professional, although there are no data to support the impression that such supplementation enhances athletic performance. Supplements are taken orally or by injection.

Some vitamins are toxic and life-threatening when taken in excess (vitamins A and D). In 1971, vitamin supplements were second only to aspirin in the frequency of accidental poisoning of children. With vitamin A, the margin of safety between the level of intake at which benefits end and that in which toxicity begins is small. The recommended daily allowance is 5,000 IU, and toxic reactions have been produced with as little as 18,500 IU a day.

Evidence against E

Vitamin E is a fat-soluble vitamin, stored much as fat and other fat-soluble vitamins are stored, and has been shown to be toxic for animals. Many nutritionists have assumed that it is toxic in human beings also, and now some evidence supports the supposition. Vitamin E produces coagulopathy in human beings when taken in excess. Although some athletes have taken vitamin E to improve athletic performance, vitamin E taken at a level of 900 IU daily for six months did not improve athletic performance of well-trained swimmers.

Excessive vitamin C supplementation increases destruction of vitamin C in the body. In guinea pigs pretreated with vitamin C and fed a diet deficient in vitamin C, scurvy developed sooner than it did in control animals. Scurvy has been noted in humans who have had a history of taking excessive amounts of vitamin C and who have returned to a diet that contains normal amounts. Humans who consumed 5 gm of vitamin C per day had no difference in blood levels from those who ate a similar diet but took no vitamin C. These data suggest that the increased rate of destruction of vitamin C produced by supplementation persists after supplementation is stopped, so not only the vitamin C that remains but also that taken in food is destroyed. An indication that vitamin C induces an allergic response has been noted when vitamin C was taken in high doses. The possibility of becoming allergic to a vitamin is life-threatening. Other studies on vitamin C have indicated that excessive doses of vitamin C ingested with food destroy vitamin B_{12}. Excess vitamin C in some individuals increases the risk of renal stone formation.

Nicotinic acid, in excess, inhibits the uptake of fatty acids by cardiac muscle during exercise. Since fatty acids are important fuels of the heart, vitamin supplements containing niacin (nicotinic acid) are contraindicated before strenuous athletic performance. Other known complications of niacin, produced when it was taken in excessive amounts for the treatment of hypercholesterolemia, include flushing, itching, hyperbilirubinemia, liver cell injury, portal fibrosis, cholestasis, dermatoses, hyperglycemia, hyperuricemia with gouty arthritis, and peptic ulceration.

Summary

When it comes to good dietary practices, the athlete is like any adult in any other occupation or profession. He or she requires calories to perform each day, and the amount needed depends on the individual's size, type of activity, and length of time engaged in that activity each day. There is no single food or nutrient that, when added to the diet, will produce special beneficial effects. The carbohydrate-loading technique will improve athletic performance, but there are disadvantages. The athlete should eat approximately 15 percent of calories as protein, 35 percent of calories as fat, and 50 percent of calories as carbohydrate. This distribution is similar to the distribution of nutrients recommended for the general population by the American Heart Association. Better athletic performance should be accomplished through physical and psychology training, not through excessive eating, special supplementation, or other food fads.

TWO

Theory and Research of Training

SECTION 2.1
HYPOXIC TRAINING AND
OTHER METHODS OF TRAINING
EVALUATED

When discussing methods of training, it seems logical to first talk about the physiological changes or adaptations that result from the various methods. But, in fact, such an approach is often limited to something like the following statement: "When you sprint, you develop speed; when you swim overdistance, you develop endurance." While this statement is true, it is certainly simplistic, and to allow our intellectual curiosity to proceed no further is to limit our understanding and possibly the advancement of training methods.

For years the exercise physiology books discussed the gross physiological changes that occur as a result of training; i.e., when overdistance work is done, the cardiovascular ability is improved, the athlete's heart can pump more blood and consequently can carry more oxygen to the muscles and take away more carbon dioxide, and so on. Such changes as these have been studied and restudied and are old hat to all of us.

More recently—just in the past few years actually—researchers have begun to examine the physiological changes at the cellular level and are making some important and interesting discoveries. These discoveries and their implications in evaluating our training methods are subjects that intrigue me both as a coach and as a physiologist. It is this area I want to explore with the reader.

First, let us examine the muscle and see what makes it contract. Astrand[1] makes a good comparison between the internal combustion engine and the human engine. The pistons compare to the muscles, and both of them must have fuel to do their work. In the automobile's engine the fuel, of course, is gasoline; in the muscle the fuel is ATP (adenosine triphosphate). When the fuel tank is empty the car's engine can no longer operate. The same is true of the muscles: without ATP they cannot contract or relax. The gasoline needs to be oxidized (or burnt) before it can release its energy. This type of energy-release is referred to as aerobic because it involves the use of air. Oxygen comprises 21 percent of the air we breath, and it is this oxygen that is needed to oxidize the gasoline. The engine can also be turned over by stepping on the starter and allowing the battery to do the work anaerobically (without air). The muscles can also contract both aerobically and anaerobically. In the absence of oxygen the car's engine can turn over for only short periods of time until the battery runs out of charge. This is also true of the muscle; the total energy it can release without oxygen is very limited compared with what it can do with aerobic work.

ATP–CP System of Energy* (Anaerobic)

The ATP immediately available in the muscle can only supply the energy demands of all-out sprinting for a short period of time (approximately 5 to 10 seconds). Since the swimmer can swim only a 25-yard all-out effort using this system, if he continues to swim hard for the next 25, 50, or 75 yards his muscles must receive their source of ATP from another system.

Lactic-Acid-ATP System (Anaerobic)

The next source of ATP is the lactic-acid-ATP system. This system is also anaerobic and is also limited insofar as the length of time it can operate, (i.e., 10 seconds to 2 minutes, as in swimming 50, 100, even up to 200 yards). The ATP during this period comes from the breakdown of muscle glycogen or glucose in the presence of certain catalysts in the cytoplasm of the muscle, resulting in an accumulation of lactic acid.† This accumulation of lactic acid along with exhaustion of the supply of glycogen becomes the main limiting factor in muscular activity and causes fatigue. The muscle also builds up an oxygen debt that must eventually be repaid. In other words, when the swimmer receives ATP from this source there is a build-up in both oxygen debt and lactic-acid concentration.

*ATP is the first-hand energy provider for the muscle. As it breaks down to adenosine diphosphate, it loses one phosphate molecule. Creatine phosphate is available to resynthesize adenosine triphosphate from adenosine diphosphate (CP + ADD = Creatine + ATP). This activity can go on theoretically until the supply of creatine phosphate is exhausted. It is likely that the level of CP in the muscle can be increased by sprint training, i.e., 10 X 25 with 20-second rest interval.

†Glycogen breaks down into pyruvic acid to provide high-energy phosphates which are available to change ADP (adenosine diphosphate) back into ATP. Pyruvic acid is then changed to lactic acid by picking up a hydrogen ion.

Aerobic or Steady-State System

The third source of ATP for the muscle comes from aerobic activity. In this type of exercise the effort is less intense, and if it is completely aerobic can be continued almost indefinitely, as in swimming a very long race, such as across the English Channel. The oxygen supply to the muscles is sufficient to oxidize and resynthesize the lactic acid into glycogen, with the release of carbon dioxide, water, and energy. The availability of oxygen to the muscle cells in the final analysis is what determines endurance in prolonged physical work. There is no lactic-acid accumulation during aerobic work and also no oxygen debt. When the body works at a level at which there is no oxygen debt build-up, it is said to be in the *steady state*.

Most swimming races involve at least two of the systems shown in Table 2.1, and some utilize all three, as in a 100-yard swim. Table 2.2 shows the relative contribution of the aerobic and the anaerobic systems at the various distances.

In events under two minutes duration (approximately 200 yards) the work is predominantly anaerobic. After this period the aerobic ability of the swimmer becomes more important. In the 1500-meter swim approximately 90 percent of the energy used is developed via the oxygen system. Obviously a person training for this event should stress training that improves his ability to transport oxygen and to use the oxygen at the cellular level, such as overdistance training and short-rest interval training.

Type of Overload Determines the Type of Change at the Cellular Level

It becomes very important to understand that there are two entirely different types of adaptations made to endurance training versus speed training. When using speed training, you are overloading the muscle in terms of intensity—this is somewhat similar to weight lifting. To test this premise, in the summer of 1974 our sprinters were trained with overdistance training, interval training, and repeti-

Table 2.1
Three Systems of ATP

System	Source of ATP	Aerobic or Anaerobic	Distance
1. ATP-CP System	ATP—CP stored in muscle	Anaerobic (without O_2)	25-yd. sprint
2. Lactic-Acid-ATP System	Breakdown of glucose or glycogen in muscle, resulting in accumulation of lactic acid and oxygen debt	Anaerobic	50 to 100 yd. at top speed
3. Steady-State or Oxygen System	Breakdown of glucose in presence of oxygen—no accumulation of lactic acid or oxygen debt	Aerobic	200 yd. and up at moderate speed

Table 2.2
Work Time at Maximal Effort
(Approximate Distance)

Process	10 sec. 25 yd.	60 sec. 100 yd.	2 min. 200 yd.	4 min. 400 yd.	20 min. 1500 m.	120 min. 4 miles
Anaerobic Work Percent	85%	60-70%	50%	30%	10%	1%
Aerobic Work Percent	15%	30-40%	50%	70%	90%	99%

Note: Adapted from Astrand and Rodahl, p. 303.

tion training*; they did no sprint training (all-out efforts for 25s or 50s). In lieu of sprint training, strength-building exercises done at a fast speed with near maximum resistance using isokinetic exercisers were substituted. The swimmers were highly successful, placing first, second, and seventh in the National AAU Championships (Long Course) and recording best times of :51.5, :51.7, and :52.6.

I don't say this is the best way to train, but

it was an experiment based on some research I had read and which I present here:

> By subjecting laboratory animals to programmed work, Dr. E. E. Gordon's group was able to confirm that functional constituents of muscle may be selectively increased ... as an adaptation either to endurance-stimulating or strength-stimulating exercises.

> Energy-liberating enzymes which are a part of the sarcoplasmic proteins of the muscle determine the endurance capacity of the muscles. On the other hand, actomyosin largely constitutes the contractile system and determines the strength of the muscle.

> They postulated that the prolonged repetitive effort of running or swimming should increase the sarcoplasmic protein while the forceful exercise of weight lifting might increase contractile protein.

---

*We distinguish between interval training and repetition training in the following manner:

I.T.—many repetitions, short rest, moderate quality, i.e., 40 X 50 with 5-10 sec. rest, 75% effort, average time for 50 m.—31 sec. Primarily aerobic work.

R.T.—fewer repetitions, longer rest, higher quality, i.e., 20 X 50 with 30 sec. rest, 90% effort, average time for 50 m.—28 sec. Primarily anaerobic work.

The endurance-building groups consisted of one group of rats which was exercised in a running wheel, running up to 5 miles per day for several weeks, and another group which was subjected to 30 minutes of continuous swimming per day. The strength-building group climbed a 16-inch pole 50 times a day carrying 100-gram packs. The animals were sacrificed and the quadriceps and gastrocnemius (leg) muscles were examined. In the swimmers and runners the concentration of sarcoplasmic protein rose, while contractile protein fell. In the weight-lifting group the reverse was observed.

What does this mean if we want to apply these results to training for swimming? Here are a few of the assumptions we could make: if we train for nothing but endurance (overdistance and interval training), we will improve the quality of the muscle for endurance work, but it will probably make the muscles weaker (as shown by the decrease in actomyosin or contractile protein in the endurance group) and there will be a negative effect on the speed of the swimmer in the short events. On the other hand, if we train the swimmers only with weight lifting or sprint training, we will make the muscles stronger and will improve the speed for a short sprint,* but there will be a negative effect on the aerobic capacity or the endurance of the swimmer, based on the decrease in sarcoplasmic protein (and a consequent decrease in energy-liberating enzymes, possibly in the mitochondria).

This means that if a swimmer wants to swim a good 1500, 400, 200, and even occasionally a good 100 freestyle, he must use more than one method of training.

The swimmer must often train many different functions at the same time—aerobic and anaerobic. Swimmers such as John Kinsella, Tim Shaw, and others who will swim anything from the 100 through the 1500 must try to develop more than just the endurance aspect of their muscles. In order to perform at least respectably in a wide range of events they need speed, strength, and endurance. They must develop all three systems of supplying ATP to some degree. There is only so much of each quality (speed—anaerobic; endurance—aerobic) that you can pack into a muscle; that is, the muscle cannot accommodate maximal anaerobic adaptations and also maximal aerobic adaptations. A swimmer or his coach must decide what quality he wants to emphasize in workouts. Nevertheless it is important for the swimmer to train all of the systems that deliver ATP to his muscles. An occasional reference to Table 2.2 will help determine approximately what percentage of the race for which the swimmer is training is aerobic and what is anaerobic.

Keeping all these elements in mind, the swimmer and coach must devise a plan of training, using a combination of the four methods of training shown in the following paragraphs.

1. *Overdistance Training*
   Definition: Continuous swimming of long distance, such as 400, 1500 yards or meters or even longer distances
   Percentage aerobic/anaerobic:
      70 to 95% aerobic
      30 to 5% anaerobic
   Physiological changes: The advantage of this type of training is that it places a great demand on the oxygen-transportation system, resulting in the following adaptations: increased cardiac output and greater stroke volume of the heart; a slower resting pulse rate; improved ability of the lungs to extract oxygen from the air; improved quality of the blood, enabling it to carry more oxygen; storage of more glycogen in the liver and muscles; increase in the number of functional capillaries in the muscle; increase in the number and composition of the mitochondria† in the muscle fibers.

---

*At the higher speeds the fast-twitch fibers are exercised while at the slower speeds only the slow-twitch fibers are involved.

†Mitochondria are small cellules in the muscle fibers (100 to 1000 per muscle fiber) that contain a system of enzymes, co-enzymes, and activators which carry on the oxidation of foodstuffs and release the

2. *Short-Rest-Interval Training*

   Definition: Swimming various repeat efforts at a moderate speed with a short rest interval between each—5 to 20 sec. For example: 15 × 100 with 10-sec. rest interval

   Percentage aerobic/anaerobic:
   55 to 85% aerobic
   45 to 15% anaerobic

   Physiological changes: The changes manifested here are similar to those mentioned above under overdistance training plus, to a lesser extent, those mentioned below under repetition training. The advantages of this method over overdistance are (1) during the short rest period some of the ATP-CP resources are partially replenished and available for use in the next repeat swim, thus delaying the accumulation of lactic acid somewhat, with the result that even though the work is more intense than in overdistance training, extremely high levels of lactic acid are not accumulated; (2) even during a short rest interval some of the lactic acid is resynthesized to glycogen (in the liver and kidneys) enabling the swimmer to work at a more intense level than he can in overdistance training; (3) during the rest interval the swimmer can restore some of the oxygen debt he has created. Oxygen debt is the main stimulus for many of the physiological changes that improve both aerobic and anaerobic capacity; thus it is not advantageous to eliminate it completely.

3. *Repetition Training*

   Definition: Hard efforts at near top speed with long rest intervals. For

   example: 4 × 150 near top speed with 5 to 10 min. rest interval.

   Percentage aerobic/anaerobic:
   30 to 50% aerobic
   70 to 50% anaerobic

   Physiological changes: During this type of training most of the ATP comes from anaerobic breakdown of glycogen in the cytoplasm. The catalysts required for this activity are also found in the cytoplasm of the muscle cell. There is apparently an increase in both the glycogen and catalyst stored in the muscles, and this is perhaps the main adaptation that results from repetition training.

   The high level of oxygen debt and lactic acid incurred during this type of training probably is the stimulus that brings about changes that cause more efficient absorption and transportation of oxygen—that is, increased number of functional capillaries, increased number and quality of mitochondria, advantageous changes in blood chemistry, and so on. This type of training adapts the muscle tissues to high lactate concentrations.

4. *Sprint Training*

   Definition: All-out sprinting for short distances. For example, 10 × 25 yd. with 20 to 30 sec. rest.*

   Percentage aerobic/anaerobic:
   85% anaerobic
   15% aerobic

   Physiological changes: This type of training improves the muscle's ability to contract fast (due to improved neuromuscular coordination) plus increased strength (due to increased levels of actomyosin). There is also probably an increase in the ATP-CP level in the muscle, resulting in the increased ability of the swimmer to sustain sprinting tempo for a longer period of time.

ATP used during aerobic work. Arcos[2] reported that rats subjected to six hours of swimming daily have a 52% increase in mitochondrial mass. It also appears that with an increase in endurance the mitochondria improve their ability to generate ATP aerobically.

*Approximately 80 to 90% of the ATP-CP used during a short sprint is replaced during this rest interval.

The four methods listed above do not preclude their use in combinations and variations such as interval training with moderate rest (i.e., 15 X 100 with 30 seconds rest interval). This type of interval training is more anaerobic than the type mentioned above under Short-Rest-Interval Training, but is not so anaerobic as that mentioned under Repetition Training.

These four methods and their variations and combinations are all based on the concept that the body has the ability to adapt itself to maintain a high level of the ATP in the muscle. Insofar as endurance is concerned, the more of the ATP that can be produced aerobically the better, since glucose can provide 19 times as much energy per gram mole aerobically as it can anaerobically. It appears that any adaptations that bring about better transportion and absorption of oxygen and tolerance to lack of oxygen would benefit the athlete. It is reasonable to assume that these changes could be facilitated by running high levels of oxygen debt in the muscle. Ordinarily the swimmer does this by working at such an intense level that he has to create the ATP for the muscle's contraction anaerobically (either via the ATP-CP system or the lactic-acid system).

Hypoxic Training

Another method by which a high level of oxygen debt may be created at even lower intensities of work is to inhale less air by breathing less often, thus making less oxygen available to the cellular level—in other words, through the use of controlled breathing, also termed hypoxic training. In training for track, the Czechs, East Germans, and even some American athletes have tried this type of training using such patterns as the following: inhale for six steps, hold the breath for six steps, exhale for six steps, and so on. Some have even practiced breath-holding when not exercising. I'm not convinced this latter practice is of much value.

Some research on hypoxic training has shown desirable effects. Kenneth Sparks,[3] in a research project at Indiana University in 1973-74, trained two groups four days a week, using interval training. One group used normal breathing, while the other trained in the same manner with the addition of hypoxic breathing. Sparks concluded that the hypoxic group showed a greater efficiency in the extraction of oxygen. "It can be concluded that training using controlled breathing can benefit the athlete in his extracting more oxygen per unit volume ventilated."

Under hypoxic conditions, at a given rate of swimming or exercising, the oxygen debt and the blood lactate (also the lactic-acid concentration in the muscles) are higher than those attained under the same training program, but using a normal breathing pattern.

Hollman and Liesen[4] tested the effect of hypoxia training on 36 subjects. The subjects breathed a mixture of air with only 12 percent oxygen content, rather than the normal 21 percent, while training on a stationary bicycle or on a treadmill. This type of breathing is not the same as the controlled breathing used in swimming or track training, but there is so little research on the subject of hypoxic training that I refer to this study for lack of other available research material. The result was that a lower amount of oxygen was available to the muscles, the same finding as under controlled breathing conditions. Reference to this study at this point might therefore have some relevance.

The maximum oxygen intake per minute rose with the hypoxia-trained group by 16.6 percent, while the control group improved only 5.5 percent. This difference of increase is significant and favors the hypoxia group. There was no detectable increase in the number of erythrocytes (red blood cells) or in the amount of hemoglobin. The heart volume also remained unchanged. The acid-base equilibrium showed a slight reduction of the negative acid excess value and a slight rise of standard bicarbonates.

The following three points can be considered as an explanation for the increased cardiopulmonal capacity under hypoxia conditions:

1. The intramuscular blood distribution can be additionally economized and hence the efficiency of the blood supply increased . . . .

2. An improved vascularization could be the result of hypoxia training. But the possibility of improved capillarization is undecided. . . .

3. An enlargement of the intracellular metabolic capacity with an increase of the energy supplying process per unit of time.[5]

It would appear from Item 3 above that hypoxia training increases the ability of the muscles to create ATP, perhaps both aerobically and anaerobically. The *intracellular metabolic capacity* could refer to (1) an increase in the mitochondrial number or composition (including enzymes, co-enzymes, etc.), (2) a possible increase in the amount of glycogen stored in the muscles, or (3) an increase in the enzymes that permit release of ATP in the lactic-acid-ATP system. All three of these changes can result in better performance in the middle distance (100 yards and above) and in longer events (400 yards and above).

A search of the literature reveals that little research on the effects of hypoxic training* in swimming has been conducted. During the past three years at Indiana University we have used hypoxic training consistently and beneficially. Prior to three years ago we had used breath-holding occasionally in practice, notably before the 1968 Olympic Games. I want to warn against breath-holding as a potentially

*Hypoxic training and hypoxia training are differentiated as controlled breathing and breathing air with reduced oxygen concentration.

dangerous practice and to emphasize the difference between breath-holding, as used in the past, and hypoxic training.

It is our experience that with a given amount of submaximal effort (for instance, swimming 10 X 100 freestyle in 65 seconds with 15 seconds rest interval) a swimmer will achieve a higher pulse rate when using hypoxic breathing than when using normal breathing. On maximal effort this is not the case, since the terminal pulse rate will be reached whether the person is hypoxic or normal breathing.

Table 2.3 depicts the results of several hundred trials at various controlled levels of breathing at the very beginning of a hypoxic training program.

For workouts consisting of swimming 5 X 200-yard repeat efforts with an average time of 2:05.1, leaving every 3 minutes (approximately 55 seconds rest interval), the Indiana swimmers recorded the following pulse-rate increases:

1. Normal breathing—pulse rate after last 200   150.4
2. Hypoxic breathing every second arm cycle   153.4
3. Hypoxic breathing every third arm cycle   167.3

An interesting aspect of the above data is that there is very little increase in the pulse rate when the breathing rate is changed from a normal to a controlled breathing pattern of once every second arm cycle. In swimming 100 efforts the increase was only 2.9 beats,

Table 2.3
Variation in Pulse Rate Due to Hypoxic Breathing.

Breathing Pattern	Average Time for 10 X 100, 15-sec. R. I.	Average Pulse Rate after Last 100
Normal breathing, once every arm cycle (av. 7.4 breaths per length)	64.13 sec.	161.4 beats per min.
Breathing every second arm cycle (av. 3.9 breaths per length)	64.20 sec.	164.3 beats per min.
Breathing every third arm cycle (av. 2.7 breaths per length)	64.18 sec.	175.2 beats per min.

while in changing from a normal breathing pattern to one of every third arm cycle the increase was 13.8 beats per minute. The same pattern can be observed in the 200-yard swims. Later in the season (eight weeks) the difference in the pulse-rate increases between the three breathing patterns narrowed considerably: for 5 × 200-yard swims with times of 2:03.4, they were as follows:

1. Normal breathing   150.8
2. Breathing every second arm cycle   152.9
3. Breathing every third arm cycle   161.4

This represents a difference between 1 and 3 after eight weeks of hypoxic training of 10.6 seconds, compared to 16.9 seconds when the experiment first started.

Unfortunately, no control group was used in this experiment, but it is reasonable to think that the decrease in heart rate after eight weeks of hypoxic training was due to some physiological adaptations. The main stimulus for this adaptation is probably a decreased level of oxygen and an increased level of carbon dioxide and lactic-acid concentration in the muscles and the blood.

Obviously the additional stress imposed on the swimmers by breathing only every second arm cycle is not so great that it causes much of an increase in the swimmers' heart rates. A high level of carbon dioxide in the blood acts on chemoceptors in the carotid artery and in the respiratory center, causing an increase in the pulse rate. Assuming that through hypoxic training we are trying to increase the oxygen debt and lactic-acid level in the body generally and in the muscle fibers specifically, it would seem that a higher pulse rate would be desirable. For this reason, once the swimmers (in this case freestylers) become accustomed to breathing every second arm cycle, I encourage them to proceed immediately to breathing every third arm cycle. For short distance repeats, such as 50s, they may try breathing only every four arm cycles.

Guidelines for Use of Hypoxic Training
Here are set down a few principles of

hypoxic training that can serve as a guide for the swimmer and coach:

1. Caution: hypoxic training is potentially dangerous. If the breath is held too long, unconsciousness will result. Remember—drowning is permanent!
2. If headaches develop with the use of hypoxic training, they should disappear within a half hour. If they persist, the amount of hypoxic training used in practice should be decreased and only slowly reinstated. Adaptation may be an individual matter; thus progression should take place with this in mind.
3. Approximately a quarter to a half of the total workout should be done hypoxically.
4. All of the pulling in a workout should be done hypoxically—breathing every second or, even better, every third arm cycle.
5. Most of the hypoxic training in a workout should be done at controlled speeds. Very little of sprinting at top speed should be done hypoxically.
6. Competitive races should not be attempted using hypoxic breathing. The breathing pattern that best suits the individual swimmer should be used.
7. The shorter the repeat swim, the more strokes the swimmer should take per breath. When swimming 10 × 50, he might breathe every third or fourth arm cycle; while swimming 4 × 500, he might breathe every second or third arm cycle.
8. When using hypoxic breathing for strokes other than freestyle, the following patterns should be used:

Butterfly—Breathe every second or third stroke on 100 and 200 swims breathe every third, fourth, or fifth stroke on 25, 50, and 75 swims
Backstroke—The same as for freestyle
Breaststroke—Breathe every second or third stroke, never failing to lift the head as if for breathing in order not to disturb stroke mechanics. Also try taking two long strokes off the wall at the turn.

9. A conscious effort should be made *not to change stroke mechanics* when breathing hypoxically. There is a tendency to shorten the pull in order to take more strokes per

breath. The swimmer should concentrate on retaining good stroke mechanics.

10. The swimmer should practice race breathing patterns when using hypoxic training. For example, if he swims a 50 taking one breath on the first and two breaths on the second 25, he can use the same pattern when swimming 5 × 50 with a 30-second rest interval. This technique would also apply to the breathing pattern for the 100-yard race, and so on.

11. Each week the swimmer should swim some overdistance training at slow to moderate speed, concentrating on stroke mechanics, but using hypoxic breathing (i.e., 1000 yards within 30 seconds of best time).

12. At the risk of being repetitious, remember the hazard involved in breath-holding drills. The swimmer should *never* attempt to see how far he can swim without breathing. When using hypoxic training for any distance over 100 yards, the swimmer should take at least two breaths per 25 yards.

Pulse Rate Related to Anaerobic Work

Most of the literature on the topic states that up to a pulse rate of 150 beats per minute the source of energy is aerobic. Above this rate the shift is toward an anaerobic source of ATP. Many factors, however, enter into determining the pulse rate. Such factors as state of emotion, age and individual differences, elapsed time since eating, elapsed time since intake of coffee, and so on, must be considered. If the swimmer and coach want to use the pulse rate as an indicator in determining roughly whether the swimmer is performing aerobically or anaerobically in practice, they should use the pulse-rate table.

Respiratory Rate and Distress Used in Evaluating Aerobic and Anaerobic Work

Along with the pulse rate, the breathing rate after an effort and the desire to breathe plus the respiratory distress felt during the actual swim are all indicators as to whether the swimmer is performing aerobic or anaerobic work or a combination of the two. In the course of the swim, if he (1) has no desire to breathe any more than he is breathing and

Pulse Rate per Minute	Percent Aerobic*/Anaerobic
Under 120	Probably 100% aerobic. Little or no benefit will be derived insofar as developing the anaerobic systems is concerned.
120-150	90 to 95% aerobic/5 to 10% anaerobic
150-165	65 to 85% aerobic/15 to 35% anaerobic
165-180	50 to 65% aerobic/35 to 50% anaerobic
Over 180	Over 50% anaerobic

*In sport sprints this table has little validity. For example: in a sprint (25 yards) the work is almost completely anaerobic, but there is little increase in pulse rate.

feels no respiratory distress, he is performing aerobic work; (2) wants to breathe more but is not feeling extremely distressed, he is performing a combination of aerobic and anaerobic work; (3) feels a strong desire to breathe more frequently and his breathing is extremely distressed, he is working mostly anaerobically.

After the effort is completed, the same indicators mentioned above apply, but the rate of breathing and the recovery of the breathing rate toward normal also can serve as additional measures to evaluate the type of work done.

Adaptation of the Nervous System and Development of Resistance to the Feeling of Fatigue

For years it was believed that neuromuscular block in voluntary effort was an important factor in the onset of fatigue. That is, the synaptic resistance at the point where the nerve and muscle meet become so great that it is difficult for the nerve impulse to get to the muscle. Transmission fatigue at the neuromuscular junction is no longer considered a plausible weak point.

Fatigue developing in the central nervous system (C.N.S.) is now considered to be one of the main limiting factors in voluntary muscular effort. Training no doubt improves the ability of the C.N.S. to adapt to moderate exercise prolonged over a period of time or to the stress of extremely intense effort over a short period of time. Each type of training must also bring about specific adaptations in the C.N.S., as well as in the muscles and organs of the body. We are conditioning the C.N.S. and the heart, the blood, the muscles, etc., simultaneously.

The ability to subdue the feeling of fatigue and the pain associated with muscular exertion varies from one person to the next and from one day to the next for the same person, depending on that person's motivation, concentration, and personality. The ability of the person to endure the unpleasant feelings associated with contracting the muscle maximally for a short period of time, as in an all-out 50-yard sprint, is different from the ability to endure the unpleasant sensations of swimming at a fairly moderate pace for 1500 meters. Both the sensations of an all-out sprint and that of a long sustained effort are different from that evoked by an all-out effort in a 200 race. The latter race, being an example of combined aerobic and anaerobic work, is probably the most difficult pain to become accustomed to and that which tests most the swimmer's ability to tolerate high levels of carbon dioxide, lactic acid, and low levels of oxygen.

For the above reasons it is important that swimmers at some time use all methods of anaerobic and aerobic training to aid in these adaptations. It appears not only that the swimmer's body in general and the tissues of his muscles specifically must become accustomed to high levels of oxygen debt but that the swimmer must also learn to tolerate the uncomfortable feelings associated with this condition. When he has done so, he may truly be said to have learned to tolerate pain. Hypoxic training appears to be a good supplement to a regular training program to accomplish this goal, as well as to facilitate the gross physiological changes and those at the cellular level.

As you may have guessed, I have felt some apprehension in writing about hypoxic breathing since it means introducing a training method which offers so much possibility for danger. I am impelled to say again—be careful in distinguishing between breath-holding, as it once was used, and controlled or hypoxic breathing, as it is discussed here.

SECTION 2.2
POWER: WHAT IS IT, HOW DO YOU MEASURE IT, AND WHAT DOES IT MEAN TO THE COACH AND THE SWIMMER?

Power is one of the most misunderstood of our physical traits. It is often considered to be synonymous with strength, but while it is related to strength, it also involves the factor of speed. A more appropriate term for this physical quality might be *explosive power*. Although it is somewhat redundant, I think it better conveys the message.

The formula for power can be expressed in an equation as follows:

$$Power = \frac{Force \times Distance}{Time}$$

In this equation, F (Force) is equal to the resistance or drag the swimmer must overcome in moving through the water, D (Distance) represents the distance of the race expressed in feet, and T represents the time it takes the swimmer to cover this distance.

Power is always expressed in units of foot-pounds (or meter-kilograms) for a given length of time, such as for one minute. A swimmer who swims 100 yards (300 feet) in 45 seconds (.75 minute) creates a drag of approximately 35 pounds. The formula for the power he generates is as follows:

$$Power = \frac{35 \text{ lb (F)} \times 300 \text{ ft (D)}}{.75 \text{ min (T)}} \text{, or}$$
$$Power = 14{,}000 \text{ foot-pounds per minute}$$

Assume we have another swimmer of the same size and shape, who uses the same stroke mechanics but who is not capable of creating as much force. He swims the same distance in 60 seconds, or 1 minute. The formula for the power he generates would be expressed as follows:

$$\frac{Force \text{ (20 lb)} \times Distance \text{ (300 ft)}}{Time \text{ (1 min.)}} =$$
$$Power \text{ (6000 ft-lb per min)}$$

Personally I have always had trouble grasping the concept of power, but I have also always been intrigued with the implications of what variations in power between individuals could mean to the coach. In 1948, as a pilot study for a possible doctoral dissertation, I measured the vertical jump of several of the Olympic track sprinters and several of the distance runners. The vertical jump has long been considered to be a good measure of explosive power. I found the sprinters attained average scores of 28 inches, while the distance runners averaged only 14 inches. The range of the scores on the vertical jump ranged from 9 to 31 inches. The technique I used then and still use today involves the jump and reach.

The subject stands sideways and next to the wall against a graph or a yardstick and raises one hand, reaching as high as he can (with his dominant hand). He then moves about 6 inches to 1 foot away from the wall and, without taking a step, jumps upward as he would in jumping for a basketball and reaches as high as he can with his dominant hand. The differences between his standing and jumping reach is noted and recorded. He He is given three trials, with the highest score being taken as his final measurement.

My graduate advisor, due to the wide spread in scores between sprinters and distance runners, believed I had not gathered my data carefully and recommended that I not let my bias enter into my testing procedure. Since that time I have measured the vertical jump of hundreds of swimmers and have found there is a positive correlation between the height a swimmer can jump and his sprinting ability. Below are listed the vertical jump scores of some swimmers, including data gathered at the 1975 National AAU Outdoor Meet:

Sprinters	
Mark Spitz	26 in.
John Trembly	28 in.
Ken Knox	27 in.
Chris Woo	29 in.
Rick Hofstetter	30 in.
John Murphy	27 in.
Jim Montgomery	25 in.
Joe Bottom	26 in.

Distance Swimmers	
James Kegley	16 in.
John Kinsella	18 in.
Bruce Dickson	19 in.
George Breen	14 in.

Others	
Greg Jagenburg	22 in.
John Naber	18 in.
Mike Stamm	24 in.
Gary Hall	25 in.

Greg Jagenburg and John Naber present two very interesting cases:

Greg won the World Championships in the 100-meter butterfly and didn't do as well in the 200 butterfly in that particular meet. At the National Outdoor Championships, after Greg had done only fair in the 100-meter butterfly, I tested his vertical jump and found he had a score of 22 inches. On the basis of his score I predicted he should swim a better 200-meter butterfly than a 100. He then won the 200 fly in near world-record time.

John Naber, who won the 100- and 200-meter backstroke, probably has the lowest vertical jump of any male swimmer who has ever won a national title at the 100-meter distance. John is not basically a sprinter and would better qualify as a distance swimmer, as evidenced by his win in the 500-yard freestyle in 4:20 plus, and in the National AAU Indoor 1650-yard freestyle in 15:05 plus, both American record times.

I have measured several track sprinters with a vertical jump of over 30 inches. In 1956 I measured the vertical jump of Paul Anderson, Olympic weight-lifting champion and considered by many to be the strongest man in the world. Even though he weighed 330 pounds at the time, he had a vertical jump of 31 inches. Sprinters in track run 60 and 100 yards (6 to 10 seconds) and sometimes 220 yards (21 seconds). In swimming, especially in international competition, the shortest event is 100 meters, which compares to a 400-meter running race in terms of elapsed time. We do not have a truly explosive swimming event as they do in track unless we consider the 50-yard race in indoor competition. It is therefore doubtful that we will see many explosive athletes in swimming, particularly in the long-course competition.

What Makes One Athlete More Explosive than Another?

For over one hundred years physiologists have been aware of the distinction between *red* and *white* muscle fibers. In humans and most animals both red (slow-twitch) and white (fast-twitch) fibers are found in nearly every muscle. The white (fast-twitch) fibers are adapted to contract quickly, but they tire easily, while the red (slow-twitch) fibers contract more slowly but are capable of greater endurance. For many years it was believed that the main difference in the two muscle fibers was the difference in the level of myoglobin. Myoglobin is a protein material in the muscle that has a strong affinity for oxygen and gives the red color to the muscle fibers. The red fibers, having considerably more myoglobin than the white fibers, consequently display the difference in color. The higher myoglobin in the red (ST) fibers permits them to have a high metabolic capacity for carrying on aerobic oxidation, which results in better endurance. These are the muscle fibers a swimmer would use primarily when swimming a long race. White (FT) muscle fibers are capable of fast release of energy and are the fibers a swimmer uses primarily when swimming a sprint. Exactly how the slow-twitch fibers are used or recruited in a sprint event, if they are, or how the fast-twitch fibers are used in a distance swim, if they are, is unknown, and the question is a source of controversy. Humans, as well as the various species of animals, show variations in the percentage of slow-twitch and fast-twitch fibers they possess in the various muscles. For example, members of the cat family, such as the lion, cheetah, and even the common house cat, have a predominant number of fast-twitch muscle fibers. They catch their prey by slowly stalking it and then finally capturing it with a fast sprint effort. If they don't catch it within ten to fifteen seconds, they give up and walk slowly away with the slow-twitch fibers because their fast-twitch fibers are out of gas. Members of the canine family, such as

wolves, wild dogs, or hyenas,* are different from the cats in that they have a higher percentage of slow-twitch fibers and they catch their prey by running it down and wearing it out.

How can this information be used by a coach in his selection and training of swimmers?

Inherent Variability among Humans in the Proportion of Fast-Twitch and Slow-Twitch Fibers

Before we make an application to actual coaching methods, let us discuss several important physiological principles concerning slow-twitch and fast-twitch fibers.

The proportion of slow-twitch to fast-twitch fibers is genetically established and apparently cannot be changed by training. The proportional percentage of the two types of fibers that make up a muscle is determined by taking a small biopsy of the athlete's muscle (usually the thigh or calf). The muscle sample is sliced, stained, and examined with a microscope. There is no great deal of discomfort from this procedure, with the athlete's performance not being detrimentally affected. Costill[6] has found that the thigh muscle is usually a mixture of these two fibers in a ratio of 50/50. He has also found that good distance runners have a higher percentage of slow-twitch fibers. Here are a few examples of the distance runners' results, as measured in the gastrocnemius muscle.

Runner	Slow Twitch	Fast Twitch
Ndoo	80%	20%
Prefontaine	82%	18%
Shorter	75%	25%

Sprinters usually have a higher percentage of fast-twitch fibers, with Costill reporting some as having as high a proportion as 90 percent of white fast-twitch fibers.[7]

That this proportionality is an inherent characteristic seems to be an accepted fact. Bengt Saltin reports that identical twins, one a weight lifter and the other a distance runner, were identical in their proportion of

*Hyenas are not really dogs but are a separate branch of the canine family.

fast-twitch and slow-twitch fibers. Costill tested the father and two sons (Stetina), all three prominent bicyclists, and found the father had 60.5 percent slow-twitch fibers, one son had 60.8 percent, and the other son 61 percent. From the few samples taken of fathers and sons, there is some evidence to believe that sons tend to inherit this trait from their fathers. This must be substantiated by further research, but my mention of it here may stimulate some doctoral candidates to try to prove I am wrong through a research study in this area. I am, after all, a coach first and a physiologist and scientist second; on this basis I permit myself some license to draw broad conclusions from little data in an effort to explain certain phenomena.

A More Recent Classification of Muscle Fibers

Physiologists no longer classify muscle fibers simply as red or white, but rather as fast-twitch or slow-twitch fibers. Table 2.4 shows the prevailing concept concerning this classification and the interconvertibility of these fibers and makes it clear why the simple differentiation by color is inadequate.

What Happens When 2a Fast-Twitch Red Fibers Are Converted to 2b Fast-Twitch White Fibers, or Vice Versa?

If we take a sprinter and train him as a distance swimmer, what will happen to his speed and what will happen to his fast-twitch white fibers? Some research plus an application of the physiological adaptation principle would seem to indicate that with distance training the athlete would change some of the fast-twitch white fibers into fast-twitch red fibers. It would also seem logical to believe that, once these fast-twitch white fibers are converted into fast-twitch red fibers, they increase their endurance but lose some of their speed. I believe that if you train a runner who runs the 100-yard dash on primarily the same schedule as a marathon runner he will lose much of his speed. I don't think this explosive runner can train as hard as a marathon runner; his muscles are not physiologically adapted for this type of training. He literally cannot take the work.

In the past we have gotten by with training what we call sprinters and distance swimmers on essentially the same program and with

Table 2.4
Classification of Muscle Fibers
As Slow-Twitch-or-Fast-Twitch

1-Slow-Twitch Fibers *	2-Fast-Twitch Fibers Two Types	
1-Red Fibers Cannot be converted into fast-twitch fibers. Adapted primarily for slow, prolonged, or repeated contractions	**2a-Red Fibers, Fast-Twitch** These fibers contain more myoglobin than *2b* and can sustain activity longer than *2b* white fast-twitch fibers, but probably do not contract as fast as *2b* fibers	**2b-White Fibers, Fast-Twitch** These fibers are histologically different from *2a* red fast-twitch fibers and probably contract faster, but fatigue more easily than *2a* fibers.

Training
⟶
⟵

It is believed that these two types of fibers cannot be converted into slow-twitch fibers, but some seem to have the ability to be converted into the other type within their classification of fast-twitch fibers. The interconvertibility of these fibers depends on the type of training the fibers undergo or upon sex hormone activity.

* Frequently referred to as intermediary fibers

some success because, as I mentioned before, we do not have a true sprint event in swimming, our shortest international event being the 100 meters which compares to the 400-meter run in terms of time. As competitive swimmers become more advanced in their performances we can expect to see more variation within a training program as swimmers, in order to win a single event, are forced to specialize in training either for the shorter distance, the middle distance, or the distance events. This has already happened in track. The detrimental effect that endurance training has on explosive power is shown by the following two illustrations:

1. Amby Burfoot, winner of the 1968 Boston Marathon had a vertical jump of only 9 inches when he won this race. Two years after retiring he was once again tested by Costill who found his vertical jump had increased to 20 inches. Costill also reports that he has never tested a world-class distance runner during the time he is in training who has had a vertical jump of over 13½ inches.

2. John Kinsella, when not training, had a vertical jump of 20 inches; during the season, when training for distance events, John showed a decrease in vertical jump to 17 or 18 inches. This pattern has also been noted in other distance swimmers at Indiana University. In the past two years we have found we are able to prevent this decrease in power of the muscles as measured by the vertical jump by the use of isokinetic exercise and some sprint training, such as adding a few all-out sprints to each distance swimmer's workout.

Jim Montgomery has a vertical jump of 25 inches and while not extremely explosive is above average in this quality. He probably will never win an NCAA Title in the 50 free. He is to a great extent like Mark Spitz (vertical jump: 26 inches) in that the proportion of FT to ST fibers best suits him for the 100 and 200 distances. Both of these swimmers can swim a good 50-yard and a good 400-meter race, but they are better suited for the longer sprints and the middle distances.

Jim Montgomery likes to work hard and in previous summers has trained like a distance swimmer with the concept of *speed through endurance*, training about 16,000 meters a

day. He thought that if he got in great shape for the long races he could certainly hold up for a 100- and 200-meter race. On the surface this seems a logical assumption. In the summer of 1975 he trained with our middle-distance swimmers and, at times, with our sprinters, averaging only 10,000 meters a day. He did more sprint work and more anaerobic work than in previous years. The result of this type of training on his speed became obvious when he set a world record of :50.59 for the 100-meter freestyle.

Mark Spitz had a vertical jump of 22 inches as he trained for the 500-yard freestyle and set the American record in his freshman year at Indiana. In subsequent years I trained Mark for the sprints and put him on isokinetic exercises. As a senior in 1972 he increased his vertical jump to 26 inches, and although he never won an NCAA title in the 50-yard event, I believe the shorter sprint training and the isokinetic exercise program improved his explosive power and strength with the resulting success he experienced in the 1972 Olympic Games.

Are Athletes either Explosive-Type or Endurance-Type, or Can They Be Both?

I believe that scores on the distribution of the traits of speed and endurance if measured carefully on a large segment of the population would distribute themselves in a normal bell-curve pattern. In Figure 2.1 I have set up such a hypothetical curve with the range of scores on the vertical jump for adult men, 18 years to 25 years of age, from 9 to 31 inches, with the mean average score being 20 inches; this, incidentally is approximately the mean average for this age group.

Earlier I compared the explosive athlete to the cat and the endurance athlete to the dog. These animals need the traits they possess to survive. How about their prey—such animals as the zebra—who must have enough speed to get away from the cats and enough staying power or endurance to outrun the hyenas? These animals usually do manage to avoid capture by both of these predators. They try to avoid the lions and cheetahs by grazing in open land and by keeping a given distance between themselves and the cats. The cats can outsprint them for short distances, but if the zebras can see the cats and keep enough distance between themselves and the cats before the race begins, they know the cats will tire before the distance between them is completely closed. If they misjudge this distance or are unaware of the nearness of the cats, they become a meal for them and assure the survival of that species of cat.

Fig. 2.1. *Normal distribution curve of adult males on vertical jump*

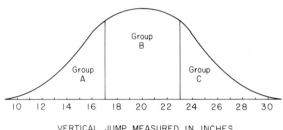

VERTICAL JUMP MEASURED IN INCHES

Group A. Not explosive, primarily red-fibered muscles. These athletes will be relatively better at distance events.

Group B. Average in explosive power and endurance. These athletes will be relatively better at middle-distance events.

Group C. Explosive, predominantly white-fibered muscles. These athletes will be better at the short sprint events.

To avoid the endurance-type predators, such as hyenas or Cape Town wild dogs, the zebras must count on their superior speed in the sprints to save them when the hyenas are near. Eventually the persistent hyenas will wear out many of the zebras because of their superior endurance. The perspicacity of the zebras can be seen by the fact that they will allow the hyenas and wild dogs to get much closer to them than they will allow the cats.

I believe the majority of athletes would fall into the zebra category, being average in endurance and average in speed and not excellent in either. Over the years I have been coaching I have always seemed to have one or two swimmers who can't work exceptionally hard and can't swim distances very well but who are able to sprint well. These athletes have always had an above-average vertical jump of 27 inches or more. Such athletes are commonly called *drop-dead* sprinters. John

Murphy, Ken Knox, and Mel Nash would fall into this category.

I have also always had a few boys on the team who have been able to take tremendous amounts of work and who can swim good distances but who can't sprint exceptionally well. Examples of these would be George Breen, Alan Somers, John Kinsella, James Kegley, and Bruce Dickson, all of whom have had a vertical jump under 20 inches. Most of the members of any group of men that I have coached, however, fall in the middle category of swimmers who can take an average amount of work and can swim sprints and distance events moderately well but who excel at the middle-distance events. They also have had average scores of 20 to 25 inches on the vertical jump. I do not want to imply that there are only three categories of swimmer. That human traits vary on a continuum is apparent. For example, two athletes already mentioned, Montgomery and Spitz, while not extremely explosive, are above average in explosive power and consequently are better adapted for the longer sprint and middle-distance events but are definitely not adapted for distance swimming.

According to Costill, "Training the . . . muscles to perform endurance work increases the number of mitachondria and related enzymes, but it does not alter the character of the muscles."[8]

A swimmer is born with a given amount of potential for sprinting and a given amount of potential for endurance work. If we develop him to his fullest potential in endurance, it is impossible to develop him to his fullest potential at the same time for sprinting. Coaches who make such brash statements as "anyone who comes out for my team becomes a distance swimmer" had better reexamine their training programs and be aware of the fact that not only do dogs, cats, and zebras vary in their endurance and speed potential but that humans also vary in the same traits and in their ability to handle hard training.

Hormonal Influences on Power

Gutmann, a German researcher, states that certain muscle fibers are sensitive to the influence of sex hormones. The transition from red fast-twitch fibers to white fast-twitch fibers under hormonal influence has also been observed. The implications here are obvious. If a girl were to be given a male hormone, such as testosterone or the anabolic steroids, her speed would improve, but her endurance would be detrimentally affected. Little work has been done with biopsy studies of females. On the basis of their performances at the various distances women appear to be better suited for endurance activities. If we were to take a large group of world-class women swimmers and give them male hormones, we would expect them to perform well and possibly to set world records in the sprint events, but to do less well in the distance events.

Is the Vertical Jump a Good Test of Power?

The vertical jump is generally considered to be a good test of power. Margaria and Kalamen are critical of it as a measure of power unless speed and weight are part of the measurement. Speed is a part of the measurement since the height that the subject jumps depends on his speed as he leaves the ground. The weight factor should be given some consideration, but most competitive swimmers are a rather homogeneous group insofar as general body-build is concerned and we do not run into many obese or overweight swimmers. At present there is no simple way to equate the weight factor; so, in principle, do not expect the heavier swimmer of a given height and age to jump as high as he would if he were lighter. Margaria and Kalamen suggest that their test be used to measure power. In this test the subject runs up a flight of stairs and the time it takes him to complete the last six steps (three steps at a time) is measured electronically. The power of the person is calculated from the formula

$$Power = \frac{F \times D}{T}$$

in which F=Force (weight of the person)
      D=Distance (height of the six steps in feet)

T=Time it takes him to go up the six steps

The end result is measured in foot-pounds per second.

Kalamen found a high relationship (r. 974) between this test and the time it took the subjects to run an all-out 50-yard dash, after a 15-yard running start. I do not think most coaches want or have the time or equipment to have their swimmers running 65 yards or running up and down steps and timing them electronically. For these and other reasons I would suggest that coaches use the vertical jump as a measure of power. This test can be easily administered in the pool area. Lines one inch apart can be drawn on the wall, a chart can be nailed to the wall, or even a yardstick will suffice.

Does a High Power Factor in the Legs Also Mean a High Power Factor in the Arms?

The swimmer receives most of his propulsive force to pull him through the water from his arms. Wouldn't it be better to measure the power in his arms? The answer to this question is a definite yes. At the present time it is difficult to measure arm power. Eventually we will have an electronic digital analyzer that will attach to the Mini-Gym Swim Bench and which will be able to analyze the power factor in the arms. In the meantime we will continue to use the vertical jump.

I believe that it is highly unlikely that a person could have endurance-type muscles in his legs and speed-type muscles in his arms, any more than we would expect a cat to have slow hind legs and fast front legs. In the next few years we will see the birth of all sorts of electronic analyzing isokinetic equipment that will be capable of measuring the power output of almost any muscle group. At that time I hope to be able to report to you on the use and effectiveness of this type of equipment.

I think at this time, however, it is safe to say that the power of the muscles in the leg is indicative of the potential power in the rest of the muscles of the body.

Have Many Studies Been Done on the Muscle-Fiber Typing of Swimmers?

Very little has been done on the muscle-fiber typing of champion swimmers. However, under the supervision of Dr. David Costill, Director of the Human Performance Laboratory at Ball State University, we have taken biopsies of the Indiana University swimmers.

The biopsies (muscle samples) are taken from the swimmer's posterior muscle. This muscle is used during the finish of the arm pull, but is not as important a muscle in swimming as the pectoralis major or the latissimus dorsi. In taking muscle samples, however, it is important to stay away from large blood vessels and nerves, and the posterior deltoid is well qualified in this respect.

Fig. 2.2. *Muscle biopsy and fiber typing*

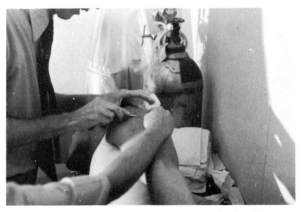

A. Dr. David Costill, Director of the Human Performance Laboratory, Ball State University, is shown taking a muscle biopsy of an Indiana University swimmer and Olympic team member. A biopsy needle is being inserted into the deltoid muscle.

B. The biopsy needle has a solid point but a hollow shaft. After the needle is inserted into the muscle, some muscle fibers fall into a groove in the shaft and are then cut off by the chopper inside the shaft. A piece of muscle about half the size of a pea is left in the needle when the needle is withdrawn. This muscle sample is then picked out with a tweezers and frozen in liquid nitrogen. It is then ready to be sliced and stained for whatever tests are proposed, such as the presence of enzymes, and so forth.

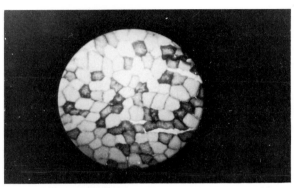

C. The stained cross-section of a muscle sample under a microscope distinctly reveals the muscle fibers. In this slide, the red fibers (slow-twitch) appear as the lighter colored and the white (fast-twitch) as the darker. This coloration is the result of the stain being used. This slide is of a cross-section from a distance athlete's muscle and shows that approximately 70 percent of his fibers are slow-twitch, while 30 percent are fast-twitch.

Are There Norms or Averages for Boys and Girls at the Various Age Groups for the Vertical Jump?

I have been able to find no up-to-date norms or even rough estimates of the averages for boys and girls of the various ages. In our summer swimming camp at Mercersburg Academy, Pat Barry and I have tested hundreds of age-group swimmers in order to develop a set of norms for both boys and girls and for the various age levels. The age-group coach will find that if he takes the vertical jump of his team and accumulates some data from a number of children of the same age and sex, he will be able to construct his own norms. Table 2.5 shows a fairly reliable prediction of men's (age 17 to 25) best events, based on their vertical jump.

Table 2.5
Vertical Jump as a Predictor of
Sprinting or Distance-Swimming Potential

Vertical Jump in Inches	9-22 in.	20-24 in.	23-26 in.	25-31 in.
Best Events	Distance 400—1500	Mid-Distance 400—800	Long Sprints 100—200	Short Sprints 50—100
Fringe Events	200	100—200—1500	50—500	200

Some Questions and Answers about Power

Question: If Swimmer *A* has a vertical jump of 27 inches and Swimmer *B* one of only 18 inches, does this mean that Swimmer *A* will beat Swimmer *B* in a sprint event and that Swimmer *B* will win the distance event?

Answer: No. Swimmer *A* may win both, or Swimmer *B* may do so. If all other factors are equal (which they never are), such as stroke mechanics, buoyancy, size and shape, level of training and competitive attitude, Swimmer *A* would win the sprint, and Swimmer *B* the distance event. The purpose of measuring the vertical jump is to determine whether the swimmer is better suited for sprints, middle-distance, or distance swimming. Swimmer *A* with the high vertical jump is better adapted to sprint, and Swimmer *B* is better adapted to distance swimming.

Question: What are some examples of athletic events that require power?

Answer: Any form of sprinting, shot-putting, high jumping, the speed required in football or basketball, the knock-out punch in boxing, Joe Namath's quick release in football. Most athletic events that require a fast burst of speed or that require maximum effort for hurling, kicking, or pushing an object require power. Other examples are hitting the home run, driving a long ball in golf, throwing the javelin, spiking in volleyball, and so on.

Dr. Ernst Jokl accounts for the large percentage of American blacks in athletics, where power and speed are required—football, basketball, and baseball—by the fact that they are more explosive due to the presence of a larger percentage of fast-twitch fibers. This is particularly obvious in professional football and basketball in which over 50 percent of the players are black in a total population of the United States of which under 15 percent are black.

Question: If John Naber and John Kinsella lack a high degree of power as measured by the vertical jump, why do they have such good turns and push-offs?

Answer: There are two possible explanations: 1) The push-off involves power but is performed at a slower speed than the vertical jump. This permits the swimmer to recruit more slow-twitch red muscle fibers to help him in his push-off. 2) Both of these men are very big, weighing over 200 pounds and being well over six feet tall. During the push-off they get farther out because of their height, their weight permits them to develop more momentum, and they can effectively hold their push-off longer than can a more slightly built person who has a higher vertical jump.

Question: Can you improve power, strength, and endurance of muscle at the same time?

Answer: Yes. Under certain conditions, improving the power and strength of muscle can improve its endurance. This is true of nearly every age-group swimmer, every girl swimmer, and most adult male swimmers. It is not true when the swimmer uses the wrong exercises or when he is already strong enough and any additional increase in strength will cause an increase in bulk. If a swimmer is so weak he can barely pull his arms through the water, his pulling muscles will tire very soon, whereas if he strengthens them, his neuro-muscular system will alternate the fibers. In this manner the endurance of the muscles is improved by increasing strength. This is the reason I believe it is important for all competitive swimmers to do strength-building exercise. In our program most of the strengthening exercises are done on the isokinetic exercise equipment.

Question: What is the best way to develop power?

Answer: One of the best ways to increase power is to improve strength. Strength can best be improved through progressive resistive exercise. The best way to build strength is through isokinetic exercise. Every research project that has compared isokinetic exercise with weight lifting has shown isokinetic exercise to build strength faster than any of the weight-lifting methods, including use of the Universal gym or the Nautilus equipment. But, even more important, the use of isokinetic exercise improves speed of muscular contraction, and that means power. In an experiment at the University of California at Davis a group of students on isokinetic exercise improved their vertical jump by two inches and improved their time on the 40-yard run by two tenths of a second, while the group that did weight lifting showed no improvement in these two test items.

In 1975 I measured the vertical jump of the Indiana University Basketball Team. The seven-foot center, Kent Benson, had a vertical jump of only 22 inches and during the season never jumped center for the basketball because of his low jumping power. I put him on an isokinetic exerciser called the Mini-Gym Leaper. During the summer he improved his vertical jump by 4 inches and according to his coach, Bob Knight, is an entirely different player. He is much faster and can jump much higher on the backboard. Coach Knight then put all his players on the Mini-Gym Leaper and adopted a complete isokinetic exercise program for all the members of his team.

Using this same Leaper with a group of swimmers over a period of eight weeks, we noted an average improvement of 3½ inches on the vertical jump, with a corresponding improvement in their ability to get better racing starts and better push-offs.

Question: Why does the isokinetic exercise improve power so much?

Answer: Because isokinetic exercise permits the muscles to work maximally through the full range of movement even at a fast speed. It permits the neuromuscular system to recruit more muscle fibers—both slow-twitch and fast-twitch. The muscles are taught to exert all the possible force that is intrinsically theirs, and the muscles themselves become stronger. The exact histological changes that occur in a muscle as a result of isokinetic exercise are unknown. This is another area of study which we hope to pursue at Indiana University in the near future.

Question: Should sprinters in swimming train as do sprinters in track?

Answer: No, on two counts: (1) Runners walk around all day using the same muscles they will use when participating in track events and in a similar manner. If swimmers lived in Venice and had to swim to school, to the store, and from one class to another, they could get by with training for only an hour or so a day. When a track runner plays a game of tennis, soccer, football, and so on, he is acquiring some conditioning for running, just as a swimmer does who plays water polo. (2) As previously mentioned, track sprinters run for only six to ten seconds, while swimming sprinters swim two to four times as long.

Practical Application to Training Methods

I do not want anyone to think I advocate eliminating all overdistance swimming for sprint swimmers. I feel they should do some overdistance swimming, some short-rest-interval training and, obviously, some high-quality work, such as repetition training and sprint training. I have the sprinters swim such sets of repeats as 4 × 400 or 8 × 200 or 20 × 100, but I never have them do such sets of repeats as the distance men use, such as 3 × 1500, 8 × 800, or 10 × 200. I believe that a steady diet of long sets of repeats or constant use of overdistance training would be detrimental to the sprinter's explosive power and would have a negative effect on his speed. Any program that includes swimmers of national caliber should provide three different programs:

1. For distance swimmers—events of 400 yards and up
2. For middle-distance swimmers (this includes most breaststrokers, backstrokers, and butterflyers)—events of 100 yards through 400 yards
3. For sprinters—events of 50 and 100 yards or meters and sometimes the 200

The sprinters do much less total distance, but do more high-quality work (i.e., more anaerobic work in which there is a build-up of oxygen debt). Any swimming coach who has tried to develop sprinters by doing nothing but sprinting has failed. Even sprinters must have a combination of training methods in their program. They need speed, but they also need some endurance.

Conclusion

I hope this discussion has confused you as much as I have been confused by the concept of power for the past twenty years. I also hope that through the use of muscle biopsy and other related research methods to be able to shed a little light on this subject in the next few years.

SECTION 2.3
"THE USES AND ABUSES OF INTERVAL TRAINING," BY ROBERTA ANGELONI

Interval training is an abused and misused term. Many track and field athletes believe that all fast running interspersed with rest/recovery periods is interval training. It is not. Some of it is interval work, and there's a vast difference between them.

What is that difference and how does it affect training for the various events? Perhaps we'd better start with definitions from a couple of experts.

Tony Nett, a top German coach who is editor of *Die Lehre der Leichtathletik* (The

Teaching of Track and Field) published in Berlin, describes interval work as sprinting, and speed work as being primarily concerned with the training of the nerve/coordination of the muscles. The adaptation to the stress of exercise occurs during the period of work. The rest interval merely serves for recovery of the muscles and nerves after exertion.

Kenneth Doherty, one of the best known coaches in the United States, discusses interval training in his book *Modern Training for Running*. He describes it as a system of repeated efforts in which a specific distance is run on the track at a timed pace, alternating with measured recovery periods of low activity. There are no actual recovery pauses, merely a slowing down of speed (jogging or walking) during the intervals. This system primarily trains the heart, and it is during the pauses or intervals that this takes place.

So, the basic difference in the two systems is that in one case the training effect occurs during the rest period, in the other during the time when the athlete is exerting himself.

This gives us a broad outline, but it still doesn't fully clarify how these systems work. Let's examine each in more detail, starting with interval training.

The identity of the man who originated interval training is obscure, but a pioneer in the field was Finnish coach Lauri Pikhala, who in 1920 stressed the rhythm between work and rest and whose principles were applied by the great Paavo Nurmi.

Then Drs. Herbert Reindel and Woldemar Gerschler of Germany examined the optimum amount of physical exertion necessary for a systematic improvement. After many experiments they extablished the Gerschler-Reindel law of interval training which states:

1. A warm-up should be used which brings the heart rate up to 120 beats per minute.
2. The runner then covers a given distance—100, 150, or 200 meters—in a given time which must bring the heart rate up to 170-180 beats per minute. He then takes a rest interval.
3. When the heart rate returns to 120-125, the runner starts again. The maximum time this recovery should take is a minute and a

half, and it can be shortened by highly trained individuals.

Interval training is the ideal method for increasing the efficiency and size/strength of the heart.

The two major factors which enable it to do this more efficiently than continuous training (running a given distance at a steady pace) are

1. More work can be performed with less fatigue and in less time.

2. A greater stimulus to improvement of the aerobic capacity (oxygen transport system) is provided.

The explanation for the first factor is a bit complicated, involving the ATP-PC and lactic-acid systems of the body. ATP is adenosine triphosphate, which is simply the prime source of the energy for muscle work, while PC is phosphocreatine which is stored in the muscles and instantly manufactures ATP. ATP can provide enough energy to keep the muscles working at maximum intensity for 10 seconds.

In the lactic-acid system, glucose is chemically broken down to lactic acid when the oxygen supply is inadequate, and then ATP is manufactured.

Energy

In their book *Interval Training*, Edward L. Fox and Donald K. Mathews state that less energy is supplied via the lactic-acid system in interval training than via the ATP-PC. This results in less fatigue, because during the rest periods the muscular stores of ATP-PC are replenished via the aerobic system, and part of the oxygen debt is repaid. This makes more ATP-PC energy available once more and "spares" energy from the lactic-acid system.

By contrast, they say, in a continuous run the stored ATP-PC is exhausted in a few minutes and cannot be replenished until the run is over. This means that energy from the lactic-acid system will be called upon and lactic acid will soon accumulate to exhausting levels, bringing the runner to a halt.

This is why one can perform more intensive work when running intermittently than when running continuously. It also has important considerations for training for specific events which will be dealt with later.

Drs. I. Astrand, P-O Astrand, E. H. Christensen, R. Hedman, and others have shown that in interval training as much as two and a half times the intensity of continuous running can be maintained before comparable blood lactic-acid levels (fatigue) are reached.

As to the second factor mentioned earlier—the improvement of aerobic capacity—Fox and Mathews point out that the stroke volume of the heart is higher during recovery than during exercise. Stroke volume refers to the amount of blood pumped by the heart with each beat. The more blood that is pumped, the more oxygen is transported to the working muscles.

Therefore, they say, interval running is more efficient than continuous running in developing aerobic capacity because of the many recovery periods which enable stroke volume of the heart to reach its highest levels as many times as there are intervals. In continuous running, there is only one rest interval: at the end.

Running Speed

Dr. Reindel suggests that the speed of the runs in interval training should not be too high because the heart reacts to high speeds not by pumping more blood but by increasing the number of beats. Stroke volume, therefore, is not trained and the stimulus for enlargement of the heart muscle is limited by the smaller number of repetitions (and consequently rest intervals) possible at higher speeds.

This implies that it is impossible to do interval work to improve the efficiency of the muscles and at the same time do interval training to improve the efficiency of the heart.

There seems little doubt that interval training, while improving aerobic endurance, has little effect on anaerobic capacity (the ability to do work without oxygen—while in oxygen debt).

Therefore, short and middle distance events require less interval training and more interval work, which does improve aerobic capacity.

Nett states that in the sprints and middle distances it is the skeletal muscles, rather than the heart, which should receive the "stress stimulus." This, he says, is brought about by fast—perhaps all-out—running speeds in which the stress stimulus affects the cross-section of the muscles, making them thicker, stronger, and faster while at the same time stimulating the muscle metabolism. Muscle metabolism is what gives muscles endurance while in oxygen debt.

Differences

Tempo work, he says, also improves muscle metabolism while having less effect on muscle bulk and should form the basis of training for the middle distance runner. Tempo work differs from interval work only in that the distances covered are longer. Instead of sprinting all out for 100 or 150 yards, the tempo trainer might cover anywhere from 400 to 1,000 meters as fast as possible (at race pace), rest and then repeat.

Similar improvements cannot be achieved with interval training, Nett says, because of the slower pace required to allow for a number of repetitions to be run in order to train the heart.

Although interval training should form the basis of training for distances above 1,500 meters, it should not be the only form of training for distance runners. They also require speed, strength, and muscle endurance. These are achieved not by interval training but by interval work, overload training such as hill running, and tempo running.

This is why the modern method of training for almost all distances is complex training. This utilizes all the different methods, emphasizing the particular one which brings about the desired results for the specific distance. The runner uses an optimum mixture to tone up all his different biological systems.

While interval training is a heart conditioner and hence useful for the endurance runner, we should keep in mind that more than a strong heart is required to win races. The ability to withstand pain is a vital asset, particularly the pain of competition associated with the demands of all-out, steady running. Interval training does not develop this, because the athlete stops before the pains of fatigue become a major factor.

Only by subjecting himself in his training to the stresses of competition can the athlete learn to handle the mental aspects of competition. This can best be done through tempo running—running long distances at race pace.

Stability

According to Nett, continuous running may not be quite as efficient as interval training in enlarging the heart and improving endurance in the shortest possible time. But, he says, it has a more stable effect.

And Doherty warns that attempting too much too fast, too soon in interval training can endanger muscles, tendons, and morale. Apparent success in interval training does not guarantee success in competition, he points out, and the athlete may be deluded into a sense of stamina which in actual fact is best achieved by a sound base of well-rounded gradually developed endurance through continuous running.

Doherty believes that the systematic analysis of all aspects of the training situation possible in interval training can be considered a great asset if the athlete anticipates each separate run and enjoys overcoming its challenges. But, he warns, having to face the challenges of interval training day after day can become a drudgery and a stress factor.

Different methods of training, therefore, not only tone up the different biological systems but help to provide variety and prevent boredom and staleness.

Another weakness of interval training, according to Doherty, is that it can develop excellent interval trainers without developing excellent competitive runners. The athlete's performance in training becomes the primary concern and he finds himself unprepared for the physical and mental aspects of competition.

Specificity in both the physical and psychological preparation of the athlete is important.

Warning

Although the problem with most athletes is

doing too little work, not too much, Reindel also has some reservations about the unlimited use of interval training. He says that over-emphasized interval training—such as repeating 100-meter runs 50 or 100 times—has in recent times led to heart injuries. He advises that pulse rates be taken after a certain number of repetitions to ensure that injury does not take place.

This is not to overlook the positive aspects of interval training. It can form the basis of conditioning for all sports, it permits the intensity of the workout to be adapted to the individual athlete, and it has great importance in sports medicine for prophylaxis and rehabilitation.

Its specific application is the improvement of circulation and the heart, and that's the purpose for which it should be used.

SECTION 2.4
"CHAMPIONSHIP MATERIAL,"
BY DR. DAVID COSTILL

Over the years a great deal of public attention and physiological effort has been directed toward superior endurance athletes. Our early studies with Derek Clayton, Amby Burfoot, Ron Daws, and others served to illustrate the unique physiological qualities required for championship-level performance in distance running. It is now common knowledge that distance runners possess a highly developed oxygen transport system and are capable of exercising at high rates of energy expenditure with little accumulation of blood lactic acid.

Following our studies of Clayton, the world's fastest marathoner, it became obvious that factors other than maximal oxygen uptake might play an important role in successful distance running. At the suggestion of an English colleague, Harry Thomasin, we attempted to determine what laboratory mea-

Dr. Costill is the director of the Human Performance Laboratory, Ball State University, Muncie, Indiana.
This article is reprinted from *Runner's World*, Vol. 9, No. 4 (1974).

surements might be most accurate in predicting one's performance in distance running.

The subjects for our study were 16 runners from the Manchester-Liverpool region of England. Unlike in our previous studies, these men were not all of championship caliber. For example, the runners' best times for 10 miles ranged from 49 to 69 minutes. All of the runners were in good to excellent running condition, averaging 8—12 miles daily. In order to make comparisons between laboratory measurements and running performance, each runner was first tested on the treadmill at four different speeds during a maximal run. After this testing, the men competed in a 10-mile road race under nearly ideal conditions (flat course, no wind, 50 degrees, mist).

In an earlier study, we had reported that there was a very low correlation between maximal oxygen consumption and the runners' best marathon running time. Those observations were complicated by the fact that the runners' best performances were attained over different courses and varied environmental conditions. With these factors controlled, we found that oxygen uptake capacity was highly related to the runners' 10-mile time (correlation of -0.91 from a possible 1.0).

The maximal oxygen uptake for the best runner was roughly 82 milliliters per kilogram of body weight per minute, a value quite similar to those reported for Jim Ryun, Ron Clarke, and Kip Keino. It is also interesting to note that the slower runners have oxygen uptake values that are not much higher than those commonly measured in sprint and moderate endurance athletes (basketball, football, etc.). It is unlikely, however, that a man with a value of 55 ml/kg/min can run 10 miles in 67 minutes without specific training in endurance running. We were led, therefore, to view other factors that might serve as prerequisites for success in distance running.

One quality we observed in Derek Clayton was his ability to run at better than five minutes per mile without accumulating blood lactic acid, a waste product of anaerobic metabolism. The muscles only pour out lactic acid when the tissues are deficient in oxygen. Most trained athletes show an increase in blood lactic acid when their demands for oxygen exceed 70 percent of their maximal oxygen uptake. Clayton, however, was able to work at 85-89 percent of his oxygen uptake capacity (4:53 per mile) without accumulating lactic acid. After reviewing all of Derek's laboratory tests, we were unable to explain this unique ability to satisfy the muscles' oxygen demands at such severe levels of effort.

Our next step was to determine whether this quality was typical of world-class competitors and to see if we could differentiate this quality in runners with varied abilities. For that reason, we measured blood lactic acid at varied running speeds and related our findings to their 10-mile running performance.

We found that the best runners were able to use a larger percentage of their oxygen uptake capacity without accumulating lactic acid—confirming our findings with Clayton. From a physiological point of view, this fact was quite intriguing. But it really did not explain how these men were able to prevent the build-up of this waste product, thereby enabling them to run faster, longer.

All indications seemed to suggest that the ability to utilize a large fraction of the aerobic capacity for prolonged periods is dependent upon some unique quality of the runner's leg muscles. Having made such a vague assumption, we found it relatively difficult to prove our point. In the fall of 1972, Drs. Bengt Saltin (Stockholm), Phil Gollnich (Washington State University), and I were able to examine the muscle tissue from the thigh and lower leg of some talented and not so talented distance runners.

Very small samples of muscle tissues were obtained with a biopsy needle from the thighs of 10 runners before and after a 30-kilometer cross-country race. This procedure is relatively painless and did not affect the runners' performance.

These muscle samples were subsequently sectioned (sliced) and chemically stained to reveal the character of the muscle fibers. Human muscle is characteristically classified into two distinct muscle-fiber types. Some fibers are quick in their response and are equipped to work anaerobically, such as is expected during sprint running. These fibers are termed fast-twitch (FT). Their counterparts, slow-twitch fibers (ST), are designed to perform aerobic work, but respond more slowly than the FT fibers. Most muscles are a mixture of these two fiber types—usually a 50-50 ratio in the thigh muscles.

Our biopsy studies with the distance runners revealed a very interesting relationship. Those runners who finished in the fastest times had a greater percentage of slow-twitch fibers than the slower runners, which showed that there was a good correlation between running time and percentage of ST fibers.

Since maximal oxygen uptake and distance running time are also highly related, it is not surprising that the runners with large aerobic capacities also had a large number of ST fibers. In retrospect, it seems only logical that good endurance athletes should have more ST fibers. These fibers have the structural necessities required for aerobic metabolism. ST fibers have more of the enzymes and mitochondria needed for the production of energy with the aid of oxygen.

Training the leg muscles to perform endurance work increases the number of mitochondria and related enzymes, but it does not alter the character of the muscle. That is to say that training can improve the endurance qualities of the muscles, even the FT fibers, but it will not change a FT fiber into a ST fiber. This point is well documented by Gollnich and Saltin, suggesting the proportions of ST to FT fibers that compose your muscles are genetically determined. In a sense, superior endurance ability is determined at birth. But like intelligence, only with training can that capacity be developed to its full potential.

You probably wonder how all this relates to your running success, and what it means in terms of improving your performance. These studies serve to emphasize the individual variations in athletic ability and the innate qualities possessed by the superior distance runner. As you may already have deduced, the muscle-fiber-typing methods could be employed to identify those young athletes with superior endurance potential. Just as IQ tests are used in screening for superior intellect, the muscle biopsy technique may hold equal predictive potential in pointing out those individuals of "super" athletic ability.

Are you interested in knowing how you might rate? There is no way of knowing for sure unless such tests are performed. However, our data provide a means of estimating your maximal oxygen uptake and percentage of ST muscle fibers, providing you have performed a 10-mile run for time. Before making such predictions, you must presume that the 10-mile performance was representative of your distance running ability, that you are a relatively efficient runner, and that you were at a high level of fitness at the time of the run.

These factors assumed, it is possible to use the following pregression equations to estimate your maximal oxygen uptake percentage and ST fibers:

Maximal oxygen uptake = 138.6 − 1.278
    × (time in minutes for 10 miles)
Percentage of ST = 1.424 × (maximal oxygen uptake) − 38.28

If such information leads you to conclude that you may never be a world record holder in the distance events, it may at least give you some excuse for running failures you previously blamed on poor training or lack of intestinal fortitude. You might gain some satisfaction from knowing that your inability "to win the big ones" is the fault of your parents and not your own.

SECTION 2.5
"WHY YOU CAN INHERIT SPEED AND ENDURANCE," A RESEARCH REPORT BY ROBERTA ANGELONI

Toomsalu stated in 1963 that in individuals where white fibers predominate, greater speed of muscle contraction is possible; thus, one individual will have a higher maximum speed of movement than another.

Benjamin Ricci states that both red and white muscle fibers are found within every muscle, but the predominance of one fiber type or the other determines whether it is a "white" or a "red" muscle. The proportion is genetically established and apparently cannot be changed by training.

It is the amount of myoglobin contained in the muscle which determines the color, according to Matthews, Stacey, and Hoover. Red muscle has more of this protein substance which is chemically related to hemoglobin and like hemoglobin possesses an attraction for oxygen. It is therefore aerobic in character, while white fiber is anaerobic; endurance events are considered aerobic events in that they require an efficient oxygen transport and utilization system, while sprint events are anaerobic in that oxygen transport is of little or no importance, depending on the distance.

Since muscles differ in their ability to produce fast movements, those which are required to produce fast movements have a greater proportion of white fibers. Those which do not have this requirement have a greater proportion of red. For example, such muscles as the anti-gravity muscles, the trunk and leg extensors, the cardiac muscle, and the diaphragm are predominatly red muscle. The flexor muscles, on the other hand, are fast-contracting and possess a predominance of white fibers.

Degree
There are also relative degrees of redness, according to Ricci. For example, within two muscles of the calf—both anti-gravity muscles—the soleus possesses greater amount of myoglobin per unit area than does the gastrocnemius.

This also applies to white muscle.

L. E. Smith (1961) showed that speed is 87-88 percent specific to a limb. Henry (1960) found that individual differences in the ability to execute a fast movement are 70 percent specific and 30 percent general. Letter (1960) found speed within a limb to be 88-90 percent specific to the direction of movement in a particular limb.

These findings indicate that a fast runner may not necessarily be a fast thrower, and vice versa. They also explain why a transitional period is usually required before even a well-trained athlete can achieve maximum efficiency when making a change from one sport to another.

Some interesting experiments have been done to see if muscle characteristics can be changed. For example, Bach (1948) attached a red muscle to a white muscle tendon. This resulted in a decreased myoglobin content and endurance in the red muscle. He concluded that it is the function of a muscle which determines its chemical nature.

Buller et al. showed that the red, slow-contracting soleus muscle in a cat could be transformed into a fast-acting muscle merely by replacing its neural pathway with that of a fast-acting muscle. His conclusion was that the differentiation of slow muscle activity is influenced by neural pathways in the spinal cord.

Although there are many factors which influence speed and endurance, muscle as well as the neuromuscular coordination are hereditary factors which place a limit to maximal speed. The relationship between speed, endurance, and race is something which needs further study before definite conclusions can be drawn.

Success

However, Jokl, who is probably the world's foremost authority on the physiological basis of records, believes that Black American athletes have been dominating sprint events for the past 30 years because they have more white muscle fiber than Caucasians. The success of Caucasians in middle and long distance events, conversely, can be credited to their red fibers.

Sociologists disagree with this theory. They attribute the supremacy of the Negro sprinter to the drives produced by their socially disadvantaged position in American society.

The recent victories by east Africans and Ethiopians in middle and long distance races has also been accounted for by Dr. Jokl. He says there are profound genetic differences between American Blacks, who are descendents of West African Negroes, and East Africans such as Keino, Jipcho, Bayi, and Bikila, who have Hamitic genetic mixtures from the North of Africa.

All this does not mean that your speed and endurance cannot be improved whatever the color of your skin or muscle fibers. Training, of course, can make startling changes in strength, coordination, neuromuscular reactions, heart efficiency, and other things which affect your physical capacities in important ways. But it does help to explain differences in potential between individuals and perhaps between racial groups.

SECTION 2.6
"SOME THOUGHTS ON THE SPECIFICITY OF TRAINING," BY ROBERT L. BARTELS

The concept of specificity of training is not a new one to coaches. Although it would probably have been expressed in different terms, coaches and the athletes with whom they work have for many years been aware that in order to do well in a sprint event one needs to do a substantial part of his training utilizing comparatively fast swimming. The evolution of the record in the 100-yard freestyle since the time of John Weissmuller has closely paralleled the incorporation of an element of specificity into training routines. It can be noted that Weissmuller's record time of 51.0 for the 100-yard distance stood for nearly 20 years, until Alan Ford of Yale broke it. Ford was trained, in addition to his water training, with dry-land conditioning which was intended to increase his strength: a prime prerequisite for sprint swimming. Further progress was made by Dick Cleveland of Ohio State who broke Ford's record when he included heavy weight training into his training routine. His strength was thus increased, and, although weight training was a taboo among his contemporaries, Cleveland became a world record holder because of it.

Thus it has continued. The rise of interval training in the 1950s allowed a further application of the principle of specificity until modern sprinters of international class are

Robert L. Bartels is Professor of Physical Education at Ohio State University.

capable of times around 45.0, literally beyond the wildest dreams of sprinters of the Weissmuller era.

What Is Specificity?

In order to completely understand specificity, one has to understand the requirements of the various events: those things prerequisite for success. Assuming skill to be constant, it should be profitable to examine the physical needs of the swimmers in two categories of events, the sprints and the distances.

Metabolic Fitness Needs

One of the primary reasons for training is to improve the capacities of the metabolic systems which furnish the energy used in the particular event to be swum. This energy is furnished by the three different metabolic systems, two of which are called "anaerobic" (i.e., without oxygen), and another which is "aerobic" (i.e., with oxygen). The cost of an all-out 50-yard freestyle is paid nearly entirely by the anaerobic system, whereas the cost of a four-mile swim is paid for nearly entirely by the aerobic system. The cost of a 1650-yard swim by a topflight competitor is paid for approximately 80 percent aerobically and about 20 percent anaerobically. It is obvious, therefore, that any training program for the sprinter must be designed to increase the capacity of the anaerobic systems, and that any program designed for the distance man must increase the capacity of the aerobic system. This is done by designing workouts to stress the appropriate system, thus increasing its capacity by forcing it to adapt to a progressively greater need.

A close look at the metabolic systems reveals that the energy for all muscular work is furnished when the following reaction takes place: energy is released so that work can occur.

$$ATP = ADP + P$$

So that repeated contraction can take place, another compound, phosphocreatine (PC) is broken down to phosphorus and creatine, with the release of sufficient energy to resynthesize ATP from ADP + Pi. These two reactions make up the ATP - PC system, with which the cost of short, explosive events like the 50-yard freestyle is paid.

In order to reform phosphocreatine, energy is derived from ATP produced by the breakdown of foodstuffs, in this case glucose. Glucose is broken down in a series of steps to pyruvic acid. If the energy requirement per unit of time of the event being performed is great, as it is in 100- to 200-yard events, pyruvic acid is changed by the addition of hydrogen to lactic acid. The net result of the series of reactions whereby glucose is changed to lactic acid is sufficient to produce a small amount of ATP furnishing energy for work. This system which does not use oxygen, and is thus anaerobic, is the primary means by which the energy cost of the 100- to 200-yard events is paid. It has as its end product lactic acid and is called the lactacid system.

Lactic acid is important for it is thought to be the end product of anaerobic work. Each individual is thought to have only so much tolerance for lactic acid, and when this level is reached, the individual is exhausted and can do no more work. The amound of lactic acid which can be tolerated, however, can be changed by training.

The work done by these energy systems can be related to stress levels indicated by heart rate. A highly trained distance swimmer might be able to work at a heart rate of 160 beats per minute without accumulating a significant amount of lactic acid. However, at the greater stress levels of 170 or 180 beats per minute lactic acid is being rapidly produced and will surely soon produce exhaustion.

If the event is a long one and the energy requirement is less, the heart rate at 150 to 160 beats per minutes, sufficient O_2 may be present to shunt pyruvic acid into the energy-rich Kreb's cycle rather than to have it undergo the reaction to become lactic acid. Kreb's cycle in which O_2 is utilized breaks pyruvic acid down to CO_2 and H_2O. The energy produced is used to resynthesize comparatively large amounts of ATP. The aerobic pathway, however, is the predominant metabolic pathway only if enough O_2 is available in relation to the amount of pyruvic acid and the energy requirement of the work is low. A little more than half of the cost of a 500-yard swim is paid for by the aerobic system; the remainder, by the anaerobic system. Thus, part of the training of the 500-yard swimmer should stress specifically the aerobic system, and part must stress specifically the anaerobic system. The 50-yard sprinter, who should do some aerobic work early in his training season, must do progressively heavier work, and as the time for his peak performances approaches, he must be doing some hard sprinting at or very near race pace with enough rest to allow him to do the next repetition at nearly the same pace.

While it is beyond the scope of this paper to outline specific examples of interval training programs, some principles of training should be discussed.

Training the Sprinter

The swimmer who swims only the sprints should begin his pre-season training by doing some fairly heavy aerobic work. However, he should be doing, by the end of the pre-season period, a substantial portion of his work in fast interval training with some repeat and sprint work added occasionally. Progressively more and more of his training should shift from slow interval training to fast interval training to repeat training to sprint training across his training season. Stress should be added to his program progressively by increasing the rate at which he swims and not by adding distance or decreasing only the rest interval.

A sprinter, who is trained properly, does very heavy work during his season but should do so only 3 or 4 days a week and always with a day of comparative ease in between to allow time for repair of damaged tissues. The rest period in any interval training the sprinter does, following his initial pre-season period of aerobic work, should probably not be less than 30 seconds. This allows adequate time for partial resynthesis of the ATP-PC systems so that repeated heavy work may be attempted. To shorten his rest period is to force him to slow down and to work aerobically, thus defeating the purpose of his training program.

Training the Distance Swimmer

The swimmer who trains for the 1000-yard to the 1650-yard swims must do a great deal of aerobic work progressively nearer the rate at which he will wish to compete. He should train at least on a six day per week basis at first with some elements of distance training and Fartlek training, but then predominantly with the slow interval training. Distances from 8,000 to 15,000 yards per day are desirable and probably necessary for peak adaptation. Across his training season the amount of fast interval training he does should be increased, but the bulk of his program should be slow interval training, at first with rest periods long enough to permit him to do the work at the required rate but gradually lowering the rest period below 30 seconds, thus forcing him to do aerobic work. In some kinds of training schemes, his rest period may be as short as 5 to 10 seconds. He must thus adjust the rate at which he swims to allow him to swim aerobically, as the rest period does not allow adequate time for resynthesis of the anaerobic systems. If he swims hard enough to utilize the anaerobic metabolic systems, an accumulation of lactic acid in the muscles will soon force him to stop.

THREE

Dry-Land Exercises

A swimmer should do dry-land exercises for one or more of the following reasons:

1. To improve strength
2. To improve speed
3. To improve endurance
4. To improve flexibility

The coach and swimmer must realize that not all dry-land exercises are beneficial to the swimmer and that some not only are not beneficial but may have a negative effect on the swimmer's performance in the water. For this reason it is very important that the dry-land exercise program be carefully planned.

It is important that both coach and swimmer have some knowledge of certain physiological and anatomical principles which help determine what exercises the swimmer should include in his program. For this reason a review of some of these principles follows.

SECTION 3.1
ANATOMY OF THE MUSCLE

For the purposes of this discussion, instead of looking at the muscular system as one system, let us consider it as two. Muscles are composed of a mixture of two types of fibers: slow-twitch (red) fibers and fast-twitch (white) fibers. These fibers are very different in many respects, each type even having a different nerve supply. How do we know they have a different nerve supply? In experimental animals, when the nerve fiber that supplies the white (fast-twitch) fiber is transplanted to a red (slow-twitch) fiber and the red fiber's nerve is transplanted to the white fiber, the fibers change their characteristics: the white fiber becomes a red fiber, and the red fiber becomes a white fiber. Figure 2.2 in Chapter 2 shows the cross-section of a human muscle (see p. 100).

The red fibers, because of their chemical nature, are well-adapted for endurance. They contain more myoglobin than the white fibers and are able to carry on aerobic work efficiently. They contract more slowly than do the white fibers and are not used to any great extent when the movement is a fast all-out effort. The red fibers would be those a swimmer would use when performing a long race at a slow or moderate tempo. They would also be the fibers a swimmer is exercising when he lifts a weight or performs an exercise at slow or moderate speed.

The white fibers are markedly different

from the red in adaptation for fast movements and quick energy release (anaerobic work). They tire quickly and are not used to any great extent except in fast movements. These fibers are used in swimming a sprint, when lifting a weight quickly, or when performing any exercise at fast speed.

It is not known precisely how the fibers co-operate to perform these movements that begin slow and finish fast, such as a racing start. It is postulated that the red fibers help the white fibers overcome the inertia of the body at the beginning of the movement, but that after the movement becomes too fast for them to contribute any force to the muscle's contraction they phase out.

Every person varies from every other in the proportion of red to white fibers that exists in their muscles. Each is born with this proportionality and it cannot be changed through training or by any other means.

The fibers do not change from red to white, or white to red, but the quality in the fibers can be changed somewhat, depending on the type of training to which they are subjected.

How Can the Red Fibers Be Changed?

1. The red fibers can be increased in size (hypertrophied) and strength by exercising with heavy resistance at a slow or moderate speed. This is especially true if negative exercise (letting the weight down) is used. This increase in size of the muscle fibers is due to an increase in the size of the myofibrils (the contractile element of the muscle fiber) and results in a bulkier muscle—actually a larger cross-sectional area. The endurance of the muscle is not improved, because there is no beneficial change in the mitachondrial mass of the muscle. The mitachondria are cellules in the muscle fiber which carry on the metabolism of the muscle, and an increase in their mass improves endurance. The use of a certain piece of equipment—a rocker-arm weight-lifting arrangement—or of weight-lifting exercises with heavy weights at slow speed has limited merit for swimmers and other athletes who are interested in acquiring speed, because they build big, but slow muscles. Because the exercises are done at

slow speed, the white fibers are not involved and thus remain unchanged and do not increase in size. The increase in the size of the red fibers with no corresponding increase in the size of the white fibers causes a shift in the proportion of total mass of the muscle in favor of the red fibers. This is another reason for emphasizing to all athletes who are interested in building speed or endurance that they should avoid slow-movement types of exercise, such as that developed by the Nautilus and similar equipment.

Body builders use this type of exercise to "bulk up" since they are not interested in speed or endurance. Competitive weight lifters, because they are interested in speed, avoid this type of work.

2. The red fibers can be improved in endurance by performing many repetitions of an exercise against moderate resistance, such as by doing 300 repetitions on a pulley-weight exerciser. This type of exercise may not improve the size of the muscle to any great extent, but it will improve the muscle's endurance. The improvement results from changes within the red fiber—primarily in the mitachondria—which permit a more efficient enzyme action and improve the muscle's ability to utilize oxygen.

The swimmer, however, builds endurance in the red fibers when he swims overdistance or when he uses interval training and does not need to build a lot of muscle endurance in his dry-land exercise program. The dry-land exercise program is necessary to improve strength, speed, and flexibility.

HRFS Exercise
and How It Can Change the White Fibers

1. The white fibers can be increased in size and strength by exercising against high resistance at a fast speed. The increase in the size of the white fibers is desirable since it increases the white fibers' mass relative to that of the red fibers and therefore increases the speed potential of the muscle.

This type of exercise (HRFS—high resistance at fast speed) can best be done by actually getting in the water and sprinting or by doing isokinetic exercise at a fast speed. HRFS exercise is virtually impossible to do on the Nautilus or the Universal or with barbells. The reason is that these three forms of exercise are all done by lifting weights against gravity. If the weight is lifted at a fast speed it soon becomes ballistic, and the momentum it develops during the first part of the lift carries the weight upward, with the result that the lifter gets little benefit from the last part of the movement. For this reason the makers of the Nautilus and the Universal Gym recommend that the exerciser do the exercises at relatively slow speed. The movements in most athletic events involve speed and are done in a fast, explosive manner.

2. The white fibers can be improved in their endurance through the performance of a lot of distance work. A paradox exists in this area: why do some white fibers change in some of their characteristics and become more like red fibers (they are never *completely* converted into red fibers)? If the white fibers are not involved in slow movements, why should they adapt to distance work and change their characteristics? This change has been noted by so many researchers that it is considered a valid change, and there is no doubt it is compensatory in nature. The fibers that change improve their endurance, but they do so at the expense of some of their speed. The application of this knowledge is that sprinters should avoid excessive over-distance work, especially at the peak of the season when they want to develop optimum speed and explosive power.

For more information on muscle-fiber typing and the physiological changes resulting from training, see Chapter 2, *Theory and Research of Training.*

Does Building Strength Harm or Improve Endurance?

It can do either, depending on how strong the person is when he begins a strength program and whether or not he hypertrophies the red fibers to an excess. If a swimmer is so weak in the muscles that pull the arms through the water that he has to use every muscle fiber he can activate to perform the movement properly just a few times, these fibers will tire quickly, and obviously their endurance will be low. If the muscles are sufficiently strong that only half or less of the muscle fibers have to be used each time the proper movement is made, the fibers can be alternated in performing the movements, and the endurance of the muscle will be enhanced.

In this instance, increasing strength improves endurance and is the reason that all age-group swimmers and most senior swimmers can improve their swimming performance by improving their strength. Again it is necessary to caution the reader that some exercises, particularly the type I mentioned earlier—those done at a slow constant speed—can result in excessive increase of the size of the red fibers and that their constant use should be avoided.

Use Only the Correct Exercises!

No swimmer should use a general body-building program. He should use the specific exercises that will strengthen and develop speed in the muscles that pull him through the water (prime movers). If indiscriminate exercise is used, the swimmer may increase muscle bulk in the muscles not used in the swimming movements. It is possible to add as much as 15 to 25 pounds in these unused muscles. This muscle bulk has to be carried along during the race, and since it is not paying its way, the prime movers have to work that much harder and their endurance is decreased as a result. This is one reason we see so few distance swimmers who look like weight lifters and also the reason that weight lifters have difficulty in performing endurance activities.

Later in this chapter I will list the prime movers in swimming and describe the exercises that will effectively strengthen and develop speed in them.

SECTION 3.2
THE THREE R's OF EXERCISE

When doing exercises there are three items that should be considered:

1. Repetitions—how many times the exercise should be repeated

2. Resistance—how much weight or force the person should work against

3. Rate—how fast the exercise should be done

With the foregoing material as a guide some principles can be formulated that will determine the type of exercise best suited to aid the swimmer:

1. Speed and strength are best built in a muscle by doing low-repetition, high-resistance exercise at fast speed.

2. Endurance is best built in a muscle by doing high-repetition, moderate-resistance exercise at moderate speed.

3. Bulk and strength in the red muscle fibers are best built in a muscle by doing low-repetition, high-resistance exercise at slow speed. The use of this kind of exercise should be limited because of its detrimental effect on speed and endurance.

SECTION 3.3
ISOKINETIC EXERCISE

The importance of HRFS (high-resistance, fast-speed) exercise in developing the qualities needed for swimming has already been discussed. Another factor that is important in deriving the optimal benefit from the exercise is that the muscle fibers be permitted to contract maximally through the entire range of movement of the limb.

As any limb of the body travels through its full range of movement, the amount of force it can create varies at different points. This variation is due to the constant change in the angle at which the muscle is pulling on the limb. In addition is the fact that at the beginning of the contraction, when the muscle is stretched, it can create more force. This means that every time a weight is lifted the muscle is working maximally only at the weakest point of the limb's movement.

The ideal form of exercise would be one in which the force that the muscle worked against would change as the muscle's capacity to create force changed. In this manner the muscle would always be working against

maximum resistance through its full range of movement. This type of exercise has recently been developed and it is referred to as *isokinetic exercise*. Another name for this exercise is *ARE*, accommodating-resistance exercise. The manufacturers of certain weight-lifting equipment have tried to achieve ARE by using a rocker-arm method of weight lifting. This equipment is expensive, the exercises must be done at a steady speed, and the manufacturers emphasize the importance of the negative action (letting down of the weight). This equipment should not be used to any great extent by any swimmers or athletes who want to build speed or endurance in their muscles. As mentioned before, this type of equipment builds strong but slow and bulky muscles because it causes hypertrophy of the red (slow-twitch) fibers. Other weight-lifting equipment has the same deficiencies as the rocker-arm equipment, and none of them can provide HRFS exercise through the full range of movement.

Does this mean that all weight-lifting exercises are of no value? No! Barbell exercises can be used when isokinetic exercise equipment is not available. When a swimmer has only average or below-average strength in the swimming muscles, he can gain in swimming performance by doing some of his exercise work at moderate speed. He can also do his weight-lifting exercise at a faster speed, but, as he will become aware when he tries, the weight will develop so much momentum when it is lifted fast that he will get little benefit from the exercise once the inertia of the barbell has been overcome. The use of barbells provides a good way of testing the strength of the various swimming muscles. Figure 3.1 illustrates the basic barbell exercises.

Fig. 3.1. *The five basic barbell exercises for swimmers*

How often should they be done? Once a day, five days a week—either before or after practice, depending on the swimmer's schedule.

How many repetitions? Two or three sets of exercises with 10 to 30 repetitions in each set.

How much weight? Between 15 and 80 pounds, depending on the strength of the swimmer.

What rate of exercising? If the exercises are done

at a slow rate of speed, the strength developed will not transfer to swimming movements. Exercises should be done at a brisk speed.

1. Elbow extensor

A. *Starting position*: Kneeling on cushion or pad (this exercise can be done while standing erect if the ceiling is high enough). Barbell is held straight overhead with the elbows extended, palms forward gripping the bar 6 to 12 inches apart.

B. *Action*: The barbell is lowered by flexing the elbows without lowering them. Then return to starting position.

C. *Muscles developed*: Elbow extensors: triceps.

Variation of elbow extensor

Follow the instructions for exercise above except lower the barbell only half way down. Then return to Starting Position.

2. Supine straight arm pullover

A. *Starting position*: Lying on the floor on the back, barbell held in wide grip, palms up, arms extended overhead.

B. *Action*: Without bending the elbows pull the barbell in an arc up to a vertical position. Return to starting position.

C. *Muscles developed:* Arm depressors: pectoralis major, latissimus dorsi, teres major.

3. Arm rotator

A. *Starting position*: Lying on back with top of head almost touching bar. Grasp barbell with palms up and wide grip, so that the elbows are bent 90° and are on the ground at shoulder level.

B. *Action*: Raise bar to vertical position in an arc by rotating upper arm. Keep elbows on floor. Return to Starting Position.

C. *Muscles developed*: Medial arm rotators: pectoralis major, subscapularis, latissimus dorsi, teres major.

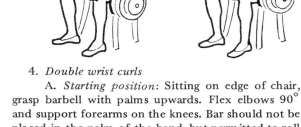

4. Double wrist curls

A. *Starting position*: Sitting on edge of chair, grasp barbell with palms upwards. Flex elbows 90° and support forearms on the knees. Bar should not be placed in the palm of the hand, but permitted to roll down the fingers.

B. *Action*: Raise and lower weight through the fullest possible range of movement by flexing and extending the wrists.

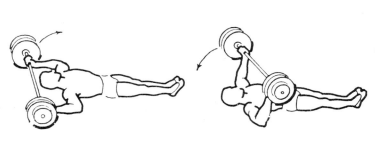

5. Jumping quarter squats

A. *Starting position*: Stand erect with bar resting on shoulders at back of neck. With one foot slightly in front of the other, grasp barbell firmly so that it does not bounce up and down on the shoulders.

B. *Action*: Bend knees only slightly, raise heels slightly off floor. Jump up and down, emphasizing a vigorous drive of the legs and extensors of the ankles and reverse feet on each jump.

C. *Muscles developed*: This exercise develops speed and power in the hip and knee extensors and the plantar flexors of the ankles: gluteus maximus, quadriceps extensors, gastrocnemius, and soleus.

SECTION 3.4
THE SWIMMING MUSCLES

Following are listed the main muscles used in the propulsive phase of swimming movements, the exercises with the barbells that should be used to strengthen the muscles, and the manner in which to test the strength of those muscles.

1. *The Arm Depressors* (the latissimus dorsi, pectoralis major, teres major, long head of the triceps). These muscles pull the arm through the water. They can be tested and strengthened by doing the supine pullover (see Fig. 3.2).

Fig. 3.2. *Supine pullover*

A. Starting position: Lie on the floor on the back, barbell held in wide grip, palms up, arms extended overhead.

B. Action: Without bending the elbows, pull the barbell in an arc up to a vertical position. Return to starting position.
    Muscles developed: Arm depressors, pectoralis major, latissimus dorsi, teres major

2. *The Arm Medial Rotators* (pectoralis major, latissimus dorsi, teres major, subscapularis). These are almost the same as the arm depressors, but they are used in a slightly different manner. They rotate the upper arm medially, and it is necessary for these muscles to be strong if the swimmer is to maintain the high-elbow position so desirable during the first part of the arm pull of all four competitive strokes (see Fig. 3.3).

Fig. 3.3. *Arm medial rotators*

Action: Lying on back with top of head almost touching bar, grasp barbell with palms up and a wide grip in order that the elbows be bent 90 degrees and will be on the ground at shoulder level. Raise bar to vertical position in an arc by rotating upper arm. Keep elbows on the floor. Return to starting position.

3. *The Elbow Extensor* (triceps). This is the muscle that extends the elbow during the last half of the arm pull in the crawl, butterfly, and backstroke. A strong triceps enables the swimmer to finish the last half of his arm stroke with a strong pushing action (see Fig. 3.4).

Fig. 3.4. *Elbow extensors* (25 to 60 pounds)

4. *The Wrist Flexor Muscles* (plantaris longus and all digital flexors). See Figure 3.5.

Fig. 3.5. *Double wrist curls*

Action: Kneeling on cushion or pad (this exercise may be done while standing erect if the ceiling is high enough), hold barbell straight overhead with the elbows extended, palms forward and gripping the bar 6 to 12 inches apart. The barbell is lowered by flexing the elbows without lowering them. Return to starting position.

Variation of elbow extensor
(preferred for swimmers)
Follow the instructions for exercise above except lower the barbell only half way down. Then return to starting position.

Action: Sitting on your haunches, grasp barbell with palms upward. Flex elbows 90 degrees and support forearms on the knees. Bar should not be placed in the palm of the hand, but permitted to roll down the fingers. Raise and lower weight through the fullest possible range of movement by flexing and extending the wrists.

SECTION 3.5
DO-IT-YOURSELF BARBELLS

Few swimming teams can afford enough conventional barbells to permit the whole team to do exercises at the same time. With the use of barbells made of cans filled with concrete and galvanized pipe, barbell weights can be made very cheaply.

The use of this type of barbell at Indiana permits our whole team to do their barbell exercises together. We have over one hundred such barbells varying in weight from 35 pounds to 70 pounds. *Heavier ones than these are not needed for the type of exercises we do.*

One big advantage of these weights is that many of them can be stored in a small area by standing them on end in a vertical position. At Indiana University most of the boys also have one of these barbells in their dormitory rooms. They roll them under their beds for storage. Table 3.1 lists the necessary ingredients.

Table 3.1
Barbell Construction

Weight of Barbell	Ingredients (Always fill pipe with concrete mixture)
18 lb.	1″ pipe 44″ long and 2 regular-size fruit-juice cans (1 qt., 13 oz)
35 lb.	1″ pipe 48″ long and 2 #10 cans (commercial fruit and vegetable cans—pick up at restaurant)
42 lb.	1-1/2″ pipe 48″ long and 2 #10 cans
52 lb.	2″ pipe 48″ long and 2 #10 cans

How to Make the Barbells
1. The concrete mixture should have the following proportions—2 parts of sand or gravel and 1 part of cement. Mix with enough water to make the mixture thoroughly wet, but not so wet that water will stand on the top. Or you can buy a bag premixed.

2. After filling one can with this mixture, take the pipe and set it into the mixture, pushing it all the way to the bottom of the can, *taking care to set the pipe in a straight vertical line.* Tie the bar to the back of a chair or a table top to stabilize it until the concrete sets. Wait 24 hours for the concrete to set.

3. Fill the second can and place the other end of the pipe into it. Be careful when lining up the bar that it is in an exact vertical position in order that the weights may be stored by standing them on end.

4. Paint the cans and concrete with team colors. Use two or three coats of paint. After the concrete has set for several days (to allow the water to evaporate), weigh the barbell on a bathroom scale and mark the amount of weight on each end.

For Age-Group Swimmers—Barbell Party
Have the whole team meet at the home of one of the swimmers. Mix a large amount of concrete and have each swimmer make his own barbell. The next day, after the concrete has set, add the other one.

Fig. 3.6. *Do-it-yourself concrete barbell*

SECTION 3.6
EXERCISE EQUIPMENT

Latissimus Device
Possibly one of the best pieces of weight-

lifting equipment for swimmers and one that can be cheaply made is the Latissimus device, shown in Figure 3.7. It exercises the arm depressors, the arm medial rotators, and the elbow extensors if the exercises are done properly.

The weight used in this equipment can also be made with food cans filled with concrete. The cans should be bigger than in the case of the barbells and the weight should vary from 20 pounds for young age-group swimmers to 120 pounds for a few senior swimmers. A large 8- to 12-inch eyebolt should be imbedded in the wet concrete, and an anchor arrangement should be made by bolting several large washers at two or three different levels on the shaft of the eyebolt that is to be submerged.

Fig. 3.7. *Latissimus device*

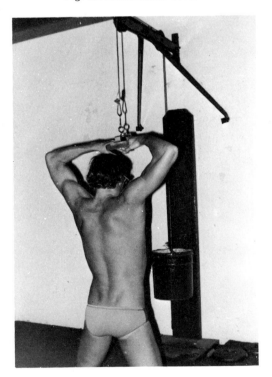

SECTION 3.7
AN ISOKINETIC EXERCISE PROGRAM FOR SWIMMERS

Isokinetic exercise involves the use of special equipment. The equipment that we use at Indiana University is called the Mini-Gym isokinetic exerciser. It has several advantages over the use of barbells and other types of weight-lifting equipment.

The fact that the use of weight-lifting equipment develops slow, bulky muscles whereas the use of isokinetic exercises at a fast speed develops muscles that *are strong and can contract at a fast speed* has been discussed earlier in this chapter.

In developing an exercise program for swimmers, it is important to stress the specificity of these exercises. Specificity is of primary significance if maximum transfer of training effect is to occur. An athlete must try as far as possible to simulate the conditions in his exercise program that he will encounter in his athletic activity. If a muscle develops strength by being exercised at slow speed, it will adapt by becoming, as mentioned earlier, strong at slow speeds. Little of this strength can be used in fast movements because the slow weight-lifting movements have strengthened only the red muscle fibers. If the athlete wishes to strengthen the muscle fibers that contract quickly—the white fibers—he must do his exercises at fast speed. This is an example of the specificity of speed of movement.

Other Examples of Specificity

When doing strengthening exercises the swimmer must work his arms in the same pattern in which he will pull them when he is propelling himself through the water. This will assure him of maximum transfer of training effect. Another very important factor insofar as specificity is concerned is that the force the muscle contracts against at the various points throughout its range of movement should be similar to the force it will encounter in swimming movements. The arms, however, must work against a greater force out of water than they will work against in the water, in order that greater strength will be developed in the arm-depressor muscles. This is an application of the overload principle.

One of the most important factors to consider in evaluating the specificity of exercise is that when the arm is pulled through the water the muscles (particularly in an all-out sprint) work maximally at every point in the pull and do not work against a constant force. This was shown in a study conducted by me in 1951 and was reported on pages 46 and 47 of my book *The Science of Swimming*.

As the arm is pulled through the water, the lever system of the arm changes and the muscles are capable of creating greater force at certain points of the pull, this phenomenon being an example of biomechanical principles. This accounts for the fluctuating force the arms create. *When a swimmer pulls his arms through the water, he is contracting the arm-depressor muscles isokinetically*, not isometrically, because movement is involved; not isotonically, because the muscles are not working against a constant force nor can they develop a ballistic movement.

When a swimmer exercises his muscles isotonically by lifting weights or working against a friction rope exerciser, the amount of resistance the muscles must work against is held constant. There is no possible way that these two methods can simulate the conditions the swimmer will encounter in the water.

Since a swimmer contracts his muscles isokinetically when pulling his arms through the water, why not exercise them isokinetically when doing strength-building exercises? This, of course, has been impossible until recently when a whole new generation of exercise apparati was designed that will exercise the muscles isokinetically.

Isokinetic exercisers are available in single units that attach to the wall, such as those shown in Fig. 3.8 in which Mark Spitz, as a student at Indiana University, is shown exercising on the Mini-Gym, performing the arm-rotator exercise. Mark never did any weight lifting, but limited his strengthening exercise to the Mini-Gym isokinetic exercisers.

In Figure 3.9 American record holder of the individual medley, Fred Tyler, is shown

doing the Latissimus pull with a single wall unit.

Fig. 3.8. *Mark Spitz performing arm-rotator exercises on an early model of the isokinetic exerciser*

Figure 3.10 shows Fred Tyler using the Mini-Gym isokinetic leg press machine to improve the strength and speed of his quadriceps extensor muscles. These muscles help in performing the racing dive, the push-off after the turn, and the leg drive of the breaststroke kick.

Exercises on the Mini-Gym Isokinetic Swim Bench*

With the use of the Swim Bench the swimmer can imitate the swimming move-

*For more information about Mini-Gym isokinetic exercise equipment for swimmers, including price list, write: Counsilman Co., Inc., 2606F East Second Street, Bloomington, Indiana 47401.

ments of all four competitive strokes on land exactly as he should perform them in the water and *at a fast speed*. This piece of equipment is used by most of the world-class swimmers in the United States, as well as by the East German swimmers. The Indiana University swimmers chose this piece of equipment as their favorite, believing that it helps them more than any other. Jim Montgomery, Olympic champion in the 100-meter freestyle, has worked daily on the Swim Bench and thinks it helped him achieve world-record times.

Many coaches use this equipment as a means of teaching their swimmers correct stroke mechanics. The swimmer can perform the stroke on the Swim Bench, watching to see that he has good arm position: the right amount of elbow bend, good hand position, and so on. This learning transfers to his stroke mechanics when he performs in the water.

Fig. 3.9. *Fred Tyler performing latissimus pull with single-unit isokinetic exerciser*

Fig. 3.10. *Fred Tyler performing quadriceps extensor exercies on the leg-press isokinetic exerciser*

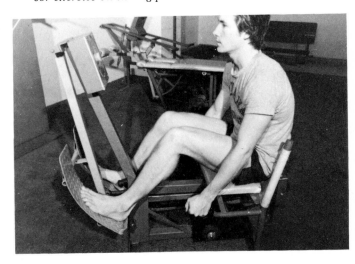

Fig. 3.11. *The Swim Bench as a teaching aid*

A. Simulating the crawl stroke

B. Simulating the back stroke

The Leaper

This piece of equipment received a great deal of publicity in *Sports Illustrated* for its importance in improving the vertical jump of Indiana University's All-American center, basketball player Kent Benson, by 5 inches. It is used by swimmers to improve their starts and push-offs after the turn. In 1976 the average improvement of the vertical jump of our team members was 3 inches after ten weeks of work on this apparatus.

Fig. 3.12. *The Leaper* is used in swimming to improve the start and the push-off after the turn

SECTION 3.8
A METHOD OF MEASURING EXPLOSIVE POWER—THE VERTICAL JUMP

Over the past twenty-five years I have used the *vertical jump* to measure the explosive power of swimmers. Results show that swimmers who have a high vertical-jump score for their age and sex make better sprinters, while those who have a low vertical-jump score make better distance swimmers. Those near the norm make good middle-distance swimmers. For example, the vertical jump of one of our sprinters, world record holder Jim Montgomery, was 26 inches (as was that of Mark Spitz); that of world record holder in the distance events, John Kinsella, was 18 inches. The following is a rough estimate of the classification of adult males according to their scores in the standing vertical jump:

24 to 31 inches — sprinters
18 to 25 inches — middle-distance swimmers
11 to 22 inches — distance swimmers

While it is obvious that there are many factors involved in swimming any distance and no coach is so naive as to take a sprinter who has a vertical jump of only 14 inches and yet holds the world record in the 100-meter freestyle, and suddenly change him to a distance swimmer, still the predictive value of the vertical jump is amazingly accurate, causing the case above to be highly unlikely. Tables 3.2 and 3.3 give the norms for swimmers of the various ages and both sexes.

Fig. 3.13. *The vertical jump*

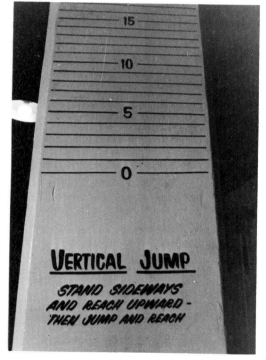

A. The vertical-jump testing chart: A series of lines should be painted on the wall, with every fifth line painted a different color and numbered, using the English measuring system.

B. The subject stands at a right angle and next to the testing chart and reaches as high as he can with one hand, keeping his heels flat on the ground. The tester notes the line to which his hand reaches.

C. The subject steps back from the wall 6 to 12 inches and without taking a step dips slightly and jumps as high as he can, reaching with the same hand he used before and throwing the other hand downward as shown in this figure. The tester notes the highest point reached by the subject in three trials and subtracts the first number from the latter number to obtain the height of the vertical jump. Do not allow the subject to take a step before jumping.

Table 3.2
Norms for Strength Tests
for Both Sexes and Age Groups

Age (Number Tested) Sex	Latissimus Pull	Supine Pullovers	Rotators	Elbow Extensors
15 (13) M	2 reps.* w/80 lb. to 1 rep. w/60 lb.	7 reps. w/65 lb. to 2 reps. w/35 lb.	3 reps. w/75 lb. to 6 reps. w/45 lb.	7 reps. w/55 lb. to 2 reps. w/35 lb.
Average	1-5 reps. w/70 lb.	1-5 reps. w/55 lb.	1-5 reps. w/55 lb.	1-5 reps. w/45 lb.
16 (22) M	7 reps. w/90 lb. to 3 reps. w/70 lb.	5 reps. w/75 lb. to 5 reps. w/55 lb.	6 reps. w/85 lb. to 1 rep. w/43 lb.	3 reps. w/75 lb. to 8 reps. w/40 lb.
Average	1-5 reps. w/80 lb.	1-10 reps. w/60 lb.	1-10 reps. w/60 lb.	1-10 reps. w/45 lb.
17 (15) M	2 reps. w/110 lb. to 4 reps. w/70 lb.	10 reps. w/85 lb. to 10 reps. w/53 lb.	8 reps. w/80 lb. to 4 reps. w/50 lb.	4 reps. w/75 lb. to 8 reps. w/45 lb.
Average	1-5 reps. w/80 lb.	1-5 reps. w/65 lb.	1-10 reps. w/60 lb.	1-10 reps. w/60 lb.

Note: These tests were taken from swimmers attending "Doc" Counsilman Swimming camps: Indiana University and Mercersberg Academy, Summer, 1975. Compiled by Jan Prins.
*Repetitions.

Table 3.3
Norms for Tests of Power and Flexibility
for Age Groups and Both Sexes
(Measurements in Inches)

Age (Number Tested) Sex	Vertical Jump		Vertical Shoulder Stretch		Horizontal Shoulder Stretch		Ankle Plantar Flexion		Forward Flexion		Squat	
	Avg.	Range	Avg.	Range	Avg.	Range	Avg.	Range	Avg.	Range	Pass	Fail
17 (15) M	22.5	17-23 cluster 21-22	—	—	5 cross	14 apart 15 cross	4	2.5-6	—	—	10/15	5/15
16 (44) M	20	14-26 clusters (21) (15)	14	7-26	5 cross	16 apart 19 across	4	2.5-5	5	T*-12.5	23/44	21/44
(7) F	14.5	14-16	13	5.5-26	—	—	2.25	.75-3.5	3	T-8	6/7	1/7
15 (44) M	19	13-23 clusters (21) (16)	12.5	6-20.5	10 cross	6 apart 24 cross	3.75	3-4.5	3.5	T-7.75	32/44	12/44
(6) F	13	11-16	11.5	6.5-16	—	—	2.25	1.25-4	2	T-2.25	6/6	0/6
14 (26) M	17	12-21 clusters (19-20,14)	13.5	5-25	—	—	3	.5-5.5	3.75	T-8.5	13/26	13/26
(11) F	13.5	9-19	13	8-22	—	—	2	5.-3	2	T-5.5	8/11	3/11
13 (33) M	15	11-24 clusters (19) (13)	11	3-18.75	—	—	4	1.25-4.75	4	T-8.25	20/33	13/33
(16) F	12.5	8-15 clusters (14) (12)	12	0-18.5	—	—	2.25	T-4.75	1.75	T-5.5	13/16	3/16
12 (28) M	12.5	9-16 clusters (16) (12)	13.25	5.5-19.5	—	—	3.25	1.75-4	4	T-7.5	25/28	3/28
(18) F	12	7-16 clusters (13, 7-8)	11.5	2.75-18.5	—	—	2.5	1.5-4.75	1.5	T-5.3	15/18	3/18
11 (5) M	13.75	11-17	15.5	11.4-19.5	—	—	2.5	1.5-3	1.3	T-3.5	4/5	1/5
(3) F	11.5	8-15	8.25	7-10.25	—	—	1	1-2.25	2.5	T-3.5	3/3	0/3

*Touch

SECTION 3.9 FLEXIBILITY

Flexibility—What Is It?

Flexibility refers to the degree or range of movement of a joint. The two limiting factors that determine flexibility are (1) bone structure and (2) the degree to which the muscles around a joint will permit it to move (the muscle's elasticity).

1. *Bone structure.* The person with large bones and with large protuberances on those bones will—everything else being equal—be less flexible than his small-boned counterpart. Large-boned males have poorer flexibility than a light-framed male, a female, or a child. As a person matures his bones get larger, and many a flexible youth finds when he reaches adulthood that he needs to "stretch himself out" to attain the flexibility he had as an

age-grouper. Some light-boned people, such as Mark Spitz, have unusually flexible joints and need little or no flexibility exercises throughout their competitive careers, while others need them daily.

2. *Elasticity of muscles.* Muscles are only so long: they extend from where they originate on one side of the joint to where they attach on the other side. Their length cannot be changed, but their ability to permit the joint to move freely in the opposite direction from which they pull the joint can be improved. To do this the connective tissue that surrounds and goes throughout the muscle must be stretched. The muscle literally becomes more elastic so that it will stretch out and then return to its original shape, much like a rubber band does when it is stretched. The muscle can be made more elastic if this is desirable by engaging in a special exercise program.

Flexibility—Who Needs It and Why?

Every athlete needs flexibility in a specific joint or joints. The hurdler in track needs above-average flexibility in forward flexions of his upper leg in order to be able to go over the hurdles and still keep his center of gravity low. The swimmer can get by with only average flexibility in the hip joint, but he must have well-above-average flexibility in his ankles to have an exceptionally good kick. Butterfly, freestyle, and backstroke swimmers need flexibility in the shoulder joints and in extension (plantar flexion) of the ankle. The freestyler and butterflyer need shoulder flexibility in order to be able to recover their arms over the water easily. A tight-shouldered freestyler will have to roll more to recover his arms and/or use a wide, flat arm recovery, both of which stroke defects will be harmful to body position and will increase drag. A flyer lacking shoulder flexibility will either have to climb too high in the water to recover his arms over the water or will skip them along the surface of the water, creating more drag. The breaststroker needs only average shoulder flexibility since his arms always work within the normal range of movement.

During the leg kick of the freestyle, back stroke, and fly the ankles should extend as far backward as possible in order to thrust the water backward and downward in the case of the flyer and freestyler, and backward and upward in the case of the backstroker. The ankle-stretcher exerciser is used to improve this plantar flexion of the swimmers' ankles. The breaststroker needs to flex his feet in the opposite direction, that is, dorsiflexion. This permits him to apply the force of his kick in a more backward direction and is best improved by the Achilles-tendon-stretcher exercise.

Swimmers' Flexibility Tests

1. *Shoulder Flexibility—Horizontal*

Sit with back erect, legs extended, and knees straight. Raise arms to sides at shoulder height, palms facing forward. Keeping arms at shoulder height and without bending forward or turning palms downward, pull arms backward as far as possible. *Do not lower arms as you pull them backward, but keep them at shoulder height. Keep elbows straight.*

Tester: Measure the distance in inches or centimeters between the fingertips of two hands.

Fig. 3.14. *Shoulder flexibility test (horizontal)*

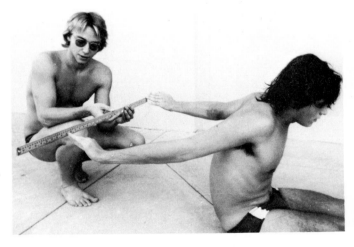

2. *Shoulder Flexibility—Vertical*

Lying on chest with face in a vertical position and chin touching the ground, grasp a broom handle or some other small wooden stick at shoulder width. Without bending the elbows or the wrists, lift the stick as high as you can.

Tester: Measure the height the stick is lifted from the ground.

Fig. 3.15. *Shoulder flexibility test* (vertical)

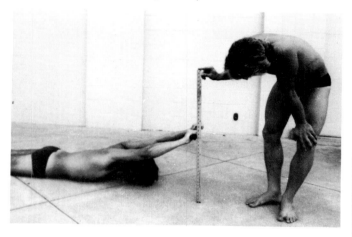

3. *Forward Trunk Flexion*

Sitting down, with legs extended, spread feet 1 foot apart. Interlace fingers behind neck, and bend trunk forward as far as possible. *Do not bend knees.*

Tester: Measure distance from forehead to ground.

Fig. 3.16. *Forward trunk flexion test*

4. *Ankle Flexibility—Plantar Flexion*

Sit down with legs together and extended

and with trunk in an erect position. Without bending knees try to touch big toe to ground. *Do not rotate leg or ankle inward* (medially).

Tester: Measure closest distance from the bottom of big toe of least flexible foot to the ground.

Fig. 3.17. *Ankle flexibility— plantar flexion test*

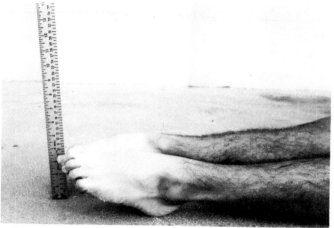

5. *Dorsiflexion*

Assume same position as in previous exercise, but place sole of foot firmly against a wall. Keeping the heel against the wall, dorsiflex ankle so that all but the heel of the foot is pulled away from the wall as far as possible.

Tester: Measure distance from bottom of least flexible big toe to the wall.

Fig. 3.18. *Dorsiflexion test*

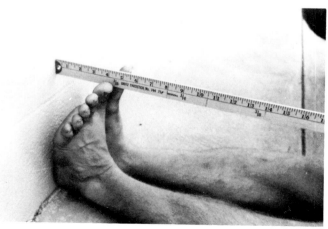

6. Breaststrokers Sit-down (Pass or Fail)

Stand erect with hands behind neck and fingers interlaced. Keeping toes, heels, and knees together, do a full squat without letting the heels leave the ground. *This must be done barefooted.* If you lose your balance and fall backwards or if your feet leave the ground, you fail the test. Be sure that you reach a full squat position and that you do not remove your hands from behind your neck.

Tester: Score on a pass/fail basis.

Fig. 3.19. *Breaststrokers' sit-down test*

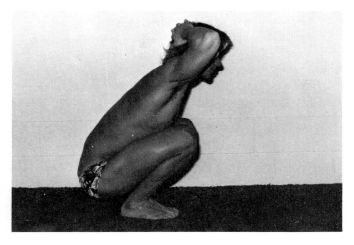

Flexibility Exercises for the Ankles

1. Ankle Stretcher—Plantar Flexion

Sitting on the ankles, lift the knees up and shift weight so as to place stretch on the ankles. Repeat 10 to 20 times, holding for 3 to 5 seconds each repeat.

Fig. 3.20. *Ankle-stretcher exercise*
(plantar)

2. Achilles-Tendon Stretcher—Dorsiflexion

This exercise should be used by all breaststroke swimmers and individual-medley swimmers. It can be done in several ways: (A) on an inclined plane, (B) on alligator shoes, (C) standing on a curbing of some type, and (D) with no equipment. When doing any of these four exercises, the swimmer should keep the knees bent slightly. This causes a greater stretch in the calf muscle/and in the Achilles tendon than in the hamstrings. The swimmer bends forward as far as possible and bounces 4 or 5 times, then straightens. He bends forward and repeats the bouncing action again. He does this for a total of 5 to 10 efforts.

A. *Achilles-Tendon Exercise As Performed on Inclined Plane*

Lean forward as if to touch the toes, bend knees slightly and shift weight of body forward so calf muscle and Achilles tendon are stretched. Hold position for 3 to 5 seconds. Repeat 10 to 20 times. The angles of the inclined plane can be made 35° or 50°—the lower angle for swimmers with normal or subnormal flexibility, the higher angle for those with above-average flexibility.

Fig. 3.21. *Achilles-tendon exercise on inclined plane*

B. *Achilles-Tendon Exercise As Performed on Alligator Shoes*

The exercise described above can also

be done on a pair of alligator shoes, as shown in Figure 3.22. These shoes can be built easily in an evening and can be made adjustable to accommodate to the swimmer's improving flexibility. Be sure to make them sturdy and to use high-top sneakers.

Fig. 3.22. *Achilles-tendon exercise on alligator shoes*

C. Achilles-Tendon Exercise As Performed on a Curbing

If neither of the above pieces of equipment is available to the swimmer, by simply standing with his toes and the balls of his feet on a curb or elevation of at least 4 inches, then relaxing his legs so his heels drop as low as they will go, he can do the Achilles-tendon exercise. The swimmer should feel the stretch on the calf muscles and the Achilles tendon. He should hold the position for 3 to 5 seconds, then rise slightly on his toes, repeating the action 10 to 20 times. I want to emphasize that this method and the next to be discussed are not as effective as using exercises A or B.

D. Achilles-Tendon Exercise As Performed with No Equipment

Another form of this exercise that swimmers use before competition to stretch out the Achilles tendons is used with no equipment except a wall to push against. Stand back from the wall 3 to 4 feet. Lean forward and place one foot half way between the wall and the back foot, and the hands against the wall. Bend the knee of the back leg just slightly so that the heel of the back leg is elevated. Push against the wall and press the heel of the back leg to the ground, feeling the stretch on the Achilles tendon and the calf muscle. Repeat several times and gradually increase the stretching action, bouncing each leg 10 to 15 times. Reverse legs and stretch the opposite leg. Repeat with each leg 3 to 5 times.

Fig. 3.23. *Fourth way to stretch the Achilles tendon*

SECTION 3.10
ISOMETRIC STRETCHING—
EXERCISES FOR THE SHOULDERS

1. *Horizontal stretching—arms straight.* The subject sits with his back erect, legs extended forward and knees straight, arms raised to shoulder height with the palms facing forward. The person who is going to stretch the subject grasps him by the wrists and pulls the arms backward in a horizontal plane until the arms are fully stretched and there is some tension but no pain. The subject then contracts his muscles as if to pull the arms forward. The stretcher continues to hold the arms firmly so the subject cannot move them forward.

This contraction of the muscles against the tension of the stretcher's resistance is the stress factor that causes the muscles to be stretched. This type of stretching has been called by various names depending on the system in which it is used. We call it *isometric stretching.*

Fig. 3.24. *Horizontal stretching*
(arms straight)

This action should be repeated 5 to 8 times for a period of 4 to 7 seconds for each effort. The person being stretched can relax the muscles and even shake out the arms between each of the isometric stretches.

2. *Horizontal stretching—hands interlaced behind the neck.* This exercise is done in a manner similar to the first exercise except that the subject places his hands interlaced behind his neck and the stretcher (the person who is stretching him) grasps the inside of his elbows with his hands and places his knee against the middle back of the subject. The stretcher pulls backward until he feels some resistance, once again avoiding such a hard backward pull that the subject feels pain. The subject then contracts his muscles as if to bring the elbows forward, while the stretcher resists and permits no movement. This action is repeated 5 to 8 times for a period of 4 to 7 seconds for each effort.

Fig. 3.25. *Horizontal stretching*
(hands interlaced behind the neck)

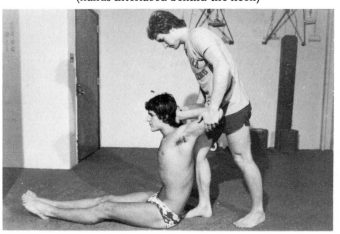

3. *Vertical Stretching.* The subject sits erect and reaches overhead, interlacing his fingers behind the stretcher's neck. The stretcher places his hands on the subject's shoulders at the base of the neck and pushes forward with his hands while pulling backward with his neck against the hands of the subject. The subject tries to pull the stretcher's head forward. Repeat 4 to 7 times, holding each effort for 4 to 7 seconds.

Fig. 3.26. *Vertical stretching*

Part Two

STROKE MECHANICS

FOUR

Practical Considerations of Stroke Mechanics

SECTION 4.1
TEACHING STROKE MECHANICS

How a Swimmer
Learns Stroke Mechanics

It is important for any person who plans to use any of the material in the subsequent sections on stroke mechanics to read this section first, to keep it in mind as he reads the next five sections and, later, as he tries to help swimmers develop proper stroke mechanics.

I have watched many swimmers who have developed good stroke mechanics with no help from any coach or, as a matter of fact, from anyone. Mark Spitz would be a good example of this type of swimmer. When he came to me as a freshman in college, he held two world records and had near-perfect stroke mechanics. When I asked him how he pulled his hands on the crawl stroke, he gave me a detailed description of a nearly straight elbow pull down the middle line of the body. Underwater movies of his pull show him to be using a zigzag pull with his elbows bending up to almost 90 degrees.

The obvious question: "If he didn't know how he swam, how come he developed such good mechanics?" The answer is that most physical skills are learned through a trial-and-

error process. When a child is a year old and learns to walk, he does not evaluate the physical laws that govern movement, such as the principles of balance, the three laws of motion, and so on. He observes an adult walking and he pulls himself up and tries it. After many failures and some successes, he develops the coordination that permits him to walk properly. He has never said to himself, "All right, now to walk I must first lean forward, lose my balance, then flex my hip and my knee and catch my weight with the front leg, etc."

In essence, trial and error is the way we learn to swim except for one important difference. Walking and running are more natural activities than is swimming, and our bodies are better adapted for them.

Am I saying that the coach and teacher should not teach stroke mechanics but should let every swimmer develop his stroke mechanics strictly on a trial-and-error basis, as did Mark Spitz? No, that is not what I have been implying. This system worked for Mark Spitz because insofar as swimming stroke mechanics is concerned, Mark is a motor genius. Few of the swimmers you will encounter will be motor geniuses of Mark's caliber. Most will be average, with an exceptionally talented few who will learn skills easily and who will, in

133

fact, learn properly in spite of their coaches. A few will also be exceptionally slow in learning skills and will have to be guided more carefully because their neuromuscular coordination has trouble distinguishing between poor and good mechanics.

Guided Trial-and-Error Learning

The answer to teaching and coaching stroke technique is to guide the trial-and-error process without forcing the swimmers into a good stroke pattern prematurely. By this I mean you should not take a child who has never swum and tell him exactly how to swim before he has had a chance to let his neuromuscular system go through a period of trial-and-error learning. A few years ago the father of a five-year-old boy came to me and said his boy couldn't swim and he had kept him from learning because he feared that the boy would learn bad techniques. The boy was now ready to learn and he wanted me to teach him correctly from the very beginning. I told the father to allow the boy to learn to swim first; after he could swim a half mile continuously, I could help him. My point here is that if we take a child or any person of any age and teach him a new physical skill by outlining precisely how he is to perform the skill and without letting him, or rather his neuromuscular system, play around with solving the problem of proper mechanics we force him into a synthetic pattern that may never seem completely natural to him.

While the foregoing is important, it does not rule out some guidance from the teacher or coach in this learning experience, with very specific descriptions of correct stroke mechanics being offered at the right time. For example, instead of making a general statement such as "During the pull I want you to bend your elbows," be more specific: "The pull begins with the elbow straight; then, as the arm pulls, begin bending the elbow until, half way through the pull, the elbow is bent 90 to 105 degrees. From that point backward the elbow should begin extending until, at the end of the pull, it is once again almost completely extended." To show exactly what is meant, demonstrate the arm pull (on land) as you describe it. Show movies, charts,

pictures, etc. Let the swimmer get a good visual image of what you expect. Although you may describe the stroke exactly as you want it swum, do allow for slight individual differences. In other words, be specific in your description of the stroke mechanics, but do not hold the learning swimmer to a rigid pattern.

Here are several other points whose importance I like to emphasize in teaching stroke mechanics to a swimmer:

1. There are so many details in stroke mechanics that if a swimmer tried to think of all of them at one time he would be immobilized. It is better to instruct the swimmer to think of only one or two points at a time. For example, when he is swimming the crawl stroke, he can ask himself, "Am I keeping my elbows high during the first part of my pull, and am I finishing my pull long—below my swim suit?"

2. The most important part of the stroke occurs under water so most of your time must be devoted to telling the swimmer how to perform this part of the stroke. You don't need an underwater window or expensive photographic equipment to check this part of the stroke. Get a face plate and hop into the pool.

3. Read the whole section on each stroke and have your swimmers read each one. At first the description may seem complex. Things will become clearer with rereading and discussion.

4. The best way to present a discussion of stroke mechanics to swimmers is in the classroom, using movies, charts, pictures, and drawings on the blackboard. A good teaching drill in the pool is to have the swimmers work in pairs and direct them to watch one another underwater using goggles. By watching for specific details in one another's stroke pattern that you have discussed and shown in films, double learning will result, as well as a clearer impression of what you have been stressing in your explanations.

5. During practice, remind the swimmers of certain stroke-mechanic details. Speaking to the whole group: "Now we are going to do 10 × 50 butterfly. On the first five I want

you to concentrate on using the hourglass pull and on the second five I want you to watch your breathing, keep your chin in the water while you are inhaling, and breathe every other stroke."

Fig. 4.1. *Classroom lectures on stroke mechanics emphasize the important points*

Fig. 4.2. *Showing movies of the record holders in order that the swimmers may get a better idea of the best method of performing the strokes—especially the underwater mechanics*

6. Don't be afraid to lecture your swimmers and then to work with them on stroke mechanics. You learn to swim by swimming and you learn to coach by coaching. Do your homework. Prepare yourself carefully; outline your lecture. Don't be afraid to make a few mistakes. You may mess up a few, but

eventually you will learn to help a lot.

7. Don't be a perfectionist. Emphasize the important points, such as high elbows, proper pull pattern, etc. Once these have been established, you may work on relatively unimportant details, such as fingers together during the pull, etc. Learning to distinguish the important from the less important means learning the laws that govern movement and especially movement in water. It requires study of physical laws, observation of highly talented swimmers, and application of what you have learned in practical terms.

8. Just for emphasis, let me repeat: Do not force the swimmer into a rigid pattern of stroke mechanics. Let him vary his stroke mechanics within a range of movement that will allow for individual differences in strength, flexibility, and buoyancy. What is a good pulling pattern for one swimmer may not be the exact pattern that a weaker or stronger swimmer may use most efficiently. Remember, however, that most swimmers, when not coached at all, will not develop proper stroke mechanics through trial-and-error learning. You must guide the learning process by mentioning and emphasizing certain aspects of stroke mechanics.

9. Require that the swimmer do exercises that will help him learn proper stroke mechanics. If he is using isokinetic exercise equipment, emphasize the duplication of the stroke mechanics he will use when swimming, such as elbow bend, high elbow action, line of pull, and so on. Remember that when a swimmer is weak he cannot swim with proper mechanics for a long period of time, because he is not able to handle all of the force his hands create. As the workout progresses he will lose his stroke. However, as he gets stronger, the swimmer will be able to handle this force and keep his stroke for a longer time. He should try to keep his stroke even when he tires, thus placing stress on the correct muscles and conditioning them. If, for example, he drops his elbows when he gets tired and doesn't try to keep them up, he will never condition the arm rotators to develop the endurance and strength to keep the high elbow position during the arm pull for the entire race.

10. Let the swimmers use mirror dry-land drills.

11. Swim on impressions; so occasionally—not often—use general statements such as "Feel light as a canoe."

12. Allow the swimmers to work with one another, doubling the learning process.

SECTION 4.2
PRINCIPLES COMMON TO ALL FOUR COMPETITIVE STROKES

There are slight and sometimes not-so-slight differences among the stroke mechanics of champion swimmers. These may be relatively unimportant idiosyncracies, such as a peculiar flip of the hand during the recovery phase of the arm pull, or major differences, such as one crawl swimmer's using a two-beat kick while another uses a six-beat kick. Such major differences need not lead the reader to think that these swimmers are applying different principles of fluid mechanics. All great swimmers obey certain principles of fluid mechanics, or they would not be great swimmers. For the same reason there are certain of these principles that are common to all four competitive strokes. Before discussing each stroke individually I would like to mention several of these principles, explain why they are important, and show their application during the actual swimming movements.

1. *The hands are not pulled through the water in a straight line, but in some form of elliptical pattern.* For many years crawl swimmers were told—and sometimes still are told—to pull their hands in a straight path down the center line of their bodies. In the butterfly, swimmers were told to put their arms in the water in front of their shoulders and to pull straight back. Fortunately, most swimmers, at least the better ones, did not follow these instructions, but pulled in the elliptical patterns shown in Figure 4.3.

Why isn't a straight-line pull effective? Or

put it this way: why is the elliptical (zigzag) pull pattern better than the straight-line pull? It seems reasonable to believe that if you push the water directly backward, as in Figure 4.4 you will be obeying Newton's third law of motion ("For every action there is an equal and opposite reaction") and will be pushing yourself directly forward. If the athlete were on a solid surface, such as the ground, this would be true, but the swimmer is pushing his hand against water, and when he does so, the water naturally moves in the direction the hand pushes it. If the hand continues to maintain a straight path, it can get little propulsion from pushing against water that is already moving in the same direction. Thus the hand must alter its path in order to contact still water. The best way for the hand to accomplish this is for it to move in some form of elliptical pattern, such as that shown in Figure 4.3.

Another reason for the hand to pull in this manner is that it is able to combine its elliptical pull pattern with a pitch in the position of the hand that will contribute a lift force generated by the hand. This sculling action is discussed more extensively in "The Application of Bernoulli's Principle to Human Propulsion in the Water" (Chapter 5, Section 5.2), "The Role of Sculling Movements in the Arm Pull" (Chapter 5, Section 5.1), and "A Biomechanical Analysis of the Freestyle Aquatic Skill" (Chapter 5, Section 5.3).

Careful study of underwater movies of champion swimmers has shown that none of them pull in a straight line, no matter what competitive stroke they are swimming. Each champion swimmer may have a pull pattern slightly different from that of any other swimmer. In fact some backstrokers and crawl swimmers have a slightly different pull pattern from one arm to the other. The only swimmers I have photographed who pulled their hands through the water in a straight line were beginning swimmers or those who were poor swimmers and had had difficulty learning to swim.

In Figure 4.3 the pull pattern of four champion swimmers performing the various strokes is shown.

Fig. 4.3. *Elliptical pull patterns of the four competitive strokes*

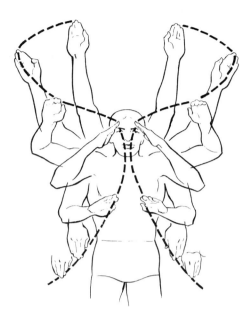

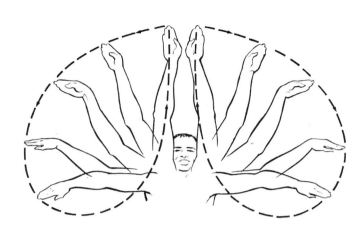

A. The butterfly-stroke pull pattern as seen from directly underneath

C. The breaststroke pull pattern as seen from underneath

B. The backstroke pull pattern as seen from the side

D. The crawl-stroke pull pattern as seen from underneath

2. *The swimmer does not pull with a straight arm, but uses a straight-bent-straight elbow action.* If the swimmer were to pull with a straight arm, the hand would not be in a good position to exert force backward except during the middle of the pull (Point *C*); at Points *A* and *B* the force would be directed primarily downward, not backward; at Points *D* and *E* the force would be directed primarily upward.

Fig. 4.4 *Straight-line, straight-arm pull*

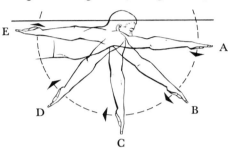

When swimming any of the four strokes, the swimmer starts his pull with the elbows straight (or, in a few cases, with just a slight degree of bend). As he pulls his arms through the water, the elbow (or elbows) starts to bend and continues to bend until it is in a vertical position (90 to 105 degrees) at which point the maximum degree of elbow bend should occur. From this point on backward, the degree of elbow bend begins to decrease until, at the very end of the pull, the elbow reaches almost complete extension (except in the breaststroke), at which time the arm recovery begins.

Fig. 4.5. *Maximum elbow bend in the four strokes*

A. Olympic swimmer John Murphy's elbow reaches maximum bend of 90 degrees in the crawl when the hand is directly under the shoulder.

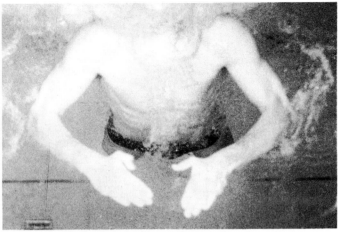

B. Mark Spitz's butterfly stroke also shows a maximum bend of approximately 90 degrees.

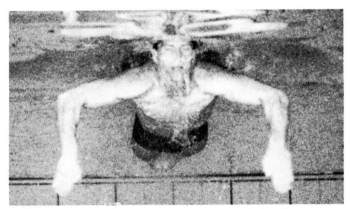

C. Chet Jastremski's breaststroke pull also shows a similar degree of bend.

D. Olympic champion Charles Hickcox bends his elbows a little more than 90 degrees when swimming backstroke.

3. *The elbow is carried in a high position during the pull.* As the pull begins and the elbows bend, the upper arm should rotate medially (inwardly). This keeps the elbow in a high position during the first half of the pull. This action, plus the bend in the elbow, places the hand in a good position to push the water backward.

Fig. 4.6. *High elbow action of some champions*

C. The high elbow action of Karla Linke, world record holder in the breaststroke, is shown here.

A. Jenny Turrall, world record holder in the freestyle, shows high elbow position in the crawl stroke.

D. Mike Stamm, Olympic silver medalist, is shown doing the backstroke with an "inverted" high-elbow action.

B. The high elbow action of Mark Spitz's butterfly stroke is seen from head-on.

The best way to illustrate this medial arm rotation action is to hold your arms out directly in front of your chest at shoulder height, palms together. By rotating your arms inwardly, turn the hands around until the knuckles of each hand are touching one another and the palms are facing outward. During the actual swimming stroke, you will not medially rotate your arms this far, but you can begin to understand the action through the use of this drill. To get a better idea of how this action feels when swimming, do the same drill as mentioned above, but begin with the elbows bent slightly. Keep the elbow bend constant and rotate the arm only half way, so the palms are facing downward instead of out. In performing this action in the manner described you have imitated the high elbow position that is desirable in the first part of the pull in the butterfly, crawl, and breaststroke. In the backstroke, medial arm rotation is also desirable, but with the difference that the swimmer is inverted and his arms are pulling laterally instead of beneath him.

4. *The hands should be pitched properly upon entry into and exit from the water.* Upon entry into the water the hands should be pitched in such a manner as to knife the water cleanly and prevent dragging air bubbles after them. The entrapment or dragging of air bubbles after the hand decreases the amount of lift that the hand can create and thus decreases the effectiveness of the pull. In swimming the backstroke, the hands should enter in a vertical position directly over the shoulder with the little finger entering first and the palms facing outward. The entry of the hands should not be made with a relaxed hand that slaps the water. The fingers should be closed and in good alignment in order that the hand may knife into the water cleanly. The hand should not be tense, but should be controlled. Figure 4.7 shows the desired hand position when swimming backstroke.

Fig. 4.7. *Backstroke*

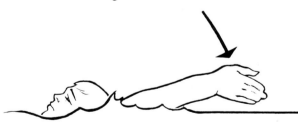

Correct entry of the hand, with little finger entering the water first and the hand in a vertical position. This permits the hand to enter the water without pulling a lot of air with it.

Figure 4.8A depicts the hand of a backstroker that has entrapped a large amount of air because of the improper pitch of the hand upon its entry into the water. Figure 4.8B shows the correct pitch of entry, with the consequent entrapment of less air.

Fig. 4.8. *Backstroke*

A. The hand has entered the water improperly and has entrapped too many bubbles.

B. The entry of the hand has been properly accomplished, and fewer air bubbles have been entrapped.

In swimming the butterfly and the crawl strokes, the hands enter the water pitched at a 35 to 45-degree angle, palms facing outward. If they enter the water flat, they will entrap air bubbles. Figure 4.9 shows the hands of an Olympic champion butterflier at the instant they enter the water.

The pitch of the hands as they leave the water is also important. They should be lifted out of the water in a streamlined position in order that they may not pull the swimmer down or create a water turbulence against the swimmer's body. The swimmer should not intentionally push the water upward at the end of his pull on any of the strokes. Figure 4.10A shows the position of the hand as it leaves the water in the crawl; Figure 4.10B shows hand position in the backstroke.

Fig. 4.9. *The pitch of the hands*

Upon entry into the water the pitch of the hands should be as shown here—the hands pitched at an angle with the palms facing diagonally outward.

Fig. 4.10. *The pitch of the hands*
As they leave the water the hands should not be in such a position as to push water upward but should slide or knife out in order to create little resistance.

A. This photo shows the typical position of the hand of a good crawl swimmer as it leaves the water. The palm is facing inward toward the body and the little finger is leaving the water first.

B. In the backstroke the palm is also facing toward the body with the hand in a vertical position, but the thumb is leaving the water first.

5. *The hands should be pitched properly during the pull in order to obtain maximum lift.* The pitch of the hands during the pull is also important. It should not be at right angles to the direction of the pull. They rather should be pitched at an angle of approximately 37 degrees with relation to their path through the water. The pitch of the hands during the pull of each stroke will be discussed in detail in the section for that stroke. However, in order that the reader may understand exactly what pitch is and why it is important, I would like to elaborate upon this topic in more detail.

The hands can be used to push the body forward in the water without ever moving backward themselves, through the use of sculling action. To prove this the swimmer need only lie on his back and, keeping his hands at his sides at hip level, use a figure-eight sculling action to push himself forward. In this case the swimmer is using hydro-dynamic lift (the Bernoulli principle) to propel himself forward.

When swimming the four competitive strokes, a swimmer also uses a sculling action of his hands as they are pulled through the water in an elliptical pull pattern. He is actually using his hands in the same manner as a propeller that is pushing a boat or an airplane forward. For this reason he must pitch his hands in a manner that will provide maximum lift. This angle, as I mentioned earlier, is approximately 37 degrees, as measured in relation to the path of the hand through the water.

Figures 4.11 and 4.12 show how the hands are pitched in the butterfly stroke.

Fig. 4.11. *The pitch of the hands during the butterfly pull*

A. This shows the angle of pitch of the hands as viewed from directly under the swimmer.

B. To provide a better perspective of the pitch, I have included another view of the stroke at the same position, but taken from almost directly head-on. The hands are pressing outward and downward, and the palms are facing diagonally outward.

Fig. 4.12. *Another view of the pitch of the hands in the butterfly*

A. The hands are farther into the pull than in Fig. 4.11 and are now pulling downward and inward toward one another. They have changed pitch and are facing diagonally inward.

B. Another view of the same phase of the arm stroke as in Fig. 4.12A.

6. *The principle of streamlining has application in swimming, as in other methods of propulsion.* A careful study of underwater movies of good swimmers as compared with those of poor swimmers shows that good swimmers are streamlined and create less resistance or drag than do poor swimmers.

Resistance or drag is composed of three types: (*a*) head-on or frontal resistance, (*b*) eddy resistance, and (*c*) skin friction or resistance.

a. Head-on or frontal resistance is the resistance offered by any part of the body that faces forward in the direction in which the swimmer is progressing.

b. Tail suction or eddy resistance is the result of the inability of the water to flow around the body in a laminar pattern and to fill in all of the curves, indentations, and parts of the body facing backwards. Water in these areas is therefore pulled forward and forms eddies.

c. Skin friction is the resistance resulting from the thin layer of water that encounters the skin as this water flows over the body.

Fig. 4.13. *Three types of resistance*

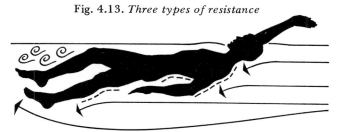

1. The arrows indicate frontal or head-on resistance.
2. The curlicues represent eddy resistance.
3. The dotted line represents skin resistance.

Good swimmers create less frontal and eddy resistance than do poor swimmers and literally trade it for skin friction. Poor swimmers frequently swim slowly because they are inclined in the water at an angle and drag a lot of water along with them.

Fig. 4.14. *More examples of resistance*

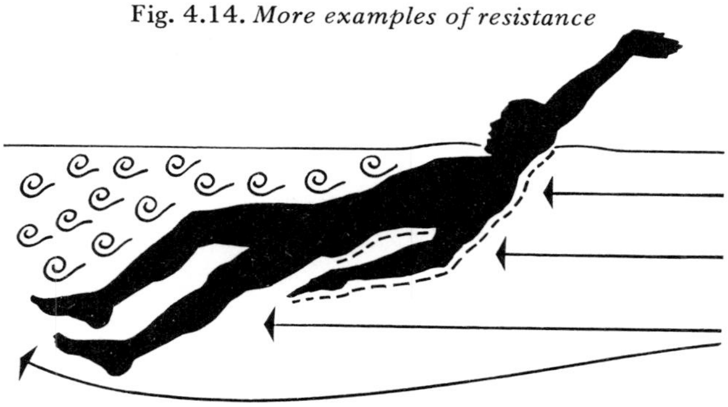

The backstroker has lifted his head farther out of the water than in Fig. 4.13 and his hips have dropped. The result is increased frontal and eddy resistance and the loss of his streamlined position.

To create as little drag as possible, a swimmer should try to keep his body in a horizontal position and to develop as little sideward movement of his body as possible. Lateral or sideward movement of the body also increases frontal and eddy resistance. Sometimes a swimmer must sacrifice decreased resistance somewhat to achieve a more effective stroke. In the backstroke the swimmer will not swim in a completely flat horizontal position or his kick will be ineffec-

tive because it will be too high out of the water. He must therefore drop his hips a few inches to keep his feet underwater where they can be effective.

The reader will also see that the swimmer has to sacrifice streamlining in the breaststroke kick in order to achieve a more powerful kick. More about that in the section on the breaststroke.

7. *The swimmer should not throw water against his body.* If the swimmer is not aware of the consequences, he may unknowingly increase the amount of water resistance he must overcome by throwing water against his body or legs with his hands and/or arms. To move forward the swimmer must push water backward. As we have seen earlier in this section, the water moves backward at an angle and not directly backward. If this backward-moving water is pushed against any part of the swimmer's body, it will increase his drag and slow him down. The swimmer should never be able to feel any turbulence created by his arms against his body or legs.

In Fig. 4.15 the swimmer's forearm and hand are so close to his body that some of the water turbulence created by them is bound to be directed against his body. This may happen when the hands get too close to the body in the crawl or butterfly stroke, particularly during the middle part of the arm pull. It also tends to happen during the last part of the

Fig. 4.15. *Another example of increased resistance*

In this picture the swimmer has let his forearm and hand get too close to his body. The water he is pushing backward against his body will increase his total resistance.

long arm pull after the turn in the breast-stroke. At the end of the backstroke pull there is a tendency for some swimmers to push the palms of their hands directly toward the upper legs instead of toward the bottom of the pool. As will be shown later, in Section 4.4, "Backstroke," this technique creates a turbulence against the legs and results in increased resistance.

SECTION 4.3
THE CRAWL STROKE

The prerequisite for understanding this and the next three sections (The Backstroke, The Butterfly, and The Breaststroke) is a good understanding of Section 4.2, "Principles Common to All Four Competitive Strokes." Once this has been accomplished, the materials in Sections 4.3-4.6 will become clear. An occasional rereading of Section 4.2 may also be helpful.

I have tried, insofar as possible, to use photographs and drawings of champion swimmers to illustrate and document the stroke mechanics that I advocate.

There are slight variations in the stroke mechanics of champion swimmers. For instance, some world record holders use a six-beat kick with the crawl stroke, while others use a two-beat crossover kick, and still others a straight two-beat kick. The same is true of slight variations in the pull pattern. Some crawl swimmers use an inverted-question-mark pull pattern, while some use an S-shaped pull pattern. The fact that such variations exist does not mean that each swimmer should be left alone to devise his own stroke mechanics. The swimmer must obey certain mechanical principles to swim efficiently. I will attempt to apply these mechanical principles to the stroke mechanics advocated in this section and will try to emphasize the important points and minimize the relatively unimportant factors. Anyone wishing to delve further into a more detailed account of the research and theory of stroke mechanics should read Chapter 5.

Figure 4.16 provides the reader with a mini-analysis of the important aspects of the crawl stroke mechanics.

Arm Recovery

There is a lot of confusion about where the pull finishes and where the recovery begins in the arm stroke. The arm recovery begins when the hand and forearm are still in the water. Many coaches and swimmers believe the hand is pushing backward during the entire time it is underwater; as a result, they also believe the hand should finish the underwater pull with a vigorous thrust backward and upward with a flip of the hand. Careful study of underwater films of champion crawl swimmers reveals that none of them does this, even though some have stated that they do. All, however, finish the pull and begin the recovery in the manner illustrated in Figure 4.16. The transition from the pull into the recovery occurs when the hand position changes. The momentum of the arm and hand, developed during the pull phase of the stroke, continues without interruption into the recovery phase, but at the end of the arm pull, the palm of the hand is positioned facing directly backward (Fig. 4.17A). During the transition from pull to recovery the palm of the hand starts to be turned inward, so that it faces the thigh (Figs. 4.17B and 4.17C). As the hand lifts upward, the little finger leaves the water first and the hand knifes out of the water, creating very little resistance (Fig. 4.17D).

A good way to describe this action is to liken it to sliding the hand out of a pants pocket.

The out-of-water arm recovery is made as the elbow lifts upward and is swung forward. Too little attention is paid to the out-of-water recovery phase of the total stroke. The often-repeated statement "The only part of the stroke that counts is what happens underwater" is an oversimplification of the complexities of stroke mechanics. A particular stroke defect prevalent among women swimmers is the use of the straight-arm recovery. In this type of recovery the elbow is not bent much, and the arm is carried over the water in a wide swinging movement (Fig. 4.18). This type of recovery results in excessive lateral movement of the body; the hips and legs wiggle back and forth sideways in an application of Newton's third law of motion: "For every action there is an equal and

Fig. 4.16. *The crawl-stroke arm-pull pattern*

1. *Zigzag pull*: On all competitive strokes some form of elliptical pull is used.

2. *Elbow bend*: Straight-bent-straight elbow action is used. Maximum elbow is 110 to 90 degrees.

3. *High elbow*: During first part of pull elbow is carried in an elbow-up position.

4. *Pitch of hands*: Hands are pitched 45 degrees as they enter water, so they create fewer air bubbles. They are also pitched as they leave so they create less resistance.

5. *Three types of kick* are used: (1) six-beat kick, (2) two-beat kick, and (3) two-beat crossover kick.

1. As one arm begins the pull with the elbow straight, the other arm begins its recovery by bending and lifting the elbow upward. The legs kick up and down in a flutter kick.

2. The pulling arm bends at the elbow. As it is pulled under the body the elbow is held high.

3. The pulling arm reaches maximum elbow bend as it passes under the shoulder and chest. Recovering arm enters the water directly in front of the shoulder.

4. As the arm pull nears completion, the head is rotated to the side for breathing.

5. Breath is taken as arm leaves water. Inhalation is through the month.

opposite reaction." This movement causes an increase in frontal and eddy resistance and slows the swimmer's progress.

When the arm is recovered properly, the elbow is bent and carried in a high position, with the hand being held close to the body. This action keeps the radius of rotation close to the body and results in less lateral displacement of the hips and legs (Figure 4.19).

Fig. 4.17. Olympic champion Jim Montgomery demonstrates the transition from the pull to the recovery phase of the arm stroke.

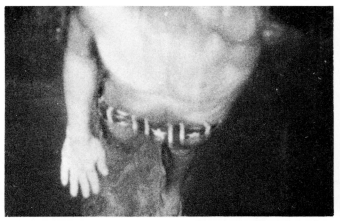

A. The hand, palm facing directly backward, and the arm are still in the pulling phase of the stroke.

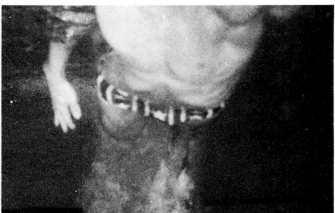

C. The palm is facing directly inward and the recovery phase has begun.

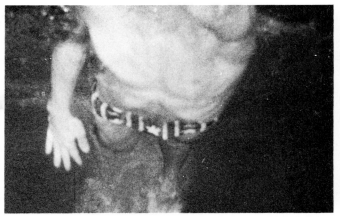

B. The hand and forearm start to rotate, with the palm facing diagonally inward toward the thigh. This is the point at which the pull ends and the recovery begins.

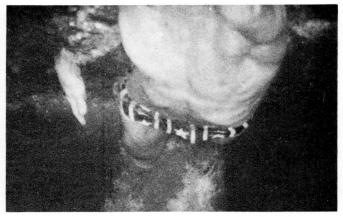

D. The forearm is completely out of the water, and the hand, with the little finger up and the thumb down, is ready to be lifted out of the water.

Fig. 4.18. Stroke defect

The wide arm recovery causes lateral movement of the hips and legs and increases resistance.

Fig. 4.19. *Arm recovery of world record holder Tim Shaw*
These pictures were taken during a race on the way to a world record.

A. As the finish of the pull occurs, the elbow is almost completely extended.

E. The fingertips enter the water about 12 inches in front of the head, with the elbow bent and carried in a high position.

B. As the arm is swung forward, the elbow bend increases.

F. As the hand goes underwater, the elbow is still out of water as it continues to extend.

C. The maximum elbow bend is reached as the hand passes the shoulder.

G. The hand is now several inches underwater, and the elbow is still not completely submerged.

D. As the hand is swung forward, the elbow starts to extend slightly.

H. The out-of-water recovery phase of the stroke is now completed. Underwater movies of Tim Shaw show that once submerged he fully extends his elbow before beginning his arm pull.

Common Mistakes in Arm Recovery

1. The most common mistake in arm-recovery technique is the one already mentioned: too wide an arm recovery (Fig. 4.18).

2. Swinging the hand too high—allowing the hand to swing so high that it is carried higher than the elbow—is another common stroke defect. It tends to cause body displacement, uses more energy, and may break the rhythm of the stroke (Fig. 4.20).

Fig. 4.20. *Stroke defect—carrying the hand too high during the recovery phase*

3. Breaking rhythm—this can be done either by excessive acceleration or deceleration of the arm during the recovery. It cannot be shown in a picture, but it can be noticed by observing the swimmer's arm recovery and watching for any jerky movements or any sudden changes in velocity during the recovery phase of the stroke. The most common cause of this break in rhythm is late breathing. The swimmer breathes so late in the stroke that he must rush his arm forward. More about this later.

Arm Pull

Hand Entry into the Water

As shown in Figure 4.19, the hand enters the water immediately before the elbow becomes fully extended.

Pitch of the Hand upon Entry

The hand is pitched so the palm is facing diagonally outward. If the hand is held flat in a horizontal position as it enters the water, it will drag air bubbles underwater with it. Such air entrapment decreases the efficiency of the pull and should be avoided. By positioning the hand's entrance into the water with the palm held at approximately a 45-degree angle to the surface—the thumb entering first—the hand can become submerged underwater without dragging a lot of air with it (Figs. 4.21 and 4.22).

Fig. 4.21. *Correct entry of the hand into the water*. A world record holder is shown as his right hand enters the water. Notice that the palm of the hand is not held in a flat position but is knifed into the water in a diagonal position. This permits the hand to become submerged without much air entrapment.

Fig. 4.22. *The pitch of the right hand as it appears from underneath the surface*

The Underwater Pull

The underwater pull is a complex movement which I will describe first in a very general manner, analyzing each aspect of it later.

In the process of discussing the pull, I want to dispel a common misconception that the hands and arms should be pulled in a straight line directly underneath the body. I have photographed many swimmers, and while they use a variety of elliptical pull patterns, they never pull in a perfect straight-line pattern. Figure 4.29 shows the elliptical pull pattern of a champion swimmer. Some swimmers may use a variation of this pattern in which the pattern may assume more of an *S* shape. The width of the pattern may also vary slightly from one swimmer to the next, due perhaps to variations in strength, flexibility, or other factors of which we are not cognizant. (See p. 156.)

Another common misconception is that the elbows should be kept straight during the pull. The pull begins with the elbow straight or almost straight, but during the pulling phase, it bends in the manner shown in Figures 4.16 and 4.24.

The Beginning of the Arm Pull

Once the hand and arm become completely submerged, the palm of the hand is turned from the diagonal position by rotation of the forearm, the action occurring between the radius and ulna bones. As soon as the swimmer starts his pull he should concentrate on bending the elbow immediately (Fig. 4.23).

Wrist Flexion during the Beginning of the Pull

During the very beginning of the pull in movies of such great swimmers as Mark Spitz, Jim Montgomery, and John Murphy, I have noticed a marked flexion of the wrist. This places the palm of the hand in a favorable position to push the water backward at a better angle than if the wrist were to remain in straight alignment. This wrist flexion is shown in Figure 4.23 along with the elbow

bend. I make our swimmers aware of this action and have them try to flex the wrist as they bend the elbow.

Fig. 4.23. *Wrist flexion during the first part of the pull*

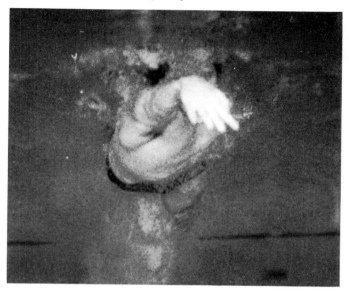

A. As the pull begins, the wrist should flex.

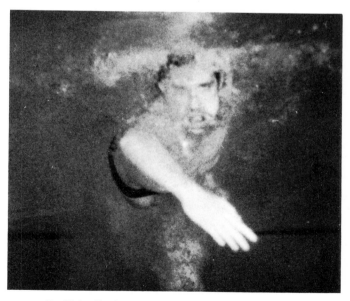

B. Wrist flexion plus elbow bend place the hand in a good position to push water backward.

Elbow Bend during the Pull

As the arm is pulled down and back, the bend in the elbow increases until it reaches maximum bend when the hand is directly under the body and the upper arm is at a 90-degree angle with the body (Figs. 4.24C and 4.25). From this point backward the hand is pushed backward by extension of the

Fig. 4.24. *Front underwater view of Mark Spitz's crawl stroke*

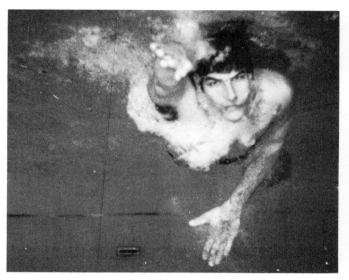

A. The right hand has just entered the water, with the palm turned diagonally outward in order not to entrap air bubbles.

C. As the pull is made, the elbow starts to bend. Note that the water line is not at the forehead, but several inches above the hairline. Air bubbles are being gently exhaled from the mouth.

B. The palm of the hand is turned to face down and back. The wrist is flexed.

D. As the arm is pressed downward, the elbow bend is increased and the arm is carried in a high elbow position (over-the-barrel pull).

elbow until, at the end of the pull, the elbow reaches almost complete extension.

For a careful analysis of the arm pull of Mark Spitz, winner of seven gold medals in the 1972 Olympic Games, study Figure 4.24 carefully.

E. The elbow bend continues. Notice that the eyes are open.

G. The pull is over half completed, and the head starts to turn to the side in preparation for inhalation. The exhalation of the air underwater increases as the head continues to turn to the side.

F. The pull is half completed and the fingertips of the hand across the center line of the body. The elbow bend is 90 degrees at this point. From this point backward, the elbow will be extended. Air begins to be forceably exhaled from the nose.

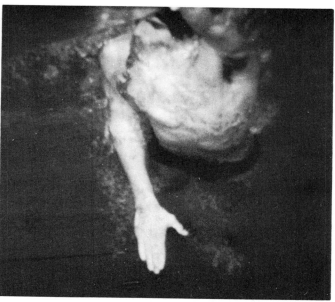

H. The wrist extends in order that the palm may continue to face backward. The amount of air being exhaled increases.

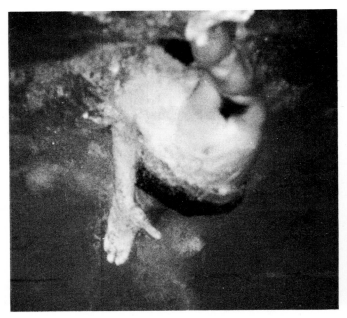

I. The hand is nearing completion of the pull. The face is turned sideward and is now out of water. The inhalation (not shown) begins.

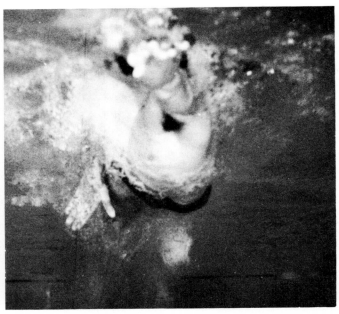

K. The hand continues to turn, with the little finger up and the thumb down.

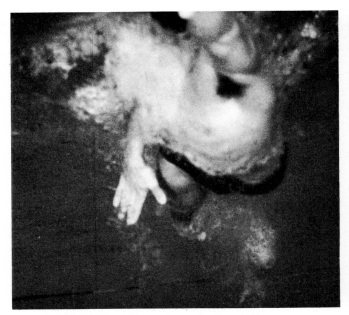

J. The transition from the pull to the recovery begins as the palm starts to turn inward to face the thigh.

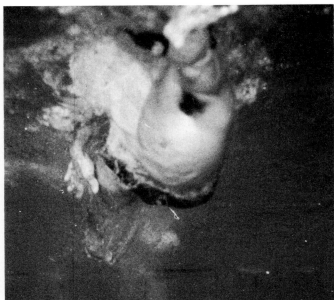

L. The underwater portion of the arm recovery nears completion as the hand lifts out of water as if it were being lifted out of the pants pocket, with the little finger exiting first.

Summary: Study these pictures carefully. They illustrate many important principles. Review the following phases of the stroke.

1. Elbow bend: When does it start and how does it vary during different phases of the stroke?

2. Breathing: When does exhalation start and when does the head begin to turn to the side in preparation for inhalation?

3. What position is the head carried in?

4. What is the pitch of the hands at various phases of the pull? What direction is the palm of the hand facing during the entry of the hand in the water? during the exit? during the pull?

Elbow-Bend Variation

Included in this section is a series of pictures of a number of championship-caliber swimmers taken from different angles in order that the reader may perceive the variety of pull patterns that may function efficiently without disregarding the mechanical principles that prevail. Figure 4.25 shows the underwater pull of three world-record-holder female swimmers.

Fig. 4.25. *The underwater arm pull of three world-champion girl swimmers.* The pictures are taken from 35-mm sequence pictures and were shot when approximately half of the arm pull was completed.

B. *Jenny Turrall.* World record holder at the 800- and 1500-meter distances, she has a slightly wider pull than Babashof, but both use a 90-degree maximum elbow bend.

C. *Kornelia Ender.* World record holder for 100 meters, she uses a wider pull than any record holder I have photographed. Kornelia carries her arm in a very high elbow position during the pull. The angle between her forearm and upper arm never reaches 90 degrees, but stops at 103 degrees before extension begins.

Summary: Observation of the above pictures may make the reader question if there is a particular pull pattern or style of stroke mechanics that is the best for everyone. I believe that there are and should be slight differences. However, I also believe Kornelia Ender's pull (Fig. 4.25 C) is too wide and that she would swim faster with her arms pulled in a pattern that extended farther under her body. From observing underwater movies of many swimmers I believe that either for anatomical reasons or from lack of strength most women swimmers do and perhaps should use a wider pull than their male counterparts.

A. *Shirley Babashof.* A world record holder is shown on her way to a new world record. Every third stroke her arm swings under her body as show above. On the other two strokes her arms are pulled in a wider arc. She breathes every third stroke, and it is during this stroke that her pull crosses the center line of the body.

Figure 4.26 shows the half-completed pull of some champion male swimmers at the point at which maximum elbow bend should occur. A comparison of these pictures with those of the women in Figure 4.25 reveals that the men tend to pull their arms farther under their bodies. Various angles are presented in order that the reader may acquire a correct impression of the proper positioning of the arm.

Fig. 4.26. *Elbow bend of some champion male swimmers*

A. *Olympic champion Jim Montgomery.* Elbow bend of 90 degrees.

B. *World record holder Tim Shaw.* The angle between the upper arm and forearm forms an angle of 105 degrees at its maximum bend. The angle of the other arm is 97 degrees.

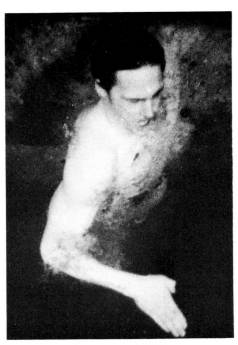

C. *John Kinsella.* The angle between John's forearm and upper arm on both arms is about 90 degrees.

D. *Peter Sintz.* Crawl stroke as seen from head-on.

E.

G.

F.

H.

E,F,G,H, *John Murphy*. These four pictures show
various views of John's arm pull.

Common Mistakes in the Arm Pull

1. Pulling with too little bend in the elbow—compare Figure 4.27 with Figure 4.26.

2. Pulling the arms outside the body too wide—this defect is shown in Figure 4.25C (Kornelia Ender's arm pull).

3. Pulling too far across the midline of the body (Fig. 4.28).

Fig. 4.27. *Stroke defect—pulling with too little bend in the elbow*

Fig. 4.28. *Stroke defect—pulling the hand too far across the body*

In this picture the left hand has pulled so far across the body that the fingertips are outside of a line on the opposite side of the body.

Pull Pattern

The hand is pulled through the water in some form of elliptical pattern as shown in Figure 4.29. This pull may appear to be almost straight-line, but the reader must remember that the pull is three- not two-dimensional.

Fig. 4.29. *The pull pattern of Don Schollander.*

The path of the middle finger of the hand is traced throughout the pull.

A better representation of the actual pull pattern of a swimmer is shown in Figure 4.30. These pictures were taken with the swimmer wearing a flashing light on the middle finger of each hand. The lights flashed at a rate of 20 per second. The swimmer swam in total darkness, and the lens of the camera was left open. A strobe light was flashed at one point in the stroke, and an image of the swimmer's body was thus exposed on the film, as well as all of the flashes of the blinking light.

Fig. 4.30. *The pull pattern of Rick Thomas's crawl stroke*. A flashing light has been placed on the middle finger of each hand.

A. The head-on view shows the zigzag pull pattern as seen from in front.

B. The side view shows how little the swimmer actually pulls his arm backward.

High Elbow Position

The elbow should be carried in a high position during the first half of the pull. This permits the hand to be in a good position to push the water backward at an efficient angle. This action is accomplished through two

separate movements of the upper arm and the elbow. The upper arm is rotated inwardly (medially) and the elbow is simultaneously bent, placing the arm in the position shown in Figure 4.31.

Fig. 4.31. *High elbow action during the first part of the pull*

A. Head-on view

B. Side view

Figure 4.32 is a sequence of pictures of matching side and head-on shots of Jenny Turrall. Her arm action is notable for the high elbow position she maintains during the first half of her pull.

Fig. 4.32. *High elbow arm action of world record holder Jenny Turrall*

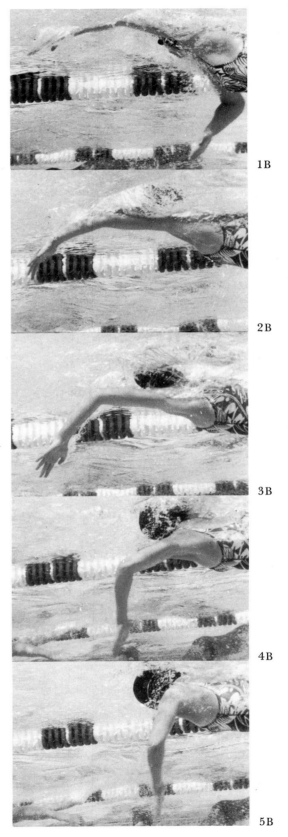

1A

2A

3A

4A

5A

1B

2B

3B

4B

5B

The mistake most commonly seen in poor swimmers is the dropped elbow during the pull, as shown in Figure 4.33. This type of pull does not permit a good application of force. Due to poor positioning of the hand, the direction of the force is downward and not backward, resulting in little forward thrust.

Fig. 4.33. *Stroke defect—a dropped elbow*

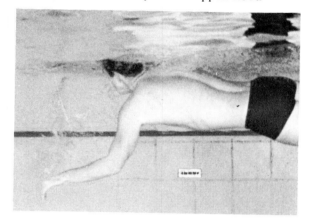

Head Position

A great deal of misunderstanding prevails concerning the position in which the head should be carried. A careful study of the underwater pictures in this section will give the reader a good idea of the proper placement of the head. The head should not be carried in a high position with the water line striking the swimmer at the forehead, but should be lower so as to achieve a more streamlined position. Figure 4.34 depicts a swimmer who is carrying his head too high.

Fig. 4.34. *Stroke defect—carrying the head too high out of water.* The head is so high that the water line is at the forehead.

Fig. 4.35. *Correct placement of the head*

Tim Shaw carries his head noticeably lower than the swimmer in Fig. 4.34. The bow wave formed in front of his head is followed by a concavity in the water, referred to as a trough. Proper placement of the head places the mouth and nose so the swimmer can breathe at the bottom of the trough without having to turn his head too far to the side. Also note the desirable bend in the recovery arm.

The swimmer in Figure 4.35, Tim Shaw, carries his head in an ideal position with the waterline at the correct position. Proper placement of the head permits the swimmer to breathe at the bottom of the bow wave. Carrying the head too high (Fig. 4.34) causes a slight drop of the hips and increases drag or resistance. In addition it places the head in a position such that when the swimmer turns his head to breathe, his mouth will be in the bow wave. He will then have to turn his head farther to the side than he would have to do if his head were lower.

Breathing

The air is inhaled in the very short period of time that the mouth is out of the water. As seen in Figure 4.24, the underwater sequence of Mark Spitz, the air is exhaled almost continuously during the time the face is underwater. The air is forced gently out of the mouth during the first part of the exhalation. During the last part of the underwater exhalation, exhalation becomes more vigorous as air bubbles can be seen leaving the nose as well as the mouth. The final exhalation is a sudden push of air out of the mouth as the mouth breaks the surface. This action forces the drops of water away from the lips so the swimmer can inhale without sucking in water.

One formerly held opinion about breathing that has recently been revived is that of "explosive breathing." I would like to suggest the reasons that this is not a beneficial method. In this technique the breath is held during most of the time the head is underwater and then is forcibly exhaled in a violent explosion of air immediately before the mouth leaves the water. This method of breathing was first advocated forty years ago and has been rejuvenated by coaches who want to develop a "new" technique. It provides poor ventilation and causes too much tension in the breathing muscles. The rhythmical breathing method used by Mark Spitz and described above is the preferred type of inhaling and exhaling.

A common defect in breathing concerns the timing of the head movement with relation to the arm stroke. In Figure 4.36 Mark Spitz is shown using the correct timing in coordinating the head movement with the arm pull. The breath (inhalation) should be taken when the body is at its maximum roll to the side. This point occurs when the hand on the breathing side is beginning its recovery. Figure 4.37 illustrates the correct timing of the breathing in the arm stroke. Figure 4.38 depicts a stroke defect, that of late breathing.

Fig. 4.36. *Mark Spitz's crawl stroke at the time of inhalation*

In this photo of Mark's crawl his head placement is excellent. His mouth is open and he is breathing near the bottom of his bow wave. One arm is being recovered with the elbow bent and carried high.

Fig. 4.37. *Two-time Olympic champion Mike Burton demonstrates good timing of inhalation and arm action.*

Fig. 4.38. *Stroke defect—late breathing.* The swimmer is breathing so late in his stroke that the forward action of his arm is pushing his face under water.

Body Roll

The body rolls 35 to 45 degrees on each side as the swimmer makes a complete arm cycle. The swimmer rolls more on the side on which he breathes than on the nonbreathing side. He should not roll intentionally, but he should allow the roll to come as a natural reaction to other parts of his stroke. He also should not try to swim flat and inhibit the roll.

The Kick

Swimmers use various types of kick with the crawl stroke. In 1976 I photographed all of the swimmers in every freestyle event in the United States World Games Trials. I came up with the following data: In the finals of the men's 100-meter freestyle seven of the eight swimmers used a six-beat kick with their strokes, and the eighth used a two-beat crossover kick. This was also true in the case of the women's 100-meter freestyle; seven of the finalists used a six-beat kick, but the

winner, Shirley Babashof, used a straight two-beat kick. In the finals of the men's 1500-meter freestyle, the winner, Tim Shaw, as well as six of the eight finalists, used the two-beat crossover kick, while only one swimmer, Mike Bruner, used a six-beat kick. In the women's 800-meter freestyle event, seven of the finalists used the straight two-beat kick, and only one of the finalists used a six-beat kick.

It would appear from these data that the six-beat kick is better adapted for sprinting, and the two-beat kick for distance swimming. Indeed this seems to be true. This may be due to the fact that in a distance race the heart cannot continue to supply enough blood to the arms and legs. The swimmer may therefore automatically modify his kick to make blood readily available to the main source of propulsion—the arms—or it may be that the swimmer who adopts this style of kicking tends to be more successful in distance events due at least partially to the fact that he has made more blood available to his arms.

Some swimmers have the ability to switch back and forth from a two-beat to a six-beat kick. Ken Knox and Tom Hickcox are two swimmers on the Indiana Team who do so. Others can swim only with the two-beat kick (Tim Shaw, Jenny Turrall, Steve Holland, and Shirley Babashof), and still others use only the six-beat kick (Mark Spitz, Kornelia Ender, Jim Montgomery).

At the World Games Trials to which I referred earlier we found only a few swimmers who could use both types of kick. The data are given in Table 4.1.

Table 4.1
Swimmers Using Two-Beat or Six-Beat Kick

	Used Only Two-Beat Crossover Kick	Used Only Straight Two-Beat Kick	Used Only Six-Beat Kick	Could Use Either
Men	43%	2%	48%	7%
Women	1%	52%	30%	17%

No matter what kick is used in the stroke, it is hard to practice anything but the straight flutter kick on the kickboard in conditioning drills. Figure 4.39 shows a sequence of the flutter kick as practiced in kicking drills.

Fig. 4.39. *Flutter kick as performed in kicking drills*

The knee is kept straight on the upbeat and is bent on the downbeat. On the downbeat the pressure of the water forces the ankles to hyperextend. The more flexible the ankles, the more effective the kick.

The Two-Beat Crossover Kick

This kick is used most by men swimmers; the straight two-beat kick predominates among women. In this stroke one kick is given by each leg during each arm pull. This gives a total of two kicks per complete arm cycle. During part of the kicking phase one leg crosses on top of the other, and during the next kick the position of the two legs is reversed.

Figure 4.40 pictures the two-beat crossover kick as seen from the back. The timing of the kick is probably tied in with the arm recovery, although this is a source of controversy. The timing ends up the same for all swimmers, and the swimmers using it need not worry about the timing, since they will automatically fall into the correct pattern.

The Straight Two-Beat Kick

Swimmers using the straight two-beat kick also use only two beats of the kick per arm cycle (one stroke per arm). In this case the legs do not cross on top of each other, but kick almost straight up and down.

Which of the two kicks is the better for a swimmer to use? I don't know if this question can be answered or if it has a definitive answer. Some coaches have speculated that the straight two-beat kick is superior to the two-beat crossover kick because the crossover action is wasted motion. I feel the crossover action of the legs may serve some purpose such as cancelling out the reaction of the arm recovery and in this way preserving body alignment. The fact that few men use the straight two-beat kick and few women use the two-beat crossover kick implies the responsibility of some anatomical difference or the role of some variation in buoyancy, flexibility, or strength.

Both of these kicks contain a definite pause when there is no movement of the legs. In the two-beat crossover kick the pause occurs when the feet are crossed one on top of the other and are in a streamlined position. In the straight two-beat kick the pause occurs when the feet are at their farthest spread. The pause at this point would seem to cause an increase in drag and therefore be detrimental. As I have watched the kick in underwater movies, however, I have gained the impression that the pause of the legs in this drag position serves the purpose of ruddering or holding the body in position, possibly to maintain good alignment and to prevent wiggling. Research and some good conceptual thinking of the fluid mechanics of the two types of kick are needed to answer these questions.

Fig. 4.40. *The two-beat crossover kick*

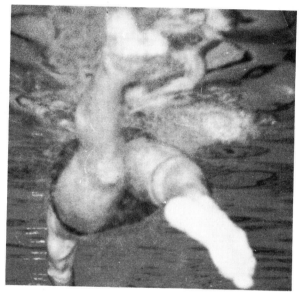

A. The legs are at their maximum spread.

B. The right leg kicks down and inward on top of the left leg, while the left leg kicks up and inward. Together they assume a crossed position.

The Six-Beat Kick

In a six-beat kick, each leg completes three kicks for a total of six kicks per arm cycle. This method appears to be used more by sprinters, even though some world-class sprinters have used either form of the two-beat kick (Shirley Babashof, Michael Wenden). The timing of the kick into the arm stroke also occurs automatically; the swimmer need not think about it. In fact, the timing is so precise and occurs so fast that it would be almost impossible for the swimmer to think of it and react quickly enough to coordinate these movements consciously.

The timing of the leg and arm strokes that all types of crawl strokes have in common is illustrated in Figure 4.41. These three pictures reveal that the downward thrust of the kick occurs during the end of the arm pull. This happens with nearly all champion swimmers. The purpose of this timing is to allow the downward thrust of the kick to counteract and neutralize the tendency of the last part of the arm pull to pull the swimmer underwater.

Fig. 4.41. *Timing of the arms and legs in the three types of kick*

B. A straight two-beat-kick crawl swimmer is shown finishing the pull of her left arm, and the left leg is kicking downward.

A. A two-beat crossover crawl swimmer is shown completing the pull of his left arm, at which time the left leg is kicking downward.

C. A six-beat crawl swimmer is shown completing the pull of his left arm; his left leg is also kicking downward.

Eyes—Open or Shut?

A careful examination of both the out-of-water and underwater pictures of crawl swimmers in this section will show the reader that champion swimmers keep their eyes open, both under and out of water. This is the desirable technique and should be followed by all swimmers. There is a brief period in which the eyes close as the swimmer's eyes enter or leave the water. This is due to the "blinking" reflex. Today's competitive swimmers do most of their training while wearing goggles to prevent eye irritation. It is a good policy for swimmers to practice without goggles some of the time in order to learn to keep their eyes open without goggles, as described above.

Acceleration of Arms during the Stroke

The hands do not move at a constant rate during the pulling phase of the stroke. When the catch or the beginning of the pull is made, the speed of the hands is relatively slow. As the pull begins to overcome the inertia of the body, the hands accelerate. A more detailed description of the acceleration phases of the pull can be found in Chapter 5 (Section 5.3), "A Biomechanical Analysis of the Freestyle Aquatic Skill."

Poor swimmers will often either lunge into the pull too fast and get too much acceleration at the beginning of the pull and too little acceleration later in the stroke or, in some cases, will make the entire pull with no acceleration, maintaining the same speed throughout.

SECTION 4.4
THE BACKSTROKE

Before beginning this section, another reading of Section 4.2 might be helpful. There is also more detailed information about the mechanical aspects of the swimming strokes to be found in Chapter 5.

The backstroke rules state that the swimmer must start the race in the water and must swim the race entirely on his back (see Section 4.7 for information on the backstroke starts and turns).

Figure 4.42 presents a mini-analysis of the important considerations of the backstroke mechanics.

Recovery

The arm recovery begins while the hand and arm are still in the water. There is a transition from the pull to the recovery which is shown in Figure 4.43. This sequence pictures Olympic medalist Mike Stamm pushing downward at the finish of his arm pull (A). This downward push causes the body to roll and results in the shoulder being elevated out of the water for the recovery (D and E). After the downward push of the hand (B), the palm is turned inward to face the thigh, thumb upward, and the recovery begins (C). The hand breaks the surface with the thumb leading the rest of the hand. Many swimmers push deeper at the end of the pull than does the swimmer in Figure 4.43.

Fig. 4.42. *The backstroke arm-pull pattern*

1. *The S pull*: All backstrokers should use some form of S pull pattern.

2. *Elbow bend*: Use straight-bent-straight pull elbow action—maximum elbow bend 90 to 110 degrees.

3. *Inverted high elbow*: Carry elbow in an inverted high elbow position during first part of pull.

4. *Pitch of hands*: Enter hands in water, little finger first, at 90-degree angle to prevent entrapment of air bubles. Pitch hands so thumb leaves water first in order to create less resistance.

1. The arm has just entered the water at a point directly over the shoulder. The legs are kicked up and downward in the flutter kick.

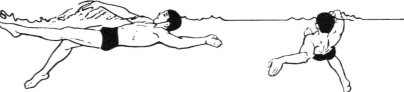

2. The left arm sinks downward as the pull begins and while the right arm starts its recovery directly upward.

3. The elbow of the pulling arm continues to bend as it is pulled backward. The recovering arm recovers directly upward.

4. The pulling arm pushes back and downward, while the legs continue their flutter kick.

5. The pull ends with the palms pressing water toward the bottom of the pool, while the recovering arm enters the water in a line directly over the shoulder.

Fig. 4.43. *The transition from the pull phase to recovery phase of the arm stroke*

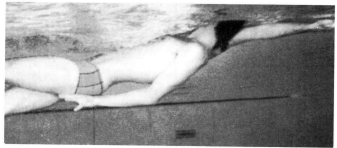

A

B

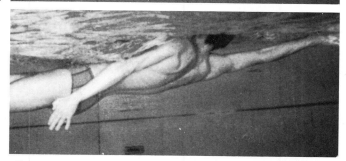

C

D

E

Figure 4.44 shows the depth of the hand at the end of the pull and at the beginning of the recovery phase of two world-ranked backstrokers.

The out-of-water recovery is made with a straight elbow. The arm is swung directly upward and forward in a vertical plane. Figure 4.46 depicts the arm recovery of Mike Stamm.

Fig. 4.44. *Depth of hand at the beginning of the underwater arm recovery phase of two champion swimmers*

A. Ulrike Richter, world record holder

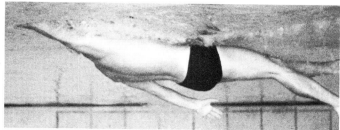

B. Tom Stock

Figure 4.45 shows the correct arm recovery of two swimmers during the 200-meter backstroke race at the 1975 World Games.

Fig. 4.45. *Correct arm recovery of two backstrokers during the 200-meter event in the World Games*

Fig. 4.46. *Arm recovery of Mike Stamm*

A. The arm breaks the water and is lifted straight upward with no bend in the elbow.

B and C. The arm continues upward.

D, E and F. The arm rotates so the palm faces diagonally outward.

G and H. The arm enters the water directly over the shoulder. The hand is turned so the little finger enters the water first.

Common Mistakes in Arm Recovery

1. The most common mistake in arm-recovery technique is bending the elbow at the end of the recovery. This places the hand in a position in front of the opposite shoulder instead of directly over the shoulder when it enters the water (Fig. 4.47). This detrimentally affects the arm pull.

Fig. 4.47. *Stroke defects*

A. Arm entering water, with elbow bent and arm crossed in front of the head. The palm is not facing sideward but diagonally upward.

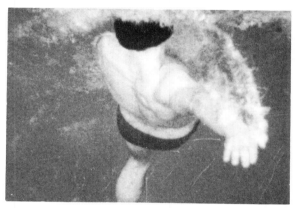

B. This type of hand entry pulls air after the hand, decreasing pull efficiency.

2. Allowing the hand to enter the water with the palm facing upward and the back of the hand striking the water first (Fig. 4.47 A). This action causes air entrapment (Fig. 4.47 B) and decreases pulling efficiency. To prevent the entrapment of air behind the hand, the hand should knife into the water with the little finger first and the hand held in a vertical position.

3. Recovering the arm over the water in a

wide swinging motion and not directly upward in a vertical plane.

4. Breaking rhythm during the recovery. The recovery should be made with a smooth, almost constant rhythm. Some swimmers rush or accelerate the movement too much, while others break rhythm by slowing the natural flow of the movement.

Arm Pull

It is very important for the swimmer to check constantly that his hand is pitched in a vertical position as it knifes out of the water, with the thumb leaving the water first, and that the hand enters the water pitched in a vertical position with the little finger entering the water first. This puts the hand in a good position to begin the arm pull. Figure 4.48 shows the correct technique of both hands of a world record holder.

Fig. 4.48. *Correct hand entry into and exit from the water of a world champion*

The arm pull begins after the arm has entered the water and sunk to a depth of 8 to 12 inches. Figure 4.49 shows the arm pull of Olympic medalist Mike Stamm. The pull starts with the elbow straight. As the arm is pulled down and back the elbow starts to bend. The elbow bend increases as the arm is pulled backward. The maximum bend of 90 to 100 degrees is reached when the arm has completed half of the pull. During the last half of the pull the elbow is extending until, at the end of the pull, the elbow is fully extended.

Fig. 4.49. *Arm stroke of Olympic*
silver medalist Mike Stamm

A. The right hand has just finished its pull and is starting to be recovered upward, with the palm facing inward and the thumb up. The left arm, elbow straight, has just entered the water, little finger first.

B. The left hand continues to sink with no bend in the elbow.

C. The hand, palm facing outward, continues to sink with no apparent bend in the elbow.

D. The elbow starts to bend as the arm is pulled down and backward.

E. The elbow bend continues to increase with the arm at maximum depth.

F. The body roll is apparent in the plane of the shoulder which at this point is 45° from the horizontal.

G. The arm reaches its maximum elbow bend of 90° at this point. The pull is half completed.

H. The elbow begins to extend as the hand enters the second half of its pull.

I. The hand reaches the highest point in the S pull pattern and from this point will start to push downward.

J. The downward push of the hand begins.

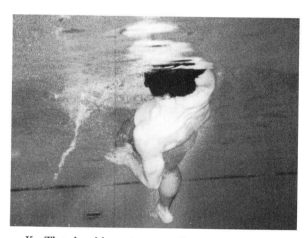

K. The shoulders start to roll toward the horizontal plane as the hand continues to push downward.

L. The finish of the pull is completed with the final push of the hand downward as the shoulders roll toward the horizontal plane.

During the first half of the pull the upper arm is rotated medially. This rotation and the elbow bend place the arm in the inverted "elbow-up" position. I use this term because it corresponds to the terms *high elbow* and *elbow-up* used to describe this action in the other three strokes. The action here is similar, but, of course, the swimmer is on his back instead of on his chest. Figure 4.50 shows the inverted elbow-up arm position.

Fig. 4.50. *Inverted elbow-up arm position during the first part of the pull*

Maximum Elbow Bend

The maximum bend in the elbow should be from 90 to 100 degrees. Figure 4.51 shows the elbow bend at this point of three world-class swimmers.

Fig. 4.51. *Maximum elbow bend of three world-class backstrokers*

A. Roland Matthes

B. Ulrike Richter

C. John Murphy

Backstroke Arm-Pull Pattern

The backstroke arm-pull pattern as seen from the side under water describes an S pattern. Figure 4.52 pictures the pull pattern of an Olympic silver medalist. The elbow bend and early part of the pull pattern are good, but the finish of the pull is probably too deep, extending as it does over one foot lower than the hips. The pull pattern as depicted by the flashing-light photographic technique described in Section 4.2 is shown in Figure 4.53 A and B. The light tracings show the true path of the hand through the water. We have found that all good backstrokers produce a light-tracing pattern similar to those shown in Figure 4.53.

Fig. 4.52. *Backstroke S arm-pull pattern of an Olympic silver medalist*

Fig. 4.53. *Backstroke pull-pattern tracing as recorded by the flashing-light photographic technique*

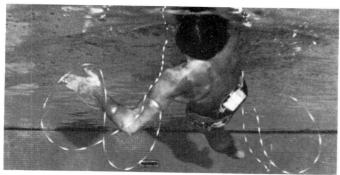

A. Rick Thomas as seen from head-on

B. Rick Thomas, sideview

Fig. 4.54. *Light tracings of another world-class backstroker*

Figure 4.54 is the pull-pattern light tracing of another world-class backstroker who pulls more shallowly than the swimmer in Figure 4.53. The difference in the patterns is apparent.

Common Mistakes in the Arm Pull of the Backstroke

1. The most common mistake is that of pulling with a straight elbow (Fig. 4.55).
2. Pulling with a straight-line pull and not using the S pull pattern.
3. Dropping the elbow and not using the inverted high-elbow action.
4. Not finishing with a downward push at the end of the pull.

Fig. 4.55. *Stroke defect—pulling with a straight arm*

The Kick

The six-beat flutter kick is used by nearly all backstroke swimmers. The swimmer should practice flutter-kick drills by lying on his back in the water with his arms extended overhead and with his hands clasped together. The head is held back, with the ears in the water and the chest elevated. The swimmer should try as much as possible to imitate the exact body position he will assume when he swims. When performing the flutter kick, the swimmer should try to keep his legs straight on the downbeat and bent on the upbeat. This is exactly the opposite of the action in the crawl flutter kick, but, once again, the swimmer is inverted and actually the kick is the same. Figure 4.56 shows the backstroke kick from in-back.

Fig. 4.56. *The backstroke flutter kick*
as performed in kicking drills

A. The right (bottom) leg is at the lowest point of the kick and the left (top) leg is at the highest point.

C. The right leg continues upward with increasing extension (plantar flexion) of the ankle, while the left leg, still straight, continues downward.

B. The right leg starts upward with a bent knee as the left leg kicks downward with the leg completely straight. Notice the ankle on the bottom foot is starting to extend due to the pressure of the water against it.

D. The right leg, toed inward, passes the left leg as the knee starts to extend.

E. The right leg is close to extension as it nears the top of its upbeat. The left leg bends as it nears the bottom of its downbeat.

F. The kick is completed. The right leg will now start downward and the left leg upward.

Timing of the Arms and Legs

The correct timing of the arms and legs in the backstroke occurs automatically in the average swimmer. It is the result of the evolvement of an action-reaction pattern. During the second half of the arm pull the hand will be pulling the hips to that side. To keep the hips from being pulled sideways the swimmer kicks his leg diagonally sideways on the upbeat to cancel the distorting influence influence of the pull. This is exactly what is happening in Figure 4.57 A and B. In both illustrations the left hand is about to start into the second half of its pull and the right leg is positioning itself to kick diagonally upward and inward.

Fig. 4.57. *Timing of arm pull and leg kick*

A

B

In both illustrations the left arm is starting to go into the second half of the pull, and the right leg is positioning itself so it can kick upward and diagonally.

Head Position and Breathing

The head should be carried so the ears are slightly submerged and the water line breaks approximately at the middle of the head. The head position to a great extent determines the body position. Laying or tilting the head farther back in the water will raise the hips, while dropping the chin down on the chest will lower the hips. There is some variation in the position in which the head should be carried for each swimmer. If the swimmer is very buoyant, he should carry his head with the chin tucked slightly in toward the chest. This will help to keep his hips from rising too high in the water, thereby causing the feet to break the water excessively during the kick. If the swimmer is below average in buoyancy, he may have to lay or tilt his head back slightly more than shown in Figure 4.58. This will tend to keep his hips and legs from sinking too low in the water and creating too much drag.

Fig. 4.58. *Correct head position*

Air should be inhaled through the mouth and exhaled through the mouth and nose. It should be inhaled on the recovery of one arm and exhaled on the recovery of the other. This pattern of breathing ensures that the swimmer will not be panting or merely taking a series of short breaths.

Body Roll

The body rolls almost 45 degrees to each side in the backstroke. This maximum roll occurs when one arm is half through the pull and the other arm is in the middle of its recovery, as in Figure 4.57. The purpose of the roll is two-fold: (1) to permit the recovering arm to recover high over the water without creating a lot of drag as it moves forward, and (2) to facilitate a stronger pull. The greater the angle between the shoulder and the arm, the weaker the arm depressors become. If the swimmer tries to swim with his shoulders flat, he will have to pull his arms in a shallow pull pattern and will have a poor application of force. He will also create more drag when he recovers his arms. The swimmer should not force his roll but should rely on the downward push of his hand at the end of the arm pull to give him the desired 45-degree roll to each side.

SECTION 4.5
THE BUTTERFLY

The butterfly is swum with both arms recovered over the water, while the legs kick upward and downward in a dolphin or fishtail kick. Two kicks of the legs are completed with each arm cycle. It is important for swimmers to remember that the rules state that the action of the arms must be similar and simultaneous. This is also true of the leg action.

Section 4.2 contains much background information which will help to gain an understanding of the stroke mechanics that will be discussed in this section. Chapter 5 also contains more advanced material on stroke mechanics that will give the reader further information.

Figure 4.60 provides a mini-analysis of the butterfly stroke (see p. 178).

The Arm Recovery

The rules state that the arms must be recovered out of the water in the butterfly stroke. The arm recovery actually begins underwater, as in Figure 4.60.

The arm recovery of Mark Spitz is shown in Figure 4.59. This is a good picture of the correct mechanics of the arm recovery. The arms are swung in a flat line close to the water, yet they are not dragging through the water. The elbows are almost straight and there appears to be no tension in the arms. They are not totally relaxed, but display some controlled tension. The chin is carried low next to the water and Mark is not climbing high out of the water. He is ending his inhalation, and as his arms swing forward from this position, his head will drop under water.

The arms are recovered sideways over the water. The elbows should be fully extended (Mark had a tendency to bend the right elbow slightly, as shown here). The inhalation is being made as the arms swing forward. As soon as the arms swing forward in a line even with the shoulders, the inhalation will end and the head will be tilted downward with the face going under water.

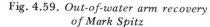

Fig. 4.59. *Out-of-water arm recovery of Mark Spitz*

Fig. 4.60. *The butterfly arm-pull pattern*

1. *Hourglass pull*: Do not pull in a straight line, but use an hourglass or keyhole pull pattern.

2. *Elbow bend*: Use straight-bent-straight elbow action—maximum elbow bend of 90 to 110 degrees.

3. *Pitch of hands*: Pitch hands at 45 degrees as they enter water, so they create fewer air bubles. Pitch hands as they leave the water so they create less resistance.

4. *Kick*: Use two-beat kick. Keep legs straight on upbeat, bent on downbeat.

1. The arms enter the water at shoulder width with the elbows straight. The feet kick downward in the first kick.

2. The hands press in an outward and downward direction with the elbows held high and kept bent.

3. The hands almost come together under the chest and the elbows are bent at right angles.

4. As the arms finish the pull, the second kick is made and the breath is taken.

5. The arms are recovered over the water and the head is lowered so the face is down.

Fig. 4.61. *Transition from the pull phase
to the recovery phase of the butterfly arm stroke
of Gary Hall*

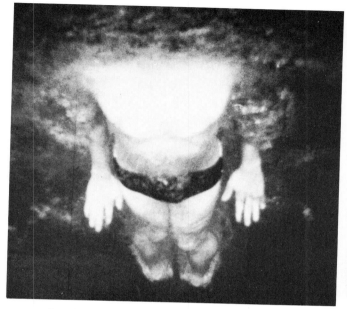

A. The arm pull is about to end as the hands, palms backward, are still pushing backward.

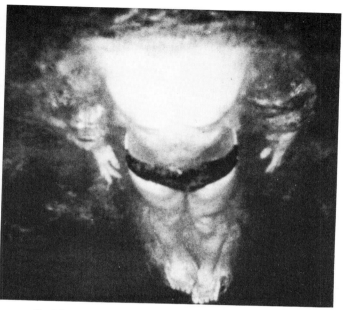

C. The palms turn inward as they are lifted out of the water.

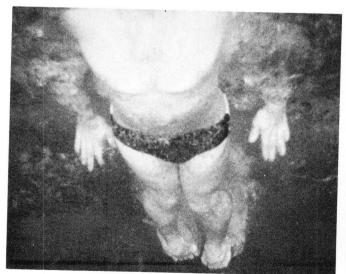

B. The arms are completely out of the water except for the hands.

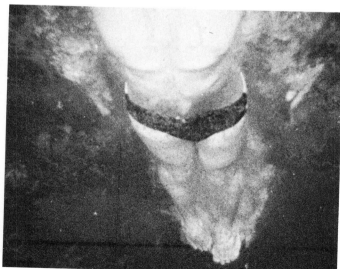

D. Fingertips leave the water last.

A. The inhalation of air begins even before the arms are out of the water.

E. The arms have almost half-completed their recovery, and the face starts to sink into the water.

B. The arms are swung forward out of the water as the inhalation continues.

F. The hands swing by the shoulders, and the swimmer's face goes underwater.

C. The arms, elbows straight, continue forward.

G. The head is dropped down by tilting the head forward (neck flexion).

D. The mouth starts to close.

H. The hands enter the water a little outside the shoulder line.

The out-of-water recovery ends when the arms enter the water. They should enter at a little outside of shoulder level, as in the out-of-water pictures of Rosemarie Kother (Fig. 4.62). Figure 4.63A shows the correct arm entry as seen from directly below the swimmer, and Figure 4.63B shows the arm entry of Mark Spitz. These pictures also show the pitch of the hands as they enter the water.

Fig. 4.63. *Correct arm entry*

A. Gary Hall, as seen from directly underneath.

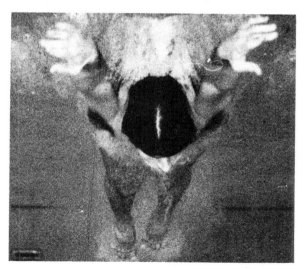

B. Mark Spitz, as seen from head-on underwater. The hands are pitched diagonally outward as they enter the water.

Common Mistakes in Arm Recovery

1. Letting the arms enter the water too far outside the shoulder width (Fig. 4.64—A as seen from out of water, B as seen from underwater).

2. Recovering the arms with a bend in the elbows.

3. Recovering the arms too high over the water.

4. Rushing the recovery so much that the arms slap the water with too much velocity. This rushed arm action is harmful for two reasons: it breaks the rhythm of the stroke and it increases drag in accordance with the theoretical-square law.

Fig. 4.64. *Stroke defect—wide arm entry*

A and B. Arms are entering the water too widely positioned.

Fig. 4.65. *Mark Spitz's butterfly stroke
as seen from directly underneath*

Several important stroke mechanics principles are revealed in this series of pictures.

1. Notice the hourglass pull pattern of Mark's hands as the pull goes first out (A, B, and C), then in (D and E), and then out again (F, G, and H).

2. The exhalation is forceable as Mark exhales air from his mouth after the pull begins (B) and continues as his head lifts out of the water (C and D).

3. The hands come so close together (E) that they seem to be touching.

4. The arm pull begins with the elbows straight (A); they reach a maximum bend of about 90 degrees underneath the chest (E); then they appear to almost fully extend at the end of the pull and beginning of the recovery (G and H).

C

A

D

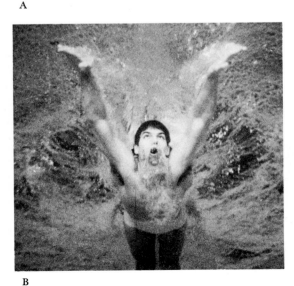

B

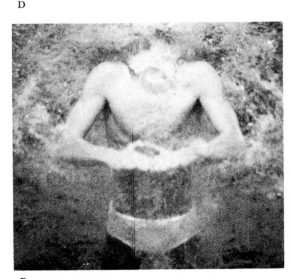

E

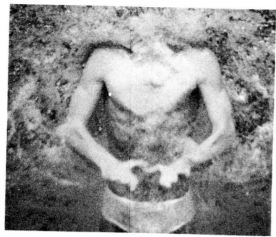

F

G

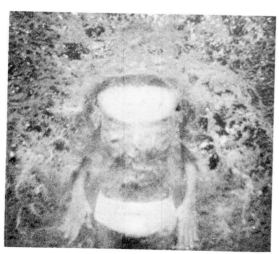

H

The Arm Pull

The arm pull begins after the hands have entered the water and have sunk several inches beneath the surface. Figure 4.65 depicts the butterfly stroke as seen from directly underneath and presents the reader with a very unusual view of the near-perfect stroke mechanics of Mark Spitz.

Width of Pull

As can be seen in Figure 4.65, once the pull begins the arms are pressed down and outward. How wide should they press before they start inward? Figure 4.66 shows the maximum width of the arm pull of four world-class butterfliers, including three world record holders. Of the four swimmers I prefer the width of pull of Mark Spitz (A). I think the pulls of Gary Hall (B) and Kevin Berry (C) are too wide and that of Rosemarie Kother (D) is too narrow.

Fig. 4.66. *Maximum width of arm pull of four world-class swimmers*

A. Mark Spitz

B. Gary Hall

C. Kevin Berry

Fig. 4.67. *Head-on view of the high elbow position of Mark Spitz*

Fig. 4.68. *Side view of high elbow position in the butterfly pull*

A. Olympic individual medley champion Charles Hickcox.

D. Rosemarie Kother

High Elbow Position during Arm Pull

   During the first half of the pull the arms are carried in an elbows-up position. This high elbow position is accomplished by bending the elbows and then rotating the upper arms medially. Figure 4.67 shows the high elbow position of Mark Spitz's arm pull as seen from head-on. Figures 4.68 A and B show the high elbow position as seen from the side.

B. Nationally ranked age-group swimmer. Notice the elbows-up position and the outward pitch of the hands.

Narrow Point in Pull Pattern

We have seen in Figure 4.65 that Mark Spitz's hands almost touch during the middle of the arm pull. How close should they come together? Figure 4.69 shows the narrowest point of the arm pulls of three world-class swimmers.

Fig. 4.69. *Narrowest part of the arm pull of three world-class swimmers*

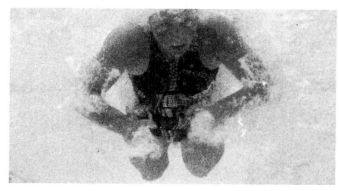

A. Rosemarie Kother

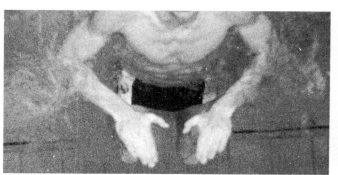

B. Gary Hall

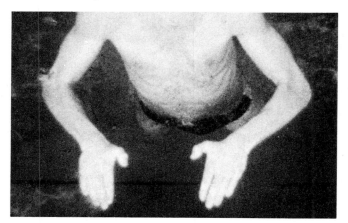

C. Charles Hickcox

The Arm-Pull Pattern

The arms are pulled through the water in what has been called a *keyhole* or *hourglass* pattern. This is shown in Figure 4.60. The actual path of the hands through the water is best shown by taking a time exposure picture in a dark pool with a flashing light attached to the middle finger of each hand. A strobe light is flashed at one point during the stroke so that a picture of the swimmer is also shown on the film. Figure 4.70 is the pull pattern of Rick Thomas as measured in this manner. Figure 4.71 is the pull pattern of Charles Hickcox as taken from directly underneath the swimmer. This pull-pattern picture is taken by making a tracing from a sequence of moving pictures taken from a camera held in a static position. Figure 4.72 is a sequence of eleven pictures of Mark Spitz's butterfly stroke. Study it carefully for all of the points that have been discussed so far.

Fig. 4.70. *Butterfly arm-pull of Rick Thomas as recorded by flashing-light technique*

Fig. 4.71. *Butterfly arm-pull pattern of Charles Hickcox as seen from directly underneath*

Fig. 4.72. *Underwater picture sequence*
of Mark Spitz's butterfly

A. The fingertips are just starting to enter the water as the arms end their recovery. The head is down, with the legs bent at the knees to kick downward.

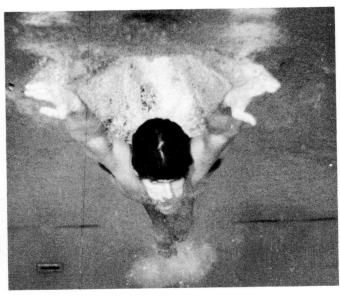

C. The palms start to turn slightly downward as the hands press out and down. The head starts to lift as the neck is extended.

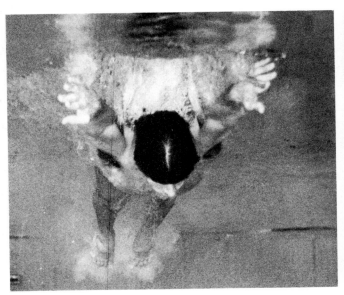

B. The arms have entered the water with no bend in the elbows, at a line slightly outside of shoulder width and with the hands turned so the palms are pitched outward. The legs have kicked downward.

D. The hands continue to press down and outward as the pitch of the hands changes so the palms are turned down. The wrists also flex slightly. There appears to be a slight bend in the elbows. Air is being exhaled gently from the nose.

E. The head continues to be raised by flexion of the neck. The elbows-up position of the arms is noticeable at this point as the elbow bend increases.

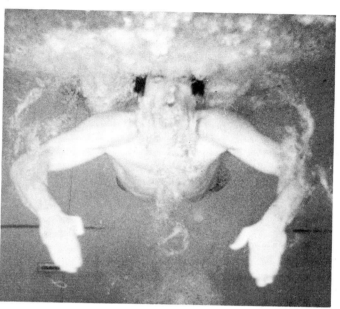

G. The hands pull back and inward as the head breaks the surface. The blinking reflex caused by the eyes leaving the water closes the eyes. Once the eyes are clear of the water, they will be opened again. The exhalation of air is now at its greatest force.

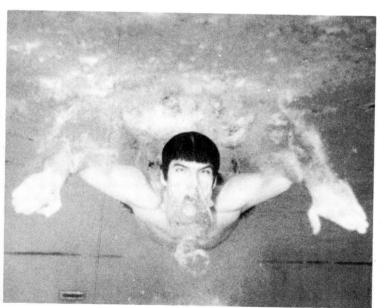

F. The mouth opens and air is exhaled from both the mouth and nose. The arms are at the widest part of the pull and from this point onward will pull inward toward the center line of the body.

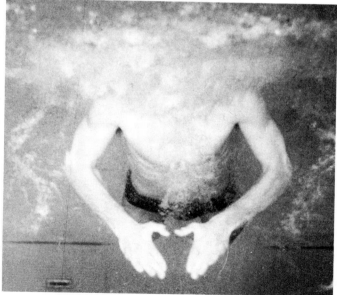

H. The head is clear of the water and the inhalation is about to begin. The thumbs almost touch as the hands pass under the chest. The elbows reach maximum bend of 90 to 100 degrees. Although not visible from this view, the second downbeat of the kick has begun.

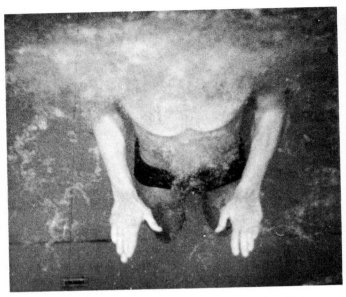

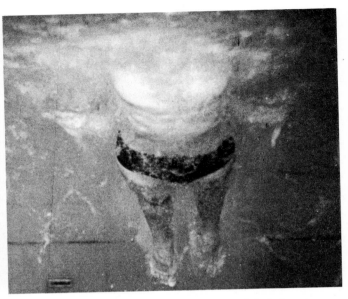

I. The air inhalation has begun and will last through the final phase of the underwater arm action and half of the arm recovery. The palms continue to push backward to facilitate recovery. Research indicates no propulsion is gained from the last push of the hands (H through K). This long push back, however, is needed for an efficient recovery.

K. The head is dropped after the inhalation is made and will be kept in this position with some slight changes during the next arm pull, since the swimmer breathes only every second stroke.

Review of This Sequence: The reader should make frequent reference to this sequence of pictures to study the various phases of the stroke.

1. The arm pull pattern—keyhole or hourglass.
2. The pitch of the hands during the pull.
3. The timing of the breathing—head movement and exhalation.
4. The timing of the arm pull with the two kicks. In this sequence the second kick appears to be bigger than the first. This is often true when the swimmer is sprinting.
5. When are the eyes open and when are they closed?
6. The bend in the elbows. When does it begin? At what point does it reach maximum?
7. Note the high elbow position at the first half of the stroke.

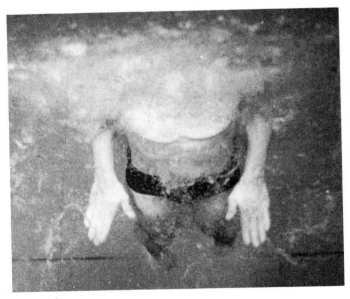

J. The hands, with palms turned inward, are finally lifted out of the water, with the fingertips of the left hand noticeable on the right side of the picture. The downward thrust of the second kick is near completion. The head is still held up as the inhalation continues.

The Dolphin Kick

The dolphin, or fishtail, kick is made by keeping the legs together and kicking them upward and downward in the vertical plane. When practicing the kick the swimmer should use a kickboard and emphasize keeping the legs straight on the upbeat and bent on the downbeat. Figure 4.73 illustrates the mechanics of the correct technique. Figure 4.74 shows the light-tracing kick pattern of the fishtail kick. The feet hardly ever move backward, so the thrust of the kick must be explained in terms of the Bernoulli or "lift" effect instead of the drag principle (Chapter 5, Sections 5.1 and 5.2).

Fig. 4.73. *Dolphin kick drill on a kickboard*
The kickboard should be held in front of the swimmer, elbows fully extended. Notice that there is no perceptible change in the position of the kickboard. When the swimmer does his kicking on the board, there should be as little bobbing up and down of the head, the shoulders, and board as possible.

The sequence begins with the legs at the bottom of the downbeat (A). The legs kick upward with no flexion in the knees (A and B). As the feet near the top of their upward movement, the knees start to bend (C and D). The feet continue upward as the knees start downward (E). The ankles extend as the feet start their downward thrust and the knees reach maximum bend (90 degrees) (F). The feet move downward as the upper leg starts to move upward (G). The downward beat of the kick finishes as the knees become fully extended (H).

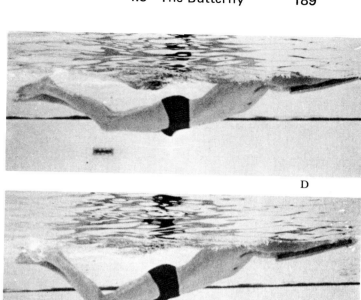

D

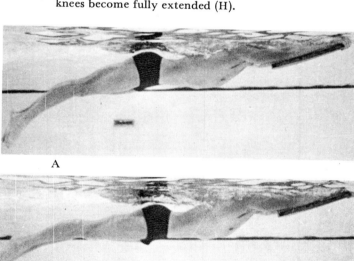

A

B

C

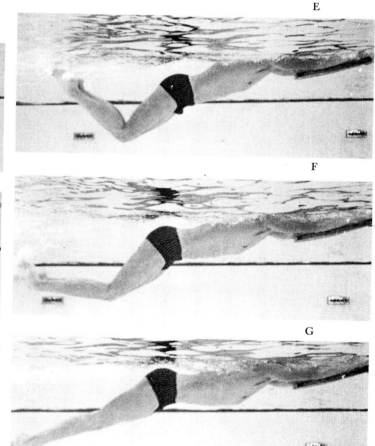

E

F

G

H

Fig. 4.74. *Light tracings of the pattern of the fishtail kick*

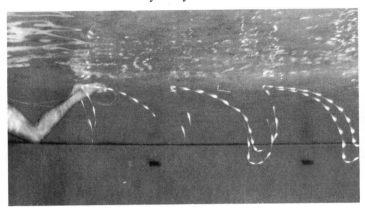

The lights attached to the feet of the swimmer leave a pattern of the movement of the feet through the water. The upbeat of the kick is recorded by the curved line going upward; the downbeat pattern by the almost vertical line. It appears that the feet never move backward to any great degree. On the basis of this photograph it is clear that the source of propulsion of the kick cannot be explained as resulting from pushing the water directly backward or from the drag effect. It must be explained in terms of the "lift" principle or "sculling" effect.

Timing of the Arms and Legs

In Figure 4.72 we have seen the timing of the arm and leg movements of Mark Spitz. The downbeat of the first kick is made as the arms enter the water after recovery, and the downbeat of the second kick is made during the second half of the arm pull. The hands during the last half of the arm pull would tend to pull the hips downward. To prevent this from happening, swimmers, after they have swum enough butterfly in practice, will automatically evolve this timing. The downward beat of the second kick prevents the upward action of the arms from pulling the hips down. In Figure 4.72 the second kick of the stroke appears to be slightly bigger than the first kick. This is true when the butterfliers are sprinting, but when they swim more slowly, the first kick will be the larger of the two. Figure 4.75 shows the timing of the arms and legs of a National champion. In this case the swimmer is swimming at a slow speed, so the second kick is very small.

Figure 4.76 is an out-of-water picture of Mark Spitz's butterfly stroke.

Fig. 4.75. *Timing of arms and legs*

The first downbeat of the kick comes as the arms enter the water and start their pull (A and B). The second downbeat of the legs occurs during the last half of the arm pull (C and D). This second kick is smaller than the first when the swimmer is swimming slow (as shown here) and bigger when the swimmer is sprinting.

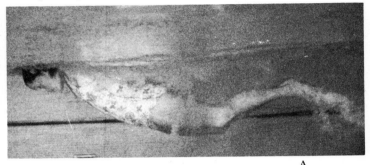

A

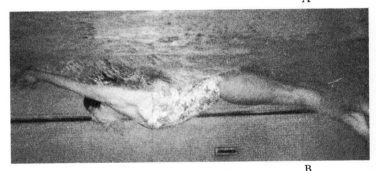

B

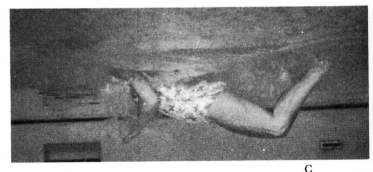

C

D

Fig. 4.76. *Mark Spitz's butterfly stroke*

This picture shows good form. The recovery of the arms is begun with the hands still under water. The air is being inhaled through the mouth. The chin is kept low in the water.

SECTION 4.6
THE BREASTSTROKE

The breaststroke rules are very specific and, while they change slightly from year to year, the changes are minor. The rules state:

1. The swimmer must swim on his chest and not dip one shoulder or any other part of the body lower than the other corresponding part.

2. The arms must move in a simultaneous and similar manner and no out-of-water recovery of the arms is permitted.

3. The legs must move in a simultaneous and similar manner. The frog, or breaststroke, kick must be used. The legs must spread outward and then squeeze together during the kicking phase. No undulating movement of the legs in the vertical plan will be permitted. This eliminates the fishtail kick, the flutter kick, and the scissors kick.

4. Part of the head must break the surface of the water at all times except for the time during the single long arm pull and kick underwater that is permitted after the dive and each turn.

5. When turning or finishing, the swimmer must touch the wall at the end of the pool with both hands at the same time and at the same level, although in high school and college swimming the swimmer's hands do not have to touch at the same level prior to turning.

None of the swimming strokes is the subject of as much controversy, misconception, and disagreement concerning proper mechanics as the breaststroke. I have included many underwater pictures of world record holders, Olympic champions, and other world-class swimmers in this chapter to document the stroke techniques that I recommend. A careful review of the articles written in the popular swimming periodicals indicates that most coaches advocate techniques that are not in fact used and that violate the principles of fluid mechanics.

Various writers have attributed a certain percentage of the propulsion to the kick and a certain percentage to the pull. A common figure is 75 percent to the legs and 25 percent to the arms. I disagree with this kind of approach to analysis of swimming propulsion. The main thing wrong with it is not only that it is unscientific and based on subjective evaluation but that it minimizes the importance of the arm pull. Unpublished research by the Dutch Swimming Federation at the Fluid Mechanics Towing Labs in Rotterdam seems to indicate just the opposite. These studies show that in world-class swimming the major source of propulsion is the arm pull. Most of the swimmers I have coached can pull a faster 100-yard breaststroke than they can kick the same distance. The best approach for a swimmer to use is to make both kick and pull as efficient as he can; this will optimize the performance of his total stroke.

The mechanical laws that apply to other strokes also apply to the breaststroke, so it is important that the reader read Section 4.2 again before he reads this section. A more technical discussion of the stroke mechanics is covered in Chapter 5 (Section 5.4), "A Hydrodynamic Analysis of Breaststroke Pulling Proficiency." It discusses the arm pull in detail and is recommended reading for all breaststroke and individual-medley swimmers.

Figure 4.77 is a mini-analysis of breaststroke mechanics and serves as an introduction.

The starts and turns for the breaststroke are covered in detail in Section 4.7.

Fig. 4.77. *A mini-analysis of the breaststroke*

1. *Inverted heart-shaped pull*: Make pull pattern as shown at the lower right.

2. *Elbow bend*: Begin pull with elbow straight. As hands are pulled backward and downward, elbow bend should increase. Do not pull with straight arm.

3. *High elbow*: Carry elbow in elbow-up position during pull.

4. *Timing of legs and arms*: Begin thrust of legs backward as arms are extended forward in recovery.

1. The stroke begins from a stretched-out horizontal position, palms facing diagonally outward.

2. Arms are pulled outward, downward and back. The head is lifted up by flexion of the neck.

3. The breath is taken as arms and the pull and legs start to recover by bending at the knees.

4. After the breath is taken, the face is placed back into the water and the heels are brought up toward the buttocks. The arms are pressed forward.

5. The leg kick is made as the arms are extended and the head is dropped slightly so eyes are underwater (but not the top of the head). The swimmer now goes into the glide position.

Out-of-Water or Head Action

The only out-of-water action in the breast-stroke is that of the head. The rule states that part of the head must be carried out of water at all times. In other words it must be breaking the surface except during the long pull following the start and turn. The head should be lifted only high enough for the swimmer to breathe, then it should be lowered back into the water so the swimmer does not have to support it out of water. He must, however, protect himself against disqualification by taking care not to submerge his head completely. His energy should be used to pull himself forward through the water, not to carry his head in a high position.

The head lift and the air inhalation should be timed to occur when the shoulders are at their highest point. This point comes at the end of the arm pull. The arms press diagonally down and back during the pull. The downward direction of the pull causes the shoulders to rise; consequently the highest elevation of the shoulders occurs at the end of the pull. The swimmer should start to lift his head by extension of the neck (posterior flexion of the cervical vertebrae). This action is initiated shortly after the pull begins and continues throughout the pull. Once the inhalation is complete, the head should be dropped slightly by forward flexion of the neck. This action will become apparent as the section progresses and the out-of-water and underwater pictures are examined. Constant reference will be made to the head action as the various parts of the stroke are discussed. Figure 4.78 is an out-of-water sequence of Olympic champion and world record holder John Hencken on the way to a new world record in the 200-meter breaststroke.

It is important to understand that the slight amount of flexion and extension of the neck that is necessary is easily exaggerated. The swimmer should not lift his head so high or drop it so much that this action causes his shoulders to bob. I have found one suggestion that helps most swimmers obtain the proper amount of head movement. The swimmer should think of the line of sight as a guide. When he lifts his head to breathe, he should

be able to look straight forward and see the end of the pool (Fig. 4.79). When he lowers his head after inhalation, the line of sight should be diagonally downward so he is looking a little below the level of his hands.

Fig. 4.78. *Out-of-water pictures of world record holder John Hencken*

A. When the arms are extended forward, the face is underwater and only the top of the head is out of water.

B. The breath (inhalation) is taken at the end of the pull, when the arms have finished their pull and the hands are almost directly underneath the chin.

C. A head-on view of the same position as in B.

Fig. 4.79. *Head action and timing of the arms*

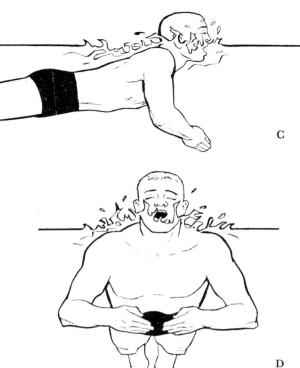

A

B

A and B. Side and head-on views of the head position when the arms are extended in front. The head is tilted forward so the line of sight is diagonally downward, as though the swimmer were looking at his hands. Notice the pitch of the hands is diagonally outward.

C and D. Side and head-on views of the head position at the time of inhalation. The hands have finished their pull and are almost directly under the chin. The head is tilted up so the line of sight is directly forward.

The Arm Pull

Elbow Bend

In the sections of Chapter 4 covering the other three competitive strokes, the arm recovery has been discussed before the arm pull. For reasons that will become obvious I will change this format for this stroke and discuss the pull first.

The pull begins with the arms fully extended in front of the body, hands touching. The hands should be at a depth of 6 to 10 inches, not near the surface as many swimmers tend to place them. At the beginning of the pull the hands should be pitched so the palms are facing diagonally outward at about a 45-degree angle (Fig. 4.79). When the pull begins, the hands are pushed almost directly sidewards with the elbows straight. After the arms have moved as wide or a little wider than shoulder width, the elbows start to bend. In many respects the breaststroke pull is similar to the first part of the butterfly pull because the direction that the arms press and the amount of elbow bend are nearly the same. Figure 4.80A compares the breaststroke arm pull of world record holder Chet Jastremski and the butterfly arm pull of Gary Hall (Fig. 4.80 B). It can be seen that the arm positions are almost identical.

Fig. 4.80. *A comparison of the breast stroke and butterfly arm pull*

A. Chet Jastremski—breaststroke

B. Gary Hall—butterfly stroke

High Elbow Position

As the arms are pulled backward, the elbow bend increases. This elbow bend, combined with the inward or medial rotation of the upper arm causes the arm to be pulled in a high elbow position, as shown in Figure 4.81. The high elbow position places the arms in a good position for proper application of a backward push of the hands. Many swimmers try to pull their elbows into their ribs. This is comparable to swimming the crawl stroke with a dropped elbow.

Fig. 4.81. *High elbow position*

A. World record holder Karla Linke with her elbows in the high position.

B. Chet Jastremski's elbow-up pull

Arm-Pull Pattern

In relation to the position of the body the pull pattern of the hands should describe the shape of an inverted heart. This pattern is shown in Figure 4.82. In relation to their path through the water the pull pattern of the hands appears as a flashing light pattern in Figure 4.83 (A and B).

Fig. 4.82. *Breaststroke pull pattern*

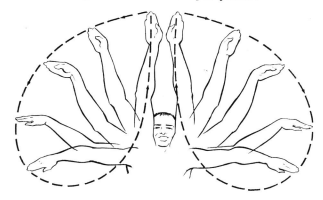

Inverted heart-shape pull pattern of the hands in relation to the position of the body.

The Total Stroke

On the following pages Figure 4.84 shows the total stroke of Catie Ball, world record holder, who had the best stroke mechanics of any girl breaststroke swimmer I ever photographed. She had a very high elbow position as shown by her arm position in Figure 4.84 (B and C). Catie held the world record for five years, and had she trained as hard as swimmers are presently training I have no doubt she would have gone under 2:30. Her pull and kick are both performed with good mechanics and her timing is perfect.

Fig. 4.83. *Pull pattern of the hands in relation to still water*
As measured by flashing lights on the middle finger of each hand.

A. A head-on view

B. A side view

Fig. 4.84. *Catie Ball's breaststroke*
from underwater

A. The pull is about to begin. Line of sight is diagonally downward with eyes open.

B. The pull has begun and the palms are turned or pitched diagonally outward. The elbows are straight. Air begins to come out of nose.

C. The elbows bend as the upper arms rotate to give the arms the elbow-up position. The amount of air coming from the nose and mouth increases. The eyes close due to the blinking reflex. The head is lifted upward by extension of the neck as the face is tilted upward.

D. The hands press backward and start to squeeze together. The air is still being exhaled. Although it cannot be seen clearly, the knees are beginning to bend slightly.

E. The head is out of water and the air is being inhaled. The hands are pitched diagonally inward and are just finishing their sculling movement inwardly. The knees continue to bend.

F. The pull is finished and the palms are facing one another (but are not facing upward). The air is still being inhaled. The knees start to move forward in the recovery of the legs.

G. The hands start forward as the legs continue their recovery.

H. The palms turn downward as they reach forward. The knees continue to move forward.

I. The feet, with the ankles flexed, start to move outward.

J. The inward rotation of the upper legs causes the heels to swing farther outward. The feet are now in position to push backward.

K. The feet start to push backward immediately before the elbows reach full extension. This particular timing is used by most world-class swimmers. The face is completely submerged. The feet are pushing out and backward.

L. The feet are pushed backward to extension of the knees. Catie Ball's kick demonstrates the desired "whip action" of the feet.

M. The kick continues as the arms are stretched forward and the head is tilted slightly downward.

N. The legs start to come together as the knees continue to extend.

O. The feet have not quite completed their squeeze when the arms start to press sideward, getting ready for the pull. The palms start to turn diagonally sideward.

P. The hands are now into their pull with the palms pitched sideward, and air is beginning to be exhaled from the nose.

Summary of Sequence: The reader should examine this sequence for the following points.

1. The pull pattern—at first outward (B), then out and down diagonally (C) and, finally, the arms scull inward (D and E) before they are recovered.

2. The pitch of the hands during the pull. The palms face diagonally outward as the hands are pressed outward (A,B, and C). As they are pulled inward (D and E), they are pitched diagonally inward (this is shown better in pictures taken from directly underneath). The arm pull is therefore not so much a pull as it is a sculling motion outward and then inward. The palms are never turned completely upward, but the palms face one another at one point (G).

3. The head begins to lift upward and the air to be exhaled shortly after the pull begins (B and C). It continues to be lifted by extension of the neck during the entire arm pull (B,C,D,E, and F). The air is inhaled as the arms finish the pull and start their recovery (E,F,G, and H). The head is then placed face down in the water by forward flexion of the neck.

4. During the first part of the pull (the outward sculling motion) the legs are extended backward and there is no movement of the legs (A,B, and C). When sprinting there is a slight overlapping of the kick and arm pull. As the hands start to scull inwardly, the knees begin to bend and the legs begin their recovery (D,E, and F). During the rest of the arm recovery the feet continue to be pulled forward as the legs recover (G,H,I, and J). Immediately before the arms are fully extended the propulsive phase of the kick begins with the feet being driven outward and backward (K and L). When using the sprint stroke, as shown here, many swimmers start their pull before the legs have completed the kick.

Common Mistakes in the Arm Pull

1. Pressing too long during the pull with no bend in the elbows, as in Figure 4.85.

Fig. 4.85. *Stroke defect—pulling too long with no bend in the elbows*

2. Dropping the elbows and pulling them into the ribs as shown in Figure 4.86.

Fig. 4.86. *Stroke defect—dropping the elbows and pulling them into the ribs*

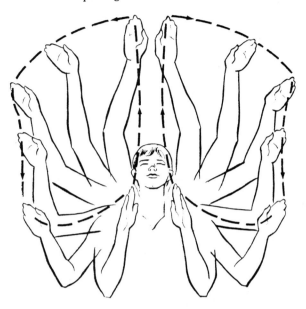

3. Turning the palms to face upward during the pull. Several articles published in *Swimming World* have stated that the palms should start to face upward during the last part of the pull and at the beginning of the recovery.

While it is true that after the hands scull inwardly the palms will be in a vertical position and facing one another, any attempt to turn them over will only result in a decreased efficiency in the pull, and the upward thrust of the hands will pull the swimmer down, not forward.

4. Pulling the legs up too late in the stroke. The legs should start their recovery during the last half of the pull (Fig. 4.90 E). Swimmers often fail to start the leg recovery until the arm pull has been completed.

5. Pausing during the arm action and not keeping the arm pull and recovery motion as one continuous action. This occurs frequently when the swimmer drops his elbows as shown in Figure 4.86. It also often occurs at the point shown in Figure 4.87. This breaks the continuity of the stroke and causes the swimmer to sink lower into the water. To correct this stroke defect the swimmer should start to exhale his air sooner—while his face is still underwater. In this way he can use all of the time his face is out of water to inhale. Most swimmers must make a conscious effort to avoid pausing at this point in their stroke.

Fig. 4.87. *Stroke defect—pausing during the arm action.* There is a great temptation among many swimmers to stop their arm action at this point. They do so to prolong the inhalation of air.

The Kick

The kicking drills should be performed while holding onto a kickboard. The board should be held out in front of the swimmer with his arms fully extended, and the end of the board should be no closer to his head than at elbow level. The swimmer should not push

the board downward and lift his shoulders upward; he should try to keep the board flat in the water and not elevate his shoulders but keep them low in the water at the same level they will be when he is performing the whole stroke. The swimmer should also kick using hypoxic breathing, that is, taking only one breath every two or three kicks. This will improve his conditioning and will enable him to practice correct head motion. When he is not inhaling, he can drop his head by the forward flexion of his neck so his face is under water and is tilted diagonally downward as in Figure 4.79.

The whip kick rather than the old-fashioned wedge kick is used today. It had formerly been believed that the forward thrust of the kick was derived from squeezing the wedge of water formed between the legs backward. Research long ago proved this to be a false assumption. The swimmer should concentrate on squeezing the legs together, but not for the foregoing reason. The propulsion from the kick actually derives from the sculling action of the feet on both their outward and backward, and inward and backward thrust. A careful analysis of some underwater movies of a breaststroke swimmer who kicked a 100-yard breaststroke in 1:04 showed that his feet never moved backward in the water during the time he was kicking on a kickboard. This proves definitely that, at least in this case, the source of propulsion from the kick was from the lift or "Bernoulli" effect (see Chapter 5, Section 5.2).

One of the finest kicks I have ever photographed is that of Catie Ball. The photographs can be examined in Figure 4.84, a sequence of her underwater stroke as seen from head-on. Her kick is truly amazing because of her good ankle flexibility and the excellent positioning of her feet for the maximum sculling effect.

Figure 4.88 is a very good set of sequence pictures of a very good breaststroker whip kick with matching rear and side view pictures. These two figures emphasize the importance of ankle flexibility, particularly in terms of flexion (dorsiflexion). This ankle flexibility can be improved by using the exercises in Chapter 3, "Dry-Land-Exercises."

Fig. 4.88. *Correct mechanics of the
breaststroke whip kick*

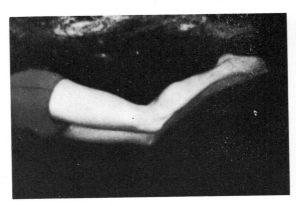
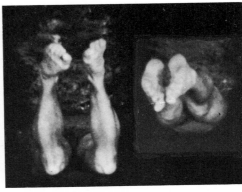

1.

2.

1. The kick starts with the legs fully extended and
toes pointed (see upper right of photo).
2—A and B. The legs start to recover by flexion of
the knees and the hips.

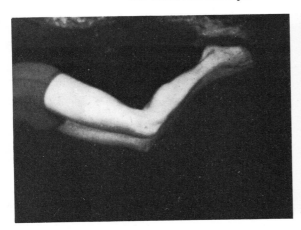
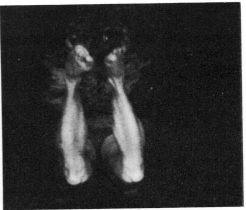

3.

3—A and B. The feet stay together as they
continue forward.

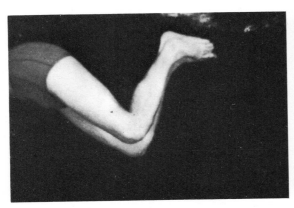
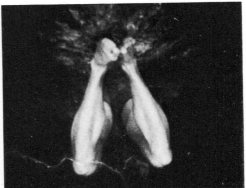

4.

4—A and B. The knees start to spread slightly, but
the feet stay together.

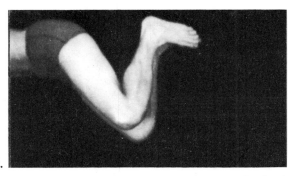

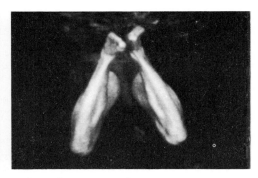

5.

5—A and B. As the heels are brought up toward the buttocks, the knees continue to spread. Note that the spread is not extreme.

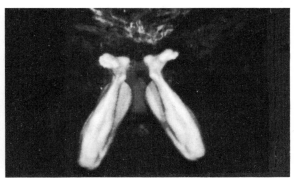

6.

6—A and B. The knees are as far forward as they will go and are at their maximum spread. The angle formed between the body and the upper leg is approximately 110 degrees. The feet are now dorsiflexed in preparation for the backward thrust.

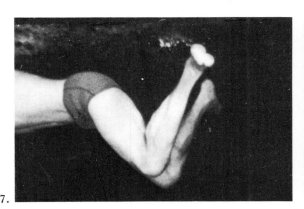

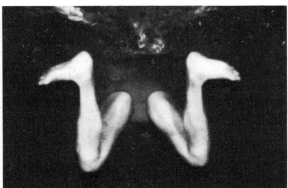

7.

7—A and B. The outward and backward thrust of the legs is beginning (that is, backward in relation to the body, but not in relation to the water, since the body is moving forward). The inside of the feet—and possibly the ankles and part of the lower legs—are in a good position to apply forward thrust via the lift effect.

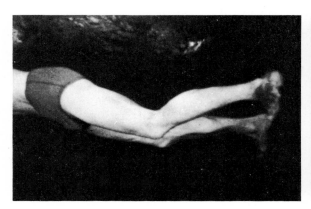

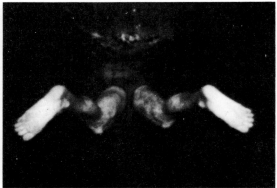

8.

8—A and B. The feet are pushed backward and outward as the knees and hips extend and the spread of the kick is at maximum width. The soles of the feet are now ideally placed to scull inward. This is the point at which the squeezing action of the kick is so important. Too many swimmers let their feet drift inward at this point and do not maintain a high velocity whereby they can receive propulsion from the sculling effect of the feet.

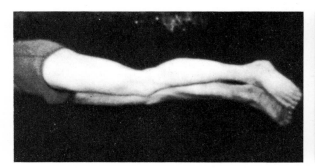

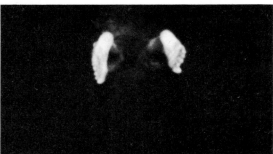

9.

9—A and B. The legs have almost completed the kick and are almost completely extended. From this point onward there is no propulsion, and the swimmer should concentrate on closing the legs together and pointing or extending the toes in order that the feet may be in the fully extended position shown in 1—A and B.

Review of Sequence: The reader should examine this sequence of pictures carefully and try to comprehend the fact that the breaststroke whip kick does not merely consist in pulling up the feet and pushing them backwards, but is a sculling action. The feet derive their propulsion from first sculling outwards (7 and 8) and then inward (9). The positioning of the soles of the feet so they face backward by flexion of the ankles is very important.

The Long Stroke after the Dive and Turn

The rules governing the breaststroke permit one complete stroke underwater (one arm pull and one leg kick) after the dive and each turn. The swimmer can take best advantage of this underwater stroke by using a long arm pull. The pull should be similar to the hourglass pull used in the butterfly stroke. The time period from the gun to completion of the long stroke and until the head breaks the water should consume from 3.6 to 4.3 seconds, as measured at the World Games, Olympic Games, and National Championships. The amount of time required when performing the turn from touch until head break after the long pull requires approximately the same amount of time. Too often the swimmer will use 5 to 6 seconds to perform this action. This causes the swimmer to slow down too much. The coach should time the swimmer frequently in meets and practice to make certain he uses the right amount of time—not too much or too little. Figure 4.89 shows this underwater stroke.

Fig. 4.89. *The long stroke after the dive and turn*

A. The swimmer pushes off (or dives) and holds the body in a streamlined glide position until he slows to swimming speed. The head is held in a position face down as though he were looking at the bottom of the pool.

B. The pull of the arms starts by pressing directly sideward with the palms facing outward and the elbows straight. This actually is a nonpropulsive movement and is more a positioning of the arms.

C. The elbows bend and the hands press deeper into the water. The elbows remain high due to medial rotation of the upper arms.

D. The elbows continue to bend as the hands are brought inward.

E. The elbows are at their maximum flexion and the hands only a few inches apart. The palms face directly backward.

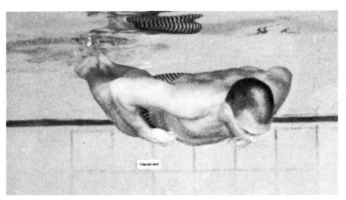

H. The arms now start their recovery as the legs also start theirs, as indicated by the slight bending of the knees. The arms should be kept close to the body as they are brought forward, in order to create a minimum of negative resistance or drag. The hands should be kept close to the chest and the elbows kept in.

F. The elbows continue to extend as they press diagonally upward and backward.

I. The hands continue forward and the heels are brought upward by flexion of the knees.

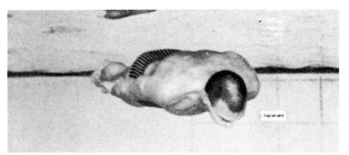

G. The final extension of the elbows is made so the palms push directly upward. This action keeps the swimmer streamlined and prevents him from popping to the surface. He should not feel any water from his hands pushing or swirling against his legs. Since the swimmer has a high velocity at this point in his stroke, this position is held for .3 to .4 second.

J. The arms push forward as the legs position themselves for their backward thrust.

The amount of time it takes from the moment the swimmer touches the wall until he turns around, pushes off, accomplishes the long pull and kick and until his head breaks the surface should be about four seconds. In the 100-meter event at the Olympic Games, John Hencken took 3.9 seconds to accomplish touch-to-head-break; in the 200-meter event David Wilkie took 4.3 seconds.

K. The backward thrust of the legs has begun as the arms extend forward.

L. The top of the head breaks the surface of the water before the legs complete the kick. In a fraction of a second the swimmer will be ready to begin his surface stroke.

Summary of Sequence: After the dive and turn the swimmer should take a long pull and kick before he begins his surface stroke. His hands will pull in an hourglass pattern (A through G). He will take a short glide when his arms are at his side (G). The arms should be recovered close to the body in order not to create unnecessary resistance as he brings his arms forward (H, I, and J). The head should break the surface immediately before the backward thrust of the legs begins (K). Although it is not clearly shown in the pictures, the arm pull accelerates as the pull progresses.

Review of the Breaststroke

In anticipation of the possible criticism that the sequence of Catie Ball shows the stroke of a swimmer who was good in her day but that that was a long time ago, I am including a photo sequence of a more recent world record holder, Karla Linke, of East Germany (Fig. 4.90). The similarity in stroke mechanics of these two girls is not complete, but the major points to be considered are quite identical and both girls exhibit very good stroke mechanics.

No stroke is more misunderstood, misinterpreted or poorly described than is the breaststroke. I have heard people talk of the Russian-style breaststroke, the Japanese, the American. I have heard them talk of the natural breaststroke versus the unnatural stroke. If all the people expressing opinions and writing articles on the breaststroke—and all other strokes for that matter—were required to document their opinions with films or pictures as shown here, there would be less confusion concerning the mechanics of the stroke.

The following sequence of Karla Linke was taken within two weeks of the time she set the world record. The reader is encouraged to study carefully this and all other sequences. The brief description below each picture may serve as a guide to point up certain major points, but it is not detailed. A close scrutiny will reveal a lot that I have not mentioned or have overlooked. Happy hunting!

A. Before the legs have completely closed together the arm pull will begin. The face is tilted downward.

D. The top of the head breaks the water as the hands begin their inward sculling movement. The upper arms are rotated inward and the elbow bend increases as the arms are carried in the elbow-up position.

B. Exhalation of air begins immediately after the pull begins. The head starts to lift upward.

E. The hands continue to scull inward as the inhalation starts. The knees start to bend slightly.

C. The pull continues as air continues to be exhaled and the head lifted. The elbows bend.

F. A slight stroke defect is revealed as the hands cross, one in front of the other.

G. The hands start forward in recovery as the legs are also recovered.

H. The hands continue forward and the legs continue to be pulled upward in recovery.

I. The feet are now in position to push backward and the arms are not fully extended in front.

J. The backward drive of the legs begins before the arms are fully extended forward. The face is completely submerged.

K. The feet push backward as the arms extend forward. The action of the legs results in a good whip action of the feet.

L. The leg kick nears completion. Before the legs have closed together, the arm pull will begin again.

SECTION 4.7
STARTS AND TURNS

The Start

The command for all starts in competitive swimming events is the same: "Swimmers take your marks" and the gun. For the freestyler, the butterflier, and the breaststroker the start is out of water and from a standing position on the starting blocks. The start for these three strokes is almost identical and either the *grab* or *conventional start with an arm swing* can be used. The angle of entry into the water for the crawl is flatter than for the breaststroke, while that for the butterfly is somewhere in between. In the breaststroke start the swimmer wants to dive deeper in order to facilitate his long underwater stroke before surfacing.

The grab start is used by most swimmers when starting from the gun. When taking off from another swimmer's touch on a relay, most swimmers will use a start with an arm swing. The advantages of the grab start are that the swimmer has fewer false starts and that he gets off the starting block faster after the gun fires. He may not dive out as far, but if the grab start is done correctly, the result will be faster than when using the arm-swing start.

The arm-swing start is better for relay starts since the swimmer is not so concerned with getting off the mark faster. He is interested in playing it safe and not being disqualified for leaving the mark before the swimmer coming in has made his touch. Since he wants to compensate for his caution in getting off the mark, it is crucial that he get as much distance as possible in his start; so most swimmers use the arm-swing start. The swimmer should, therefore, practice both types of start.

The Grab Start
Figure 4.91 shows Kornelia Ender, world record holder, performing the grab start. Her legs generate a lot of explosive power and she often gains a half body length on the field with her start.

Figure 4.92 shows the correct manner of performing the arm-swing start.

Fig. 4.91. *World record holder Kornelia Ender performing the grab start*

A. On the command "Take your marks," the swimmer leans forward and grasps the front of the starting block outside of her feet. Some swimmers spread their feet slightly and grasp the front of the block between their feet.

B. At the sound of the gun the swimmer pulls herself forward by pulling against the starting block through the flexion of her elbows.

C. As she loses her balance and starts to fall forward, she starts to swing her arms forward.

D. The body extends as the legs drive the body forward.

E. The leg drive continues. Notice that the ankles are extending to add to the final forward drive.

F. The body is now fully extended and the head is dropping slightly.

G. The hands hit the water first, as the head drop continues.

H. The head and shoulders are now almost fully submerged.

I. The body enters the water and will soon be submerged. The swimmer will hold a glide position underwater until she slows to swimming speed; she will then start stroking.

Fig. 4.92. *The arm-swing start*

A. At the sound of the gun the arms are swung forward and upward as the swimmer starts to fall forward.

D. The body is coiled in preparation for a forward spring. The arms continue to swing in a circle.

B. The head is pulled downward as the arms continue to swing upward.

E. The legs drive the body forward as the arms swing forward.

C. The knees bend and the heels lift off the block.

F. The final extension of the body is made with the arms stopping as they reach a diagonal down position.

G. The arms rise slightly as the head drops between the arms.

H. The final entry is made with the arms entering first and the rest of the body following.

The Backstroke Start

The backstroke start is made in the water and is shown in Figure 4.93. It will be noted that John Naber in Figure 4.93 uses a bent arm action when he swings his arms over the water. This is also the start used by Roland Matthes. Most male swimmers lack the shoulder flexibility to carry their arms forward in this manner. They use a similar start but bring their arms forward with no bend in the elbows, as shown in Figure 4.94.

Fig. 4.93. *John Naber's backstroke start*
This sequence of pictures is a match set taken from a diagonal head-on and diagonal side view.

1A

1B

1. On the command "Take your marks" the swimmer pulls himself partially out of water (A and B).

2A

2B

2. At the sound of the gun he lifts upward and pushes himself away from the block (A and B) by extending his elbows and pushing his hands down against the grips.

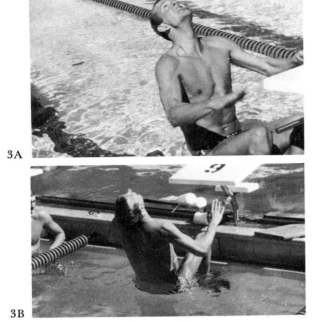

3A

3B

3. His head goes backward and his arms start to swing forward.

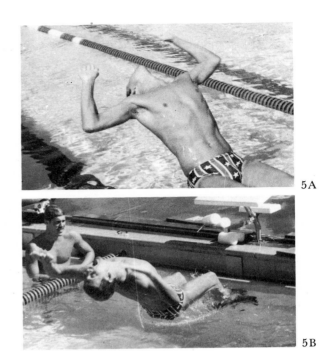

5A

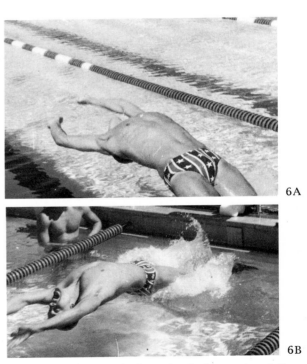

5B

5. The swimmer tries to lift himself clear of the water. Note that Naber bends his elbows as he brings them forward.

4A

4B

4. The head continues backward and an inhalation is made.

6A

6B

6. The back is arched as the body reaches full extension. The head is back.

7. The swimmer stretches out and tries for a steamlined body position.

8. The body submerges in a glide position. It will be held until the swimmer slows to swimming speed when he will begin stroking.

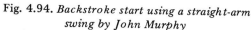

Fig. 4.94. *Backstroke start using a straight-arm swing by John Murphy*

The Turn

The butterfly and breaststroke rules concerning performance of the turn are similar in that the swimmer must touch the wall with both hands at the same level (AAU and international rules only) and simultaneously. Once he has done this the swimmer is permitted to turn off his chest and to complete the turn. When he has pushed off the wall, he must once again be on his chest.

Figure 4.95 shows Gary Hall performing a butterfly turn. In almost every respect his turn is identical to that used in the breaststroke except that the breaststroker uses a deeper foot plant on the wall (D and E). The feet should be set on the wall about 2 to 2½ feet below the surface of the water for the breaststroke rather than the depth demonstrated in the butterfly turn.

Fig. 4.95. *Butterfly and breaststroke*
turn by Gary Hall

A. The swimmer has just touched the wall with both hands at the same time and at the same level and has already started to turn his body.

D. The body rotates as the right hand pushes the upper body away from the wall. The feet, crossed so they are streamlined, are pulled toward the wall.

B. The left hand lets go of the wall in preparation for being pulled forward. As the legs start forward the feet begin to cross—left on top of right.

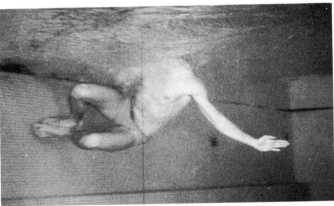

E. The right arm swings forward over the surface of the water, while the left arm is pushed forward underwater.

C. The left arm is swung forward as the right hand hangs onto the wall.

F. The right hand drives into the water. The feet are planted on the wall sideward.

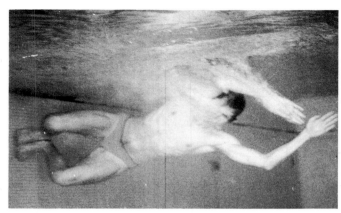

G. The hands reach for one another immediately before the legs begin the push-off.

H. As the push-off is made the body rotates so the body leaves the wall with the shoulders level. The swimmer will start his stroke as soon as he slows to swimming speed.

The Backstroke Turn

The rules governing the backstroke turn state that the swimmer must remain on his back until he touches the wall at the end of the pool. As he does his turn he may roll off his back, but his push-off must be accomplished on his back. Figure 4.96 shows Gary Hall doing the backstroke turn.

The Freestyle Turn

The rules concerning the freestyle turn merely state that the swimmer must touch the wall when turning. It is, of course, advantageous not to touch the wall with his hands, and the standard turn used by most competitive swimmers is the flip turn shown in Figure 4.97 in which only the feet contact the wall. This is in compliance with the rules.

Fig. 4.96. *The backstroke turn of Gary Hall*

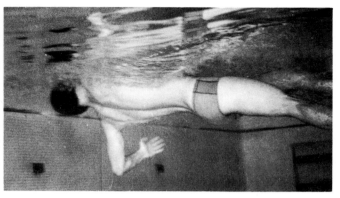

A. The swimmer is approaching the wall and reaching for it with his right hand (not shown) as his left hand finishes its pull.

B. The right hand reaches for the wall at a depth of about one foot and goes across in front of the head.

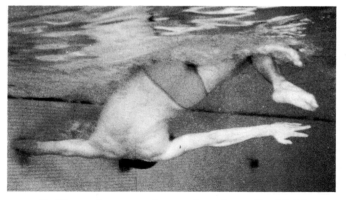

C. The swimmer pushes against the wall with his right hand as his feet start forward. The left hand, palm facing outward, positions itself to help him turn.

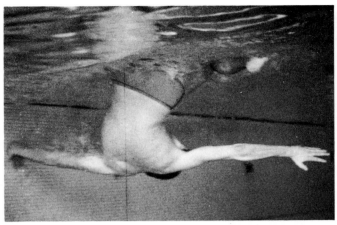

D. The elbow continues to extend as he pushes his body around with his right arm. Both feet are now out of water.

G. The left hand appears to almost be slapping the top of the head. The right hand is going forward as the legs swing closer to the wall.

E. The left hand now starts to pull toward the head. This pulling motion of the hand will help the swimmer turn.

H. The feet finally submerge as both arms start forward.

F. The left hand continues to pull toward his head as the feet swing toward the wall.

I. The hands meet overhead and the feet are planted on the wall, toes upward.

J. The legs start their thrust as the body stretches into a streamlined position.

K. The final push is made with the body fully extended. The swimmer will hold this glide position until he slows to swimming speed.

L. The pull and kick begin almost simultaneously.

Fig. 4.97. *The freestyle flip turn*

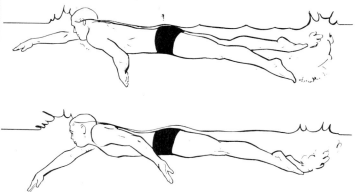

A and B. The swimmer approaches the wall with his normal stroke.

C. As he gets near the wall he positions one arm (the left in this case) as the other arm continues its pull.

D. He begins his turn when both hands are at his sides, palms facing downward.

E. The head is dropped and the knees are bent in order that he may give a small fishtail kick to help drive his hips upward.

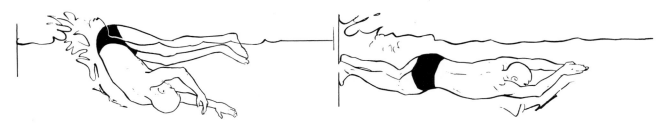

F. The palms start to press downward as the fishtail kick is completed.

J. The arms start to extend overhead as the legs begin their drive in the final push-off action.

G. One hand pulls in toward the head, as the other hand makes a small circle in an effort to get the swimmer off his back.

K and L. The final push is made with the shoulders almost level. The body is in a streamlined position.

H. The legs tuck up tightly as they are brought over. The shoulders continue to twist as the right hand continues to make a circle overhead.

I. The shoulders have completed a quarter twist, and the swimmer plants his feet on the wall sidewards. The arms meet overhead.

M. When the swimmer slows to swimming speed, he will start stroking.

The most common mistake made in turning is to fail to twist far enough off the back during the turn and to fail to get a sidewards foot plant. Many swimmers push off with their toes actually facing upward rather than sidewards.

FIVE

Theory and Research of Stroke Mechanics

SECTION 5.1
THE ROLE OF SCULLING MOVEMENTS
IN THE ARM PULL

Swimming movements in the water, particularly of the arms and hands, which seemed so very simple to swimmers, coaches, and writers of the past, now appear to be more complex and to involve principles and concepts never before considered or published. Although some rather complex descriptions of these movements have been published, when compared with the underwater sequence photographs of champion swimmers performing, they usually have been shown to be erroneous.

For example: There are two major concepts which have permeated our literature concerning the manner in which the hands and arms should be pulled when performing the crawl stroke:

1. The arm should be kept straight during the pull; that is, the elbow should not bend.
2. The arm and hand should be pulled in a straight line directly under the body. The hand should not be pulled in a zigzag pattern.

Combine these two recommendations and the result is a poor swimmer. Use a straight arm and zigzag a little, and you get a better swimmer. Drop the elbow and pull in a straight line and you have the stroke used by most beginning swimmers.

What then is the proper stroke? Coaches, how often have you heard someone say or even yourself have said to a swimmer, "Stop zigzagging your hands and letting the water slip—pull straight back and the resultant reaction will push you forward"? Years ago, when I first began coaching, I was an advocate of the pull-straight-down-the-middle-and-don't-bend-your-elbow school. After photographing many great swimmers underwater, following their pull patterns and observing their elbow bend, I began to doubt the validity of the straight-arm technique. The only swimmers who swam that way were beginning and very poor swimmers. This technique has been supported by most of our national groups who are involved in mass teaching methods. Literally millions of people have been taught to swim this way.

In 1950 Louis Alley conducted an experiment in which he compared the effectiveness of what he called the normal crawl arm stroke, which was a straight-arm pull although the elbow was bent slightly at the end of the pull to facilitate recovery, with that of the bent-elbow pull. In this study the bent-elbow pull was described as one in which the swimmer pulled his arm under the body, once again in a straight line, and bent his elbow up to 90 degrees as it was pulled directly under him. Alley figured if the swimmer pushed the water directly backward and not in an arc as was done in the straight-arm pull, he would have a more efficient pull and it would push him more directly forward.

Fig. 5.1. *Two improper crawl-stroke techniques*

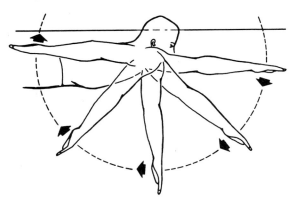

A. The straight-elbow, straight-line pull. This type of pull has been advocated by many people for many years and is inefficient.

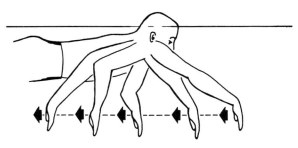

B. Bent-elbow, straight-line pull. This type of pull is even less efficient than the straight-arm pull (A).

Since, according to Newton's third law of motion, every action has an equal and opposite reaction, it would appear that this latter method would be superior. However, Alley concluded his study in this way: "The mean (force) for the normal-arm (straight) stroke was greater than the mean (force) for the bent-arm stroke." In other words the straight-arm stroke was superior to the bent-arm stroke as Alley was directing his subject to use it.

One important principle was not con-sidered in this study, and it is perhaps one of the most important we can consider in all propulsive movements of humans, other ani-mals, fish, and even boats in water. At first I will oversimplify the principle so that it may be more easily understood. It took me fifteen years to fully understand the principles and I cannot expect the reader to comprehend it in a few minutes.

Maximum efficiency in water is achieved by pushing a large amount of water a short distance rather than by pushing a small amount of water a great distance.

To use an example that would be com-parable to the study cited, we can cite an experiment conducted by an inventor almost 100 years ago. He reasoned that the paddle wheelers plying the rivers were inefficient because the force created by the large paddle wheel was improperly applied since each of its blades did not push directly backward at all times.

So he devised a caterpillar (tractor) ar-rangement of a series of paddles (Fig. 5.2). He believed that every paddle would be pushing directly backward and the resultant reaction would be for the boat to be pushed directly forward more economically than in the pad-dle-wheel method. Unfortunately for him and his financial backers the boat practically stood still when it tried this method of propulsion. It was reported that the inventor left town in a hurry and never published his findings in a scholarly journal. Perhaps we coaches are lucky that we don't have to leave town when advocating the same technique for swimmers.

Our inventor was violating the principle briefly stated above: in his conveyor belt each paddle was pushing a small amount of water a long distance. Once the water was started backward by a paddle, the paddle could no longer find any traction (propulsive force) from that moving water. Paddles, to get traction and create propulsion, must push against still water or water going in the opposite direction; they cannot effectively push against water that is already going backward. A good analogy would be that of a swimmer swimming upstream.

Fig. 5.2. *Three types of propulsion in boats*

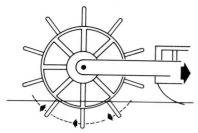

A. The Paddle Wheel, which is comparable to the straight-arm pull (Fig. 5.1 A).

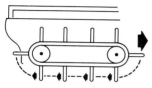

B. The Caterpillar, an arrangement of paddles comparable to the bent-elbow, straight-arm pull, which is even less efficient than the paddle wheel since the paddles push a little water a long distance.

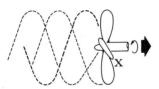

C. The Propeller, which is the most efficient arrangement because it pushes a lot of water a short distance and is comparable to the sculling type of pull of Fig. 5.3. At Point *X* the tip of the propeller is always contacting still water. The darkest line in back of the propeller shows the path of the tip of one propeller blade. This path is similar to the path of the hands of the butterfly swimmer in Fig. 5.3. Note the pitch of the propeller which is also similar to the pitch of the hands of the swimmer in the sequence of the butterflier in Fig. 5.6.

What then is the answer? For boats the answer was to go to a type of arrangement that would push a lot of water a short distance. This problem was solved by use of a screw propeller. The propeller of a boat or airplane never pushes the water or air directly backward, and it is *always moving forward into still water or air*. Every time it turns it contacts new water or air that is stationary, not moving backward.

It is my contention that swimmers also should not try to push the water directly backward but should use sculling motions of their hands and feet to propel them forward.

Assuming that all of the foregoing is valid and that we cannot gain much propulsion from water already headed backward, the swimmer must solve the problems of (1) how to evolve a stroke pattern that, once he has started the water moving backward, will allow him to get away from that water and work with still water and (2) how to pitch his hands so they will serve as propellers and not as paddles.

Fig. 5.3. *The zigzag pull pattern of 1964 Olympic butterfly champion, Kevin Berry*

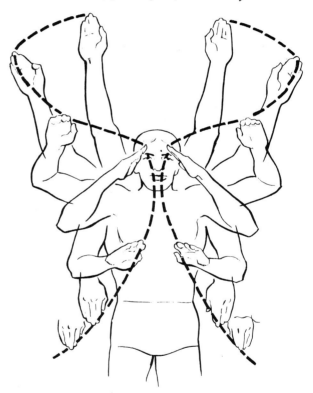

This keyhole or hourglass pull is typical of all great butterfly swimmers and is used by world record holders Mark Spitz and Ada Kok.

Figure 5.3 shows how 1964 Olympic butterfly champion Kevin Berry solved this problem in his performance of the butterfly stroke. He and every other world class swimmer naturally pull their arms in a keyhole or hourglass pattern so they are continually working in still water. They do not pull straight backward as advocated by the if-you-want-to-go-forward-push-directly-backward theorists, but follow a zigzag pattern. There is also evidence that backstrokers, freestylers, and breaststrokers observe the same principle.

Since I first published the book *The Science of Swimming*, most of the mail I receive has been from swimmers, coaches, and teachers who express surprise at the zigzag pull patterns used by the champion swimmers whose strokes illustrate the text. Although I used many actual photographs to document this principle, some readers have interpreted these zigzag patterns as stroke defects, and have difficulty accepting them as proper techniques.

Pitch of the Hands

If the hands are being used as propellers and not paddles, the palms of hands must be pitched or tilted in a manner much like that of a propeller of an airplane or boat, or a more common object with which we are all familiar, the blades of a fan.

When the hand is traveling in one direction it must be pitched at a certain angle; when it changes its direction of pull, the pitch of the hand must also be changed so that it can be used effectively as a propeller. The sequence of pictures of Kevin Berry shows how this pitch of the hands operates with the zigzagging action of the arm pull.

Summary

There is evidence to substantiate the theory that good swimmers use their hands and legs as propellers or foils to push against the water in much the same way as the propeller of a boat or the fins of a fish.

The concept that we should push the water directly backward so that we can be pushed directly forward is negated by the fact that once water is started backward, a paddle can get very little traction from this water. For this reason good swimmers invariably evolve a zigzag pattern in their pull.

To receive maximum efficiency in propulsive movements in the water, a lot of water should be pushed a short distance.

SECTION 5.2
THE APPLICATION OF BERNOULLI'S PRINCIPLE TO HUMAN PROPULSION IN WATER

It is generally assumed that the propulsive force created by the swimmer's hand is a drag force. I will examine here the role played by hydrodynamic lift in propelling the swimmer.

The use of oars to row a boat or of a paddle to propel a canoe are examples of the use of drag. The forward thrust in these two instances results from the difference in pressure between the posterior side of the paddle or oar, where the pressure is high, and the anterior side of the paddle or oar, where the wake is formed and the pressure is low (Fig. 5.4 A). In this type of propulsion the wake is necessary because, according to d'Alembert's paradox, if the flow were completely streamlined, the pressure on the paddle would add up to zero.

Examples of methods of propulsion using aerodynamic lift are the use of sculling paddles on gondolas in Venice, propeller-driven boats, and airplanes (Fig. 5.4 B). The dolphin, the whale, and most large fish all use a means of propulsion that depends on lift. These creatures propel themselves with large wing-like flukes or caudal fins.

Fig. 5.4. *Applications of Bernoulli's principle*

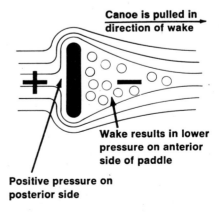

A. Wake formation from a paddle. The canoe is pulled in the direction of the wake.

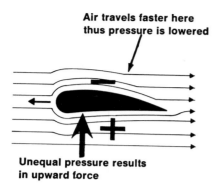

Air travels faster here thus pressure is lowered

Unequal pressure results in upward force

B. A wing provides aerodynamic lift through the camber (curvature) of its surfaces. Because the upper surface is more highly cambered than the lower surface, the air moving over the top surface is forced to move more quickly. This results in a lower pressure on the upper surface as compared with the lower surface and results in aerodynamic lift (Bernoulli's principle).

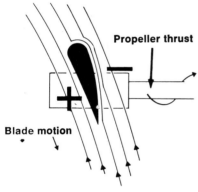

Propeller thrust

Blade motion

C. The propeller of a boat also uses Bernoulli's principle in the same manner, except that the blade moves in a vertical plane and the lift effect is used to push the boat in a horizontal plane.

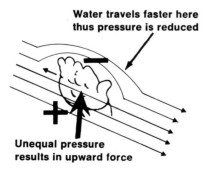

Water travels faster here thus pressure is reduced

Unequal pressure results in upward force

D. The hand of a swimmer can use lift to propel the swimmer forward by using Bernoulli's principle

instead of relying on wake formation, as the paddle does in A. The pressure differential between the palm of the hand and back of the hand is determined more by the pitch of the hand in relation to its path through the water than by its camber.

For many years it has been theorized that in the crawl stroke the swimmer pulls his arm through the water in a line straight down the center of gravity of his body. This method has been accepted as a result of the assumption that the swimmer is using his arm as a paddle and that his hand is forming a wake. Therefore, to observe Newton's third law of motion (action-reaction), if he wants to move straight forward, he should push the water straight backward.

Underwater movies of champion swimmers performing the various strokes have shown, however, that they do not pull their hands backward in a straight line, but rather in the shape of an S or an inverted question mark or some similar arrangement. In no champion swimmer was a straight-line pull ever observed in this investigation. Figure 5.5 shows the arm-pull pattern of four champions swimming the four competitive strokes. The dotted line represents the path of the middle finger.

Fig. 5.5. The pull pattern of four champion swimmers performing the four competitive strokes, as taken from underwater movies

A. The butterfly arm-stroke pull pattern as swum by 1964 Olympic champion Kevin Berry.

B. The crawl stroke arm-pull pattern of Dawn Fraser, three times Olympic champion.

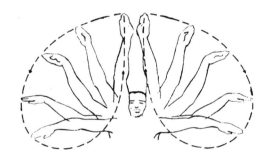

C. The breaststroke arm pull of Chester Jastremski, former world record holder.

D. The backstroke arm-pull pattern of Charles Hickcox, former world record holder.

The arm strokes of all these swimmers have a number of components in common. They are not straight-line pulls. The arms start the pull with the elbows straight, then during the pull, the bend of the elbow is increased until the arm is half way through the pull, at which point the elbows are bent about 90

degrees. From this halfway point onward (except in the breaststroke) the elbows extend until the pull is completed and they are again almost completely straight.

From study of the above pull patterns it appears that champion swimmers are not pushing directly backward, but are using a zigzag pattern of varying degrees. The illustrations are, however, deceptive in two ways:

1. The patterns are depicted in only two dimensions and are therefore represented as straighter than they really are.
2. They show the path of the hand through the water in relation to the swimmer's body. What is actually relevant in explaining the observed arm pull is the motion of the hand with relation to the still water. One way of observing this relationship is to take a time exposure, in a darkened pool, of a swimmer with a light attached to his hand. Another method is to photograph the swimmer by using a movie camera held in a static position as the swimmer moves past the camera. Both of these methods were used in this study.

Some Principles of Fluid Mechanics Applicable to Swimming

If, indeed, the swimmer is using his hands as propellers there are several principles that must be reviewed in order to obtain a better understanding of this technique.

Bernoulli's principle. This principle or law states that fluid pressure is reduced wherever the speed of flow is increased. For example, an airplane wing is so designed, and its pitch so inclined in relation to its direction as to produce a greater speed of airflow traveling over its upper surface than over its lower surface. This difference in the speed of flow causes a greater pressure on the lower surface and a lesser pressure on the upper surface (Fig. 5.4 B) and results in a lift or upward push on the wing.

The propeller of a boat acts in the same manner and uses lift to supply the forward thrust to a boat (Fig. 5.4 C).

Similarly, the hand of the swimmer, if it is

pitched in the proper manner in relation to its path through the water, can also serve as an air foil or propeller to provide forward propulsion to the swimmer (Fig. 5.4 D).

Efficient propulsion is obtained by pushing a large mass of water a short distance without much acceleration. This principle of fluid mechanics indicates why a straight-line pull is not efficient and why the lift principle is probably applied by the better swimmers.

Relevant to the study, a more appropriate way of stating this principle would be

> Greater efficiency in water is achieved by moving a large amount of water a short distance than by moving a small amount of water a great distance.

The propeller of a boat or airplane never pushes the water or air directly backward; it always moves forward in still water or air. Every time it turns it contacts new water or air that is stationary, not moving backward. This may also occur in swimming movements, especially during the early part of the arm pull. If the swimmer pulls his hand in a straight-line pattern, he is pushing a little water a long distance with great acceleration. Once the water around the hand has been started backward by the movement of the arm, the swimmer can get little traction or propulsion from this backward-moving water. He must therefore move his hand in an elliptical pattern in order to continue encountering still water. In this manner he observes the principle stated above.

Assuming the foregoing discussion to be valid, that the swimmer cannot gain much propulsion from water already headed backward, he must solve the problems of

1. How to evolve a stroke pattern that, once he has started the water moving backward, will allow him to get away from the water and work with still water

2. How to pitch his hands so they will serve as propellers and not as paddles—that is, so they will not create a wake

The Butterfly Stroke

Because there is significant change in the pitch of the hands during the butterfly stroke and because the zigzag pattern of the arm stroke is pronounced, a special emphasis has been placed on this stroke in the presentation of this study.

The pattern described by the hands as they are pulled through the water, the relative position of the arms, and the degree of bend of the elbows of 1964 Olympic butterfly champion, Kevin Berry, is shown in Figure 5.5 A. This type of pull, often referred to as the hourglass or keyhole pull, is used with slight variations by all world-class butterfliers who were studied, including Gary Hall, Ada Kok, and Mark Spitz. This pull pattern is shown in relation to the swimmer's body. The pull in relation to the still water of Olympic champion Charles Hickcox is shown in Figure 5.6. In this sequence of pictures, a 35-mm sequence camera was held in a static position on the bottom of the pool while the subject swam directly over the camera. The motion of his hands with respect to still water has been drawn into each frame. This sequence of pictures was taken at 24 frames per second. From the time the hands entered the water at Frame 1 (not shown) until they left at Frame 25 (not shown), the time involved was slightly over one second. In order to illustrate various hand and arm positions, only selected frames are used in this sequence.

The motion of the hands in Frames 1 through 17 suggests the possibility that the force exerted by the water on the hand is one of lift rather than of drag. During the outward push of the butterfly arm pull through Frame 11, the swimmer has the impression he is pulling back on the water. The pictures show, however, that his hands are actually moving forward. It is possible that a forward thrust, due to lift, is present during this phase of the stroke. This is the case with both the propeller blade and the dolphin's flukes, which exert a forward thrust while moving forward through the water.

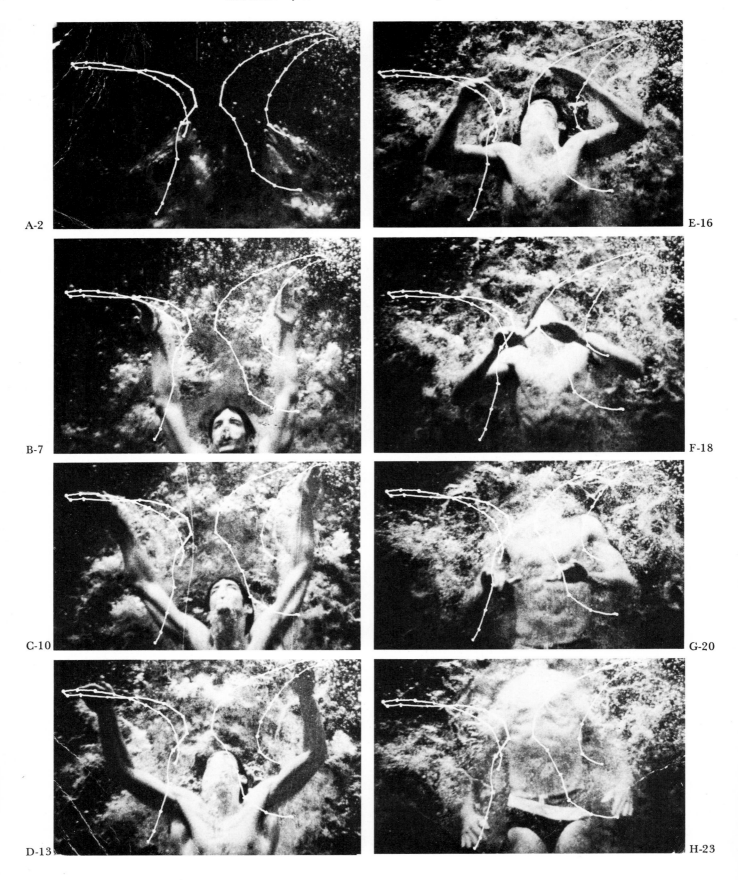

Fig. 5.6. *Underwater picture sequence*
The butterfly stroke taken from directly underneath.

To help verify that the outstanding swimmer exerts a lift force with his hands, one should also determine the angle of attack of the hand and whether or not it creates a wake as it moves through the water. Some information in this respect can be obtained from movie frames like those of Frame 7. In Frames 13 through 16 it is possible to get an impression of the angle of attack of the right hand. In some cases it may be possible to determine whether or not a wake is present on the back of the hand by observing air bubbles about the hand. Pictures of poor swimmers, for example, clearly show large bubble-filled wakes behind their hands. In general, however, a satisfactory way to determine the presence of a wake has not been found.

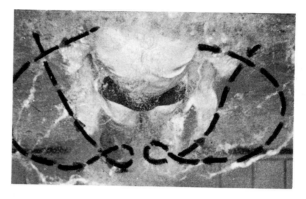

This sequence of pictures shows the underwater stroke of Kevin Berry with an overlay of the pull pattern as shown from head-on. The variation in the pitch of the hands can be seen in each of these frames. The hands are always pitched so that they provide hydrodynamic thrust. This same hand pitch is also noted in pictures of other world-class butterfly swimmers.

Fig. 5.8. Mark Spitz's butterfly stroke

Fig. 5.7. *Kevin Berry's butterfly stroke*

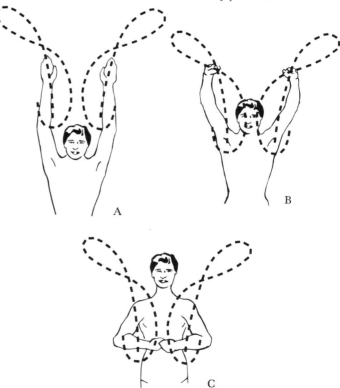

This sequence of pictures and the pull pattern represented by the dotted line were taken from 16-mm movie film taken from a static position on the bottom of the pool. His hands enter the water and leave at almost the same point. The similarity between Spitz's pull pattern and that of Hickcox (Fig. 5.5. D) is remarkable.

Fig. 5.9. *Santiago Esteva's crawl stroke*

Fig. 5.10. *Backstroke arm-pull pattern*

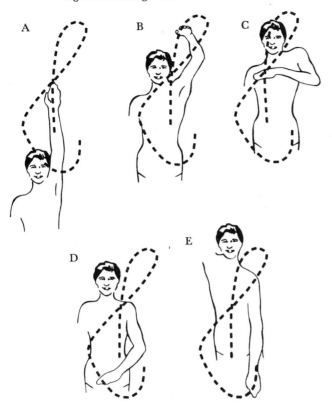

A. Charles Hickcox's backstroke pull pattern as shown in relation to still water. The pull-pattern overlay on this picture is taken from 16-mm movies.

B. Santiago Esteva's backstroke pull. The dotted white lines are made by the flashing lights described under Figure 5.9.

Fig. 5.11. *Olympic breaststroke champion Don McKenzie's arm pull*

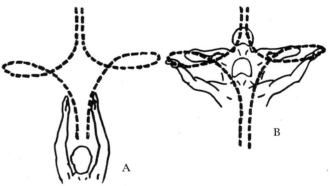

This sequence of drawings depicts the underwater pull pattern of Esteva's left arm, as taken from a static position with a 16-mm movie camera placed on the bottom of the pool. The actual photograph is a time exposure taken with the swimmer swimming across a darkened pool with a flashing light attached to each hand (the lights flashed at a rate of 20 times per second). The dotted white lines represent the pull pattern described by the swimmer's middle finger. The figure in the photograph is shown by taking one strobe flash during the swimmer's run. In the pull patterns of each hand, the hand leaves the water in front of the point at which it entered the water.

Although when watching Don McKenzie swim breaststroke one gets the feeling he is pulling backward, his hands scarcely push backward at all in relation to still water. The pull pattern above shows that, as he starts his pull outward, his hands are still moving forward (A). The first half of his pull is accomplished without any backward movement of his hands. During the inward sculling action of his hands, shown in B, his hands move only slightly backwards.

The greatest improvements in McKenzie's times were made immediately prior to the 1968 Olympic Games, when this writer (his coach) asked him to emphasize the outward and inward sculling action of his pull. Careful attention was given to the pitch of the hands and a particular emphasis was placed on not turning the palms upward during this part of the stroke or during the arm recovery. McKenzie became aware of the sculling action of his hands and tried to feel the positive pressure on his palms and the negative pressure on the tops of his hands. He stated that his whole concept and feel for the stroke changed as he began to *feel* his arm pull.

Fig. 5.12. *Elbow-up arm position*

The elbow-up position in the swimming stroke is accomplished by bending the elbow and medially rotating the upper arm. This elbow-up position permits the *P.D.* (pressure differential) between the positive (+) force on the palm of the hand and the lesser pressure (−) on the knuckle side of the hand to push the swimmer horizontally in the direction of the arrow. *R* = reaction.

A

B

C

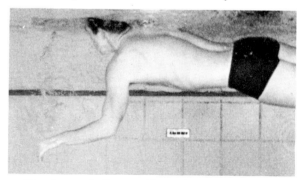

D

The high elbow position seen in A. freestyle, B. butterfly, C. breaststroke are all desirable and are typical of the good stroke mechanics of world-class swimmers. In the backstroke, D, the swimmer bends his elbow and rotates his upper arm in a manner similar to that of the other three strokes, but, since he is in a supine and not a prone position, his arm position might better be referred to as the elbow-down position. If the reader turns the picture upside down, he will see that the backstroke arm position then appears similar to the crawl elbow-up pull.

Fig. 5.13. *A common stroke defect*

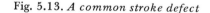

The dropped-elbow pull results in a misapplication of force and is uneconomical. The *P.D.* causes the swimmer to be forced upward instead of forward.

Summary

This study examines the possibility that the propulsive force exerted by the water on the hand is one of lift rather than drag. Through the study of champion swimmers' underwater arm-pull patterns, as determined by sequence photography and time-exposure photography with flashing lights attached to the swimmers' hands, various elliptical pull patterns were observed.

A swimmer swims more efficiently by moving a larger amount of water back more slowly than by moving a smaller amount of water back more rapidly. The champion swimmers observed in this study accomplished this by applying Bernoulli's principle. They moved their hands in elliptical patterns and changed the pitch of their hands so the flow of the water over the knuckle side of their hands was at a faster speed than that of the water on the palm side of the hand.

SECTION 5.3
"A BIOMECHANICAL ANALYSIS OF FREESTYLE AQUATIC SKILL," BY ROBERT SCHLEIHAUF

The science of biomechanics governs the study of swimming technique. Hay, in his book *The Biomechanics of Sports Techniques*, states: "Just as motor learning may be regarded as the science underlying the acquisition of skills, and physiology the science underlying training, biomechanics is the science underlying techniques."[1] The objective assessments of a science are demanded in our field where the complexities of swimming motions remain misunderstood due to varied opinions of leading authorities. It is apparent that the advancement of our field is based upon the application of the findings of science. "At the highest levels, improvement comes so often from careful attention to detail that no coach of sports in which techniques play a major role can afford to leave these details to chance or guesswork. For him, a

knowledge of biomechanics might be regarded as essential."[2]

The following analysis of freestyle stroke technique will concentrate upon the arm pull. A review of the literature indicates that a complete understanding of the factors related to the arm pull and swimming propulsion has not yet been attained. Despite the evident complexity of swimming motions, the problems of the swimming coach are often shrugged off by the nonprofessional who analyses swimming based on "intuitive knowledge." Unfortunately, reality presents many situations in swimming which would seem counter-intuitive to the layman. In the following discussion many principles of biomechanics will be mentioned and those which are counter-intuitive at first glance will be emphasized.

Freestyle Pulling Patterns

No area of sport has suffered more misunderstanding than the freestyle arm pull. The misconceptions surrounding swimming propulsion stem from an incomplete knowledge of the principles of biomechanics as well as an inability to isolate highly skilled stroke movements through the cinematographic method. Up until a short while ago, most swimming theorists advocated pulling on a straight line beneath the center of gravity of the body with the consequence of "pushing water directly backwards." It was thought that Newton's third law (action-reaction) would be satisfied and efficient propulsion would ensue. The problem with this theory was that it was based more on "intuitive" than biomechanical knowledge. In fact, the "push water straight backwards" theory is based on principles very similar to those which founded the assumption that the world was flat.

In December 1969, Counsilman published the article "The Role of Sculling Movements in the Arm Pull" and provided the first accurate analysis of swimming propulsion. An analogy was made between three types of pulling motions and three forms of navigational locomotion. Figure 5.14 illustrates a first analogy.

Fig. 5.14. *Caterpillar paddle wheel—*
straight-back arm pull

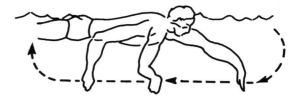

The drawing at the left in Figure 5.14 depicts a "caterpillar" paddle wheel, a device once theorized for use on riverboats. The motion of the paddles directly backwards on a straight line was supposed to produce efficient forward propulsion. The reason you have never seen such a paddle wheel on a boat is that, in reality, it doesn't work. The problem is stated: "In his conveyor belt each paddle was pushing a small amount of water a long distance. Once the water was started backward by a paddle, the paddle could no longer find any traction (propulsive force) from that moving water. Paddles to get traction and create propulsion, must push against still water or water going in an opposite direction; they cannot effectively push against water that is already going backward. A good analogy would be that of a swimmer swimming upstream."[3] As a result, pushing water on a straight line backwards is probably the worst technique for obtaining propulsion in swimming. Counsilman states, "Maximum efficiency in water is achieved by pushing a large amount of water a short distance rather than a small amount of water a great distance."[4]

An improvement on Figure 5.14 is shown in Figure 5.15.

The advantage of the circular paddle wheel is that it pushes water on a curved line, thereby continually seeking out still water for propulsion. The straight arm-down-the-middle pull is analogous. The advantage offered by propulsive efficiency is largely cancelled out in swimming by the mechanical disadvantage encountered by the pulling arm. The strength required to perform the pull increases linearly with the length of the resistance arm. In addition, the transfer of force from large muscle groups of the trunk to finer muscle groups of the arm and hand is not permitted with a stiff arm pull.

What we need is a pull which will satisfy hydrodynamic principles and also allow for some mechanical advantage in the muscles most involved. Figure 5.16 illustrates the navigational and aquatic mechanisms which satisfy the above requirements.

Fig. 5.15. *Circular paddle wheel—*
straight arm pull

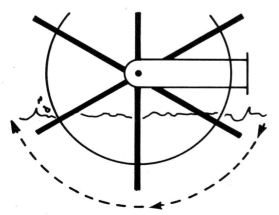

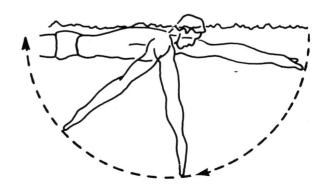

Fig. 5.16. *Propeller—curvilinear arm pull*
Graham Windeatt drawn from Counsilman's film
The Science of Swimming, adapted by James G. Hay
in *The Biomechanics of Sport Techniques.*

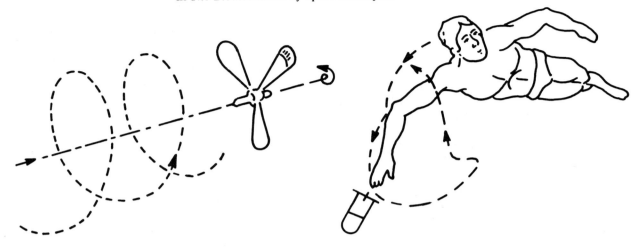

The propeller is the most efficient means of propulsion in water currently known. The propeller blades do not push any water directly backwards, but, instead, they actually move forward in the water continuously, always encountering still water. The sideways rotation of the propeller produces a force backwards in accordance with Bernoulli's principle of fluid mechanics.[5] Bernoulli's principle, or the lift principle, explains how Newton's third law of action-reaction can be met without pulling on a straight line. The lift force results from pressure differences and is directed at right angles to the line of motion of the wing or propeller blade. See Figure 5.17.

Fig. 5.17 *Lift force*

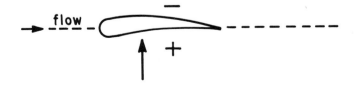

Thus, in order to produce a forward lift force a swimmer must move his hand in a sculling motion from side to side or up and down. These sculling motions can achieve the pressure difference illustrated above provided the hand is pitched so that the flow of water over the knuckle side of the hand is faster than that under the palm side of the hand.

The importance of lift forces in swimming may be accurately determined by a cinematographical analysis of highly skilled swimming motions. Mark Spitz has been chosen as the principal subject of the following analysis for it may be considered safe to assume his technique is "highly skilled." Nevertheless, the points to be made are general in nature and any other world-class swimmer could serve as an example.

First of all, to completely obliterate the notion that hand motion is predominantly backwards consider Figure 5.18. The sketch makes it evident that the right hand leaves the water *in front* of where it enters. Therefore, the resultant motion of the hand relative to the water is *forwards* not backwards. It is possible in the case of extremely poor swimmers to obtain hand motion which is predominantly backwards. In such cases, however, the swimmer is not pulling but is actually slipping his hand through the water. The swimmer, like the caterpillar paddle wheel, is pulling too far in a straight line and therefore cannot obtain traction.

Fig. 5.18. *Mark Spitz's hand motion relative to the water*

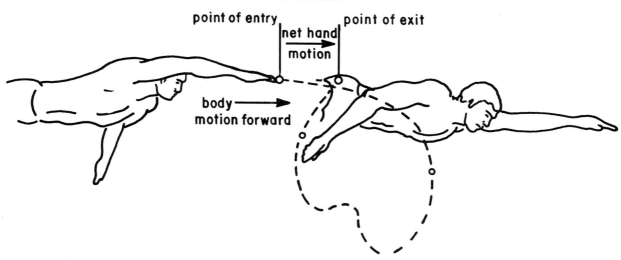

Another reason for the misconception about backward motion of the hand is that many people confuse motion of the hand relative to the body with motion relative to the water. Only motion relative to the water as shown above can describe the hydrodynamic forces acting on the hand. In the past, pulling patterns drawn relative to the body have prompted some to say that the pull is done almost on a straight line. In fact, Figure 5.19 illustrates that freestyle pulling patterns relative to the water follow a complex three-dimensional curve that in no way approximates a straight line.

Fig. 5.19. *Mark Spitz's pulling patterns*
Drawing taken from a cinematographical analysis
of Counsilman's film *The Science of Swimming.*

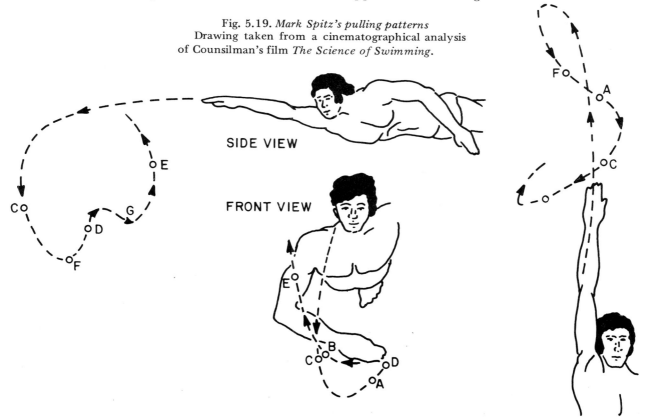

When interpreting these drawings bear in mind that the hand follows the dotted line pattern which remains fixed. The swimmer however, should be visualized as moving. For example, in the side view the body progresses from right to left, in the anterior view from page bottom to top, and in the front view the body is moving out of the paper.

In addition, bear in mind that the complexity of hand motions in freestyle is oversimplified by any two-dimensional drawing. The actual three-dimensional pattern assimilates the curvature of all three of the illustrated patterns at once.

It is interesting to note that the drawings above provide only a partial description of swimming movements. The study of pulling patterns alone limits understanding of aquatic skill to three-dimensional space. An additional factor, crucial to the understanding of propulsive forces, is hand velocity, the fourth dimension in aquatic skill.

Hand Velocity

Hand velocity has been conspicuously overlooked in the current field of swimming literature. The push-water-straight-backwards theorists imply that hand speed accelerates continuously in a unidimensional motion backwards. A study of cinematographical data however, indicates that hand speed is best described relative to a three-dimensional reference frame. For each dimension in space a separate component of hand velocity may be measured. In Figure 5.20, the variation in velocity in sideways, up-down, and forward-backward dimensions for a single arm pull is shown.

The first impression gained from the velocity curves is that hand speed does not uniformly increase in the backwards direction, or, for that matter, in any direction. In fact, a basic principle of aquatic skill is disclosed: peaks in hand speed may only be held briefly and must be followed by changes in direction for efficient propulsion. Too much velocity held for too long will only result in slippage. This explains Counsilman's observation that Spitz actually decreased his turnover rate in order to speed up during some of his races.[6] By spending more time on each underwater

pull, Spitz must have devoted more effort to sideways and up-and-down hand speeds. In fact, inspection of velocity curves V_y and V_x indicates that the highest velocity values occur in the plane perpendicular to the direction of forward progress. Since lift forces result from motion in this plane, and since the magnitude of lift forces increases with hand velocity, we have convincing evidence that lift forces dominate swimming propulsion.

A more detailed look at the velocity curves in conjunction with the stroke patterns will give the reader a better understanding of what is actually taking place during a freestyle arm pull. Looking at sideways hand motion (V_x) and the front and anterior patterns it is seen that the hand moves rapidly inward at midstroke (point A) as well as outward on the finish (point B). This change in direction keeps the hand working in still water. The magnitude of velocity values at these peaks represents a balance between two separate extremes. Too little speed supplies diminished propulsion and in an average swimmer indicates insufficient strength. Poor swimmers may also exceed velocity values shown for Spitz; this indicates that the hand is rapidly sliding through the water.

Similar interpretations may be applied to the V_y curve. Spitz's up-down hand velocity is dramatic proof of his ability to vary hand speed to maintain purchase on the water. The side view pulling pattern shows that the hand moves down on the press (point C) then rapidly sculls upward (point D), pulls down again and then pulls rapidly upward once more on the finish (point E). There is a considerable amount of work going on which is not acknowledged by the push-water-straight-back theorists.

The forward-backward velocity curve yields a different interpretation from those above. The peak below the time axis does not indicate a strenuous pulling action but instead an easy stretch-and-glide forwards. These initial V_z values are more indicative of linear motion of the body forwards than of hand speed. The point at which the velocity curve crosses the t-axis is significant, however. A poor swimmer will obtain positive hand speed earlier in the stroke cycle than shown, thus indicating slippage. The remainder of the V_z

curve shows efficient peaks (points *F* and *G*) depicting change in direction of the hand.

Thus we see that while pulling patterns define where to pull, velocity curves define how much to pull. Going through the motions is not sufficient to insure propulsive efficiency. It is the variety in emphasis placed on each part of the stroke which separates the champion from the also-ran. Through the velocity curves a display of the abstract quantity of motion reveals a fourth dimension in aquatic skill.

While efficient swimming propulsion is dependent on a curvilinear stroke pattern and a fluctuating hand velocity, there is still another variable of paramount importance in efficient performance. It is the swimmer's complex orientations of the hand and forearm when pulling, and it may be considered the fifth dimension of aquatic skill.

Fig. 5.20. *Mark Spitz's hand velocity*

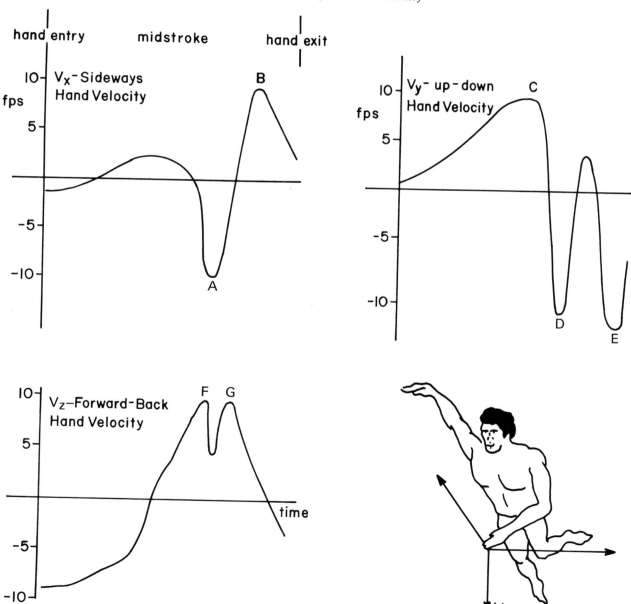

Fig. 5.21. *Swimmer's hand-edge view:*
Lift-drag force interaction for
three angles of pitch

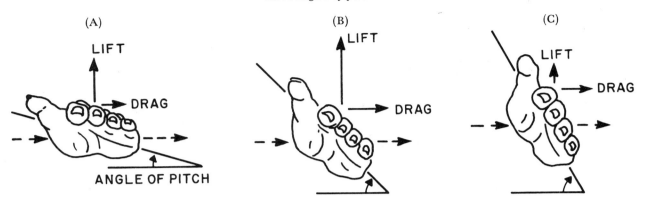

Hand Pitch

The swimmer's "feel for the water" is determined by his ability to pitch his hand and forearm. Contrary to popular opinion, "feel for the water," or the ability to maintain purchase on the water does not imply that the hand is held at 90° to the direction of motion of the pull. In order to produce lift forces the hand must be pitched or angled as illustrated in Figure 5.21.

The hand, like the wing in Figure 5.17, is moving from right to left on the page. As a result the flow of water generating forces on the hand is from left to right.

The vertical, or lift force, components vary with hand pitch as shown. The largest lift force (Fig. 5.21 B) corresponds to the burble point in the airfoil. Either less or more pitch will result in a decrease in lift force. In the case of too much pitch an airfoil is said to be stalled, and in swimming (Fig. 5.21 C) this indicates that the hand is being used as a paddle instead of a propeller blade. With too little pitch both lift and drag forces diminish and the hand is in effect sliding (Fig. 5.21 A). Thus we see that in order to produce maximum lift forces a swimmer must strike a delicate balance in hand pitch based on his sensitivity or feel for the water.

The horizontal, or drag force, components increase continuously with the angle of pitch. It is through the use of the interaction of both lift and drag forces that the swimmer achieves straight forward progress from his

widely fluctuating pulling patterns and hand velocities. Figure 5.22 A shows how direct forward propulsion results from diagonal hand motions.

Note that the size of the lift and drag force components entirely determines the orientation of the resultant propulsive force. Figure 5.22 B shows that too steep an angle of pitch will produce a force angled to the side, and possibly introduce lateral hip motion in the swimmer.

Thus, efficient propulsion is dependent on lift-drag force interaction. For the swimmer, this means that the pitch of the hand must be continuously adjusted to ever changing directions of pull. Even the forearm can be pitched to increase propeller-like pulling surfaces. High elbow position, common among talented swimmers is shown in Figure 5.23.

It is interesting to note that the hand and forearm may not always be oriented to produce a force directly backwards. At times, extraneous inertial and kicking forces must be canceled by the pull in order to produce straight forward propulsion upon the swimmer's free body diagram.

That the arm pull adjusts lift-drag force interaction in response to the kick sheds light upon the variation in style between six-beat and two-beat freestyle. Carlile[7] observed that at the Munich Olympics the six-beaters had a low stroke frequency (as low as 39 strokes per lap in a 400-meter race) and the two-beat kickers had a high stroke frequency (as high as 54 strokes per lap). That the two groups swam equally well appears mysterious at first, especially when one considers Counsilman's conclusion that the kick does not directly provide propulsion in freestyle[8]. An understanding of lift-drag force interaction does provide an explanation, however.

Fig. 5.22. *Mark Spitz's hand pitch*
Drawn from Counsilman's film *The Science of Swimming.*

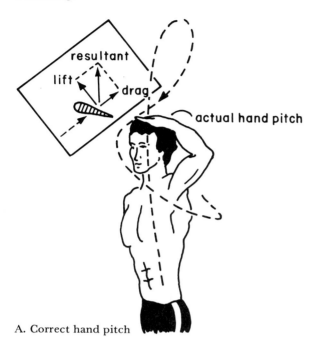

A. Correct hand pitch

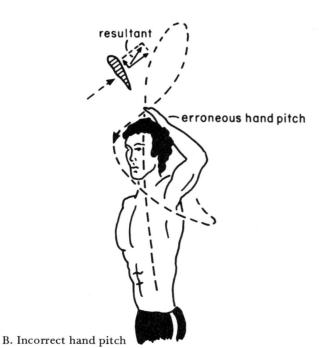

B. Incorrect hand pitch

Fig. 5.23. *High elbow position*

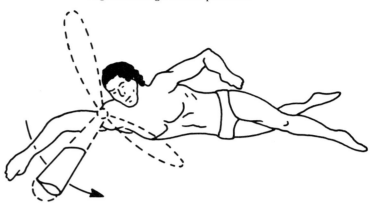

Fig. 5.24. *Mark Spitz's lift-drag interaction*

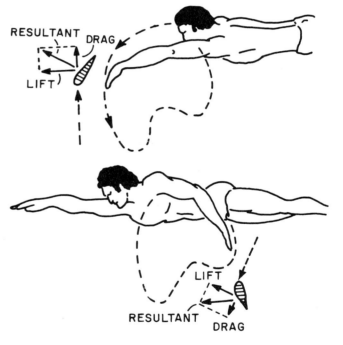

It seems that a six-beat kicker could achieve higher sideways and up-and-down hand speeds at midstroke because of the availability of lateral and vertical kicking forces. The drag component of the hand could neutralize eccentric kicking forces and the lift component could approach its maximum value. For example, the explosive hand speed at point D on Spitz's V_y curve (see Fig. 5.25) would be sure to cause a lowering of hip elevation if powerful downward kicking forces were not available. In contrast, two-beater Kinsella shows much less hand speed upward at midstroke, indicating omittance of a sculling action.

Thus Kinsella, by varying hand pitch and speed, is using a stroke which requires less energy per arm pull but demands a higher rate of turnover. The situation is similar to the problems in ship design discussed by Tallman[9]. For a given ship and motor the pitch of the propeller blade will define the rpms required by the motor. In aquatics, swimmers with different strengths and weaknesses can modify the pitch of their hands and the rpms of their strokes to arrive at an optimum combination of lift-drag force interaction.

The success enjoyed by both two- and six-beat freestylers is proof that although specific key concepts govern swimming propulsion, the application of these concepts will vary from swimmer to swimmer. The extra-polation of the foregoing biomechanical principles to a wide variety of swimmers is beyond the scope of this paper. However, a more extensive research project is currently underway at Lehman College in New York City, and it is designed to arrive at quantitative conclusions from the qualitative material presented above. In particular, the use of hand-pitch measurements and hand-velocity curves as potential analytic techniques in stroke evaluation will be investigated. Specific guidelines for the analysis of all swimming styles will be sought.

Before the coach can make specific applications, however, a basic background in biomechanics is required. An understanding of the importance and interdependence of a curvilinear stroke pattern, a fluctuating hand velocity, and a precisely oriented hand and forearm is basic. This knowledge, in combination with the expertise of the coach may allow the essentials of aquatic skill to be communicated to the swimming world at large.

Fig. 5.25. *A comparison of the lift-drag force exerted by a six-beat and a two-beat swimmer*
Drawn from Counsilman's film *The Science of Swimming.*

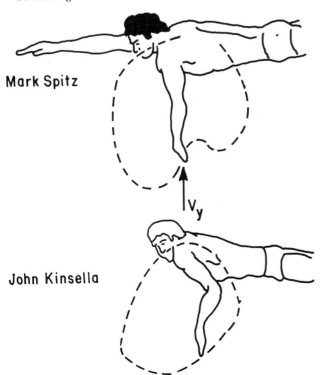

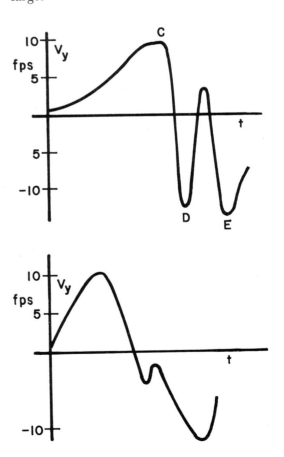

SECTION 5.4
"A HYDRODYNAMIC ANALYSIS OF BREASTSTROKE PULLING PROFICIENCY,"
BY ROBERT SCHLEIHAUF

The breaststroke arm pull is probably the simplest propulsive action used in the world of competitive swimming. In spite of this, controversy exists regarding such basic coaching questions as: should water be pulled backwards or sculled sideways? should the elbows be pulled into the ribs or should the pull be short? and finally, should the hand accelerate uniformly backwards or not? Although these questions must have simple and straightforward answers, they remain unresolved because a lack of objective data on the subject.

The most obvious source of information on breaststroke lies in cinematographic data. Such stroke parameters as pulling pattern, hand velocity, and hand pitch may be measured from films with scientific accuracy. These measures by themselves provide very good, but indirect evidence of pulling proficiency. More direct measures of performance can be supplied by the application of hydrodynamic principles to cinematographic data. Using the "hydrodynamic analysis" the actual forces produced by breaststroke swimmers may be calculated for both size and direction. The resulting data present the coach with an extremely objective basis for the evaluation of breaststroke pulling proficiency.

Model Pulling Patterns

The "McKenzie Style Breaststroke" will be used as a stroke model in this paper (Don McKenzie was an Olympic gold medalist at Mexico). For the purpose of visualizing McKenzie's technique the reader may refer to films by Counsilman[1], Speedo[2], and Sunkist[3]. Drawings of Subject 1, a good college breaststroker, are shown in Figure 5.26, for they bear remarkable resemblance to McKenzie's style of swimming. His anterior view pulling pattern is nearly identical to the drawing shown in Counsilman[4] for McKenzie. Furthermore, his front and side views match closely with the model breaststroke swimmer shown in Counsilman[5].

Looking more closely at Figure 5.26 we see that the pull is three-dimensional. Note that the path of the forefinger of the right hand relative to the water is shown. In other words, the force-producing actions of the hand on still water are shown by the dotted lines. For the purpose of visualization the reader should imagine that the hand follows the fixed pulling pattern while the body moves: from left to right in the side view, from page bottom to top in the anterior view, and out of the page in the front view (see Fig. 5.26).

For example, the anterior view is usually obtained from films taken with the camera man lying on the bottom focusing straight upwards at the pool ceiling. Then, as the swimmer passes into and out of the range of vision of the camera, the hand follows a pattern typically similar to that of Subject 1. Note that the anterior view shows that without a doubt breaststroke pulling is a sculling action. Hand motion is predominantly sideways (hands press out at point 3-10, and scull in at points 10-15) with only slight motion backwards (points 6-11). Actually what motion there is in the forward-back dimension must be considered predominantly forwards when comparing progress from pull beginning (point 3) to pull end (point 15). This information leaves little support for any contention that water is pulled backwards in breaststroke.

All values shown are relative to three-dimensional space. It should be noted that although carefully collected data on McKenzie are not available, approximate measures on hand speed for a number of world-class swimmers (McKenzie, Jastremski, and Dahlberg) all bear close resemblance to those in Figure 5.27. This is not surprising, for the pulling patterns of these three swimmers, particularly McKenzie, are very similar to those of Subject 1. Actual values of peak velocities may be expected to vary with hand size, arm length, and hand pitch, but the form and distribution of the velocity curves seems to remain similar among good swimmers.

Fig. 5.26. *Subject 1—breaststroke*

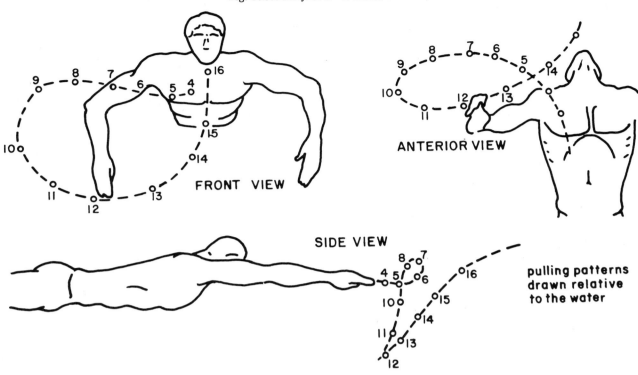

Fig. 5.27. *Subject 1—hand velocity*

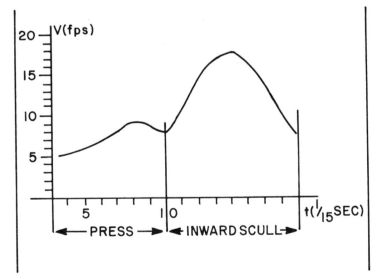

Looking at the velocity curve in conjunction with the anterior pulling pattern for Subject 1 we see that there are two peaks in hand speed. The first occurs two-thirds of the way into the press (frame 8) indicating hand acceleration outwards. The second velocity peak occurs near the end of the inward scull

and indicates the culmination of the most forceful action in the breaststroke pull. It is interesting to note that at the point where the hand moves backwards (frame 10) that hand speed is at its lowest. It seems that the swimmer is subconsciously aware that pushing water directly backwards will be futile. As a result very little effort is expended sideways until the hand is maneuvered to a position where a powerful sideways sculling action can again predominate. Interestingly enough, these data show that the hand does not accelerate uniformly backwards in breaststroke, but instead moves sideways in two discrete pulses of speed.

Hand Pitch

The final, and most critical, parameter of swimming proficiency is hand pitch. Technically, hand pitch is the angle between the hand's orientation and its line of action,[6] although it may be viewed subjectively as a measure of a swimmer's "feel for the water." This "feel for the water" is of critical importance to force production in swimming. For example, it is possible for a swimmer to pull on near-perfect pulling patterns, using ideal representation of hand velocity, and still be partially unproductive due to an erroneous choice of hand pitch. His problem would be that he is going through the motions but not the actions of proficient stroking. In order to differentiate between a stroke that looks good and a stroke that is good the coach must gain an understanding of force production in swimming.

Force Production

As an example of the effect of hand pitch on force production consider the airplane wing analogy in Figure 5.28.

Fig. 5.28. *Wing analogy*

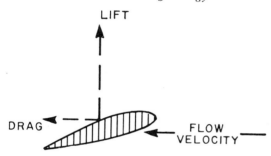

A typical airfoil, if held at an angle of inclination of approximately 18 degrees will produce maximal lift force. This lift force, with airplanes is always directed upwards. With propulsion in water, however, "lift" should not be considered synonomous with "upward" forces. For example, the propeller in a boat directs lift forces forwards for propulsion. Similarly a swimmer's sculling motions derive propulsion from lift forces which usually are oriented forwards.

Another type of force created by wing or hand motion is drag force (see Fig. 5.28). With a wing or a swimmer's body this force may be regarded as retarding. In the case of the motion of a canoe paddle or a swimmer's hand, however, drag force may make a positive contribution to propulsion. For example, pulling water straight backwards is an attempt to provide propulsion purely through drag force's action on the hand.

Measurement of these lift and drag forces

in swimming may be accomplished in the same way that propulsion and flight characteristics are calculated for boats and planes. At the New Rochelle Aquatic Club we have completed some preliminary research in the application of hydrodynamic principles to swimming proficiency, and as a result have been able to generate propulsion vector diagrams and resultant force curves for competitive swimmers. Our technique is called the hydrodynamic analysis and, using it, the coach's role in the stroke-correction process may be likened to an architect involved in the stroke design of swimmers. The following examples should shed some light on the strength of the hydrodynamic analysis in the interpretation of swimming technique.

Hydrodynamic Analysis—Subject 1

Looking at the results of a hydrodynamic analysis of Subject 1 we see that force production is very similar between airfoils and swimmers' hands (see Figs. 5.28 and 5.29).

Fig. 5.29. *Subject 1—force production*

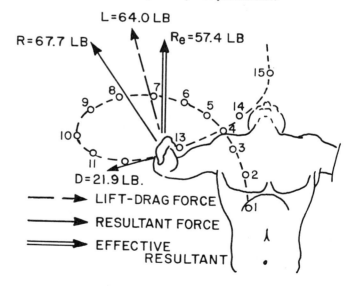

There are slight differences, however. First the ideal angle of inclination is greater (37°) due to the difference in shape of a swimmer's hand and a plane wing. Second, the lift force is now directed approximately forwards relative to the swimmer's body, and finally, the drag force does not retard body motion, but instead tends to pull the body to the side. The opposite hand, of course, will counteract sideways motion, and the net effect on the body will be straight forward propulsion.

The combined effect of lift and drag forces is represented by the resultant R and is equal to the amount of effort in pounds exerted by the swimmer, The amount of force which is translated to forward propulsion for the right hand is R_e the effective resultant. In breaststroke, since both hands act simultaneously the total propulsion created is equal to two times R_e. We shall see in the next section that plots of R_e for the entire pull yield a very objective basis for the evaluation of stroke technique.

Before moving on, however, we should look at typical force production on the press phase of the stroke. Although this force is not as powerful as the inward scull (described above) it is nevertheless important and follows the same hydrodynamic principles.

Fig. 5.30. *Subject 1—press phase*

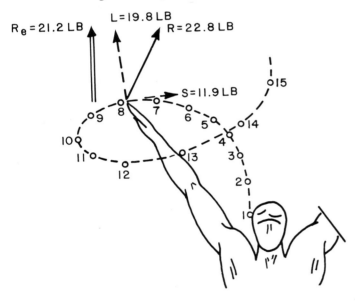

Inspection of Figure 5.30 shows that the resultant is directed predominantly forwards with a small component inwards. Again, this inward component is cancelled out between the right and left hands, and net propulsion is straight forwards. The effective resultant shown is the largest force generated during the press, for it occurs at the point of peak

hand velocity. It is interesting to note that this peak force and hand velocity occurs at a point in the stroke where the pulling pattern orientation and hand pitch yield a resultant which is predominantly forwards. In other words, the three parameters of swimming proficiency (hand pitch, velocity, and pulling pattern) combine at this point to illustrate the skill of this subject.

Stroke Guidelines

We now have a fairly detailed description of the McKenzie-type breaststroker. But what about swimmers who use styles which differ from McKenzie's? To what extent can individuals vary from our stroke model without violating hydrodynamic principles? An absolute answer to this question depends on each case at hand; however, the following two case studies should help define some general stroke guidelines in breaststroke.

Hydrodynamic Analysis—Subject 2

This subject exhibited a long and seemingly powerful arm pull in early season. As he was a talented high-school breaststroker, I was tempted to ignore the fact the his elbows pulled into his ribs with each stroke. The results of a hydrodynamic analysis shown in Figure 5.31 B quickly changed my mind.

The extended length of his arm pull caused a poor orientation of his pulling pattern on the inward scull (frames 12-15). As a result, his resultant force is angled too much to the side, causing a diminished portion of his effort to be translated to forward propulsion (see Fig. 5.31 B). Of the 26.1 lbs exerted by the swimmer only 16.0 lbs are effective with the remainder of the right and left arms.

As a correction, a shorter pull, more similar to McKenzie's was advocated. Particular care was taken to keep the hands in front of the shoulders and the elbows away from the ribs. The subsequent hydrodynamic analysis showed an improvement in pulling proficiency (see Fig. 5.31 C). Note that for similar physical positions of the arm the resultant force orientation has rotated forwards with the short stroke. As a result, a greater percentage of effort was directed forwards (33.1 lbs). The dramatic increase in propulsion is also due to the occurence of peak hand velocity near frame 13. With this stroke everything seemed to "click" for this subject, and his times dropped 5 seconds on the 100 over a three-month span.

A rationale for the subject's improvement in performance is supplied by the effective resultant force curve (Fig. 5.31 D). Note that the average resultant created on the inward scull increased from 8.2 lbs (long stroke) to 12.5 with the short stroke. This data seems to supply positive confirmation of Doc Counsilman's recommendation that the elbows should never be pulled into the ribs in breaststroke[7]. As long as pulling patterns are generated similar to Figure 5.31 B it would seem impossible for efficient propulsion to ensue from long arm pulls.

Fig. 5.31. *Subject 2—proficiency comparison*

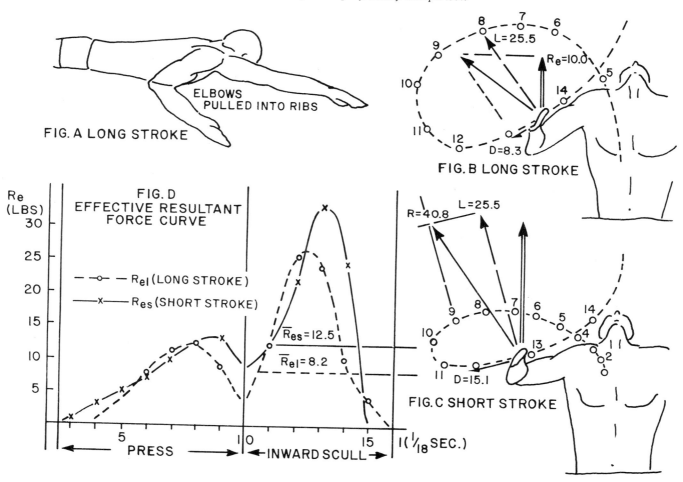

Hydrodynamic Analysis—Subject 3

This subject used a narrow but seemingly effective arm motion for our initial analysis. His arm pull was circular, but his hands pulled just barely outside the width of his elbows at the end of the press (see Fig. 5.32 A). The results of an hydrodynamic analysis showed a good pulling pattern orientation and hand pitch, with resultant forces generated in approximately the right direction (see Fig. 5.32 B) The peak hand speed is significantly low, however (10.3 fps versus 17.7 and 14.6 for subjects 1 and 2). This information came as a surprise for this swimmer was strong and well conditioned. It was hypothesized that the error in hand velocity was related to the narrow pulling pattern. As a result, a wider arm pull was suggested to give the hand time to accelerate to higher values on the inward scull.

The results of the subsequent hydrodynamic analysis showed a significant increase in hand speed to 13.1 fps and a corresponding increase in propulsion with the wider pull (see Fig. 5.32 C).

It is interesting to note that although the wider stroke is more powerful for the subject, it is not necessarily more efficient. Figure 5.32 C shows that in order to gain an 8.3 lb. increase in effective propulsive force, an additional 16.7 lbs. of effort (R force) was required. In other words, this swimmer had to pay the price for increased speed. The investment was good, however, for the swimmer improved his best time by 5 seconds on 100 yds. that season.

Looking at Figure 5.32 D, we see a graphic rationale for this swimmer's improvement in performance. The 4.7 lb. gain in the average propulsive force on the inward scull is due to the fact that R increases in proportion to velocity squared (i.e., only a 41 percent increase in V will cause a 100 percent increase in R). As a result, we see that swimmers should strive for maximum hand velocity wherever possible, providing hand pitch and pulling pattern orientation remain good.

In the case of breaststroke, all requirements can be met with a wide arm pull. It seems, again, that Doc Counsilman's recommendation that the hands should pull outside the width of the elbows[8] is well founded.

Fig. 5.32. *Subject 3—proficiency comparison*

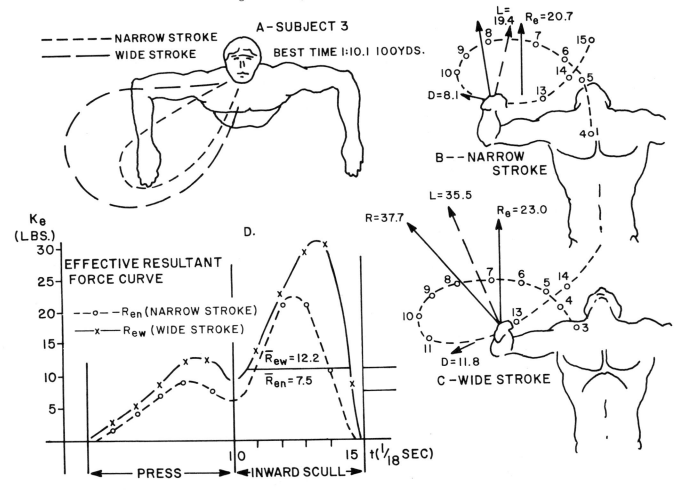

Conclusions

Thanks to the application of the hydrodynamic analysis, the following objectively determined conclusions may be drawn on breaststroke:

The pull is a sculling motion, deriving propulsion from sideways hand motions; little if any water is pushed backwards.

Hand acceleration occurs in two pulses, first to the side and then rapidly inwards.

Hand pitch magnitude governs the size of lift force production just as wing and propeller pitch affect flight and navigation.

A long arm pull, with elbows pulling into the ribs, seems to rely on an inefficient application of hydrodynamic principles.

A narrow arm pull, with hand pressing only as wide as elbow width, seems to supply insufficient hand speed sideways for significantly large lift force production.

These conclusions should supply the coach with a general framework with which he can design stroke technique. The specifics of the stroke correction process must vary with individual strengths and weaknesses. Nevertheless, the hydrodynamic principles outlined here may be expected to govern proficiency in all styles of breaststroke.

Part Three

COACHING

SIX

The Principles of Coaching

SECTION 6.1
THE SEARCH FOR A PHILOSOPHY OF COACHING

Whether we are aware of it or not, whether we have actually sat down and written it out or not, all of us coaches have a philosophy toward our profession. If you would like to examine your own, a good place to begin might be in asking the question "Why coach?" While there are many answers to this question, they may finally be seen to center on the basic need to establish status, both in the eyes of other people and in your own eyes.

We are motivated to action and adopt a certain line of behavior in order to satisfy basic needs: we eat when we're hungry, we drink when we're thirsty, we are stimulated to activity when we are bored, we investigate when we are curious, we want to fight when our aggression is aroused, we seek out other people when our group instinct is stimulated and—crucial to this discussion—we desire esteem within our communities and within ourselves. All of us respond to the needs listed above, but we respond in different ways and in varying degrees. Sometimes we are forced to inhibit our response in our own interest or in that of the group of which we are a part.

For example, if a person is overweight, he must override his hunger pangs and avoid satisfying his appetite, or risk suffering a coronary. When a coach allows his appetite for acclaim and personal glory to be satisfied at the expense of the opinion of his associates and the athletes in his program, he is allowing one need to dominate another—that is, the need for status to override the need for social acceptance.

How do you define and recognize the basic needs of the group and of the individuals with whom you associate, and how do you decide on the lines of action that you should adopt to see that the needs of most of these are fulfilled? The answers to these questions should be among the first considerations in the formation of a coach's philosophy. Next, how do you define your basic needs and decide the means by which they are fulfilled? If the answers to both sets of questions parallel one another and have identical elements, your philosophy is probably very sound. If they do not, you may either be too self-seeking or, at the other end of the scale, too self-sacrificing.

Most people admire maturity in a person; yet I have seen some twelve-year-old swimmers who were more mature than their parents or coach. Some people never mature

251

in their behavior patterns or develop a mature philosophy. Let me give you an example of an immature young man who swam for me. He wanted the best for himself, as we all do. He wanted all the headlines, all the world records, to win all the races and get all the glory. He swam poorly on relays in order to save himself for his individual events. He talked only of himself and took no interest in the other swimmers on the team. He was so concerned with fulfilling his needs that he failed to an unnatural degree to consider the needs of anyone else. Yet, in common with us all, he shared the need to be part of a group—which in this case was the team—to be liked and respected. His immaturity lay in the fact that he failed to recognize that he had to help others satisfy their needs to best satisfy his own. Owning all the world records would fail to make a person happy if he knew no one cared for him. Our team member was unhappy, but he had no inkling of the reason why. He only knew that here it was happening again, so he asked me for help. I told him that he had to take an interest in other people, had to consider their feelings, had to talk about them. Specifically, we decided that he could begin by being interested in the swimming times of his teammates. He could put out on relays and not just be concerned with how he swam in the individual events, in practice, and in meets. He could try congratulating the swimmers when they did well. I told him to remember the word "TATNAM"—Talk about them, not about me." I gave him a dollar-fifty paperback copy of a very simple book which outlines the mechanics of behavior. The book was Dale Carnegie's *How to Win Friends and Influence People*, and it is as timely today as when it was written many years ago. Translated into over thirty languages and sold in the millions of copies, this book is designed to teach people how to fulfill the needs of others while satisfying their own.

After reading this book, the swimmer made no overnight transition, and often he found it hard to adopt the proper mechanics of behavior. Eventually, he developed a more mature attitude and was accepted by the team. He became happier and better adjusted in all aspects of his life and was able to break the cycle of behavior that had plagued him for so long. He became part of the group, his self-esteem increased and gradually affected all his relationships beneficially.

Swimmers and other young people are not the only ones who suffer from a lack of maturity. A mature person is one who understands that to achieve the best for himself he must first see that the needs of the group and the needs of the individuals he serves are fulfilled. If he wants to be a mature person, the coach must learn to consider the needs of the group before he considers his own, but without totally sacrificing himself and his needs.

There will be many times in your career, chiefly when you are in the process of formulating your philosophy, when you will have to make choices that have no clearly defined right or wrong. Your decisions should be based on a clear understanding of yourself and the others who will be affected by them. For example, one group, your team members, needs you at the pool seven days a week to get them into top physical condition and to help them perfect their stroke mechanics; another group, your family, needs you at home to fulfill its need for love, affection, and guidance. Each of us responds differently to the demands made upon us, depending on our level of energy, our interest, and our goals and needs. In the situation just described, one person will compromise and scrupulously divide his time between the two groups. He may or may not feel guilty about his decision. Another highly goal-oriented person may decide to sacrifice his family for his team: if he feels guilty about his decision, he can as easily rationalize it as the third person who decides to neglect his coaching responsibilities in order to devote more time to his family. None of the three is right or wrong; he has simply made his decision in light of his needs.

I think you get the point, but I want to present two extreme cases that will further illustrate it: a completely dedicated—even fanatic—coach once told me he never took a vacation, never delegated any responsibility because he felt no one else could do anything right (he even filled out entry blanks). He worked twelve to fourteen hours a day and passed out twice on the deck from overwork in one season. He had an ulcer and was so nervous that if someone had goosed him, he'd have set a high-jump record. On the other extreme is the coach who wrote me that he loved his wife and children a great deal and wanted to spend a lot of time with them and would I please send him a workout that his team could do in one hour a day and still get into top shape. These two types of coach and their divergent philosophies do exist and no one can say that either is wrong. We can safely say that they belong in different programs. An energetic and ambitious coach with a strong desire to achieve success should not get into or, once in, stay in a low-pressure program where the predominating philosophy of the program is to swim for recreation and fun. Occasionally such a coach can change this philosophy, sometimes not. If he can't change it, he should not sacrifice himself or his needs by adopting the group's philosophy. He should look for a team or situation where his philosophy will parallel theirs. I did this when I left the State University of New York at Cortland, N.Y., to go to Indiana University. There should be no stigma associated with a move of this sort.

On the other hand, the coach with the "one-hour-a-day" philosophy does not want to put himself into a high-pressure program where the stress will be so great that he will certainly be unhappy. Unfortunately for the people who hire the personnel, coaches do not walk around with a rating scale of 1 to 10 tattooed on their foreheads. Even if they did, the tattoo mark might have to be changed occasionally. Most of us are familiar with the young coach who starts out with enthusiasm and sets a fast pace early in the race, only to slow down or even decide to give up the race and become an aquatic director.

Theoretically, a very simple solution to the problem of conflicting philosophies between the coach and the group he serves—parents, team members, and administration—is to move to another position. It's easier to move him than to move all the others. But if his philosophy is shared by a majority of the group and conflicts with that of only a few,

perhaps the minor portion of the group should switch situations.

Sometimes swimmers jump from one club to another. These events can be embarrassing, but they do occur. Other factors, such as social incompatibility between coach and swimmer, or between parent and coach, contribute to club-jumping, but I believe the primary reason is a conflict of philosophies. It is important that a coach adopt a philosophy that is somewhat flexible, but for him to force himself to change his philosophy, compromise his beliefs, and change his goals is to invite discontent and probably disaster.

I have said that all humans are controlled in varying degrees by their basic needs or drives. It would be easy, if this were not the case, to map out a standard approach for all coaches to follow. It would also be dull; but that is not the point I want to emphasize now. What I want to stress is that what is good for one person may be disastrous for another. The assistant of one coach I know so admired his boss that he adopted the head coach's goals and emulated him in every aspect of his coaching duties. The head coach was strongly motivated, with a high compulsion to achieve and a high tolerance for stress. The assistant coach had a lower ego drive and a lower tolerance for stress. In adopting the philosophy of the head coach, the assistant was establishing a situation incompatible with his personality and needs. After becoming a head coach in a high-stress situation, he recognized this incompatibility and settled for a coaching job in a less stressful environment.

In recognition of my needs, I sought a stressful situation, but I was largely influenced in the formation of my philosophy by my coach, the late Ernie Vornbrock, of the St. Louis Downtown YMCA Swimming Team. His primary obligation was to the swimmers; to see that they achieved their potential academically, athletically, and socially. In other words, he tried to conduct his program in such a manner as to help his swimmers gain self-fulfillment. That I feel the same obligation as a coach is due to his example.

I will now outline the needs that are basic to all humans, as I see them, in the context of a coach-athlete team situation. A list of twenty to thirty could be made, but I will confine myself to the primary ones that concern an athletic coach.

1. *Love and affection.* A primary need is for love and affection—to like and be liked. I want the swimmers to know that I have a genuine affection for them and convey it when I can. If I see a former swimmer many years after his career with me has finished and I find that he has retained a strong tie with me and with his former teammates, I am pleased. In many cases we have established lifelong friendships. I think this is one of the greatest things going for us in athletics.

I try to know every swimmer's grade-point average within a fraction of a point. I try to know their best swimming times in a meet and in a workout. I know their problems, their girls—sometimes these two are the same. I know their goals and aspirations. This is one way I have of showing my affection and concern. Affection is a two-way street; to receive it you first must give some of it away. Feigned affection is like flattery, it is counterfeit and eventually will be detected. If you do not genuinely like and understand children, do not try to become an age-group coach. I have always liked young adults and am, at least in this area, well adapted to coaching college-age swimmers. Some outstanding age-group coaches have tried college coaching and found it distasteful, while others have done well at both levels. Some coaches find they are better suited to coaching girls than boys, or vice versa, or some coach both equally well. Once again, every coach should consider this factor before determining what type of job he looks for. He and those under his charge will be unhappy if he makes a wrong decision.

2. *Security.* Within all of us is a need for security. The security of knowing we will not go hungry, we will have an opportunity for a job, and so on. Consider the average freshman student in a large school of several thousand students. He goes from class to class, seeing very few people he knows. He deals with many people whom he knows only casually. He finds himself in a new and strange environment where the leader of the group is someone he has never met. The students in his class are competing with him for grades. He may lack status in the group, he feels insecure. He goes to the pool for a workout. He walks in the door and the coach greets him with a "Hiya, Jim, how are things going?" and gives him a smile. He is in a familiar environment where he knows what to expect. He belongs to the group and is accepted by the team members. He can predict that the coach will be enthusiastic and have a positive attitude. He also knows that the coach is an emotionally stable, mature individual. What a feeling of security these factors generate! An athlete does not get the same feeling from a coach who is hot and cold, who is by turns unpredictably friendly or abusive. No one can feel secure in an atmosphere of worry, fear, anxiety, and resentment. A coach should be a stable person the athlete can count on—another example of the importance of maturity in a coach. If a person is contemplating coaching as a career but knows that he responds poorly to stress, he should face the fact that his athletes will be affected by his instability, and either learn to control his reactions or not coach. His highs and lows are too bewildering to his young athletes who haven't learned to be objective and to recognize that the moods of others may have little relation to themselves.

3. *Status.* Whether we like it or not, each of us has a certain rank order in the groups of which we are a part. These relative ranks in society comprise our status. It has been said that life is a struggle for status, and I tend to agree. We are always trying to elevate our self-image and the image that we present to the world. The swimmer is a member of his team, he is also a member of the student body and probably of many other groups. He may have the lowest rank order on your team, but his membership on the team may raise his status in the student body. Thus he has raised his status in one group merely by being a member of another. This is especially true if the team is successful and has high prestige. If you want to help your

swimmers achieve high status, give them a good program in order that they may be successful. Then make sure they receive recognition of their success in the form of publicity, awards, trips, and anything else you can think of. An innovative and successful program is not the result of "good breaks," as many would have us believe. It is the result of hard and consistent effort to learn and then carry out what you have learned. An aspiring coach must decide if it is worth the work. Before he decides that it is not, he should consider the alternatives and ask himself if he will be content with the results of a half-hearted effort. Whatever he decides will strongly influence his evolving philosophy.

4. *Achievement.* Within each human resides the desire to achieve whatever he undertakes. It is the coach's responsibility to see that his program provides the swimmers with a feeling of accomplishment, even of creativity. After a practice session in the pool, a workout in the exercise room, or a stroke lecture in the classroom, the swimmer should feel he has made progress towards a goal. In order to ensure that the swimmer will acquire this feeling of accomplishment, the coach must educate him concerning the theories of training. This information about the physiology of training will stimulate him to work more conscientiously than if he is merely following orders.

For example, I have heard uninformed people question the value of hard training. Such remarks as "Why do you need to go 12,000 yards a day in order to swim 100 meters in a race?" are quite common. This is no mystery to a swimmer who knows what occurs in the muscles, the heart, the lungs, and blood vessels of an individual in training. His knowledge will make the swimmer more cooperative in workouts.

Part of the job of the swimming coach is to set goals that are compatible with the abilities of the individual and the team in order that they may achieve this feeling of accomplishment. If he is unrealistic in the goal-setting process or if he tries to protect himself by setting goals that are too low, he will only lose the confidence of his athletes.

The coach also must help the athlete evaluate what has been achieved. This evaluation must be truthful and not only serve as an estimate of what has been achieved but also indicate what lines of action must be adopted for the future.

5. *The group instinct.* All of us need to be part of a group. I think every individual, if handled properly, is team-oriented. Some psychologists refer to this phenomenon as the group instinct. It is the coach's job to foster team spirit, to form strong bonds among team members and between them and himself. This is mostly done by setting common goals, such as to win a certain meet. Even though humans are self-interested, they are also group-oriented, and it is up to the coach to establish a program that considers both of these aspects.

Remember, however, that team spirit should be brought about through positive and not negative means. The cheapest method of instilling team spirit is through the use of hate psychology: hatred against other teams, an opposing coach, certain individual athletes, and so on. The use of hatred is the worst form of psychology and, on a moral basis, belongs in no one's philosophy.

Another negative approach that should be avoided is to foster the impression that the team is "my" (the coach's) team rather than "our" team—the swimmers', the managers', assistants', and coach's—with the resulting guilt feelings if an athlete fails. Such shotgun tactics can be effective, and if you believe that the end justifies the means, you may employ them. However, you have then put yourself in a class with those who should not be guiding young people.

There are many positive methods by which a coach may enhance the feeling of "our team." One is to allow the athletes a voice in decision-making. A lot of the things we do at Indiana have been decided by the whole team. I don't want to convey the idea that a coach should avoid his responsibilities by asking the team to vote on every issue. The result of continual use of this kind of conduct is to risk losing authority, and there are many times when authority is needed and there are certain decisions only a coach can make.

Because I believe this latter point is important, let me diverge here to present a quote from Freud concerning the importance of authority:

> A great majority of people have a strong need for authority which they can admire, to which they can submit, which dominates and sometimes even ill-treats them. We have learned from psychology of the individual, whence comes this need of the masses, this longing for the father that lives in each of us from his childhood days.

All people vary somewhat in their need for authority. This is why we will hear some swimmers say "Coach is too easy on us and doesn't discipline us enough," while the other swimmers will say just the opposite about the same coach, such as "He's too strict."

An authoritarian coach who permits the athletes no voice in decision-making is as bad as the overly permissive coach who never disciplines and sometimes doesn't seem to care enough to rebuke bad behavior.

6. *Recognition.* Recognition is important to all individuals, but it is essential to a hard-working athlete. It satisfies the ego drive. The worst type of coach is one who displays indifference, never showing enthusiasm for an athlete's performance.

The coach's second responsibility is to obtain recognition for the athlete through the medium of the sports page, radio, or television—or just by his approval in workout or after a race. A slap on the back if he does well or a constructive kick in the pants—these are forms of recognition. If he is not trying hard enough, the athlete is probably really saying to you, "I'm here; be aware of me."

When talking to the press after a successful competition, spread the acclaim around. Never mention "me" or "I," but say, for example, "The boys worked hard for this victory. We want to give credit to our divers and our diving coach. Their points made the difference."

After a disappointing loss don't be the kind of coach who always tries to protect himself and place the blame on someone else. Don't say such things as "We were disappointed in Joe's performance. We thought he'd take two firsts," or "The kids just didn't want to win badly enough." This kind of statement puts a terrible burden of guilt on the athletes and reflects badly on your own ability to accept responsibility for failure. Rather say "Both the swimmers and I are going to have to work harder," or "We swam well, but not quite well enough."

It is unwise to be so self-effacing as to completely submerge your ego, but you must be able to suppress it. Telling the media "how it is" immediately after a race or meet may be a great method of letting off steam or temporarily getting rid of your aggressions, but the repercussions of such behavior include diminishing the respect of your athletes and eventually losing your self-respect.

The place to wash your linen is in the team meetings and individual conferences, not in front of the public and particularly not in the press.

7. *Self-esteem.* People have a strong desire for self-esteem. It's the coach's job to help the athlete form a good opinion of himself. Do not belittle, ridicule, or humiliate the athlete. Try to make him see the best in himself, and, as the song so appropriately says, "accentuate the positive, eliminate the negative." Do not let your team break into cliques or allow some team members to make a scapegoat of any person.

The late Maxwell Maltz, author of *Psycho-cybernetics*, a book all coaches and athletes should read, and popularizer of the concept of "Self-Image Psychology," told me that after years of success as a surgeon and lecturer he continued to lack self-confidence in many situations. If this is true of such a person, think how fragile is the self-esteem of a young teenager and what harm can be done if he is not permitted to retain his dignity.

Here are some variations of Dale Carnegie's principles about how to get along with people. They are chosen to serve as guides in protecting another person's self-esteem.

1. Make every swimmer, assistant coach, and manager on your team feel he is

an important, contributing member. By giving praise and recognition when it is warranted, you will convey that message.

2. Be genuinely interested in the other person, know his name, his interests, and his needs.

3. Before you talk about a swimmer's mistakes, allow him to rationalize them by sharing the blame with him: "John, you went out too hard in that race, and that was my fault for not telling you to control the first hundred."

4. Never prove another person wrong. Don't say to an assistant coach, "I told you we shouldn't have swum Jim on the relay. Now we've lost the meet just because you insisted he would do better than Harry."

8. *The role of challenge.* While it may be an overstatement to say that everyone welcomes a challenge, it is probably true that people who are attracted to athletics welcome a challenge, like to test themselves, and invite an opportunity to face new experiences.

The coach should plan his program to be dynamic and innovative. He should keep abreast of the latest training techniques, even adding to them or improving on them. While it is true that challenge places stress on an individual, most of us like to take a few chances, to gamble a little bit, to initiate a new method, or to get a thrill when we prove something. If a new technique doesn't work out, it's back to the drawing board and start over again. Even when a coach can't be creative, he can be enthusiastic, and his workouts can be interesting, not boring.

The eight needs just discussed are primary ones that we as coaches must consider in evolving our philosophy. In addition there are a number of other factors that should be mentioned, because a fledgling coach must make some decisions regarding them. If some seem too obvious to mention, let me state that I have met coaches who have disregarded them or lost sight of them along the way. There is a place for *honesty, truthfulness,*

and *integrity* in your philosophy. Most coaches, if they are admired and respected by their athletes will serve as models for them to emulate. If you display dishonest practices, are argumentative, dispute decisions constantly, or are ill-tempered, many of your athletes will also tend to adopt these traits. When a person accepts the responsibility of becoming a coach, he must accept the obligations that go with it. He owes this not only to the athletes but to his profession and himself, as a matter of self-esteem.

Early in my coaching career, if I had encountered troubles at the pool, I tended to bring them home along with a negative attitude. The whole family had to hear my complaints and problems. The results were pretty sad: my wife got upset at the children, who would soon sour toward one another, and someone would end up kicking the cat. The entire household suffered just because I had come home with a negative attitude. The same atmosphere was duplicated at the pool if I wasn't in a good mood. Then I woke up to what was happening and tried a different approach: even if the day hadn't been the best, I came into the house and shouted, "Hey, Marge, lover-boy is here!; hey, kids, the world's greatest dad is here!" The whole family responded and I started to feel better too. Later, my wife and and I might discuss problems I had had at work. You don't want to be a clown and phony, but it is amazing how a sense of humor and a positive attitude can bring a little perspective to a problem.

As a coach, you are the leader of your group, the head baboon, so to speak. It's up to you to set a positive mood. No one likes to be around a person who is sour and negative all the time, except perhaps other sour and negative people. Some of the coaches I admire the most are enthusiastic and positive—Jack Nelson, George Haines, and Don Talbot, for example. Just watch Jack Nelson and you can quickly see his enthusiasm and positive attitude, and sense his affection for his swimmers. Everyone has a different way of showing affection and other emotions; just don't be guilty of hiding them.

The following events took place in the year 1938, during the Big Depression. Every day before going to swimming practice at the YMCA I would spend several futile hours in the employment lines, trying to get a job. I came to the pool bitter and depressed, but I was always greeted by a friendly "Hiya, Jim, how are things going today?" and a big smile from Coach Vornbrock. I said to myself, "What's he so happy about? I wish he wouldn't give me that phony smile." One day I came in and Ernie didn't notice me for a while, and when he did, he only greeted me in an off-hand way. I said to myself, "What in the hell is wrong with him? He sure got up on the wrong side of the bed." A couple of days later I walked into the pool and got the old enthusiastic "Hiya, Jim" and the smile I had thought was so phony. This time I said to myself, "Thank God he's got himself straightened out."

Coach Vornbrock either purposely or unintentionally taught me the value of keeping a positive attitude.

Frankly, I'm no Ernie Vornbrock, nor would I try to imitate him; but there have been times in my career when I tried to think of what Ernie would have done because he was able to maintain a cheerful and positive manner in most circumstances. I am sure my philosophy has been affected by my association with him.

None of us can be completely positive and enthusiastic all the time, but we can try. Before going to practice adopt the policy of Houdini the Magician. Before he went onto the stage for a performance, he imagined he was going to see some old friends he hadn't seen in a long time and that they would be as happy to see him as he was to see them.

An example that demonstrates the importance of showing approval and affection is in an event that happened to me in 1966 in Mexico. I was there to work with the Mexican team for a couple of weeks. Every day the swimmers came in the pool and every member came to shake hands with me before going into the pool. After practice each one also shook hands with me before leaving. I decided to eliminate all this ridiculous handshaking and one day positioned myself on the opposite side of the pool. As the swimmers came in for practice, I told them to get into the water

immediately and start their warm-up. After practice was over I ended it by waving to them all and shouting "See you tomorrow" and left without shaking hands. In a few days I could see there was a barrier between us, and I didn't understand the reason until one of the parents asked me "Why don't you like the Mexican swimmers?" I assured her that I did like them and wondered why they thought that I didn't. She said I would not shake hands with them and consequently they thought I didn't like them. I promptly started shaking hands all over the place and the barrier disappeared. Do not dismiss ritual and ceremony as useless and a waste of time. It does serve a purpose. Remember, the most beautiful sound to a person is the sound of his own name. The most interesting subject of conversation is himself.

I have talked a lot about being positive, but for many people this is easier said than done. Inhibited people have to adopt the mechanics of such behavior to suit their personalities. There are some pitfalls to avoid: Don't substitute sarcasm for humor; don't exaggerate your mannerisms to the point that they appear insincere. As I mentioned before, you must find your own style. Everyone is capable of finding a way of showing people that he likes them. Don't be afraid to communicate your feelings.

Nowhere in this discussion have I mentioned the development of champions as a goal. Only a fraction of one percent of your swimmers will ever swim in the Olympic Games, but all who participate in your program can gain the benefits of competitive swimming.

It happens too often that a coach is guilty of concentrating his efforts, attention, and hopes on only a few of his team members, at the cost of ignoring the others. This practice becomes so obvious to all who are involved: to those who are on the receiving end, the pressure becomes too great; to those who are neglected, the frustration becomes demoralizing.

The philosophy of a coach should contain room for developing the abilities of all the participants, not only those few who have proven their talents. You do not have to sacrifice the rest of the team to develop the exceptional few. Don't let yourself get caught in the trap illustrated by the remark of one swimmer's parent, "In a race there is one winner; he's the champ, the rest are chumps." Develop a state of mind that will concern itself with everyone on the team. If you do this you will have more than your share of champions, and fewer of these champions will have a distorted idea of their own importance. Teach the swimmers to respect one another by your own example.

The high divorce rate of successful coaches is possibly related to the amount of effort and energy required to be devoted to the job. Coaching swimmers on the international level is time-demanding, self-sacrificing work! The ambitious young coach as well as his wife must understand this.

We are living in a time when divorce has been made easy, not legally but morally. We have largely forsaken the belief in the necessity for maintaining a commitment, come what may. I don't have much advice for young coaches and their wives just because my marriage has survived twenty-seven years of coaching. I can only say that it makes it easier if your wife is involved in your career and finds it as fascinating as you do.

Learn to *organize, delegate,* and *supervise.* People who complain about never having enough time to do everything fail to separate what is important from what is unimportant. These people are trying to do everything themselves. A coach's job involves so many tasks that he cannot hope to get them all done unless he delegates some of them. For example, I never have much to do with the running of meets, arranging for officials and timers, ordering of equipment, and so on. I assign one of my managers to do these things and I try to check to see that they have been done. Out of season I try to accomplish many routine tasks in order to be free of them during the season. A coach must allow himself some free time during the season to evaluate and plan his workouts, plan his talks for team meetings, decide on strategy, consult with swimmers, and so on. Delegating jobs to

people who do them poorly or not at all is worse than not delegating them in the first place. Obviously you must choose responsible people, organize them effectively, and then supervise them consistently to see that your plans are carried out. Much of the success of your program depends upon your ability to do these things. Andrew Carnegie had a friend state to him that he (Carnegie) probably knew more about the steel business than any person in the world. He told his friend, "No, *I* don't, but the people who work for me do." Although no swimming coaches of my acquaintance are in the position of an Andrew Carnegie, the point is still valid.

Some head coaches like to take care of the details and leave the actual coaching of the swimmers to their assistant, while other just put up the workout and let the swimmers do it "on their own." This type of office coach has certainly misplaced his emphasis, for few of his swimmers' needs can be fulfilled unless the coach is on the deck. There may be a few exceptions, but I have found that if you show me an office coach, I'll show you a loser.

If you should discover that you are inclined to be an office coach, you have two choices: (1) when you have the opportunity to hire an assistant, be honest with yourself and hire someone who will be an effective deckside coach or (2) if you are not in a position to hire an assistant, consider that you may be in the wrong profession because you are probably short-changing the swimmers in your charge.

The buck stops here. I often get letters from coaches who want to move to another job. If a coach is miserable in his job and if, as I discussed previously, there is a basic incompatibility between the coach's philosophy and that of the team, the parents, and the administration, then he should leave. Sometimes, however, we rationalize our failures by making excuses—some reasonable and some not. Here are a few that are pure rationalization: the athletic director doesn't care about swimming, the kids are lazy and won't work hard, the parents are a pain in the neck. Nobody in the community is interested in swimming—it's all football and basketball.

When Harry Truman was president, he had a sign on his desk, "The Buck Stops Here." We cannot keep passing the buck and rationalizing our deficiencies. Other people are not interested in excuses, only in results. It is your job to see that the community or institution becomes interested in swimming or to make the athletic director care. Show that you are sincere in building a good program, and convince people of the benefits that can be derived from it. It is part of your job to motivate the swimmers, no one else's. You are bound to find some swimmers whose talents exceed your first estimation. At one time or another everyone becomes discouraged, but if you persevere and refuse to blame others when things go wrong, you will have your share of successes.

My mother believed in the benefits of prayer, but she also thought that God helped those who help themselves. She explained it this way: A lot of people pray to God, then sit back and wait for God to come through for them. According to her, God might show the way but you had to follow through and do the job yourself. There is no heavenly welfare, and this is true of a coaching situation. You may need help and seek it out in order to do a better coaching job, but after you have talked to other coaches, read books and articles, and looked at successful programs, it will be up to you to fulfill the many functions of a good swimming coach. No one else can do it for you, and people get tired of listening to excuses.

Recently I have become disturbed by the growing number of beginning coaches who write to me wanting workouts, manuals of procedure, in short, to eliminate the long road taken by most coaches who read, study, and experiment throughout their working lives, and instead want to be handed a blueprint to winning. Their letters reveal their preference for the shortcut of having a proven coach set up their program for them. They also want to be given a magic formula, and it's a shock to them to find there is none. Even if I had the time to do all this letter-writing, because of all the reasons I've stated before, it wouldn't work. One coach's style will not work for another.

On decision-making. It is obvious that a person in the position of leadership must develop confidence in his ability to make decisions. Perfectionists live in fear of making mistakes, but their biggest mistake is often that they never make a decision. The general who broods and worries over all the mistakes in the last battle is likely to lose the battle he is currently waging. Make decisions and expect some of them to be wrong, but don't be too critical of yourself, at the risk of losing your self-esteem.

When you have a problem and all of the pertinent facts to solve it, make the decision, don't put it off. Procrastination will only compound your dilemma. If your decision is wrong, don't let it discourage you from being decisive in the future.

On taking criticism. "Show me a man who is never criticized and I'll show you a man who has never done anything, nor ever made a decision. Even Jesus was nailed to a cross; why should coaches be an exception?" This statement certainly illustrates an important point for coaches or for anyone in a position of leadership.

During the Civil War, Lincoln was constantly bombarded with criticism and condemnation from all sides concerning his conduct of the government and the war. His reply is a classic: "If I were to read, much less answer, all the attacks made on me, this shop might be closed for any other business. I do the very best I know how—the very best I can; and I mean to keep on doing so until the end. If the end brings me out all right, then what is said against me won't matter. If the end brings me out wrong, then ten angels swearing I was right would make no difference."

I was very sensitive when I first had some success and heard that I was being criticized. I've learned to overlook most of it. Recently a very young girl swimmer who was attending my summer swimming camp came to me and said, "Doc, you don't seem as bad as my coach said you are. He said if your boys don't swim fast, you punch them in the stomach." I couldn't help but laugh. I said, "What do you think?"

The best way to handle unjustified criticism ninety percent of the time is to laugh at it and forget it. Try not to get caught in a name-calling contest. Remember, unjustified criticism is often a compliment. A couple of years ago a writer in Belgium published an entire book, not stating what he thought about stroke mechanics, but devoted entirely to criticizing a book I had written. He sent me a copy and signed the book, "With my compliments and condolences," and his name. My first reaction was one of anger, but in thinking it over I proceeded to read the book—at least the part written in English—with what I hoped was an open mind. I dropped the author a brief note in which I stated that I hadn't seen too many compliments in his book, but I wanted to thank him anyway. The book has an honored position on my shelf since it is the only book I know of that is totally and completely written about me and my ideas; I am indeed flattered.

On changing. While everyone is a unique individual, the only one of his or her kind in the world, certain things about ourselves we can and might want to change. I'm sure all of us have heard people say "That's the way I am, I can't change." "I'm a night person, I can't get up at 6:00 A.M. to go to practice," or "I can't stop smoking."

You can change. You can go to bed earlier and alter your biorhythmic sleep patterns. You can give up smoking if you are sufficiently convinced of the need. If you believe, as I do, in the free will of humans to affect their destinies, you can do a lot to change the attributes that you believe damage you. How does this concern us as coaches?

You and I have heard the coach who says "They say I have a bad temper and am too stubborn. Well, I can't help it, that's the way I am." I've said before that you shouldn't alter your basic needs to suit the situation. However, if you find that there is no situation in which your particular personality as a coach is acceptable, better take a long look at yourself and consider that you might be to blame. If you are convinced that you want to coach, you must be prepared to behave acceptably to the majority of people you encounter. I could

name you fifty—maybe a hundred—people who sincerely wonder why they have problems wherever they go. There are fifty—or a hundred—reasons, but they involve an inability to recognize the obvious and to change. I'm that way too, but if sufficiently and repeatedly hurt, I try to sit down and figure out why. That is why my philosophy is still subject to alteration. You and I can only hope we will continue to be perceptive enough for that to be true to the end of our careers.

Satisfying the coach's needs. Let me repeat, within us all is the need for recognition, for love and affection, for achievement, and so on. We should not submerge them to the point of becoming self-effacing, sacrificing martyrs, filled with self-pity. We must also realize that we are not perfect and that sometimes we will trip on our egos. A coach must develop a high sensitivity to the effects of his behavior, his words, and his actions on other people. He must at some point in his career stop shooting from the hip and reacting emotionally in every situation.

Summary

The coach must adopt a game plan, a list of do's and don'ts, a set of principles that will guide his actions, a philosophy that will not subordinate the interests of the team, the assistant coaches, and so forth to his own. He must develop an understanding and empathy with the athletes in his charge. He must be capable of forgiveness, but must also demonstrate firmness and the ability to discipline when it is necessary.

As I stated in the beginning, even though most of us have the same needs, we also have different personalities, energy levels, and goals. Therefore, it is necessary for each of us to formulate an individual coaching philosophy. I believe the guidelines I have stated, the examples of my own decisions and those of others that I have presented will help you in the formulation or evaluation of your own.

> There is a time in every man's education when he arrives at the conviction that envy is ignorance; that imitation is suicide; that he must take himself for better, for worse, as his portion; that

though the wide universe is full of good, no kernel of nourishing corn can come to him but through his toil bestowed on that plot of ground which is given him to till. The power which resides in him is new in nature, and none but he knows what that is which he can do, nor does he know until he has tried.—Ralph Waldo Emerson, "Self-Reliance."

SECTION 6.2
THE "X" FACTOR

Is there any one factor or trait that determines a successful swimming coach? If there is, could we teach a coach to have this particular trait? The business world has long wondered what makes a good executive, a good administrator, or a good salesman. Research into this ingredient of success has led to the use of million-dollar testing bureaus. For example, the executives of U.S. Steel are given personality tests, intelligence tests, leadership-ability tests, and others, in every possible measurable area. So far they have had very little success in identifying any single trait that their subjects have in common. For instance, they sometimes find the lowest-paid filing clerk to have more basic intelligence than the highest-paid executive. They have determined that once a person reaches a level of intelligence somewhere above average, that higher intelligence by itself is not necessarily a determinant. So, we cannot give all coaches intelligence tests and determine that the most intelligent will be the best coach. If this were true, then all we would have to do to select a good coach is hire the man with the highest IQ. It might be just the opposite—a man with a high IQ might be too smart to get involved in coaching.

Let's get back to the business world. I personally feel that intelligence has a lot to do with success in coaching, in business, in almost any field of endeavor. However, the type of intelligence I am speaking of is not the type that can be measured by academic testing. It could better be called a type of *perception*. The business school at Indiana University have found their search for a common denominator from which to predict success to be rather fruitless. They have, however, isolated an unidentifiable factor which they have named the "X" factor. They can't sharply define this factor, but they talk about it, and they feel they are closing in on a definition.

I would like to apply this X factor to swimming coaches. They know a little about this factor in business, and I would like to mention a few of the dangers encountered by business in attempting to build a perfect administrator. Business has sent its top administrators to training courses—very much as you go to a coaching clinic, they send them to universities and sometimes to the Menninger Foundation in Kansas. The most outstanding business training course is given in Kansas at the Menninger Psychiatric Clinic. Here, three times a year, a course is offered to top executives at a fee of $1200. Entrance is limited to 20 per group in three groups, and is called "Understanding Man." Business sends its top executives to this clinic, the theory being that with this type of training they will return and do a better job, just as many of you go to a clinic and hope to return to your swimmers and do a better job with them.

Unfortunately, business has found that many of its executives go back from such a clinic and do worse. Likewise many of our coaches go home from these clinics and do a worse job of coaching than before. I can see some of your kids now saying, "Oh my God, Coach has been to one of those screwy clinics again. Now we get all of those strange workouts and those crazy ideas on stroke mechanics." I believe that we must continue to experiment, to continually change our programs and our methods. Therefore I do not recommend that we stop attending such clinics, but I would caution you about one thing.

There are examples of men who have trained themselves to be coaches, devoted their entire lives to that end, and failed miserably. Some of these men have been warned before they start that they will fail, just as I warn some of my graduate students that they too will fail. Why do they fail? Let us take a partially true case and synthesise an individual, give him a false name—call him Frank Zilch.

Frank Zilch came to me some years ago and said, "I want to study under you, learn all that you know, take all the scientific courses available, so that I can become the greatest swimming coach in the world." Of course, this approach was wrong.

As his graduate advisor, I set out to plan his education. Theoretically, he had everything going for him; he was good-looking, he had desire, he had lots of energy, he was intelligent, and with good planning we would have been able to make a great coach out of him. But, as it turned out, it was impossible to do. Frank lacked the X factor.

Frank Zilch read all the research on swimming that he could find; he read the *Research Quarterly*, *Swimming Technique*, *The Journal of Applied Physiology*, and many, many others. He attended all the coaching clinics he could find, he did research, he lived, he ate, he breathed swimming. In short, every waking minute he devoted to swimming. We designed his courses to cover every area of knowledge that could possibly contribute toward making him a great swimming coach. He knew more facts about swimming than any person in the world. His brain was crammed with swimming knowledge. In setting up his course of study we tried to give him a full education in the areas necessary to make him a great swimming coach.

He had to be a great physiologist—to understand the process of conditioning; what happens to the swimmer's body when he trains. The perfect coach should know that the swimmer's body changes as he trains; he should know how and why these physiological changes occur. In preparing the perfect coach for this area of knowledge, he should certainly read Dr. Selye's book on Stress and Adaptation. Frank Zilch studied all of this.

The thought must occur to you, "Does all of this really seem necessary?" We all wonder if we should not concentrate on just training the swimmers and let Dr. Selye and others do this type of research. Maybe we should learn by trial and error—by either overworking or underworking our swimmers. Most of the United States progress in training technique has occurred through trial and error. The Europeans, in particular those from the Iron Curtain countries, are usually surprised and disappointed when they visit training sites in the United States and fail to see the American coaches taking pulse rates and electrocardiograms. They expect American coaches to be more scientific, to see us taking pulse rates and electrocardiograms, and measuring all the physiological changes in our swimmers. During a recent trip to Russia, I gave an hour lecture at the Russian Institute for Physical Education in Minsk. During the question-and-answer period the questions were entirely on minute details such as "Do the swimmers take vitamins?" or "How many miligrams of Vitamin C do they take?" or "Do you measure their electrocardiograms?" They asked no questions on training of swimmers, on repeats, and so forth.

Later we had a special conference with officials of the Russian sports field. There were about six or eight sitting around the table; they had a nutritionist, an expert on fluid mechanics, and a physiologist, but missing from the group was a swimming coach. Again the questions asked were, in my opinion, irrelevant. Their favorite question is on the T-wave. Then they asked the 64-ruble question. They wanted to know why they were not getting better swimmers in spite of spending millions of rubles. They asked if they were behind the times. They asked what we in the United States were doing that they were not. I told them that they were actually far ahead of our country in scientific methods, but they did not understand. I think the Russians are missing the X factor.

We had similar experiences with the East Germans. They too were going about their swimming on a very scientific basis. They selected their future athletes on a scientific basis, just as they would go about chosing their future scientists, mathematicians, and physicists. When an East German child shows promise in any area—math, science, sport, etc.—he and his family are often moved so that the child can be enrolled in a special school or institute that is designed to nurture this skill. The East Germans, like the Russians, wondered why they were not having greater success in swimming. The answer is again, I believe, the X factor. Since that time, however, the East Germans have had tremendous success by combining both the scientific methodology with a broad-based age-group program such as we have here in the United States, and the results are obvious.

In the United States we throw our 500,000 age-group swimmers into the pool and let the best survive. The ones that come out on top have the physical ability and have fought their way to the top through hard, merciless work. We do not coddle our swimmers; our swimmers, as well as the Canadian and Australian swimmers, are not pampered. We expose them all to the same conditions, and the best survive and excel. I favor this system over the scientific approach of the Russians and East Germans. They approach things too scientifically and forget that it is a dog-eat-dog competition. The Americans, the Australians, the Canadians, and a few others, produce the toughest swimmers because of the system that forces them to fight their way to the top. This is why these swimmers are the toughest in the Olympics and other international meets.

In business they have a saying, "You never see a good-looking salesman." I don't know how true this really is, but possibly he doesn't sell much because he is too busy with the farmer's daughter. The point is, I believe, you want to stay away from people who have everything going for them. I have yet to have a good swimmer who was talented physically and also well adjusted. A person can have all the most promising physical and mental attributes and yet not do well, because the person with everything going for him does not have a strong ego drive. Perhaps this ego drive is part of the X factor we've been talking about.

Now back to Frank Zilch. He had everything going for him. We trained him to be a good physiologist, and now we would train him in stroke mechanics. He studied physics, fluid mechanics, he examined and re-examined underwater movies, he learned all about Bernoulli's principle, he studied every aspect of stroke mechanics. This is another area in which the Europeans seem surprised to find that American coaches are not spending more time on the deck with stroke mechanics. I do not believe any coach could teach Mark Spitz to swim the way he does. Much of this he has done on his own. The better a swimmer is, the less he really has to be coached. If you have a Mark Spitz, just sit back and enjoy him and try to learn from him.

How does a swimmer learn? He learns through trial and error. Why doesn't everybody learn the same? Because we all have varying abilities. We have photographed dogs swimming, and have learned that not all dogs swim naturally—in fact some nearly drowned. We found that at first most dogs tried to swim with all four feet, then gradually learned to pick up the hind feet and swim with only the front feet. However, in the case of the Labrador Retrievers, they learned to swim this way usually during their second time in the water, much sooner than other types of dogs. We studied the dachshund and on the twentieth time in the water he was still trying to work all four feet and nearly drowned.

I believe the Gary Halls, the John Kinsellas, the Mark Spitzes, are the Labrador Retrievers. Unfortunately, most of you will get a lot of Dachshunds in your programs. So, many of our swimmers swim well in spite of lousy coaches. Those of us who work only with the Labrador Retrievers have a real advantage. So you club coaches keep on sending us the Labrador Retrievers and keep the Dachshunds.

Those of us with the top twenty college teams just go out and recruit the Labrador Retrievers from the local coaches, so we don't have to know very much about stroke mechanics. The better the swimmer, the less you have to work on stroke mechanics. I believe stroke mechanics is important, but at the lower levels. The best stroke mechanic men in the United States are the lesser known coaches in the local programs.

We now have Frank Zilch well qualified in physiology and in stroke mechanics. Next we go to what I feel is the most important area of all—psychology This is one area about which the Russians and East Germans were very complimentary to the Americans. They marveled at the rapport the American coaches have with the American swimmers. They have remarked on what great psychologists the American coaches are, how we can motivate the swimmers in spite of the fact that we don't do scientific testing and don't work with stroke mechanics. I believe that if you gave three different coaches—one a psychologist, one a stroke-mechanics expert, and one a physiologist—identical teams that the psychologist would win every time. A good psychologist can motivate his swimmers to work hard and to dedicate themselves to the sport. He can keep the swimmers happy so they will enjoy the sport and stay with it; he can recruit the best swimmers; he can handle the city council and the parents. The good psychologist in time will become a good organizer and administrator; he will have a large team and attract good swimmers to his team. So, this is the way to become a good coach.

Finally, let me tell you what I think the X factor is in successful coaching. The X factor is, to quote an old saying, "the ability to separate the wheat from the chaff." Another way of expressing it is to say, "You must be able to recognize the important things and work on them; to minimize the unimportant." Let me give you an example: we have seen mothers and fathers, and a few coaches, walking up and down the pool deck as the swimmer is swimming with dropped elbows, overkicking like mad, and he is being yelled at to "kick, kick, kick." In other words, they ignore the important item—the dropped elbows—and emphasize the unimportant by yelling "Kick, kick."

I feel that the present trend of doing everything for the athlete is not good. For example, I could put a timer on every swimmer in my practice, keep all their splits for them with the managers, but I do not, because I want them to be aware of what they are doing. Too often we do so much for them that they stop using their brains—they stop thinking about their own activities. It is important for the swimmer to know his own times so that he understands the significance of what he is doing.

Another place in which the coach fails the swimmer is when he allows parents and others to come on the pool deck and engage him in conversations during practices. The coach's responsibility is to the swimmer, not to the parent or others. The swimmer is important; the parents are not important. This is another example of where the coach must recognize the important thing—the swimmer—and ignore the unimportant—the parent.

The X factor is then, in other words, the ability to see what has to be done and doing it. The great coach recognizes what is needed to do the job and then does it. This applies not only in coaching but in business, in administration, in every aspect of life. Another way of saying it is "Cut through all the detail and get to the heart of the matter." The perfectionist usually does not make a very good coach; he is too busy taking care of the little details and seldom gets to the heart of the matter.

At the present stage of development in swimming, the great coach must have two basic abilities—he must be a good organizer and a good psychologist. The good organizer will have the large team, will attract the good swimmers from other teams, and will develop the Mark Spitzes and Gary Halls of the future. The good psychologist will be able to handle the parent problems, will get along with the city council, will be able to communicate and get along with the swimmers—he will have the "super" team.

The good coach today need have only an elementary knowledge of the areas of conditioning physiology and stroke mechanics. He does not need these to get the job done. However, nothing remains static, and in the future these two areas will become more and more important. As more superior athletes come out for swimming, as more talented people go into coaching, as more and better facilities become available, all of the aspects of knowledge that we have discussed will become important.

I frankly feel that we are on the verge of a tremendous knowledge explosion in the area of competitive swimming which will make the more technical areas of knowledge more important to good coaching. The meetings we attend should help us separate the important from the unimportant and make us better coaches. I would like to attend such a clinic a hundred years from now to see what is being discussed. By that time they should have simple electronics devices that can be put in the swimmer's ear to monitor pulse rates, blood lactate, and other physiological data. We are not ready for this sort of thing today, but even a hundred years from now the inherent behavioral patterns of the swimmers will be the same as today, and the good coaching psychology of today will still apply.

SECTION 6.3
PSYCHOLOGY OF COACHING

Much has been said and written of the actual physical training routines of the swimmer in order that he may be in good physiological condition when the big competition is imminent. At the present time we appear to have pushed the swimmers as far as we can physically. For example, we know that it takes somewhere between 6 and 20 kilometers of training per day to achieve maximum fitness. Tim Shaw and Bruce Furniss train about 12,000 meters, Jenny Turrall, the Australian world record holder, trains around 20,000 meters a day. Some great sprinters train as little as 6000 meters a day. Most of the swimming is done in the interval-training method or some related form. The factors of time, fatigue, and logic seem to indicate that we cannot ask the swimmers to go further to improve perfor-

mance. The immediate future improvements in swimming may come, not from better physical preparation, but from better mental or psychological preparation for both practice and competition.

Little has been said or written of mental preparation for competition, and even less has been said of the mental preparation for practice sessions. Without meaning to minimize the roles of the coaches and the officials, I would like to stress the importance of the actual swimming program itself in conditioning the swimmer's mind for competition.

Foreign coaches who visit the United States to observe the swimming programs of our successful teams have expressed surprise at how little the coaches work with and, in some cases, how little they appear to know of stroke mechanics. Because these coaches had world-class swimmers, they expected them to be thoroughly knowledgeable in all phases of swimming, including fluid mechanics, physiological concepts, research, etc. Our coaches are often not trained in coaching or physical education: they become coaches because of their love for the sport, and sometimes chance seems to be the important factor. Few courses are offered in our universities in which a person who wants to study all phases of aquatics can enroll. We hope to correct this eventually and offer a degree or at least a minor specialty area in the coaching of swimming. This would do much to elevate our knowledge of swimming in the United States.

If most of our good coaches are not experts in mechanics or physiological conditioning, how do they achieve such success? They are intelligent, ambitious, and energetic people who understand human psychology and the importance of creating a good environment through proper organization of their program. The answer to training the mind for swimming is not to hire a psychologist, to use hypnosis, or to take personality tests, and so on. We have tried most of these at Indiana University. We have tested over 1200 swimmers with the Cattell 16 PFI Test and have found no significant trends from our data. The answer is, not to develop new principles of handling our swimmers, but to use principles already established and apply them to our programs.

The essence of discovery becomes more and more a matter of applying previously known principles to new situations.

I have visited many countries as both a consultant and an observer and I have seen them try to build successful programs by emphasizing only a few aspects of a total program. For example, they might (1) build more pools, (2) bring in experts for clinics, (3) conduct research, (4) send the better swimmers to training centers, and so on. While all of these contribute somewhat, in the final analysis they will avail these countries little unless they become part of a more complete program; a well-conceived and well-organized program is the only way the athlete's body and mind can be trained for swimming. The officials, coaches, swimmers and their parents must work toward the development of all phases of a swimming program. I will now discuss these phases.

Just as a house is built of a frame, a siding, roof, windows, doors, and so on, so a good swimming program is made of its component parts:

1. Good pools available for practice
2. Good coaches, well-trained and keenly interested in their jobs—and well-paid
3. Good officials, interested in the welfare of the swimmers and coaches, not just the power they can derive from the sport
4. Good publicity—not too much, not too little
5. Plenty of meets, but not so many that the swimmers become tired of them
6. Parental backing, but not of the sort that imposes undue pressure on their children
7. A general environment that is one of cooperation between all people involved
8. A physical enviromnent which is conducive to hard work: attractive lane markers, pace clocks on the wall, record boards kept up to date, bulletin boards with opponents' times listed, etc.

Everything must be aimed at making the swimmer think, "At this time in my life swimming is the most important thing I can do." If this attitude can be achieved, the coaches' job of motivating the swimmer is fifty percent accomplished.

Building a Proper Attitude toward Swimming Practice

Good mental or psychological preparation is prerequisite to optimum physical conditioning. Only if a swimmer is motivated properly will he be able to achieve physical conditioning; therefore, psychological preparation precedes or parallels physical preparation.

The coach and the swimmer should approach practice with a common goal in mind: "We are here to practice hard, accomplish something, and enjoy ourselves." I do not like to drive swimmers through workouts as though they were so many trained seals. In team meetings I tell them why they are doing a certain set of repeats, such as 20 X 100 on 1 minute 20 seconds. I think it is important that the swimmer's mind as well as his body participate in practice. I refuse to shout or get angry at a swimmer if he is not performing as well in practice as I feel he is able. I will tell him what I expect him to do, and then if he does not, I will ask him to leave the pool since he is wasting his time and mine. Each year I must cut from my squad a number of individuals who might be better playing football or the violin. Generally, I try to motivate through enthusiasm, interest, and attention to how they are swimming. I even resort to giving candy or other tangible rewards for outstanding practice performances. I think it is better to keep the practice session rather casual and relaxed, but well organized, than to have it tense and quiet. I remember one of Thorndyke's laws of learning, "We tend to repeat a pleasant experience and avoid an unpleasant one." The coach and athlete should look forward to practice and not detest it. I make every effort to make this so, and I must succeed to some extent for many of my swimmers, such as Chet Jastremski and George Breen, swam to the ripe old age of twenty-seven, an unusual situation in the United States.

Assuming Hard Work Is Necessary, and Developing Pride in Working Hard

The coach should do everything he can, sometimes in very subtle ways by casual remarks, often in talks at team meetings, to build the swimmer's pride in his ability to "put out"—even hurt himself in practice. Loafing and malingering should be made to be undesirable qualities, and anyone who displays such qualities should be socially ostracized by the rest of the team. Frequently we have used a hurt, pain, agony chart to demonstrate this concept. I try to place a halo over the head of the swimmer who has the ability to work hard. The lazy swimmer who refuses to work usually drops from our team as a result of social pressure from the other swimmers. If he doesn't, I ask him to "shape up and train hard or get off the team."

What we have left are boys whose self-image is "We're tough," and thus we have begun our mental preparation.

The whole program should be designed to emphasize this toughness and manliness (perhaps maturity would be a better word since we are talking of both men and women swimmers). All extreme emotional outbursts, crying, complaining, or other overt and obnoxious acts are taken to be signs of weakness and are discouraged. Let the swimmers take pride in their toughness. The coaches and officials must serve as examples. The swimmer should show his aggression in the pool in the way he swims, not in bad manners displayed on the pool deck or in the locker room.

The swimmer has a self-image; this image should be one of a strong person who competes well and accepts success or failure with dignity. Help him to achieve this self-esteem through example, rules, and operant psychology.

All persons vary in their ability to hurt themselves in practice. Some tend to work too hard, others to work too little and never approach the "agonistic" training phase. Examples of two extremes on our team a few years ago at Indiana University were Gary Hall and Mark Spitz. Gary tended to work too hard and often developed a guilt complex if he had to miss a day's practice, even when he was ill. He occasionally had to be reminded not to work too hard, and to learn to develop a feel or sensitivity for when he was too fatigued to exert himself. He was, in the true sense of the word, an extreme agonist, who finally developed a sense of feeling for when to work hard and when to merely get through

practice. He had an ideal mental attitude for both practice and competition.

Mark Spitz, on the other hand, did not like to hurt himself frequently or to push himself into the agony phase of exertion. If he was not watched carefully, he could go through a whole workout and never realize he was not placing enough physiological stress on himself to bring about conditioning. He therefore had to be handled differently from Gary Hall. He had to be prepared mentally for practice by having reasonable goals set for him to achieve in practice. At that time his personality would not permit him to take the continual hard swimming that Gary Hall could tolerate. Perhaps if he had learned to do that he could have lowered the 100-meter freestyle record to 50 seconds. This presented a challenge to me as Mark's coach and I had to work constantly on his mental preparation, for, as I stated before, "mental preparation must precede physical preparation."

The Coach's Role

A good coach, as I mentioned previously, is a good organizer who manipulates the swimmers' environment in order to motivate him highly to train hard and make the necessary sacrifices required to be a great swimmer. He also must have certain knowledge in several areas:

1. *A knowledge of psychology.* The coach must not only understand the psychology of constructing a good program but understand how to work with the swimmer (I will discuss this in more detail later).

2. *A knowledge of conditioning.* The coach must understand the conditioning process and how to apply the various conditioning methods to the training program of the swimmer. At present, a coach can get good results by merely learning the training schedule of some champion swimmers and having his team duplicate these workouts. He need not understand the concepts of physiological stress and adaptation or the basis of the various training techniques. But we do need more understanding and research in this area. We have arrived at this point in our training programs through a combination of trial and

error, the application of common sense, and an intuitive feeling, but we have often not understood what we are doing. We only know what gets results. Future knowledge in this area will eventually make us realize how little we knew back in the 1970s.

3. *A knowledge of mechanics.* In our programs in the United States the coach is often so busy organizing and running practice and manipulating the environment that he has no time to work with stroke technique—in fact, he has little time to learn much about stroke technique. His job as an organizer is so time-consuming that he must subordinate the job of working with stroke technique to less than five percent of his total practice time. Often no stroke correction is ever made. Therefore, the strength of the American program—the large number of swimmers—results in its greatest weakness, that of insufficient time for many coaches to work on stroke technique.

Many articles published on stroke mechanics in our monthly periodicals and swimming books defy all the laws of motion; yet they are eagerly and unsuspectingly assimilated by coaches and swimmers to the detriment of their performance. It is to be hoped that through study, research, and meetings will come knowledge which will help all of us better understand the biomechanics of swimming and, at the least, become more discriminating in what we accept.

We now have a picture of the complete swimming coach—a psychologist, a physiologist, and a physicist. It is my contention that at the present embryonic stage in the development of our sport, the psychologist-coach is needed the most. It, however, behooves each coach to acquire some expertise in the other two areas, otherwise he will lose his ability to maintain the confidence of his swimmers. As swimmers become more educated and sophisticated, it will be harder to tell them to do something that violates a principle they have learned in a physics or physiology class. For example, Gary Hall, who was an honor student in physics, took a seminar in fluid mechanics as an undergraduate. If I, as his coach, told him to use a technique that violated a fluid-mechanics principle he had studied, I would have to defend my position and I had better do it or his confidence in my knowledge of stroke mechanics would be detrimentally affected.

My first suggestion for better mental preparation of swimmers would be better educational preparation of coaches.

A coach who understands only psychology and nothing of the other two areas has already destroyed some of the psychological preparation of his swimmers, for they realize they are being coached by an incomplete coach who, as they say, "can psych us up for the race but doesn't know anything about stroke mechanics or training." A coach who has knowledge in all three areas has the ability to build confidence—a much-needed trait in psychological preparation.

Building Confidence

While it may seem a rather boastful attitude to promote in our program, I try to build the following attitude in the swimmers' minds: "There are two ways to do a thing—the Counsilman way and the wrong way." If I can establish this opinion, I can then help the swimmer to achieve his full physical potential. It is important that a swimmer have complete confidence in his coach, the coach's program, his own mental and physical preparation; it then follows he will perform near his optimum level in the big competition. A swimmer who is not sure of his coach, of his own preparation, and of how he will perform in the competition will perform sporadically, usually well below his optimal level. Athletes look to their coaches for counsel and to borrow strength. The poorest possible coach would be uninformed, weak, and emotional. He can give the swimmer no strength or confidence and his athletes must *go it alone*; still, talented and strong-willed athletes have often achieved amazing results with this kind of inept guidance.

Think of what great victories could have been won by Ron Clarke, world-record distance runner, if he had found an intelligent and strong-willed coach to lean on when his confidence began to waver. Because of an intelligent and analytical mind Clarke could find no coach whose knowledge of training could match his own and he decided to *go it alone* and train himself. Perhaps all of the gold medals at the Olympic and Commonwealth Games would not have been able to elude him, as they so easily did throughout his long, brilliant, and disappointing career.

The coach must remember that all people at some time look for leadership. They do not always look to the intelligent ones to lead them, as history shows; they look instead to the "strong-willed." Most athletes are looking for a strong-willed, knowledgeable coach who can help them build confidence in themselves. They want the confidence that a successful coach and a successful program can give them. They want to know they are in a program where everybody improves and does his best times in the big competition. *This is the essence of mental preparation.* I have had swimmers specifically come to our program because, to quote them, "Your swimmers do their best times in the big meets."

To a great extent, we are what we think we are. If a swimmer believes he is a poor competitor, he will usually prove it by swimming accordingly in meets. If he believes he is a tough competitor he usually will perform well in meets. The reason he believes either one way or the other is his previous experience.

Fig. 6.1.

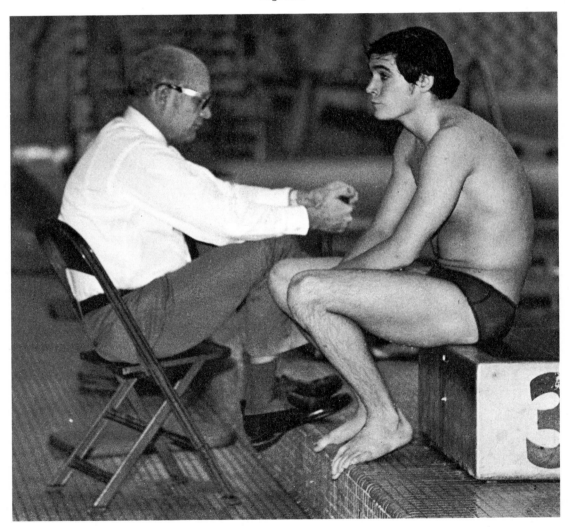

One swimmer who came into our program as a poor competitor, with a very poor attitude toward his own ability to compete, later became an Olympic champion and developed a reputation as a fierce competitor. This change did not happen overnight. A person cannot make himself a good competitor by merely saying over and over to himself, "I will be a good competitor," one thousand times a day. That is the reason that hypnosis will not, in my opinion, help in the long run. The swimmer must prove to himself that he is a good competitor by competing well, first in small meets, later in big competition. It is significant that before he has a big success he must have a series of small successes during which he can gain confidence. It is the job of the coach and the function of the program to see that he has these successes.

A coach can help the swimmer achieve the proper mental preparation by observing the following seven procedures:

1. Set reasonable goals for the swimmer to achieve and be able to predict his times accurately.

2. Use only positive statements in your discussions. For example, if you have a backstroker who swims the 100-meter backstroke in 60 seconds and who is swimming against Roland Matthes and is not near him in time but is ahead of the rest of the swimmers, don't say to him, "We will swim for second place," but say, perhaps, "If Roland makes a mistake in the race, we might beat him; if he makes two mistakes, we'll win for sure." This way you have not allowed the swimmer to approach the race negatively, but you have left hope for victory. You cannot expect to tell an athlete who is swimming 65 seconds for the 100 back that he will beat Roland Matthes. This would only insult his intelligence and undermine his confidence in you.

3. Help the swimmer to rationalize a poor performance, or at least help him to understand why he sometimes fails to perform as expected.

4. Help the swimmer plan his race intelligently. Know what his splits should be and build confidence in his ability to swim the race properly.

5. As mentioned previously, be knowledgeable about all phases of swimming.

6. Be strong-willed; don't waver in your determination, and the chances are that the swimmer will not either. Don't lose yourself emotionally during the competition. These are the times a swimmer must lean on you; be ready to help, but remember it is also important that the swimmer eventually achieve self-reliance. I do not like to hear coaches boast of their importance to their swimmers by saying, "If I'm not there he (or more frequently, she) will swim lousy."

7. As a coach don't pride yourself on being indispensable. Don't destroy the swimmer's self-confidence by making him completely reliant on you and your presence. Wean him gradually so he has strength of his own and he can compete half way round the world from you and still perform at his best level. This can be done by allowing him to help plan his workouts and his races and by letting him attend some races in your absence. I have had as many of my swimmers set world records in my absence as I have had in my presence.

Getting Mentally Ready to Swim Fast at the Right Time

Our program at Indiana, as most large programs in the United States, is organized and designed for the swimmers to swim their fastest times at the biggest meets. This is achieved in the following ways:

1. Constantly remind the athletes that this is the way the program is designed and illustrate your point with examples.

2. Keep working through all the smaller meets and don't care too much if you lose in the smaller races. In one small dual meet, Indiana versus Ohio State, Mark Spitz came in third in three races and wasn't apparently worried. Four weeks later he won three national titles in record time. Don McKenzie, another Indiana swimmer, never won a race, even a small one, until the United States Olympic Trials. He then went on to win the Olympic title—the only two wins in his short swimming career. The reason was that he trained through every meet except those two. He was indeed highly talented, but he also had the firm belief that he could win these races if he tapered only for them. He was mentally ready.

I have had many European swimmers train with us, and I am amazed at how upset they become over getting beaten or swimming poorly in little meets. They, in turn, are amazed at how casual Hickcox, Hall, Spitz, Murphy, Montgomery, and other top swimmers are about getting beaten. These swimmers are not trying to lose on purpose, they are simply at that phase of their program at which they can subordinate winning to their overall training plan. The media in the United States seem to understand this better than does the European press, and no big fuss is made if our big-name swimmers lose in smaller competitions.

3. Have the swimmers shave the hair off the arms and legs. While this technique has a doubtful physical effect, it does have a tremendous psychological effect. All of the United States swimmers do it, preferably only before the biggest meet. It has become a ceremony, a sort of mystical ritual that will drop their times as much—the swimmers say—as 1 to 2 seconds per 100 meters. I use to frown on this practice, and in 1960 one of my swimmers, Mike Troy, and I agreed he would not "shave down" before swimming in the Olympic Games. He didn't shave down, and he won the 200 fly, beating all of the shaved-down swimmers. Now I recognize the psychological advantage of this ceremony, and all of my swimmers shave down. Mike Troy, now coaching, had Mike Stamm, his swimmer, shave down before taking second place in the 1972 Olympics.

4. Get the swimmer mentally ready by showing him he is physically ready. This is done by tapering the swimmer (reducing his workout load and resting him). During this tapering period his times in practice should improve considerably. He should be capable of doing his best sprint times of the year and should feel the "power beginning to surge through his body." The statements the coach makes during this period should be encouraging, enthusiastic, and positive. If the coach feels the swimmer will not swim fast on a given day during the taper, he should not give him any maximum efforts. If he feels the swimmer is ready for a few good fast repeats, the best of the year, he can have the swimmer

go hard, and if they are indeed outstanding, the psychological effect will be beneficial. During this tapering period a coach must be extra sensitive to the mental attitude of his swimmers. He must anticipate and hope for an increase in the swimmers' nervousness and aggressiveness during this time. He must help the swimmers to control it and not lose the confidence built previously.

Summary

In this section I have tried to cover the mental preparation of swimmers for both training and competition. Most of my research and writing has been in the other two areas: those of the physiology of training and the biomechanics of swimming. It is much easier to talk of specifics such as the red-blood-cell count, the drag coefficient, the height of the T-wave, and so on, than it is to talk of such nebulous matters as motivation and mental preparation. I, therefore, get the feeling I have written much and said little. Perhaps I have given too much credit to the coach and his role. This is natural since I am a coach. Perhaps if I were an official I would talk in terms of the importance of their contributions to the swimmers' mental preparation.

Therefore, I must return to my original statement: "I would like to stress the importance of the swimming program itself in conditioning the swimmers' minds." Since we have over 500,000 age-group swimmers training and competing in a very active program in the United States, perhaps the simplest answer to the reason for the poise and toughness of our swimmers is that when we get down to the last few hundred, all of the weak-willed, poor competitors have been screened out and only the best are left to make up our national teams.

Nearly all of our champion swimmers come up through our age-group program. They compete in this program for many years, frequently swimming six to eight races a day during a meet, staying in the pool area for a period of over twelve hours. They learn to relax, read comic books between events, play cards, or just run around. Some of them compete in over thirty meets a year, certainly too many, but as much as we American coaches complain of our overemphasis on age-group swimming, it does allow us to finish with seasoned competitors who when they stand up on the starting blocks at the Olympics have years of competition behind them in addition to superb mental preparation.

SECTION 6.4
"I HAVE CONFIDENCE IN CONFIDENCE," AN INTERVIEW WITH DOC COUNSILMAN, BY PAUL JUHL

Dr. James Counsilman of the University of Indiana is a coach who believes in confidence. He believes that it can be created and that a good coach develops situations in which his athletes can be and are confident.

This is just one of the characteristics that have made Doc Counsilman one of the great medal producers of all time—from the collegiate level right up to the Olympics. He's a swimming coach, but his methods and philosophies are valid for all sports, because he has found the secret of developing winners. He does it year after year, and it's no accident.

Recently, he predicted that Indiana swimmers would win three or four gold medals at the Munich Olympics. He put it this way: "They will win gold medals because I have a great deal of confidence in myself, at least overtly.

"A kid goes to a meet. He's suffering from anxiety. He's wondering whether he's going to perform well. He looks over at me and sees I'm calm, I'm relaxed. He says: 'It must be all right, look at Doc Counsilman—he's so relaxed, he's so confident of himself.'

"If he'd only take a few physiological measurements, he'd find my pulse rate is 160 and my stomach is in a knot. But I appear to be confident. I'm a crutch for him.

This article is reprinted from "Methods of the Master Coaches," *Sports and Fitness Instructor*, Spring 1972.

"I think that this is a practical function of a coach."

Psychology
Of course, there's more to Counsilman than confidence. It is his sound background of physiological and psychological know-how which enables him to be so apparently positive and relaxed about eventual victory.

And it is his attitude toward knowledge that has helped to make him a respected figure throughout the sport world.

Any coach, he says, who does not take the time to learn enough basic psychology to understand athletes, and enough physiology to know what it is he is asking them to do, is doing a great disservice to his athletes.

The coach must always want to know and find out the "why" of the psychological, physiological or mechanical factors of his sport—not just the "how." Otherwise, he will be unable to pass them on. He must be flexible, constantly evaluating his methods to see if he can find a better way. Too many coaches are content to stick with one method.

"There is no room for coaches to sit down and be satisfied," he has been quoted as saying. The true coach is embarked on a never-ending search for new ways to maximize performance.

Respect
He also believes that the athlete must like his coach, and if he doesn't like him, he must at least respect him.

After the recent NCAA swimming championships in the United States, which his team won once again, he said: "If your athletes don't like you, you should take time off to find out why."

The coach, he says, is first a motivator and second a communicator. Though mechanics and technique are important, they don't mean a thing unless they are made important to the athlete as a person.

He tries to speak personally to every athlete at every workout—something surprisingly few coaches do, and he has made a point of finding out about the person inside each athlete.

In this way he is able to drive his athletes

harder than most other coaches. They know he is tough—even authoritarian—but that he is democratic and on their side and that he is concerned for their welfare, not just as performers but as people.

Although he works his athletes extremely hard, he gives frequent easy days in order to maintain their zest and enthusiasm for work. He believes that they must have "fun" too, and lead a balanced life. The alternative, he believes, is physiological and psychological staleness.

"There is no easy way to coaching success," he has said. "You must always do your homework so you at least give the appearance of being authentic so the athlete has confidence in you."

Counsilman is a great believer in what psychologists call "positive reinforcement"— rewards for achievement, rather than criticism and punishment for failures. It is a law of learning, he says, that people tend to want to repeat pleasant experiences and avoid the unpleasant. He tries, therefore, to make practices and training assignments as pleasant as possible within the hard work context, and to make sure an athlete knows when he has done well.

Here are two final quotations he directed at coaches in a paper he presented at the International Symposium on the Art and Science of Coaching in Toronto in 1971:

1. Are you really interested in helping yourself learn more from the other disciplines, or are you so lazy and indifferent you don't want to make the effort?

2. Are you really interested enough in helping yourself and your athletes so you will not be offended if someone shows you that you don't know everything?

SECTION 6.5
"POSITIVE AND NEGATIVE REINFORCEMENT," BY JOE TAYLOR

Like any professional or specialized group, be it of scientists or lawyers, coaches have a language all their own. It doesn't matter that much of the jargon has been begged or borrowed from other fields, almost every coach has a verbal shorthand through which he communicates with other coaches—and with which he all too often baffles the general public.

In the field of teaching, the average Canadian coach's language is increasingly studded with such catch phrases as "transfer of learning," "positive reinforcement," "game conditions," and "specificity."

All are valid terms—provided the coach is not using them merely to "show off" and is well aware of exactly what he is talking about. Take "positive and negative reinforcement" for example. Many coaches use the phrase and can discourse upon it, but have never thought about whether it has been properly embodied into their coaching techniques.

The coach who talks positive reinforcement may still be sarcastic, punish failure without praising success, tell athletes what they should not be doing ("Don't let your head drop") rather than what they should be doing ("That's good—keep your head up like that every time")—and offer compliments and rewards only sparingly for skillful performance or good effort.

Briefly, reinforcement means "strengthening." In the coaching situation, it most often is involved in the teaching of skills, although the coach will also use the technique in developing attitudes to competition, codes of sportsmanship, practice habits, etc.

Positive reinforcement, then, is strengthening the desired patterns of behavior in the athlete by praise or other reward. Negative reinforcement achieves the same objective through criticism or punishment, which the

This article is reprinted from *Sports and Fitness Instructor*, August 1973.

athlete strives to avoid by performing correctly.

Which is better? positive or negative? punishment or praise? Do we need to reinforce at all?

Tests have shown that both techniques work, but positive reinforcement will usually produce better results in the long run. The athlete is apparently better motivated to improve his skills by the thought of avoiding punishment.

On the other hand, the coach who praises without criticising may also lose his effectiveness. The effect of constant praise is soon weakened. And far too many coaches, some top sports psychologists say, are neither positive nor negative. They tend to be bland purveyors of facts, figures, and instruction who fail to understand what the athlete needs in the way of motivation to achieve his objectives.

Robert F. Singer, a leading physical educator and coach in the United States, tells of an experiment in which the effects of praise and criticism on test achievement were measured.

Problem-Solving

Four groups of students were formed—one received praise; another reproof; a third was ignored by the teacher who was present in the room; while the fourth (control) group performed in a room with no teacher. The same problems were given to all students to solve.

"Although differences in group performances were small at first, dissimilarities were apparent by the end of the fifth day," Singer writes in *Coaching, Athletics and Psychology*.

"The following conclusions were drawn: the most effective technique in improving performance is praise, followed by criticism, and then by ignoring the student. Two things should be emphasized: first, criticism leads to performance nearly, but not quite, as good as that demonstrated as a result of praise; second, the ignored group scored higher than the control group which was left alone in the room. Social presence is thus once again shown to serve as a motivator.

"The coach is therefore encouraged to use praise more often that criticism, . . . to take a positive approach."

Dr. Thomas A. Tutko, another top United States sports psychologist, warns against the dangers of criticism:

A player tends to learn quickly and repeat those reactions which are accompanied or immediately followed by something that brings satisfaction; he tends not to repeat or learn rapidly those reactions which are accompanied or immediately followed by something that is annoying.

Disapproval and criticism by the coach will be painful to the athlete and will help to increase his anxiety. If a player misses a tackle, it is already painful enough for him without the coach adding to his misery through criticism.

The important thing for the coach to remember is that criticism tends to destroy rather than build desirable traits in a person.

Many coaches tend to believe that rough, callous or caustic treatment wins the respect of the athletes and produces the best results. This is simply not true. In fact, in some instances this approach is instrumental in alienating the athlete.

Perhaps most coaches use a combination of positive and negative reinforcement. That is, they punish errors, but compliment effective or successful play. Even though this may be the case, some coaches tend to punish more than they reward, while others reward more than they punish.

Combination

If asked, coaches are apt to report that they use a combination of both simply because they have no means of checking the frequency with which they use either. Some coaches feel they use a combination, but actually do not openly express their positive feelings. They believe it is unnecessary to compliment the obvious.

The athlete, however, has no way of knowing what the coach is thinking. He is only aware of the coach's criticism.

Golf coach Gray Wiren tells of overhearing another golfer's teaching technique which left the pupil so confused it was some time before he could perform normally again. It consisted entirely of advice like "Don't lift your head,"

"You didn't shift your weight," "Don't bend your left arm," and "Don't hurry your backswing."

Says Wiren: "Everything that golfer told his pupil was technically correct. The fault was not in the observations but in the approach that was used to implement them."

In other words, the negative reinforcement of "Don't do this, don't do that" creates anxiety and uncertainty in the recipient.

Don't Say Don't

Better to eliminate the word "don't" and phrase instructions positively: "Keep your arm straight." Better to praise the things the athlete is doing right, because as he does them correctly, the bad patterns he has formed will gradually be erased.

Explains Singer:

> The process of learning a complex skill is delayed considerably if positive reinforcement is withheld until the task is performed with a high degree of accuracy and proficiency. The path to mastery of skill is filled with many blocks. Each is piled on the preceeding one until ultimate goals are reached. At first goals are general and undefined; later they become more fixed and specific.
>
> In applying this concept to the learning of complex motor skills, we would at the beginning reinforce any activity that was in the correct direction. The youngster learning the hook shot in basketball will obviously not perform with precision and grace at the onset, but any movements that bear some resemblance to the hook shot should be reinforced.

Reuben B. Frost, writing in *Psychological Concepts Applied to Physical Education and Coaching*, warns against the dangers of too much positive reinforcement, however:

> There can be so much attempted reinforcement that it becomes ineffective. When praise comes too frequently, when success becomes commonplace, when one is so completely accepted that it is no longer a concern, or when children are showered with too much affection, the reinforcing factors become no longer as

effective as when they are applied more judiciously. Some coaches interviewed by the author believe that when players know that praise must be earned they value it more, and it becomes a more effective incentive.

Principle

A good principle to follow would be to praise if there is reason for praise—and to look for those reasons. It is hard to overpraise if it's really earned. The praise itself must be sincere, otherwise the athlete will soon see through it, however.

In the case of an athlete whose morale is down to rock bottom, the coach should look for something—anything—which he can praise and build up. He should keep seeking positive reinforcements until the athlete's state of mind shows a strong upward turn.

SECTION 6.6
THE TEAM MEETING

It is my belief that a team meeting should be held at least once a week. At Indiana we have ours every Tuesday at 3:30 P.M. The meeting lasts between twenty minutes and one hour and serves to bring the team together for many purposes, which change as the season progresses. The night before the meeting I sit down for an hour or so and construct an outline of the material I want to cover the next day. I keep a file of the notes of previous meetings for my reference.

I don't try to cover a great many points in each meeting; instead I try to emphasize certain items and then avoid repeating them so often that they become tiresome and get tuned out. That is one reason for planning in advance what I'm going to say. Another reason is that I want each meeting to have significance for the team members. I would hate to think that the swimmers say or have the attitude, "Oh no, not another meeting!" It is my experience that the only meetings that have been a flop have been those that weren't planned carefully.

At the end of my remarks I ask the

assistant coach, the diving coach, and the co-captains of the team if they have anything to add. I also give the co-captains the chance to talk to the team alone. This provides a way the team members can bring up anything they want to discuss without the inhibiting influence of my presence. If the co-captains think there are some swimmers who are not putting out in practice or are breaking training rules, they will discuss the problem and decide if they can handle it or if they should turn it over to me.

As the season progresses, the nature of the meetings changes. In the following section I have listed the approximate topics of the meetings and have followed them with some of the notes I have used in past meetings. Not all topics should be discussed at one meeting.

Early Season Meetings

1. Election of co-captains.

2. Explanation of time schedule—when workouts occur—warning not to be late—penalty for being late.

3. Outline of entire year's program—how many times per week in October, how this changes in November and December and then goes to a full workout schedule from January through March.

4. Discussion of dry-land exercise program—take team to weight room—show them the exercises—explain how we are developing the same muscles when exercising as when swimming—discuss number of repetitions, amount of weight to use, attendance chart, etc.

5. Discussion of stroke mechanics—show movies, charts, explain how and why of stroke techniques. Agree on terminology—discuss recovery of arms, pull patterns, elbow bend, breathing, etc.

6. Discussion of methods of training and importance of each. Show how to take pulse rate—explain its importance in evaluating effort. Discuss and define overdistance, sprint, Fartlek, interval and repetition training. Discuss hypoxic training.

7. Explain organization of practice—swimming in circles, use of pace clock, importance of keeping times, swimming of broken sets of repeats—what to do with kickboard (no throwing in pool), pull buoys, and tubes. How to install lanes before practice, backstroke flags, pace clock, and how to remove and store them after practice.

8. Discussion of daily diet—well balanced mixed diet—diet on day of competition. Explain use of vitamins, fructose and glycogen loading. Avoidance of greasy, highly seasoned foods, salads, etc., on day of competition.

9. Discussion of value of rest and sleep—abstinence from alcohol, drugs, marijuana, tobacco, etc.

10. Value of hard, consistent, intelligent work—feeling of pride in putting out 100 percent. Promote idea of forgiveness for not winning if a person has tried his best; but we can't rationalize laziness and failure to try hard.

11. Setting of team and individual goals—completion of goal sheets by each team member. These are confidential between coach and athlete, and while they can take various forms, are usually an individual's evaluation of what times he expects to go during the year, his splits on the way, and how he expects the team to finish the year. I also have the team members fill out a form in which they estimate the times necessary to win each individual event in the NCAA Meet and the time it will take to qualify in each. The swimmers who make the best predictions get three extra team T-shirts plus a free steak dinner. Individual conferences between coach and swimmer before season and during season may also help motivate the swimmers and clarify their goals. An evaluating session after the season is over can also be a good technique to establish rapport between the coach and swimmer and help the swimmer to understand why he had a good or bad or average season. Lines of communication should always be kept open. As the phraseology of a few years ago put it, "we must have meaningful dialogue."

Below is a sample outline for an early season meeting:

The First Team Meeting

1. Discuss workout plans for the coming season:

a. This month, swim a minimum of 3 days a week, most of it overdistance; exercise 5 days a week, most of it isokinetic; increase the number of practices in the water each month to, ultimately, 11 per week.

b. Strength and flexibility tests—start today after meeting, explain tests and importance of power.

c. Explain vertical jump and difference between white and red muscle fibers.

2. Stroke mechanics—every Sunday we will photograph your stroke; next week we start on a series of stroke lectures.

3. Hand out T-shirts and assign lockers

4. Explain academic eligibility requirements

5. Discuss importance of good grades—Explain 3-point dinner. (Swimmers earning over a B average get a free dinner, those under a B average are fined $1.00—this happens after each semester's grades come out.)

6. Discuss training rules—harmful effects of smoking, drinking, drugs. Use examples. I have a biopsy display of the lungs of a smoker and nonsmoker that I bring.

7. Team goals—next Tuesday I want everyone to write down his assessment of the realistic goals of the team and the times it will take to win and make the finals in the NCAA Meet.

8. Call on Hobie (diving coach) and Gary (assistant coach) for any remarks they may want to make.

9. Turn meeting over to the new co-captains who may want to say something to the team in private.

The Midseason Meeting

As the early season meetings have a great deal of material to cover, so the midseason meetings will take less time because the emphasis has changed to less talk and more action in the water. A midseason meeting can cover such points as the following:

1. The following week's schedule: date, time, and place of the next dual meet; what time the swimmers should come to the pool for warm-up. Review what team should eat before the meet, etc. For away meets—when the team will leave, type of clothing expected, behavior on the trip, etc. What do you expect from the opposing team, the strategy we will use, who will swim in what events, whether we will swim a workout before or after the meet. Type of warm-up, etc.

2. Review of material discussed in earlier meetings—need for consistent work, the harm of smoking and drinking.

3. The purpose of changing the program as the season progresses, i.e., more sprinting and less overdistance work.

4. Discussion about the fact that team will be working more on turns, starts, and relay takeoffs—movies and explanation of technique.

5. Discussion of what the various swimmers in our conference and others are doing in terms of times in meets, workouts, etc.

6. Discussion of latest research and concepts in training methods, dry-land exercise, diet, etc. Keep team up to date on new developments.

Below is an actual meeting outline I used during midseason:

Team Meeting—January 14

1. Turn in goal sheets—compare them to occupational goals.

2. Explain change in workouts—after meeting I want to meet with IM swimmers in the pool to explain switching workouts.

3. Workout contest—from now on those making the most workouts in a week get a free dinner in the Tudor Room (smorgasbord).

4. Explain importance of morning practices.

5. Explain how some swimmers quit without even knowing it—in practice and in a race.

6. Michigan trip—leave Saturday from pool at 8:30 A.M. or meet at the University Airport at 8:45 A.M.. Dress neatly—no blue jeans—wear a coat and stocking cap. Discuss what to expect from Michigan swimmers.

7. Getting into water—stop messing around so long before getting into the

water. Practice starts at 1:30 P.M. for the first wave and at 3:45 P.M. for the second wave. I allow five minutes for socializing, then into the water. I don't want you to be five minutes late, then waste five minutes more. I want all of you to express your individuality, but I do expect certain disciplines, even at the risk of submerging your expression:

Be on time.
Do the workout.
Attend eleven practices a week.
Observe training rules.
Be neat.
Don't hurt our program or the team's image through poor manners or bad taste.

During the tapering period the coach and the team will have more time for meetings and there may be a temptation to spend a lot of time psyching up the swimmers. Meetings during this time should be devoted to final mental preparation, but they can also emotionalize the swimmers to the point that they become nervous and can't sleep. The coach should emphasize objectivity as well as winning and performing well.

The Late-Season Meeting

Discuss and emphasize their readiness for the meet:

1. "We have worked hard—you are ready both physically and mentally." Be positive in your approach.

2. Emphasize team effort—discuss importance of relays; look at movies of relay takeoffs.

3. Emphasize stroke mechanics—look at movies of stroke, starts, turns. Since you now have more time in practice for these fine points, work on them.

4. Discuss warm-up—before prelims and before finals. Have each swimmer standardize his warm-up, more or less.

5. Discuss race strategy and split times.

6. Review competition from opposing teams and individual swimmers.

7. Discuss the times it will take to make the finals.

8. Talk about what to eat before the prelims, before the finals. Have a dry run of at least one day's duration—getting up at the same time, warming up and swimming at the same time as on the days of competition.

9. Work constantly on building confidence, both of the team and the individuals. Appear calm, objective, and confident in the way you present your material. Avoid negative statements. Don't set unreal goals, but do leave the door open for a few wild dreams.

A Late-Season Team Meeting

1. Congratulations on an undefeated season.

2. "Now we must get ready for the NCAA Meet. You've worked harder than any team I've ever coached. It has been a pleasure to work with you. Thank you."

3. "We are in the middle of our taper. You should begin to feel stronger in practice and when I ask you for a little effort in your swims, you should be able to swim fast without much strain. You must now observe training rules more carefully than before. Get to bed on time, eat properly, dress adequately for the weather conditions; it is easy to catch a cold when you are working hard. If you feel tired in practice, let me know and we'll back off on your workout."

4. Discuss the possibility of winning the NCAAs, who our competition will be, what times it will take to qualify, where the strengths of the other teams lie, etc.

5. "Thursday and Friday night everyone should be at the pool at 7:00 P.M. for a dry run of the finals of the NCAA. Warm up just as you would for the finals; then each person will go either an all-out 150 time trial or a 75. We will also swim a 200-yard freestyle and a 200-yard medley relay for time."

6. "Everyone get a haircut between now and our departure for the NCAAs."

7. Explain flight or driving information on trip to the NCAAs.

Sometimes it is necessary to have a team meeting during competition. Perhaps the night before or even the morning of the meet. If it's a three-day meet, one, two, or even three meetings may be required. This is at the discretion of the coach. Some coaches cause the swimmers to become nervous at such meetings with the result that they sleep poorly and then perform poorly. Other coaches may have a calming effect on the athletes and inspire confidence. I personally like to have the team get together two or three times during a championship meet, at which time we take inventory. Some swimmers need these meetings. For example, if after the first day of the meet, your team is twenty points behind and a few of your swimmers have already adopted the attitude that it's all over, we've lost, you call the team together and point out your assets: "The first day is our poorest, remember, I told you that in a meeting last week." Then go on to the effect that perhaps you are a little behind schedule but that you are confident you can still win if everyone swims well today. Watch out for the swimmers who tend to give up easily and quickly adopt a negative attitude. The effect of assistant coaches and managers should also be observed; it can be helpful or harmful depending on the attitude of these people.

Before having such a meeting prepare your talk carefully. Use the best psychological preparation of which you are capable, even if you are in last place and only struggling for a few points. You still want to strive for the best possible performance from each individual and for the team. This is your strength—the team expects it of you and it is your obligation.

SECTION 6.7
CONTROLLING THE SWIMMER'S ENVIRONMENT

Analyze any consistently good competitive swimming program and you will find three factors in evidence: 1) a good coach, 2) good swimmers, and 3) a good environment. We now have the inevitable question of which came first, the chicken or the egg. It is my contention that in most cases the coach came first and he manipulated or controlled the environment so favorably that the following events occurred:

1. He attracted a good number of local swimmers to his team, and the greater the number of swimmers, the greater the number of these he found with talent.

2. Because he created such a good environment, he made the grass look greener on his side of the pool fence and he attracted the better swimmers from other teams.

3. Because he controlled the environment so well, the swimmers were motivated to train harder and to be more dedicated. The parents, the assistant coaches, the team managers and officials—everyone associated with the program was motivated to put out, and the morale of the whole group went up.

I believe that the young, aspiring coach misunderstands what coaching is all about. He thinks his job is merely to put in his time at the pool with the swimmers. If he trains them, works with their strokes, gives them a good dry-land exercise program, helps them with their problems and is, in general, their close friend, what else is necessary? These are the fun parts of the job and the real coaching is done at these times, but this kind of thinking causes the coach to underestimate the importance of the other aspects of his position, especially those that pertain to the control and creation of a desirable environment. Let him neglect that side of his job and he will not have the swimmers to work with, or they will not be very highly motivated and he may not even have much time in the water.

In 1957 I started to coach at Indiana University. There had never been much interest or enthusiasm for the swimming program and I, mistakenly, felt my enthusiasm for the sport would be the only environmental factor needed to get the swimming team into high gear. I called out the team and less than half showed up. I could see that because of past experience there was little enthusiasm for swimming even among the good swimmers on the team. The reason was obvious: the team had to share a 30-foot-wide pool with the faculty during their 1½ hours a day of pool time. The team policy in previous years had been for each swimmer to come in on his own and do a workout of his design and try at the same time to avoid bumping into the professors who were getting in their daily swim.

I immediately suspended the faculty swim. As could be anticipated, many letters of protest from irate professors were sent to the Dean's and President's offices—to no avail. I did not believe that a pool full of faculty was the type of environmental factor I was looking for. (Soon after, a new pool made it possible for the faculty to go back to their lunchtime swim.)

Practices were then organized and made compulsory. I feel that poorly organized practices have a bad environmental influence, but I also believe that overly organized practices can be equally undesirable. More about that later.

When we had our first dual meet, there were more swimmers in the pool than there were spectators in the stands. Poor attendance is a bad environmental factor; this I knew had to change even if it meant creating a synthetic crowd. At the time, I was teaching several courses in beginning swimming and in life saving. I made it compulsory for all of these students to attend our swimming meets. At the next meet, we had a packed house and I could see an immediate change in the attitude of the swimmers.

At first, the local news media were not much interested in our team and our swim meets and we got little or no publicity. I took pictures of the meets, wrote up the meet summaries and took them to the sports editors of our newspapers and television and radio stations. Most of the time they would use some of the material. The increased publicity also affected the swimmers' attitudes and they worked harder. It also had the effect of improving their status on campus. The following year I delegated the handling of publicity to one of our team managers. The sports publicity department began getting requests from the news media for pictures of our swimmers, so they took the pictures and I got out of another assignment.

As a swimming coach, you too must learn the joys of delegating, or you will learn the misery of a stomach ulcer or colitis.

A coach must delegate, but he must maintain control of the situation through careful supervision. People are an important part of the environment of the team and they must be used to help you and your team to achieve success. Delegate much of your paper work to them; use team managers, assistants, parents—anyone you can find who is competent and reliable and interested. They can handle such things as entries, transportation, publicity, awards, registration, fund raising, officiating, hotel arrangements, equipment orders, record keeping, and so on. The list is long; if the coach were to try to do it all himself he would soon be a basket case. My feeling is that the coach should delegate as much as he can except for the actual coaching. This, of course, depends on the coach and what he prefers. Some coaches want to do the detail work and to delegate the coaching of the swimmers to assistants. I, like most coaches, hate the paper work and enjoy the personal contact with the athlete; so I delegate as much of the paper work as I can and never delegate the coaching of the athlete.

I have just said that the environment is made up of people, publicity, etc. It is actually made up of a great many things more. Before going further I would like to define the term *environment* in the special way that I think of it. All of us are sufficiently informed to know the general meaning of the term, but it has unique ramifications when it is considered in a specific situation. I define it as anything in a person's surroundings that impinges on his senses of perception. It would include all physical objects as well as attitudes, beliefs, rituals, likes, dislikes, prejudices, and behavior patterns. A person perceives his environment primarily through sight and sound, that is, those aspects other than physical environment that are perceived through gestures and words. Changes in a swimmer's attitude toward hard work, stroke mechanics, or any other factor are brought about only by controlling the swimmer's environment.

Let me give you an example: Assume you are taking over a team that has a very poor past record, having a poor attitude towards work and a losing record, since these traits usually go together. The strongest social leader on the team is a talented athlete who is the number one swimmer but who constantly verbalizes his disdain for hard work. He is a bad environmental factor who, through his words and gestures, affects the attitudes of his teammates in a disastrous way. If you cannot change his attitude and thus eliminate his harmful effect, you will have to consider eliminating him from the environment or somehow cancel his effect on the other swimmers. This is the kind of control of the environment that I am speaking of.

The coach must control the environment in such a way as to create the attitude in the team and the individual that will bring about a consistently successful program. He wants to create an attitude that glorifies hard, intelligent work and attaches a stigma to laziness and goofing off. He does not want to do this by shouting and screaming or by using other methods of intimidation that increase his swimmers' level of fear and anxiety. He can create desirable attitudes through more subtle and effective ways by following these four processes or methods: education, group dynamics, good motivational techniques, and the athlete's respect and admiration for the coach.

1. The Use of the Educative Process

A coach who is training his swimmers on a national or international level is asking them to put in 3½ to 4½ hours daily in swimming between 10,000 and 20,000 meters per day. He must explain "why" they must train this hard to achieve the conditioning and the skills needed. The coach must be well informed and he must keep his swimmers well informed. He must know what is going on in swimming conditioning—what Steve Holland or Rick DeMont is doing in his workouts. He must explain why he requires his swimmers to train in a given way, and his reasons must make sense and not be "because I say so."

Each year as our swimming season begins I have a couple of classroom sessions in which I discuss training methods, the latest trends in conditioning, and the general pattern of training we will follow. Throughout the season I ask our swimmers their opinions and let them discuss these methods with me. It seems logical to me that they will cooperate much

better with me if I tell them why I am asking them to do a given workout, say 30 × 100 with 10 seconds rest interval, than if I merely tell them to do it.

To explain "why" I am asking them to do 30 × 100 with short rest, I would use such explanations as (a) there appears to be trend among most of the better swimmers towards using more short-rest interval training in their programs, (b) this type of training improves endurance because it opens up capillaries in the muscles, keeps the heart rate elevated to a optimum level (about 140 to 160 beats per minute depending on the effort), and causes other physiological adaptations that are beneficial to endurance, or (c) does not put the extreme stress on the swimmer that high-quality work does, such as 4 × 100 all-out efforts with 5 minutes rest, and therefore can be used almost daily, whereas the type of training that involves high-quality work of an all-out nature must be used only two or three times a week.

In working with stroke mechanics it is important to tell the swimmers why they should swim in a given manner, not just how they are to swim. We have classroom sessions on stroke mechanics where we discuss the mechanical principles involved in swimming. We use movies and draw diagrams on the board. Every swimmer on our team has out-of-water and underwater movies taken of himself in order that he may see exactly what he is doing. I would not ask him to change his stroke without telling him "why." I want "why" to become a part of my environment as much as it is a part of his.

2. The Use of Group Dynamics

The second method of creating desirable attitudes is through *group dynamics*. All of us want to be individuals and yet we also have a very strong group instinct. Life appears to be a constant struggle for status. Without a group we can have no status, because status is nothing more than a rank-order rating.

Not only individuals have status, but so also do groups. If the group to which an individual belongs has a high status, it will automatically improve the status of any of its individual members and thus contribute to the individual's self-esteem. The person will want to belong to the group and will work hard to remain a member of that group.

Let me be a little more explicit. Consider our swimming team at Indiana University as a group composed of twenty-four members. The highest-status members would be Jim Montgomery, John Kinsella, Mike Stamm, etc. They enjoy the pleasure of being near the top prestigewise in this group. How about the slowest swimmer in the group? He has the lowest status of the whole group—he's the bottom of the totem pole—why doesn't he quit? Even though he has the lowest status in this group, by just being a member of a high-status group his stature in other groups to which he belongs is increased. For instance, his status in the dormitory or his fraternity is improved by merely being a member of the swimming team. He therefore works hard to become and stay a member of a high-status group. There are other reasons he stays out for the team, such as a feeling of achievement, the joy of exercising, etc.

Along with status seeking we must consider the other aspects of fulfilling our group instincts. Man is naturally a gregarious social animal who likes to gather in groups. Any pleasant evening, whether it's in Paris on the Champs Elysée, in Barcelona on Las Rambles, in Belgrade on Skidalea, in New York on 42nd and Broadway, or in Chicago at the Democratic National Convention, people like to gather to see and be seen. These loosely organized groups fulfill a need, but certainly not the strong need nearly everyone feels for a closely knit group that has close ties and shares common goals and experiences. This need, once fulfilled by tribal meetings and ceremonies, was also fulfilled for centuries by strong family ties and family group experiences. With today's mobile society and the disruption of normal family life by television and other means of diversion and entertainment, we must replace these group experiences with new ones. People will always seek out group experiences, whether it is in a bowling league, a bridge club, a hippie commune, a pot party, or on a swimming team. If we are to attract swimmers to our group and keep them as members of our group, we must

compete for them against other groups. We must offer them a more valuable group experience than they can find anywhere else.

To do this we must, of course, make them a functional part of the group. The coach must not feel this is "my" team. The attitude that must permeate the environment is one of "our" team and the feeling of "we." Each team member must be able to achieve his own goals, but his goals must also help the team achieve its overall goals. Sometimes the swimmers and the coach must subordinate their interests to those of the group. An example of such a situation would be the star swimmer who stands a chance of winning an event tomorrow—will he or will he not put all out tonight to help the relay score third place and earn his team more points? If he is a normal human with any feelings of obligation to the group and if he has been handled right, he will not hesitate to put out 100 percent. If he has been catered to and pampered and his sense of obligation to the group has been blunted, he will think only of his race tomorrow and will hold back. This type of behavior should be considered unacceptable.

In order that the swimmers may take a more active role in the planning of training sessions, the coach should occasionally have a meeting and discuss the conditioning program with them. They should feel free to contribute suggestions—do they think they are doing enough sprinting, are they training too much, or too little? Every Tuesday afternoon I let one of the swimmers put the workout on the board. It is usually the toughest workout of the week. In this manner I bring the swimmers' ideas into the training program. I hope in this way to make the swimmers feel a more important part of the team, create a feeling that this is "our" team, and in the process I also learn something. Sometimes I retain their workouts and use them again later in the season.

The coach can give or share control of many of the decisions that affect the team. After the team has elected their team captain or co-captains, he should use their advice in deciding team strategy, discuss team workouts with them, and so on. In all situations in which I think it is possible, I allow the swimmers to take part in decision making. I allow them to choose their own events in many of our dual meets; they decide where we will train at Christmas. Before I make the team schedule for the following year, I discuss it with them. We put on a water show each year and conduct a swim-a-thon. Both of these money-raising ventures are planned and conducted by "us"—the swimmers, the managers, and the coaches. These are joint efforts in which we have common goals and share a common experience. This is the best way to form a strong bond among the members of a group.

The Use of Ritual, Ceremony, and Tradition in Bonding a Group

Team spirit or group bonding can be achieved in many ways. The use of ritual, ceremony, and tradition are the most common.

Coaches must be careful in using these methods of bonding because, while they may form a stronger bond between members of a team, they may also exclude team members from other groups. To illustrate this excluding process let me refer to the Hare Krishna movement. This group of Far East religious devotees practices group dynamics by having their members wear saffron robes and shave their heads except for a tassle at the crown. These two characteristics make them easily recognizable to one another and also to the layman, so they serve as methods of group identification. They identify with one another, but due to their strange appearance and customs, they are alienated from other groups. This condition is desired by their leaders for it reduces their contact with other groups and prevents them from leaving the group easily.

The coach should use some ritual, ceremony, and tradition to foster team spirit and group unity, but he should be careful to avoid any practices that nurture hatred and alienation. Here are a few of the devices we use at Indiana University: (1) The Indiana Swimming T-shirt; (2) Jelly Bean Day (On this day, once a season, everyone is timed for a half mile or 800 meters, using their own competitive stroke. A pound of jelly beans plus a free dinner goes to the swimmers making the standard times for their events. This has become such a tradition that we have the stands half-filled with spectators, and the results are published in the local newspaper.); (3) The Three-Point Dinner (Anyone who gets a 3-point grade average or better (B or more) gets a free dinner at one of the good restaurants in town. Last semester 18 of 23 swimmers made this average. It cost me over $100, but this is a small price to pay for attention to and pride in good grades. Anyone getting under 3-point average is fined a token $1.00); (4) Lasagna Dinner (Once a year my wife has the team out for lasagna.); (5) The Funny Film (Each year we make a short (12-minute) funny film of the swimmers doing such crazy skits as you might see in *Laugh-In*. This funny film has become a tradition and we have made an annual film since 1960.); (6) The Christmas Trip (Each year, using the money raised by the swimmers in the Water Show and Swim-a-Thon, we take a Christmas training trip. One year we went to Spain and the Canary Islands. Another year we may plan to go to Hawaii.); (7) The Campbell Bean Award (The outstanding swimmer of each meet gets a large can of Campbell's Pork and Beans plus a free dinner at my home. The origin of this award is too lengthy to explain here.); (8) Pre-meet Ritual (Before each meet we have a team meeting. I say a few words, so does Hobie, followed by the captain or co-captains. Then we have a team huddle and a cheer—nothing different from most teams, but still a very important ritual.); and (9) Other rituals or traditions such as our annual team banquet, presentation of certain awards, printed programs at our swim meets which contain pictures of the swimmers—all of these help to form a strong bond among the members of our group.

Unacceptable Bonding Methods

Certain methods of building team spirit are unacceptable. The use of hatred is one of the commonest of these—hatred for another team, coach, or team member. One of the cheapest, sure-fire ways to bond a group is to find an enemy to hate. Politicians have been using the technique for centuries.

Your team should be aggressive and want to beat another team without hating it. By setting goals of winning and achieving success over a competent opponent a coach can still capitalize upon the swimmers' aggressive tendencies without engendering hate. The problem with the use of hate is that it is double-edged and can be turned against its user. Coaches who forbid their swimmers communication with swimmers from other teams are using hate psychology even though they may not be aware of it.

The use of outlandish costumes and customs is another unacceptable form of bonding. Wearing ridiculous outfits and observing outlandish rituals may intrigue sportswriters and make good copy, but this practice is more appropriate to a nightclub act or professional wrestling match than it is to an amateur sport practiced by members of an educational institution. These methods should be avoided because they humiliate and alienate. Any ritual or procedure that causes an increase in the level of disdain or rejection from members of another team, coach, or individual does not belong in any sport. The competitive agression inherent in every person can be promoted in more acceptable ways.

3. Intelligent Use of Motivation

The coach must create an environment that is highly motivating. In setting up the type of environment that I want our team to have, two principles of motivation have been my guides:

a. Thorndyke's Laws of Learning which state that we tend to repeat a pleasant experience and to avoid an unpleasant one. Therefore, the coach should see to it that the swimmers on his team have a pleasant experience—not always necessarily a fun-and-games experience, but one in which the hard work leads to achievement and the goals of improved conditioning and better stroke mechanics, improved starts and turns, and so on. It should be a period of work towards achievement of these goals, not a period of work in which the coach shouts, belittles, and drives the swimmers into working hard. The methods discussed previously of educating

and using group dynamics can do more to motivate the swimmer than the coach can do by raising anxiety levels through the use of fear. A genuine interest on the part of the coach in the practice performance of the swimmer can do a lot to motivate him to work hard and develop a good attitude. After a swimmer swims a set of 20 × 100 on 1:15 and averages 1:02.5, imagine the effect when the coach goes up to him and says in a loud voice—penetrating enough so everyone can hear—"Congratulations, John, you just averaged 1:02.5 on those hundreds. That's the best anyone on our team has ever done. You are a physical genius and I owe you a dinner." To the other swimmer who didn't do so well the coach might say nothing or ask him if he is sick. He might even mildly reprimand him for not putting out. Always evaluate a swimmer's progress or performance objectively and use neither praise nor reproof exclusively. Some coaches only speak to their swimmers when they are performing poorly and then they may "chew them out" to jack them up so they will work harder. Such coaches perhaps feel they are expressing their masculinity by being tough. This negative approach too often fails, and at best its results are short-lived. The constant use of nothing but flattery or praise also has its limitations. The swimmers want to know how they performed in practice or in a meet. Evaluate their performance fairly and objectively. Do not ignore them—this is the worst method of motivation, if it can be referred to as a method.

b. Awareness of the fact that "nobody ever did something for nothing." This may sound a little materialistic, but upon examination, isn't the following question a logical one for anyone to ask: "Coach, you want me to train three to four hours a day, go to bed early, make all sorts of sacrifices. What do I get out of it?" Make it pretty clear what the swimmer will get out of it.

The East German swimmers' success can be attributed in part to the rewards they receive for training so hard and becoming so good. If they are successful, they live better, get a better position, improve their status, get to travel out of the country—which they can't do ordinarily because of political and financial restrictions—and, reportedly, receive money for winning international competitions such as Olympic events or World championships. It should also be remembered that the East German athletes are not competing for publicity nor are they sharing the limelight with professional sports and athletes. *They are the national sports heroes*, not Joe Namath or Arnold Palmer. This in itself is a big factor in their success.

Move a few miles west into West Germany. There are essentially the same people, but with a different environment and consequently a different motivation. In West Germany the people are extremely prosperous. There the average swimmer doesn't have to train hard to enjoy "the good life." Everyone already does have a good life, get to travel, and so on. The same is true in Japan and in the United States and, in fact, in all prosperous nations. We must look for other incentives or motivating methods than those that presently work in East Germany. The factors I have mentioned above are rewards for hard work and the achievement of success. What can I offer at Indiana University if a swimmer works hard and achieves success? I'll list a few of the rewards—at the risk of being repetitious: an athletic scholarship, a good education, good publicity in the newspapers and magazines, television and radio, good spectator attendance at our meets, lots of interest among local people, faculty, and students in the swimmers and the swimming program—even an interest on a national and international level in their accomplishments—all of which contributes to the team's status, the individual's status, and the swimmer's self-esteem. Recognition also comes in the form of banquets; for the past several years the governor of Indiana has given the team a banquet. A big incentive for any swimmer or coach is to make a foreign trip. We have been fortunate enough here at Indiana University to make at least one—sometimes two—foreign trips a year. If the swimmers are extremely successful they will also make trips as members of the United States Team to the Olympic Games or World Games. All teams should use trips as an incentive, even if it is

only an overnight trip to compete in an age-group meet.

We also offer our swimmers an opportunity to train hard in a pleasant environment where careful attention is paid to their progress, the mechanics of their strokes, starts and turns, and so on. In addition, they have the opportunity for membership in a high-prestige group where the morale is high and where there is a long tradition of success. They can train in a program that is highly motivating, but essentially low key in terms of psychological stress.

4. *The Use of the Athlete's Respect and Admiration for the Coach.*

Whether we know it or not and whether we like it or not, coaches often serve as models of behavior for their athletes. In the final analysis, we are all judged by our actions, even though at first we may be judged by our words. That is why there is something incongruous about a lazy coach who tries to talk his swimmers into working hard, or a coach who smokes during practice but urges his swimmers not to smoke, or an alcoholic coach who throws a swimmer off the team for drinking.

In an extension of this thinking, it is also incongruous to find a coach with a negative attitude towards everything in general expecting his team to have a positive attitude toward swimming. The ideal coach should, therefore, try to express the following attitudes—since we are all human and fallible we probably won't always feel and act positively, but we can try."

a. Be enthusiastic—your attitude should convey the feeling "I love my job," "I'm happy to be here," "I'm enjoying myself."

b. Be cooperative—bring across the idea that you and your team are working together: "Let's work together"; "This is our team and we have common goals"; "I care about each individual on the team and am concerned with his well-being as an athlete, a student, and a person."

c. Be positive—approach the achievement of the team's and the individual's goals with confidence. Coaches often adopt a negative attitude because they do not want to build expectations too high. They feel that by being negative, they avoid the ultimate letdown that results from failure to achieve the goals. To avoid this and still keep a positive attitude, establish reasonable goals that are compatible with the ability of the team and its members. Confidence is built on a series of successes plus a positive attitude. A swimmer who is on the team of a coach who has a history of success and who has the reputation of being an excellent coach has a built-in advantage over the swimmer of a coach who has neither. Such an athlete will immediately acquire a positive attitude and the belief that he is going to improve and succeed.

Up to this point I have discussed only that nebulous part of the environment that concerns the psychological atmosphere of the swimming team. I feel it is the most important aspect of the environment, but a team cannot function without the swimming pool and the other physical objects. I do not mean to minimize the importance of a good physical environment. No coach should be so egotistical that he feels he can develop a great team in any facility and under any conditions. A good, attractive, well-kept swimming pool with plenty of time available for practice is almost indispensable to any program.

Recently I attended the World Congress of Swimming Pool Architects in Heidelberg, Germany. After attending this meeting and seeing a few of the fine pools in Europe, I became convinced that all of us coaches and our teams could be working in much pleasanter environments if the pool designers in the United States were more imaginative and creative and had better taste. Most of our pools are concrete holes in the ground filled with overchlorinated water, surrounded by four dull-colored walls and squared-off deck areas. Since we spend a good part of our lives in these surroundings, why not insist that these areas be attractive as well as utilitarian?

With that hope for the future, we must still deal with what we presently have. Walk into many of the pool areas of our good teams and immediately you will think that this is a place where they really care about swimming and have a tradition. There may be pictures on the wall, record boards, electronic timers, pace clocks, trophy cases, special exercise equipment, or even an exercise room. So, a coach should control and even manipulate the physical environment of the swimmers, but he should also remember that living in a fine, new home with expensive furniture doesn't assure a successful family life. It is the quality of human contacts and social interchange, of motivation, leadership, discipline, compassion, and understanding that the children receive from their parents that determines the success of the family experience.

The same thing is true in the swimming pool and in the team-coach relationship. The odds of the family experience succeeding are much better in a clean, well-cared-for, uncrowded, pleasant home environment than they are in the slums or ghetto area, so we should always work for better facilities and a better physical environment, as well as for the ideal psychological atmosphere.

Building a consistently winning swimming program, one in which the needs of the participants are best served, is an infinitely complex problem. Good intentions and altruistic policy are not enough. Success or failure is ultimately decided at the grass-roots level, not by the coach alone, but by the multitude of people involved in the program who must spend countless—often boring and unheralded—hours of work and must make a multitude of major and minor, nitty-gritty decisions. The success of the program will depend on the quality of the people involved and their unselfish efforts on behalf of the entire group.

SECTION 6.8
ENVIRONMENT AND COACHING INVENTORY

Every year something new should be introduced into the swimming program. It may be a physical part of the environment or it may be nonphysical, having to do with a psychological part of the environment, such as a new ritual or ceremony or a new method of motivating the swimmers in practice. Even a new team to compete against or a new trip to take can provide a stimulus and avoid that "in a rut" feeling.

Such a small item as adding some new pictures in the office or changing the lettering on the team T-shirts will help. If you can afford new warm-ups or a new piece of exercise equipment, take the trouble to acquire them. Most of these things cannot be done without money so you may also need to find a new way to earn money, such as a swim-a-thon, a water show, a car wash, or all three, or an entirely different method, such as a bake sale held by the girl managers and timers.

In Tables 6.1 and 6.2 I have made a check list of items that can contribute in a positive way to the environment of your program. Use them as a guide; fill in the blanks, and in the process you may get some new ideas. A year after having filled out the inventory, come back and look at it again to see if you can truthfully change some of your replies.

Coach's Personality and Behavior Inventory

Table 6.3, a self-analysis chart, gives you the opportunity to evaluate your personality and behavior patterns. Don't answer the questions as you would like yourself to appear but as you really are. Don't expect to be perfect; no one is. All of us can improve in some areas. Awareness and the desire to change are the primary factors in adapting better behavior patterns.

Table 6.1.
Physical Environment
Inventory

	We Have It	We Need It	Target Date for Acquiring It	Cost	Source of Money	Manufacturer or Supplier
Lane Markers						Kiefer—McNeil 999 Sweitzer Ave., Akron, Ohio 44311
Pace Clocks						Kiefer—McNeil
Backstroke Flags*						
Starting Blocks*						
Kickboards*						
Pull Tubes or Buoys*						
Blackboard (at poolside)						
Bull Horn or Portable Speaker						
Meet Equipment Record Board*						
NCAA/H.S. Swimming Guide						
AAU Rule Book						AAU Order Dept. 3400 W. 86th St., Indianapolis, Ind. 46268
Judge and Time Cards*						
False-Start Rope						Clothesline will do

	We Have It	We Need It	Target Date for Acquiring It	Cost	Source of Money	Manufacturer or Supplier
Meet Scoring Sheets						Make your own
Stop Watches*						
Starter's Gun						Sporting Goods Store
Lap Counters*						
Divers Scored Cards*						
Divers Score Sheets*						
Clothing						
Sweatsuits						
T-shirts						
Tank Suits						
Award Sweaters or Jackets						
Subscription to *Swimming World*						8622 Bellanca Ave. Los Angeles, Cal. 90045
Trophy Case						
Publicity						
Newsletter						
Printed Schedule of Meets						
Programs						
Yearbook						
Pictures in Office						
Arrangements with Media						
Bulletin Board						
Exercise Equipment						
Exercise Room						
Barbells						Make your own
Mini-Gyms						Counsilman Co. 2606F E. 2nd St. Bloomington, Ind. 47401
Pulley Weights						
Universal Gym						
Floor Mats						
Exercise Charts						
Muscle Charts						
Achilles Tendon Stretcher (alligator shoes)						Make your own
Vertical Jump Measure						Make your own

Swimming World magazine advertisements will provide the source of many of these items.

Table 6.2.
Psychological Environment
Inventory

	We Have It	We Need It	Target Date for Acquiring It	Cost	Source of Money	Manufacturer or Supplier
Award Banquet						
Other Team Dinners or Picnics						
Awards or Recognition for Academic Achievement						
Trips						
Personnel						
Officials						
Managers						
Timers' Organization						
Announcers						

Table 6.3.
Coach's Personality and Behavior
Inventory

	Never	Sometimes	Always
1. Am I sometimes cruel?			
2. Do I sometimes belittle, humiliate, or ridicule?			
3. Am I fair with everyone?			
4. Do I talk to every swimmer every day?			
5. Do I have enough team meetings?			
6. Do I prepare for team meetings?			
7. Am I firm but compassionate in the disciplining of team members?			
8. Am I physically at practice, or do I spend a lot of time in the office, on the phone, etc.?			

	Never	Sometimes	Always
9. Am I always on time or early for practice?			
10. Do I show my affection?			
11. Do I show displeasure without losing control?			
12. Do I give the swimmers a voice in decision-making?			
13. Do I take an interest in the swimmer's academic record?			
14. Do I do something about it if I learn about academic problems?			
15. Do I know each swimmer's academic average?			
16. Do I know the areas of interest of each swimmer?			
17. Am I concerned with the future of each swimmer?			
18. Do the swimmers consult me when they have problems?			
19. After the swimmers have quit swimming for me, do they write me or come to visit?			
20. When a swimmer is sick, do I call or show concern?			
21. Do I know each swimmer's birthday and do something about it?			
22. Do I consider the athlete's self-esteem before I consider mine?			
23. Do I keep up on the latest developments in methods of training, strength, flexibility, etc?			
24. Have I attended a swim clinic in the last year?			
25. Do I subscribe to *Swimming World* and read it?			
26. Do I give the assistant coaches, managers, and officials the recognition they deserve?			
27. Do I show sufficient enthusiasm during practice?			
28. Do I seem to be enjoying practice?			

Fig. 6.2. *Inventory of equipment*

A.   Pace clock

D.   Pulling tube, kickboard, and pull buoy

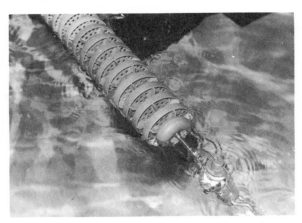

B.   Nonturbulence lane markers

E.   Lap counter

C.   Reel for storing lane marker

F.   Starting blocks

G. Record board

K. Portable public-address system

H. Do-it-yourself concrete barbells

I. Picture wall in pool office

L. Public-address system

J. Backstroke flags

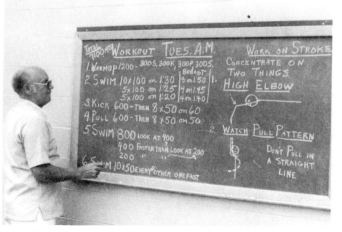

M. Blackboard (for posting workouts)

SECTION 6.9
"THE ROLE OF THE COACH
IN PLANNING A NATATORIUM,"
BY D. JOSEPH HUNSAKER

There are very few swimming coaches who do not think that they could design the world's greatest natatorium if only they had the chance. In recent years, more and more coaches are being given this once-in-a-lifetime opportunity—and ending up frustrated and disappointed. If a coach is going to make a significant impact on the design decisions of a new facility, he or she must understand the development scenario and the roles the various participants play in reaching the final design solution. Only by understanding the respective job responsibilities of the various professionals working on the project can the coach effectively articulate those points which are of the utmost importance to the aquatic program.

A natatorium is defined as an indoor swimming pool, but it can also mean an outdoor swimming-pool complex featuring spectator seating. The successful design of such a complex depends upon the interplay of many professional disciplines.

Owner. In any project there is an owner. In the case of swimming pools, the owner is usually a university, a school district, an institution, or a municipality. In any case, the owner is the entity that has decided to build a natatorium and has the money to pay for it.

Development committee. Often under a different designation, this is a group of individuals representing the owner in such areas as finance, program determination, development procedures, architecture, and construction. This committee is enlarged to include the

D. Joseph Hunsaker is executive vice-president of Counsilman & Associates. His address is 156 Weldon Parkway, Suite B, Maryland Heights, Mo. 63043; (phone 314-469-6220 or 432-1801).

architect, who will design the project, and frequently a qualified professional swimming-pool consultant who will help expedite the development of design criteria.

The architect. The term *architect* refers to the architectural firm that has been retained by the owner to design and prepare final working drawings and specifications for use in obtaining bids from general contractors. The architectural firm will usually assign an individual to the development committee with the titled responsiblity of "Project Architect." Through the project architect, the architectural firm will create conceptual drawings based upon the program requirements developed by the owner's representatives.

Following the conceptual drawings the firm will prepare developmental drawings which are used for preliminary cost estimates. This phase of the creative process is subject to review by the total development committee. This is a critical point in the process for the swimming coach because it is at this time that key decisions are made with regard to special features in the pool, the natatorium room, and satellite rooms.

In order to create accurate drawings, specifications, and cost estimates, the architect must use other technical advisors, such as specialized professional engineers: structural, mechanical, electrical, and soils, plus a number of other remote engineering specialties. The architect will also frequently use special professional consultants for unique facility areas. Such consultants are commonly used to advise on special design problems such as theatre layout and facilities, swimming-pool features, food-service facilities, elevator facilities, and sports-arena concepts, to name just a few.

Structural engineers. This profession determines the design strength and structural integrity of all primary elements of the building such as walls, foundations, roof spans, floors, beams, the pool shell, plus numerous other related features.

Mechanical engineers. All mechanical systems in the building and pool are the concern of the mechanical engineer. Such systems include the swimming-pool filter, heating and water-treatment systems, the heating and ventilating systems for the building, and the air-conditioning system if called for by the architect.

Electrical engineers. The electrical engineer is responsible for locating all electrical fixtures, for determining the proper circuitry, voltage requirements, and allocations for all mechanical equipment, and for the various safety provisions.

Soils engineers. The existence of unstable soil conditions can result in serious and sometimes devastating results when heavy structures are built. The most famous and graphic example of bad soil conditions is the Leaning Tower of Pisa.

Because a swimming pool must be absolutely level (it is obvious when it is not because the water level will identify any variances or low spots), it is understandable that the pool shell must be stable once in the ground and not subject to settlement or soil expansion. Therefore the soils engineer has a great responsibility to specify procedures and conditions that will assure a stable subgrade for the pool structure.

The swimming coach. As a representative of the owner, the swimming coach usually serves on the committee in the area of program determination and objectives. In this capacity the coach must develop a comprehensive program of current and future facility needs. Usually the swimming coach is given a literal opportunity to present his recommendations at the beginning of development studies by the development committee. Often, however, the coach is unable to present a comprehensive proposal for design criteria. In such a case one of two things usually happens. Either his influence in the project diminishes greatly or the development committee proceeds with a belief that his limited recommendations represent the best possibilities and that his concepts are infallible. Either development is unfortunate. If the coach is relegated to the status of a passive observer throughout the balance of the ongoing pro-

cess, it is a waste of valuable knowledge and experience.

If the architect-engineer team is inexperienced in natatorium design and as a result the coach is elevated to a position of infallible judge, a great danger to the project occurs. Because engineering and construction is a foreign discipline to the coach and because most humans are vulnerable to the weakness associated with "pride of authorship," the greatest danger of all develops for the project, and that is "errors and omissions." There have been many excellent ideas that have failed because they were poorly implemented. For example, everyone will probably agree that a movable bulkhead can be of great benefit to an aquatic program. However, there have been a number of bulkhead structures that were mechanically disappointing after they were built. In such cases it did not mean that such a feature was undesirable, but rather the experience emphasized that thorough research and engineering were lacking.

Very seldom does a design team blunder and make an outright mistake (although there have been a number of very embarrassing results when the projects were completed). The biggest and most common problem occurs when a critical or important detail is forgotten (omission) or improperly engineered (error). There have been several large indoor pools which have "gone out for bid" and then it was discovered that there was no provision for filling the pool(s). Another case resulted in the overhead lights casting shadows across the turning walls of the race course. A successful foot traffic pattern is sometimes overlooked, resulting in awkward and unsanitary conditions during swimming meets.

The biggest realization that all coaches should grasp when they are asked to participate in the design program for a natatorium is that compromises are inevitable due to budget limitations. Therefore, the real problem to be solved is *how to create the most efficient and effective facility with the funds available.* Obviously, a priority of natatorium features must be established, and a thorough list of alternates for each of those features must be compiled.

The professional swimming-pool consultant. A professional consulting firm is an organization which is retained by the owner and/or architect for the purpose of advising on the technical details and requirements necessary for the successful development of a natatorium. The role of the consultant is primarily that of interpretor and advisor to the design committee. The greatest interplay occurs between the swimming coach and the architect, because the experienced consultant can discuss the coach's objectives and desires and present them in technical terms to the architect with examples of how such features have been created in other projects. In this way the consultant supports the credibility of the coach's requests and likewise advises the architect about previous design solutions, thus avoiding expensive and time-consuming research.

Communication between consultant and coach. It is essential that a close working relationship develop between the coach and the consultant so that the coach's ideas are well represented to the rest of the design committee. It is also important that the consultant help clarify the coach's real objective and help him understand some of the drawbacks and negative features of his ideas before he pushes them before the rest of the design team.

One of the greatest failures in natatorium design is the all-too-frequent occurrence of a good idea which was implemented badly. Usually this occurs because the design engineers do not understand the real objective because of the way it is presented. This happens in part because the coach and the other program committee members are not aware of the secondary problems that can be encountered in achieving their objectives.

Counsilman & Associates is a professional consulting firm that applies its extensive awareness of swimming-pool features and aquatic programs to the development goals of universities, schools, institutions, and municipalities. Special techniques have been developed to expedite the development of design criteria and to make efficient use of time and money during the engineering of the proposed aquatic complexes. Having participated in the design and engineering of many outstanding natatoriums, Counsilman & Associates has extensive field history for the benefit of any coach and his associates when he is given "his chance" to build a dream pool.

Table 6.4
Basic Criteria
for Designing a Natatorium

1. Pool Structure
   - dimensions plus allowances
   - materials and structural design
   - gutter profile and material
   - mechanical systems/performance specifications
   - underwater windows

2. Natatorium Area
   - dimensions
   - clearances
       diving
       storage
       maintenance
   - materials
   - acoustics
   - lighting
       locations
       relamping/shadow lines
       intensity
   - spectator facilities
       traffic flow
       comfort
       line of sight
   - ventilation
   - air-handling distribution
   - deck equipment and anchors
   - diving facilities
   - fenestration
   - automatic scoring system
   - television provisions
   - intercom facilities
   - storage
   - exercise rooms
   - deck dimensions
   - required anchors
   - pool markings
   - appropriate office space
       allocations
   - graphics
   - food service
   - dressing rooms/fixture ratio
   - safety facilities
   - accessories
   - facility control and security

Fig. 6.3.

The items in Table 6.4 represent only a limited number of factors which must be considered when developing design criteria for a natatorium. While the list shown here is general in nature, it can serve as a partial guide for the coach. However, it should not be considered as a substitute for a qualified professional consultant. (See p. 296.)

Fig. 6.4.

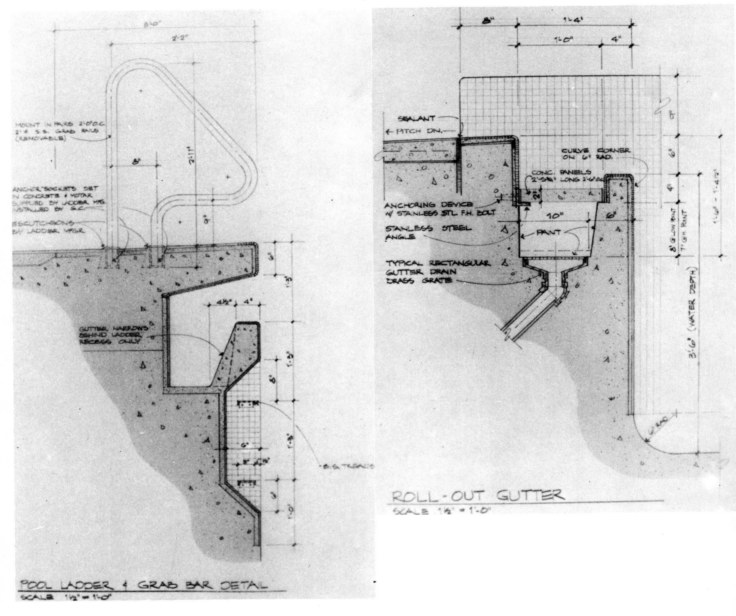

SECTION 6.10
"CHARACTERISTICS OF A FAST POOL," BY D. JOSEPH HUNSAKER

In general it is accepted that a fast pool possesses the following characteristics:

1. Excellent water quality both for swimmer comfort (temperature and chemistry) and for water clarity (underwater visibility)
2. Satisfactory tank markings
3. Illumination both above water and below water
4. Minimal wave action
5. Minimal underwater turbulence or eddy action in shallow water

Of these five items, the most discussed is *surface turbulence*. Few people will dispute the statement that a choppy water surface will retard a swimmer's progress while a calm and placid pool will maximize the same efforts. For years, controversy has surrounded the question of what is the best swimming-pool gutter design to minimize wave turbulence during swimming meets. Most coaches have felt that the deep recessed gutter with its deck overhang trapped the rolling wave and reduced the height of the echo wave that bounced back into the pool. Others, especially swimming instructors and recreation swimming proponents, emphasized the advantages of the "roll-out" or "deck-level" gutter system which provides easier egression from the water by the student swimmer or weak recreation swimmer. During swimming competition, they also point out, excessive wave action washes over onto the deck and dissipates instead of bouncing back into the pool and creating choppy surface water.

There appear to be advantages in both gutter-design concepts, with the controversy developing in the establishment of priorities. If the only purpose of gutter design were echo-wave reduction and subsequent surface turbulence control for the benefit of competitive swimming, then one of the above concepts (or some variation) would have gained prominence long ago. The fact is, however, that the gutter design is influenced by various other factors. A pool gutter must serve other purposes, such as recirculation of water, flexibility of aquatic programs, construction costs, construction materials, safety and sanitation codes.

After evaluating both concepts it is apparent that each gutter profile has its respective benefits. It is also apparent that neither provides a totally satisfactory solution to wave control.

Recent research, however, indicates that a concept unrelated to gutter profile can now produce much smoother water during a swimming race. Current AAU and NCAA official pool dimensions provide for a buffer lane between the pool wall and the outside lane. The dimension of this buffer lane is a minimum of 18 inches and sometimes is as great as several feet in long-course pools. If this lane is filled with three or more wave-dampening lane floats, the side walls of the pool are being treated in much the same way that acoustical engineers cushion large wall and ceiling areas against sound waves. By creating three or more adjacent wave-absorbing strata, the rolling wave created by the racing swimmer is trapped and dissipates as it works its way through each lane float. After making its way through the set of floats the wave strikes the wall with much less force than it would have under traditional conditions. The echo wave (already diminished) now must work its way through the set of floats again. The resulting echo wave which finally reaches the race course is subdued if at all noticeable. Such control and treatment of wave action is now easily obtained through the use of wave-dampening lane floats which have been developed in recent years.

The concept of solving the wave problem as the turbulence travels to and from the gutter is not altogether new. Dutch designers created a prototype pool at Utrecht, Netherlands, in which they installed breakwater fins or projections every few feet along the sides of the pool. The aim was to break and trap the wave action in the same way that huge engineered stone barriers break the impact of waves on the seacoast. While the concept did improve the situation, fabrication costs have proved to be a deterrent to further development.

The use of mass-produced wave-dampening lane floats provides an inexpensive, portable feature which maximizes wave control with little regard for pool gutter design. Utilization of the buffer lane is significant because it removes from the gutter the wave-quelling function. As a result the gutter can now be considered for its other purposes, i.e., ingress and egress by the swimmer, surface skimming

as part of the recirculation system, construction costs, aquatic programs, safety and sanitation codes.

Counsilman & Associates has made studies of wave control through the use of time exposures which recorded float oscillations with the use of varying numbers of wave-dampening lane floats placed six inches on centers. Because of these findings. Counsilman & Associates is now recommending to its clients that "a fast pool" surface condition be created in the buffer lanes and not solely in the gutter.

Fig. 6.5.

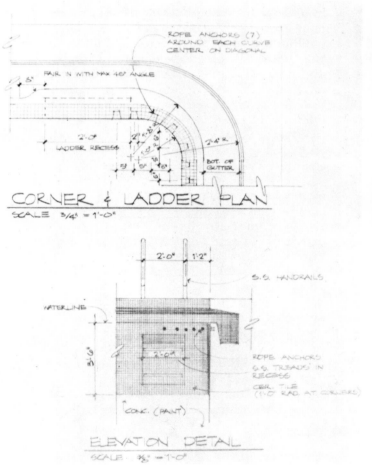

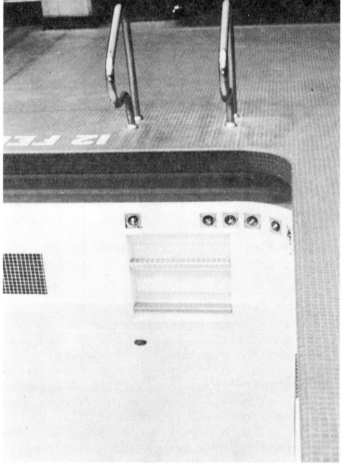

To return to the other four characteristics which are recognized as contributing factors to the "fast pool," a brief discussion may add to the value of this review:

1. *Water quality* is often taken for granted because it is seldom a problem in championship meets. However, in many cases the situation could be improved. Most coaches

and competitive swimmers agree that water temperature should be 76° to 78° F. Chemists who specialize in the field of swimming-pool water state that swimmer comfort is greatest when the chlorine count is a minimum of 1.0 and the pH is 7.2 to 7.8. The desired level of water clarity is no more than 5 PPM of turbidity (suspended quartz comparison), which results in exceptional visibility accompanied by the familiar "polish" that makes swimming-pool water so inviting.

2. *Water clarity* is important because the swimmer must be able to observe the various underwater pool markings which indicate his direction and location in the pool and which aid his depth perception when making turns. These markings are officially specified in the NCAA, AAU, and FINA regulations and they should be implemented without variation.

3. *Illumination* is a very important factor in the overall way natatoriums are lighted, and while the relative differences in light density may be difficult to notice, the overall effect of poor lighting can be a disadvantage to a swimmer who is not accustomed to the pool. It is generally agreed that the light at the water's surface should be 50 foot-candles for recreation swimming and 100 foot-candles for swimming competition. However, this specification solves only part of the problem. Understandably the reflected light on the bottom of the pool will be greater in the shallow end of the pool as compared to the deep-water end. Therefore, the sharpness of the wall target and lane strips will be less in the deep water. The problem of changing brightness is avoided in a racing tank which has a relatively consistent depth, i.e., 4 to 5 feet.

A lighting problem frequently found in natatoriums is the shadow cast over the turning wall. Because of relamping problems, overhead lights are sometimes placed over the pool deck. As a result, a shadow line falls from the gutter edge to the pool floor. This situation tends to distort the depth perception of the swimmer who is approaching the wall at a high rate of speed. Not only must the shadow line be avoided but consideration should be given to providing extra illumination at the turning walls of the race course. Both for the swimmers' benefit and that of

the judges, more light is necessary at the ends of the pool than in the center.

4. *Underwater turbulence or eddy action* is another subtle influence in swimming races. Underwater turbulence can create a negative force on the progress of the swimmer in shallow water. However, this effect is minimized in pools which are built to the dimensions specified in the AAU and NCAA regulations.

With the exception of the racing tanks built for the Olympic Games and a few university pools, design criteria must include features which benefit other aspects of aquatics besides competitive swimming. An exceptional design solution will maximize all uses with a minimum of oversights or omissions.

Fig. 6.6.

Notes and Bibliography

Chapter 1, Section 1.12

Agersborg, H. P. K., and Shaw, D. L., "Physiologic Approach to the Problem of Fatigue," *Journal of Sports Medicine and Physical Fitness* 2:217, 1962.

Asmussen, E., and Boje, O., "Body Temperature and Capacity for Work," *Acta Physiologica Scandinavavica* 10:1, 1945.

Atzler, E., and Lehmann, G., "Die Wirkung von Lecithin auf Arbeitsstoffwechset und Leistungsfähigkeit," *Arbeitsphysiologie* 9:76, 1935.

Bannister, R. G., and Cunningham, D. J. C., "The Effects on the Respiration and Performance during Exercise of Adding Oxygen to the Inspired Air," *Journal of Physiology* 125:118, 1954.

Barnes, R. H., et. al., "Effects of Exercise and Administration of Aspartic Acid on Blood Ammonia in the Rat." *American Journal of Physiology* 207:1242, 1964.

Consolazio, C. F., et. al., "Effects of Aspartic Acid Salts (mg and K) on Physical Performance of Men," *Journal of Applied Physiology* 19:257, 1964.

———, "Effect of Octacosanol, Wheat Germ Oil, and Vitamin E on Performance of Swimming Rats," *Journal of Applied Physiology* 19:265, 1964.

Cureton, T. K., and Pohndorf, R., "Influence of Wheat Germ Oil as a Dietary Supplement in a Program of Conditioning Exercises with Middle-aged Subjects," *Research Quarterly, American Association for Health, Physical Education and Recreation* 26:391, 1955.

Danowski, T. S., "Effect of Adrenal and Gonadol Steriods on Skeletal Muscles," *Archives of Physical Medicine* 47:132, 1966.

Dill, B. B., Edwards, H. T., and Talbott, J. H., "Alkalosis and the Capacity for Work," *Journal of Biological Chemistry* 97:lviii, 1932.

Erschoff, B. H., and Levin, E., "Beneficial Effect of an Unidentified Factor in Wheat Germ Oil on the Swimming Performance of Guinea Pigs," *Federation Proceedings* 14:431, 1955.

Feldman, I., and Hill, L., "The Influence of Oxygen Inhalation on the Lactic Acid Produced during Hard Work, *Journal of Physiology* 142:439, 1911.

Foltz, E. E., Ivy, A. C., and Barborka, C. J., "The Influence of Amphetamine Sulfate, d-Desoxyephedrine Hydrochloride and Caffeine upon Work Output and Recovery When Rapidly Exhausting Work Is Done by Trained Subjects," *Journal of Laboratory and Clinical Medicine* 28:063, 1943.

Fowler, Jr., W. M., Gardner, G. W., and Egstrom, G. H., "Effect of an Anabolic Steroid on Physical Performance of Young Men," *Journal of Applied Physiology* 20:1038, 1965.

Fowler, Jr., W. M., et. al., "Ineffective Treatment of Muscular Dystrophy with an Anabolic Steroid and Other Measures," *New England Journal of Medicine* 272:875, 1965.

Golding, L., and Barnard, J. R., "The Effect of d-amphetamine sulfate on Physical Performance," *Journal of Sports Medicine and Physical Fitness* 3:221, 1963.

Haldi, J., and Wynn, W., "Effect of Low and High Carbohydrate Meals on Blood Sugar Level and Work Performance in Strenuous Exercise of Short Duration," *American Journal of Physiology* 145:402, 1946.

Hale, C. J., "The Effect of Preliminary Massage on the 440-Yard Run." Master's thesis, Springfield College, 1949.

Hellebrandt, F. A., Rork, R., and Brogdon, E., "Effect of Gelatin on Power of Women to Perform Maximal Anaerobic Work," *Proceedings, Society for Experimental Biology and Medicine* 43:629, 1940.

Hettinger, T. H., *Physiology of Strength* (Springfield: C. C. Thomas, 1961), pp. 44-53.

Hill, A. V., Long, C. N. H., and Lupton, H., "Muscular Exercise, Lactic Acid, and the Supply and Utilization of Oxygen," *Proceedings of the Royal Society of London*, S.B. 96:438, 96:455, 97:84, 97:155, 1924-1925.

Hill, L., and Flack, M., "The Influence of Oxygen on Athletes," *Journal of Physiology* 38:xxviii, 1909.

Hilsendager, D., and Karpovich, P. V., "Ergogenic Effect of Glycine and Niacin Separately and in Combination," *Research Quarterly, AAHPER* 35:389, 1964.

Horwitt, M. K., "Vitamin E and Lipid Metabolism in Man," *American Journal of Clinical Nutrition* 8:451, 1960.

Johnson, W. R., and Black, D. H., "Comparison of Effects of Certain Blood Alkalinizers upon Competitive Endurance Performance," *Journal of Applied Physiology* 5:557, 1953.

Kaczmarek, R. M., "Effect of Gelatin on the Work Output of Male Athletes and Non-athletes and on Girl Subjects," *Research Quarterly, AAHPER* 11:109, 1940.

Karpovich, P. V., "Effect of Amphetamine Sulfate on Athletic Performance," *Journal of the American Medical Association* 170:558, 1959.

_____, "Effect of Oxygen Inhalation on Swimming Performance," *Research Quarterly, AAHPER* 5:24, 1934.

_____, *Physiology of Muscular Activity*, 7th ed. (Philadelphia: W. B. Saunders Co., 1965), pp. 261-278.

_____, "Respiration in Swimming and Diving," *Research Quarterly, AAHPER* 10:3, 1939.

Karpovich, P. V., and Millman, N., "Vitamin B₁ and Endurance," *New England Journal of Medicine* 226:881, 1942.

Karpovich, P. V., and Pestrecov, K., "Effect of Gelatin upon Muscular Work in Men, *American Journal of Physiology* 134:300, 1941.

Kochakian, C. D., "Mechanisms of Androgen Actions," *Laboratory Investigation* 8:538, 1959.

Laborit, H., et. al., "Influence de la composition ionique du milieu extracellulaire et influence comparée de l'acide aspartique, de l'aspartate de potassium et du glucose sur l'épreuve de nage du rat," *Comptes Rendus de la Societé de Biologie et de ses Filiales* 151:1383, 1957.

Levin, S., et. al., "Studies of Tocopherol Deficiency in Infants and Children. VI, Evaluation of Muscle Strength and Effect of Tocopherol Administration in Children with Cystic Fibrosis," *Pediatrics* 27:578, 1961.

Marbe, K., "Ueber der Vermeintliche Leistungssteigerung durch Recresal und Natrim Bicarbonicum," *Archiv für Experimentelle Pathologie und Pharmakologie* 167:404, 1932.

Margaria, R., Aghemo, P. and Rovelli, E., "The Effect of Some Drugs on the Maximal Capacity of Athletic Performance in Man," *Internationale Zeitung für Angewandte Physiologie* 20:281, 1964.

Matoush, L. O., et. al., "Effects of Aspartic Acid Salts (mg and K) on Swimming Performance of Rats and Dogs," *Journal of Applied Physiology* 19:262, 1964.

Miller, A. T., et. al., "Influence of Oxygen Administration on Cardiovascular Function during Exercise and Recovery," *Journal of Applied Physiology* 5:165, 1952.

Montoye, H. J., et. al., "Effects of Vitamin B-12 Supplementation on Physical Fitness and Growth of Young Boys," *Journal of Applied Physiology* 7:589, 1955.

Muller, E. A., "Physiological Methods of Increasing Human Physical Work Capacity," *Ergonomics.* 8:409, 1965.

Nagamine, S., "Experimental Studies on Protein Metabolism in Relation to Physical Exercise, II," *Japanese Journal of Nutrition* 9:6, 1951.

Nagle, F. J., Balke, B., and Ganslen, R. V., "Mitigation of Physical Fatigue through Spartase." Read before the American College Sports Medicine, Minneapolis, April 30, 1963.

Nelson, D. O., "Effects of Food Supplement on the Performance of Selected Gross Motor Tests," *Research Quarterly, AAHPER* 35:627, 1960.

Pampe, W., "Hyperglykämie und Körperliche Arbeit," *Arbeitsphysiologie* 5:342, 1932.

Percival, L., quoted by Consolazio, C. R., et. al., "Effect of Octacosonl Wheat Germ Oil and Vitamin E on Performance of Swimming Rats." *Journal of Applied Physiology* 19:265, 1964.

Rasch, P. J., and Pierson, W. R., "Effect of a Protein Dietary Supplement on Muscular Strength and Hypertrophy," *American Journal of Clinical Nutrition* 11:530, 1962.

Ray, G. B., Johnson, J. R., and Taylor, M. M., "Effect of Gelatins on Muscular Fatigue," *Proceedings of the Society for Experimental Biology and Medicine* 40:157, 1939.

Rosen, H., Blumenthal, A., and Agersborg, H. P. K., "Effects of the Potassium and Magnesium Salts of Aspartic Acid on Metabolic Exhaustion," *Journal of Pharmaceutical Sciences* 51:592, 1962.

Samuels, L. T., Henschel, A. F., and Keys, A., "Influence of Methyltestosterone on Muscular Work and Creotine Metabolism in Normal Young Men,"

Journal of Clinical Endicrinology and Medicine 2:649, 1942.

Schorn, M., "Ueber die Wirkung des Recresals auf die Körperliche und Geistige Leistungsfähigkeit," *Münchener mediclinische Wochenschrift* 79:371, 1932.

Simonson, E., Kearns, W. M., and Enzer, N., "Effect of Methyltestosterone Treatment on Muscular Performance and the Central Nervous System of Older Men," *Journal of Clinical Endicrinology and Metabolism* 4:528, 1944.

Smith, G. M., and Beecher, H., "Amphetamine Sulfate and Athletic Performance." I. *Objective Effects, Journal of the American Medical Association* 170:542, 1959.

Staton, W. M., "The Influence of Soya Lecithin on Muscular Strength," *Research Quarterly, AAHPER* 22:201, 1951.

Talland, G. A., and Quarton, G. C., "The Effects of Drugs and Familiarity on Performance in Continuous Visual Search," *Journal of Nervous and Mental Disease* 143:266, 1966.

Van Itallie, T. B., Sinisterra, L., and Stare, F. J., "Nutrition and Athletic Performance," in *Science and Medicine of Exercise and Sports* ed. W. R. Johnson (New York: Harper & Brothers, 1960), pp. 285-300.

Wilder, R. M., "Glycine in Myasthenia Gravis," *Proceedings, Staff Meetings of the Mayo Clinic* 9:606, 1934.

Chapter 2, Sections 2.1 and 2.2

1. Per-Olof Astrand, M.D., and Kaare Rodahe, M.D., *Textbook of Work Physiology* (New York: McGraw-Hill, 1970), p. 11.

2. J. G. Arcos et. al., *Experimental and Molecular Pathology* (1968), 8:49.
Secondary reference: "Coronary Heart Disease," *International Symposium in Frankfurt*, 1979, ed. Dr. M. Kaltenbach (Baltimore: University Park Press, 1970).

3. Kenneth Sparks, "Physiological Response with Two Types of Interval Training Programs." Unpublished study, Indiana University School of Health, Physical Education, and Recreation, Bloomington, Ind., 1973-74.

4. W. Hollman and H. Liesen, "The Influence of Hypoxia and Hyperoxia Training in a Laboratory on the Cardiopulmonal Capacity," *Limiting Factors of Physical Performance, International Symposium of Physical Performance Proceedings, 1971* (Stuttgart: George Thieme, 1973), pp. 212-218.

5. Ibid., p. 215.

6. Personal correspondence with Dr. David Costill, director of Human Performance Laboratory, Ball State University.

7. David Costill, "Championship Material," *Runner's World*, Vol. 9, Counsilman Bibliography (Continued Notes for Chapter 2, Sections 21, 22)

7 David Costill, "Championship Material," *Runner's World*, Vol. 9, No. 4 (1974), pp. 26-27.
"Championship Material" is reprinted in Chapter 2 of this book as Section 2.4.

8. Ibid.

Other References

R. James Barnard et al., "Histochemical, Biochemical, and Contractile Properties of Red, White, and Intermediate Fibers," *American Journal of Physiology*, Vol. 220, No. 2 (1971), pp. 410-414.

D. Pette and H. W. Staudte, "Differences between Red and White Muscles," *Limiting Factors of Physical Performance, International Symposium at Gravenbreeck, 1971*, ed. J. Keul (Stuttgart: George Thieme, 1973), pp. 25-35.

Donald K. Mathews and Edward L. Fox, *The Physiological Basis of Physical Education and Athletics* (Philadelphia: W. B. Saunders Co., 1971).

Personal correspondence and conversations with David Costill and Bengt Saltin.

Chapter 2, Section 2.3

Bob Anderson and Joe Henderson, eds. *New Views of Speed Training* (Mountain View, Calif. : World Publications, 1971).

J. Kenneth Doherty, *Modern Training for Running* (Englewood Cliffs, N.J. : Prentice-Hall, 1964).

Edward L. Fox and Donald K. Mathews, *Interval Training* (Philadelphia: W.B. Saunders Co., 1974).

Fred Wilt, *Run, Run, Run* (Los Altos, Calif. : Track and Field News Press, 1964).

Chapter 5, Section 5.1

1. James E. Counsilman, *The Science of Swimming* (Englewood Cliffs, N.J.: Prentice-Hall, 1967).

2. Hunter Rouse, *Elementary Mechanics of Fluids* (New York: John Wiley & Sons, 1946).

Chapter 5, Section 5.3

1. James G. Hay, *The Biomechanics of Sports Techniques* (Englewood Cliffs, N.J. : Prentice-Hall, 1973).

2. Ibid.

3. James E. Counsilman, "The Role of Swimming Movements in the Arm Pull," *Swimming World*, December 1969.

4. Ibid.

5. James E. Counsilman, "The Application of Bernouilli's Principle to Human Propulsion in Water." Pamphlet distributed at clinic at Stonybrook, N.Y., 1971.

6. James E. Counsilman, Lecture Recording at Fort Lauderdale Swimming Hall of Fame, December 1969.

7. Forbes Carlile, "Freestyle Trends at Munich," *Swimming Technique*, October 1972.

8. James E. Counsilman, *The Science of Swimming* (Englewood Cliffs, N.J. : Prentice-Hall, 1968).

9. John Tallman, "Stroke Rate," *Swimming Technique*, July 1973.

Other References

James E. Counsilman, Film: The Science of Swimming (Bloomington, Ind. :
  Counsilman Co., 1972).

Chapter 5, Section 5.4

1. James E. Counsilman, Film: *The Science of Swimming* (Bloomington,
Ind. : Counsilman Co., 1972).
2. Speedo Knitting Mills, Film: *The International Swimmer*, 1968.
3. Sunkist Corporation, Films on Breaststroke Swimming.
4. James E. Counsilman, "The Application of Bernouilli's Principle to
Human Propulsion in Water," *First International Symposium on Biomechanics
in Swimming, Diving, and Water Polo Proceedings*, Jan P. Clarys and Leon
Lewillie, eds. Université Libre de Bruxelles, Laboratoire de l'effort, 1971.
5. James E. Counsilman, *The Science of Swimming* (Englewood Cliffs,
N.J. : Prentice-Hall, 1968).
6. Robert D. Schleihauf, "A Biomechanical Analysis of Freestyle,"
Swimming Technique, Fall 1974.
7. James E. Counsilman, Lecture notes from clinic at Paramus, N.J.,
September 1974.
8. Counsilman, Film: *The Science of Swimming*.